WELCOME . . .

Welcome to this new incarnation of the first paperback magazine of science fiction and science.

In it you will find stories by established greats and those whose greatest works lie in the future—much of it, we trust, to be published in NEW DESTINIES. The mix in this first edition is typical of what you can expect in every edition, with names like Poul Anderson, Keith Laumer, Fred Saberhagen and Timothy Zahn heading the list.

But there will be more to New Destinies than great fiction. Our self-assumed mandate is to provide you with massive doses of that special kind of thinking that is the lifeblood of science fiction: scientific speculation from the far frontiers of science.

Protein computers that interface with thought; modern-day beanstalks that stretch to geosynchronous orbit and beyond; the possibility of nuclear-pulse driven pirate ships trying conclusions with anti-matter-drive vessels in the asteroid belt. Speculations about things that matter: in both fiction and fact that will be the special venue of NEW DESTINIES.

If you have been wondering whatever happened to science fiction's Sense of Wonder, wonder no more. It's right here, waiting for you.

NEW DESTINIES

EDITED BY
JIM BAEN

NEW DESTINIES

Spring Edition 1987

EDITOR IN CHIEF
Jim Baen

SENIOR EDITOR
Elizabeth Mitchell

ASSOCIATE EDITOR
Michael Banks

BAEN BOOKS

NEW DESTINIES, Spring 1987

A Baen Books Original

Baen Publishing Enterprises
260 Fifth Avenue
New York, N.Y. 10001

First printing, March 1987

ISBN: 0-671-65628-7

Cover art by Craig Farley

Printed in the United States of America

Distributed by
SIMON & SCHUSTER
1230 Avenue of the Americas
New York, N.Y. 10020

Contents

POINT MAN

Victory is a matter of being in the right place at the right time—right? Well, usually . . .

POINT MAN

Timothy Zahn

Everyone, my mother used to tell me, had a special talent. Every human being, in one way or another, stood head and shoulders above all those around him. It was, she'd firmly believed, part of what made us human; one of the few things that stood us apart from the lower animals and even from the sophisticated alien hive minds that plied the galaxy.

She never told me just what she thought my talent was while I was growing up, of course. At the time I figured that she simply didn't want to prejudice me. Looking back from the perspective of five decades, it has gradually become apparent that she hadn't told me what my talent was because she was never able to *find* any. But she was too kind to tell me outright that I was so uniformly average . . . and so I left home and spent thirty solid years looking for something in which I could excel.

Eventually, I found it. I found that I had a genuine and unique knack for being at the wrong place at the wrong time.

I remember vividly the day that conclusion suddenly came to me; remember almost as well the solid month afterwards that I fought it. But eventually I had to give in and accept it as truth. There were just too many instances scattered throughout my life to blame on co-incidence and accident. There was the time I walked into my college room just as my roommate was frying his cortex with an illegal and badly overset brain-stretch stimulator. I was eventually exonerated of all blame, but the trauma and stigma were just as bad as if I'd been thrown out of school, and eventually led to the same result. I joined the Services and had worked my way up to a very promising position in starship engineering when I was transferred to the *Burma* . . . three months before the ship's first officer attempted a mutiny and damn near made it. Again, the wrong place at the wrong time, and this time the stigma of association effectively ended my Services career. I eventually went into the merchant fleet, kicking around various ships until my special damn talent landed me in another innocent mess and I was forced to move on.

So given my history, I shouldn't have been surprised to be on the *Volga*'s bridge when it broke out of hyperspace on that particularly nasty evening.

I shouldn't even have been *on* the bridge, for starters. That fact alone should have tipped me off that my perverse talent was about to do me dirty again. Second Officer Mara Kittredge was at the command console, Tarl Fromm and Ing Waskin were backing her up at helm and scanners, and there was absolutely no reason why anyone else should have been needed, least of all the ship's third officer. But I was feeling restless. We were about to come out of hyperspace over Messenia, and I wanted to make sure this whole silly stop was handled as quickly as possible, so I was there. I should have known better.

"Thirty seconds," Waskin was saying as I arrived. He glanced up at me, then quickly turned back to his scanners. Probably, I figured, so that I wouldn't see that faintly gloating smile he undoubtedly had on his skinny face.

Kittredge looked up, too, but her smile had nothing but her normal cool friendliness in it. She was friendly because she felt professionals should always be polite to their inferiors; cool, because she knew all about my career and clearly had no intention of being too close to

me when the lightning struck again. "Travis," she nodded. "You're a little early for your shift, aren't you?"

"A shave, maybe," I said, drifting to her side and
steadying myself on her chair back. She wasn't much
more than half my age, but then, that was true of nearly
everyone aboard except Captain Garrett. Bright kids,
all of them. Only a few with Kittredge's same hard-
edged ambition, but all of them on the up side of their
careers nonetheless. It made me feel old. "Was that
thirty seconds to breakout?"

"Yes," she said, voice going distant as the bulk of her
attention shifted from me to the bank of displays before her. I followed her example and turned to watch
the screens and readouts. And continued my silent
grousing.

We weren't supposed to be at Messenia. We weren't,
in fact, supposed to be anywhere closer than a day's
hyperdrive of the stupid damn mudball on this particular
trip. We were on or a bit ahead of schedule for a
change, we had all the cargo a medium-sized freighter
like the *Volga* could reasonably carry, and all we had to
do was deliver it to make the kind of medium-sized
profit that keeps pleasant smiles on the faces of freighter
contractors. It should have been a nice, simple trip, the
kind where the crew's lives alternate between predicta-
ble chores and pleasant boredom.

Enter Waskin. Exit simplicity.

He had, Waskin informed us, an acquaintance who
was supposed to be out here with the Messenia survey
mission. We'd all heard the rumors that there were
supposed to be outcroppings of firebrand opaline scattered across Messenia's surface—opaline whose current
market value Waskin just happened to have on hand. It
was pretty obvious that if someone came along who
could offer off-world transport for some of the stone—
especially if middlemen and certain tax and duty for-
malities happened to get lost in the shuffle—then that
someone stood to add a tidy sum to his trip's profits.
The next part was obvious: Waskin figured that that
someone might as well be the crew of the *Volga*.

It was the sort of argument that had earned Waskin the half-dozen shady nicknames he possessed. Unfortunately, it was also the sort of argument he was extremely adroit at pushing, and in the end Captain Garrett decided it was worth the gamble of a couple of days to stop by and just assess the situation.

I hadn't agreed. In fact, I'd fought hard to change the captain's mind. For starters, the opaline wasn't even a confirmed fact yet; and even if it *was* there, it was less than certain what the Messenia survey mission would think of us dropping in out of nowhere and trying to walk away with a handful of it. Survey missions like Messenia's were always military oriented, and if they suspected we were even *thinking* of bending any customs regulations, we could look forward to some very unpleasant questions.

And I, of course, would wind up with yet another job blown out from under me.

But freighter contractors weren't the only ones to whom the word "profit" brought pleasant smiles . . . and third officers, I'd long ago learned, existed solely to take the owl bridge shift. Half the ship's thirty-member crew had already made their private calculations as to how much of a bonus a few chunks of opaline would bring, and my arguments were quickly dismissed as just one more example of Travis's famous inability to make winning gambles, a side talent that had made me the most sought-after poker player on the ship.

Waskin always won at poker, too. And got far too much satisfaction out of beating me.

Abruptly, the lights flickered. Quickly, guiltily, I brought my attention back to the displays, but it was all right—the breakout had come off textbook-clean.

"We're here," Fromm reported from the helm. "Ready to set orbit."

"Put us at about two hundred for now," Kittredge told him. "Waskin, you want to try and contact this friend of yours and find out about this opaline?"

"Yes, ma'am," he nodded, swiveling around to the comm board.

"Was there anything else?" Kittredge asked, looking up at me.

I shook my head. "I just wanted to make sure we knew one way or another about the rocks before anyone got too comfortable here."

She smiled lopsidedly. "I doubt you have to wor—"

"*Holy Mother!*"

I snapped my head around to look at Waskin, nearly losing my hold in the process. He was staring at the main display. As I shifted my eyes that direction, I felt a similar expletive welling up like verbal fire in my throat.

We'd come within view of the mission's base camp . . . or rather, within view of the blackened crater where the base camp was supposed to be.

"Oh, my God," Kittredge gasped as the scanners panned over the whole nauseating mess. "What *happened?*"

"No idea," I said grimly, "but we'd better find out." My long-ago years in the Services came flooding back, the old pages of emergency procedures flipping up in front of my mind's eye. "Waskin, get back on the scanners. Do a quick full-pattern run-through for anything out of the ordinary, then go back to infrared for a grid survivor search."

"Yes, sir." There was no cockiness now; he was good and thoroughly scared. With an effort, he got his face jammed into the display hood, his hand visibly trembling as he fumbled with the selector knob. "Yes, sir. Okay. IR . . . those fires have been out a minimum of . . . eighteen hours, the computer says. Could be more." His thin face—what I could see of it, anyway—was a rather pasty white, and I hoped hard that he wouldn't pass out. Time could be crucial, and I didn't want to have to man the scanners myself until we could get another expert up here. "Shortwave . . . nothing in particular. No broadcasts on any frequency. Neutrino . . . there's a residual decay spectrum, but it's the wrong one for their type of power plant. Tachyon . . . uh-oh."

"What?" Kittredge snapped.

Waskin visibly swallowed. "It reads . . . it reads an awful lot like the pattern you get from full-spectrum explosives."

Fromm caught it before the rest of us did. "Explo*sives*, plural?" he asked. "How many are we talking about?"

"Lots," Waskin said. "At least thirty separate blasts. Maybe more."

Fromm swore under his breath. "Damn. They must have had a stockpile that blew."

"No," I said, and even to me my voice sounded harsh. "You don't store full-specs that close to each other. Someone came in and bombed the hell out of them. Deliberately."

There was a long moment of silence. "The opaline," Kittredge said at last. "Someone wanted the opaline."

For lousy pieces of rock . . .? I forced my brain to unfreeze from that thought. Messenia had been militarily oriented. . . . "Waskin, cancel the grid search for a second and get back on the comm board," I told him. "Broadcast our ship ID on the emergency beacon frequency and then listen."

Kittredge looked up at me. "Travis, no one could have survived a bombing like that—"

"No one *there*, no," I cut her off. "But there would have been at least a few men out beyond the horizon from the base—that's standard procedure."

"Yeah, but the radiation would have got 'em," Waskin muttered.

"Just do it," I snapped.

"I'd better get the captain up here," Kittredge said, reaching for the intercom.

"Better get a boat ready to fly, too," I told her. My eyes returned to the main display, where the base was starting to drift behind us. "With the doc and a couple others with strong stomachs aboard. If there are any survivors, they'll need help fast."

She nodded, and that was that. If I hadn't been there, they'd have done a quick, futile grid search and

then gone running hotfoot to report the attack to some
authority or other without trying the emergency beacon
trick. We'd have missed entirely the fact that there was
indeed a survivor of the attack.

And we sure as hell would have missed getting mixed
up in mankind's first interstellar war.

His name was Lieutenant Colonel Halveston, and he
was dying.

He knew that, of course. The Services were good at
making sure their people had any and all information
that might have an influence on their performance or
survival. Halveston knew how much radiation he'd taken,
knew that at this stage there was nothing anyone could do
for him . . . but countering that was a strong will to hold
out long enough to let someone know what had happened.
The Services were good at developing that, too.

We didn't get to talk to him on the trip up from
Messenia, partly because the doc needed Halveston's
full attention for the bioloop stabilization techniques to
work and partly because long chatty conversations on
an open radio didn't seem like a smart idea. It was
nerve-racking as hell . . . and so when the captain, Kittredge, and I were finally able to gather around
Halveston's sickbay bed, we weren't exactly in the greatest of emotional shapes.

Not that it mattered that much. Halveston's report
would have been a full-spec bombshell no matter what
our condition.

"It was the Drymnu," he whispered through cracked
lips. "The Drymnu did this."

I looked up from Halveston to see Captain Garrett's
mouth drop open slightly. That, from the captain, was
the equivalent of falling over backwards with shock . . .
which was about what *I* felt like doing. "The . . .
Drymnu?" he asked carefully. "*The* Drymnu? The hive
race?"

Halveston winced in a sudden spasm of pain. "You
know any other aliens by that name?" he said. I got the

impression he would have snarled it if he'd had the strength to do so.

"No, of course not," the captain said. "It's just that—" He paused, visibly searching for a diplomatic way of putting this. "I've just never heard of a hivey attacking anyone before."

A little more of Halveston's strength seemed to drain out of him. "You have now," he whispered.

The Captain looked up at Kittredge and me, back down at Halveston. "Could it have been a group of human pirates, say, pretending they were a Drymnu ship?"

Halveston closed his eyes and shook his head weakly. "Outposts get a direct cable feed from the main base's scanners. If you'd ever seen a Drymnu ship, you'd know no one could fake something like that."

"Travis?" the captain murmured.

I nodded reluctantly. "He's right, sir. If he actually saw the ship, it couldn't have been anyone else."

"But it doesn't make any sense," Kittredge put in. "Why would any Drymnu ship attack a human outpost?"

It was a damn good question. All the aliens we'd ever run into out here were hive races, and hive races didn't make war. Period. They weren't constitutionally oriented that way, for starters; aggression in hivies nearly always focused on studying and understanding the universe, and as far as I knew the Drymnu were no exception. It was why hivies nearly always discovered the Burke stardrive and made it into space, while fragmented races like humanity nearly always blew themselves to bits before they could do likewise.

"I don't know why," Halveston sighed. "I don't have any idea. But whatever the reason, he sure as hell did it on purpose. He came in real close, discussing refueling possibilities, and when he was too close for us to have any chance at all, he just opened up and bombed the hell out of the base."

The speech took too much out of him. His eyes rolled up, and he seemed to go a little more limp beneath his safety webbing. I looked up, caught the captain's eye.

"We'd better get out of here," I said in a low voice. "It looks like he's long gone, but I don't think we want to be here if he comes back."

"And we need to report this right away, too," Kittredge added.

"No!"

I would've jumped if there'd been any gravity to do it with. "Take it easy, colonel," the captain soothed him. "There's no one else alive down there—trust us, we made a complete infrared grid search while you were being brought up. We've got to warn the Services—"

"No," Halveston repeated, much weaker this time. "You've got to go after him. *Now*, before he gets too far away."

"But we don't even know what direction he's gone in," Kittredge told him.

"My pack . . . has the records of our . . . three nav satellites." Clearly, Halveston was fading fast. "He didn't think . . . take them out. Got the . . . para-Cerenkov rainbow . . . when he left."

And with the rainbow recorded from three directions we did indeed have the direction the ship had taken—at least until he came out of hyperspace and changed vectors. But it would normally be several days at the least before he did that. "All the more reason for us to go sound the alarm," I told Halveston.

"No time," Halveston gasped. "He'll get away, regroup with other Drymnu ships . . . never identify him then. And the whole mind will know . . . how easily he got us."

And suddenly, for a handful of seconds, the pain cleared almost entirely from his face and a spark of life flared in his eyes. "Captain Garrett . . . as a command-rank officer of the Combined Services . . . I hereby commandeer the *Volga* . . . and order you to give chase . . . to the Drymnu ship . . . that destroyed Messenia. And to destroy it. Carry out your . . . orders . . . captain."

And as his eyes again rolled up, the warbling of the *life-failure* alert broke into our stunned silence. Automatically, we floated back to give the med people room to work. We were still there, still silent, when the doc finally shut off the med sensors and covered Halveston's face.

"Well?" the captain asked, glaring at the intercom and then at Kittredge and me in turn. "*Now* what do we do?"

The intercom rasped as First Officer Wong, who had replaced Kittredge on the bridge, cleared his throat delicately. "I presume there's no way to expunge that . . . suggestion . . . from the log?"

"That your idea or one of Waskin's?" the captain snorted. Perhaps he was remembering it was Waskin's fault we were here in the first place. "Of course there's no way. And it wasn't a suggestion, it was an order—a legal one, our resident military expert tells me." He turned his glare full force onto me.

I refused to shrivel. He'd asked me a question, and it wasn't *my* fault if he hadn't liked the answer.

"But this is crazy," Wong persisted. "We're a *freighter*, for God's sake. How in hell did he expect us to take on a warship with eighteen thousand Drymnu aboard?"

"It wasn't a warship," I put in. "Couldn't have been. The Drymnu don't have any warships."

"You could have fooled *me*," Kittredge growled. "I hope you're not suggesting he just *happened* to have a cargo of full-spectrum bombs aboard and somehow lost his grip on them."

"I said he didn't have any warships," I shot back. "I *didn't* say the attack wasn't deliberate."

"The difference escapes me—"

"Let's keep the discussion civil, shall we?" the captain interrupted. "I think it's a given that we're all on edge here. All right, Travis, you want to offer an explanation as to why a race ostensibly as peaceful as the Drymnu would launch an unprovoked attack on a human installation?"

"I don't *know* why he did it," I told him. "But keep in mind that the Drymnu isn't really 'peaceful'—I wouldn't call him that, anyway. He isn't warlike, but he's competitive enough, to the point of having deliberately wiped out at least one class of predators on his home world. All the hivies are that way. It's just that in space there's so much room and territory that there's no reason for one of them to fight any of the others."

"But we're different?" the captain asked.

I spread out my hands. "We're a fragmented race, which means we're warlike, and we've gotten into space, which means we're flagrant violations of accepted hivey theory. Maybe the Drymnu has decided that the combination makes us too dangerous to exist and is beginning a campaign to wipe us out."

"Starting with Messenia?" Wong interjected from the bridge. "Why? To show that his war machine can blow up a couple hundred Services men, developers, and scientists? Big deal."

"Maybe it wasn't the entire Drymnu mind behind it," I pointed out. "Each ship is essentially autonomous until it gets within thirty thousand klicks or so of another Drymnu ship or planet."

"Could this one part of the mind have gone insane?" Kittredge suggested hesitantly. "Become homicidal, somehow?"

"God, what a thought," Wong muttered. "A raving maniac with eighteen thousand bodies running around the galaxy in his own starship."

I shrugged. "I don't know if it's possible or not. It's probably more likely that Messenia was an experiment on his part."

"A *what*?" Kittredge growled.

"An experiment. To see if we could handle a sneak attack, with Messenia chosen because it was small and out of the way. You know—club a sleeping tiger or two first to get the technique down before you tackle one that's awake."

Wong and Kittredge started to speak at once; the captain cut them off with a wave of his hand. "Enough, everyone. As I see it, we have three possibilities here: that the entire Drymnu mind has declared war on humanity; that this one ship-sized segment of the Drymnu mind has declared war on humanity; or that some portion of the Drymnu mind is playing war with humanity to see how we react. Does that about cover it, Travis?"

My mouth felt dry. There was a glint I didn't at all care for in the captain's eyes. "Well . . . I can't see any other alternatives at the moment, no."

He nodded, the glint brighter than ever. "Thank you. Any of the rest of you? No? Then it seems to me that we've got no choice—ethically as well as legally. Halveston said it himself: if that ship gets back to one of the Drymnu worlds and reports how easy it was to club this sleeping tiger to death, we may very well find ourselves embroiled in an all-out war. Wong, pull the raider's direction from those tapes and get us in pursuit."

There was a moment of stunned silence. None of the others, I gathered, had noticed that glint. "Captain—" Wong began, and then hesitated.

Kittredge showed less restraint. "Captain," she said, "the last time I checked, the *Volga* was *not* a warship. Doesn't it strike you as just the *slightest* bit dangerous for us to take on that ship? Our chief duty at this point is to report the attack."

"And if Messenia was merely a single thrust of a more comprehensive and synchronized attack?" the captain said quietly. "What then?"

She opened her mouth, closed it again. "Then there may not be any human bases left anywhere near here to report to," she said at last, very softly. "Oh, God."

The captain nodded and started unstrapping himself from his chair. "Bear in mind, too, that even if we're able to guess where he'll come out of hyperspace, we'll have a minimum of several days to prepare for the encounter. Travis, as the nearest thing to a military expert we've got, you're in charge of getting us ready for combat."

I swallowed. "Yes, sir."

The wrong place, the wrong time.

*   *   *

Twenty minutes later we were in hyperspace, in hot pursuit of the Drymnu ship, and I was in my cabin, wondering just what in hell I was going to do.

A Drymnu hive ship. Eighteen thousand—call them individuals, bodies, whatever—there were still eighteen thousand of them, each part of a common mind. The concept was bad enough; the immediate military consequences were even worse.

No problems with command or garbled orders. Instant communication between laser operators and those at the scanners. Possibly no need for scanners at all at close range—observers watching from opposite ends of the ship would give the mind a binocular vision that would both make scanners unnecessary and, incidentally, render useless many of the Services' ECM jammers. The ship itself would be a hundred times larger than the *Volga*, with almost certainly the extra structural strength a craft that big would have to have. More antimeteor lasers. More speed.

In other words, warship or not, if we went head-to-head against the Drymnu, we were going to get our tubes peeled.

What in the hell were we going to *do*?

The smartest decision would be to quit right now, try to talk the captain out of it, and if that didn't work, simply to refuse to obey his order. *Mutiny*. The memory of the *Burma* incident made me wince. But this wasn't the Services, and it was nothing like the same situation. *Mutiny*. In this case, it was far and away the best chance of getting all of us out of this alive. And *that*, it seemed to me, was where my loyalty ought to lie. I respected the captain a great deal, but he had no idea what he was getting all of us into. These people weren't trained—weren't volunteers for dangerous duty like Services people were—and sending the *Volga* out to be point man in this war was mass suicide. Maybe Captain Garrett felt legally bound to carry out Colonel Halveston's dying order, but I didn't feel myself nearly so tied.

In fact, it occurred to me that by refusing the captain's orders, I might actually be doing him a favor. Halveston's order had been directed at him; but if he was prevented from carrying it out, he would be off the legal hook. Any official wrath would then turn onto me, of course, but I was prepared to accept that. Unlike Captain Garrett, I was used to having my career dumped out with the sawdust. Surely enough of the others would back me in this, especially once I explained how it would be for the captain's good, and we could just head to the nearest Services base . . .

Assuming there *were* still Services bases to head for. Assuming the Messenia attack had been a one-shot deal. Assuming the Drymnu had not, in fact, launched an all-out war.

And if those assumptions were wrong, running from the Drymnu now wouldn't gain us anything but a little time. Maybe not even that.

Which was where the crux of my dilemma lay. Saving the *Volga* now for worse treatment later on wouldn't be doing anyone a favor.

I was chasing the logic around the track for the fifth time when my door buzzed. "Come in," I called, the words releasing the lock.

I'd expected it to be the captain. It was, instead, Kittredge. "Busy?" she asked, stepping inside with the peculiar gait that rotational pseudogravity always gives people in ships the *Volga*'s size.

A younger man might have expected it to be a social call. I knew Kittredge better than that. "Not really," I said as the door slid closed behind her. "Just plotting out the victory parade route for after we've whipped the Drymnu's sauce. Why?"

The attempt at humor didn't even register on her face. "Travis, we've got some serious trouble here."

"I've noticed. What do you suggest we do about it?"

"Call the whole thing off," she growled. "We can't take on any Drymnu hive ship—it's completely out of the question."

If it had been Wong who'd tossed my own ideas back at me like this, we would have been off to lay out our

ultimatum before the captain in thirty seconds. But
Kittredge was so intense and by-the-book . . . Per-
versely, my brain shifted into devil's advocate mode.
"You're suggesting Captain Garrett disobey a duly given
and recorded order?"

She snorted. "No one in the Services would even
think of holding us to that. What, they'd rather we go
in and get blown up for nothing than come back with
valuable information?"

Maybe it was a remnant of my Services pride come
back to haunt me, or maybe it was just Kittredge and
the fact that I was the one in charge of planning this
operation. Whatever it was, something like a psychic
burr began to work its way under a corner of my mind.
"You assume the outcome would be a forgone conclusion."

"You bet I do—and don't give me that look. You
were a minor petty officer aboard a third-rate starship. I
hardly expect they overloaded you with battle tactics,
especially against an enemy we weren't ever supposed
to have to fight."

The burr dug itself in a little deeper. "You might be
surprised," I told her stiffly. "The *Burma*'s engineering
section was designed to operate independently in case
of massive destruction to the rest of the ship. We were
taught quite a lot about warfare."

"Against hivies?" she asked pointedly.

"Not exactly, no," I admitted. "But just because the
hivies weren't supposed to be warlike doesn't mean no
one ever considered what it might mean to fight one of
them. I remember one lecture in particular that listed
three exploitable weaknesses a hive ship would have
against a human ship in battle."

"Oh? I don't suppose you remember what they were?"

I felt my face getting hotter. "You mean is the old
man losing his memory at wholesale rates?"

"Well?" she replied coolly. "Are you?"

"I wouldn't bet on it if I were you," I snapped.
"You'll see what shape my memory and mind are in

when I give the captain my preliminary plan in a couple of days."

"Uh-*huh*." A faint look of scorn twitched at her lip. "I'm sure it'll be Crécy all over again. You'll forgive me if I still try and talk the captain out of it."

"That's up to you," I said as she turned around and walked, stiff-backed, to the door. It opened for her, and she left.

With an odd feeling in my stomach, I realized that I had just set a pleasant little bonfire in the center of my line of retreat. If I didn't come up with a workable battle plan now, I would humiliate myself in front of Kittredge—and probably everyone else aboard ship, too. In my mind's eye I could see Kittredge's I-knew-you-couldn't-do-it contempt, the captain's maddeningly understanding look, Waskin's outright amusement . . .

Alone in my cabin, the images still made me cringe. More undeserved shame . . . and for once, I suddenly decided I would rather die than go through all of that again. I *would* draw up a battle plan—and it was going to be the best damned plan Waskin or Kittredge had ever seen.

I would start with a concerted effort to dredge up those three vaguely remembered hivey weaknesses from their dusty hiding places in my memory. And maybe with a trip through the ship's references to find out just what the hell this Crécy was that Kittredge had referred to.

We started making preparations immediately, of course. Unfortunately, there weren't a lot of preparations that could be made.

The *Volga*, as was pointed out to me with monotonous regularity, was not a warship. We had no shielding beyond the standard solar radiation and micrometeor stuff, our sole weapon was a pair of laser cannons designed to blow away more dangerous meteors—those up to a whopping half-meter across—and our drive and mechanical structure had never been designed for anything even resembling a tight maneuver. We were a

waddling, quacking duck that could be blown into me-
sons half a second after the Drymnu decided we were
dangerous to it.

The trick, therefore, was going to be to make the
Volga seem as harmless as possible . . . and then to
figure out how we could stop being harmless when we
wanted to. That much was basic military strategy, the
stuff I'd learned my second week in basic. Fortunately,
there was one very trivial way to accomplish that.

Unfortunately, it was the *only* way I could think of to
accomplish it.

Across the room, the door slid open and Waskin
walked in, a wary expression on his face. "I hope like
hell, sir," he said, "that this isn't what I think it is."

"It is," I nodded, keying the door closed. "I'm tap-
ping you for part of my assault team."

"Oh, sh—" He swallowed the rest of the expletive
with an effort. "Sir, I'd like to respectfully withdraw, on
grounds— "

"Stuff it, Waskin," I told him shortly. "We haven't
got time for it. How much has the ship's grapevine
given you about what I've got planned?"

"Enough. You're having a meteor laser taken out and
installed aboard one of the landing boats. If you ask me,
your David/Goliath complex is getting a little out of
hand."

I ignored the sarcasm. Everyone else, even Kittredge,
had started treating me with new respect, but it had
been too much to hope for that Waskin would join that
particular club. "I take it you don't think it would be a
good idea to send a boat out after the Drymnu ship.
Why not?"

He looked hard at me, decided it was a serious
question. "Because he'll blow us apart before we get
anywhere near our own firing range, that's why. Or
have I missed something?"

"You've missed two things. First of all, remember
that this isn't a warship we're going up against. The

Drymnu isn't likely to have fine-aim lasers or high-maneuverable missiles aboard."

"Why not?"

"Why should he?"

"Because he knows we'll eventually be sending warships and fighter carriers after him."

"Ah." I held up a finger. "Warships, yes. But not necessarily carriers."

Waskin frowned. "You mean he might not know we've got them?"

I shook my head. "I'm guessing that the concept of fighters won't even occur to him."

"Why wouldn't it? You could put a handful of Drymnu bodies aboard something the size of a fighter, and as long as they didn't get too far from the mother ship, they'd still be connected to the hive mind."

And at that moment Waskin sealed his fate. Everyone else that I'd had this talk with had needed to be reminded that hivies couldn't function at all in groups of less than a few thousand . . . and *then* had needed to be reminded that the thirty-thousand-klick range meant that small scouts or fighters could, indeed, have limited use for them. "You're right," I nodded to Waskin. "Absolutely right. So why won't the Drymnu expect us to use small fighters?"

He made a face. "You're enjoying this, aren't you? This is your revenge for all the poker games you've lost, right?"

God knew there wasn't a lot about this situation that was even remotely enjoyable . . . but in a perverse way I *did* rather like being ahead of Waskin for a change. The fact that my years in the Services gave me a slight advantage was totally irrelevant. "Never mind me," I told him shortly. "You just concentrate on *you*. Why won't he expect fighters?"

He snorted, then shook his head. "I don't know. Maybe a single ship-sized mind can't handle that many disparate viewpoints. No, that doesn't make sense."

"It's actually pretty close," I had to admit. "It's loosely

tied into the reason for that thirty-thousand-klick range. That number suggest anything?"

"It's the distance light travels in a tenth of a second," he said promptly. "I'm not *that* ignorant, you know."

He was right; that part of the hivies' limitation was pretty common knowledge. "Okay, then, that leads us immediately to the fact that the common telepathic link behaves the same way light does, with all the same limitations. So what do you get when you have, say, a dozen high-speed fighters swarming out from the mother ship vectoring in on your target?"

"What do you—? Oh. Oh, sure. High relative speeds mean you'll be getting into relativistic effects."

"Including time dilation," I nodded. "A pretty minor effect, admittedly. But if a section of mind can't handle even a tenth of a second time lag, it seems reasonable that even a small difference in the temporal *rate* would foul it up even worse."

He nodded slowly and gave me a long, speculative look. "Makes sense. Doesn't mean it's true."

"It is," I told him. "Or it's at least official theory. We've observed Sirrachat and Karmahsh ships occasionally using small advance scouts when feeling their way through a particularly dense ring system or asteroid belt. The scouts behave exactly as expected: they stay practically within hugging range of the mother ship and keep their speeds strictly matched with it."

"Uh-huh. I take it this is supposed to make me feel better about going up against Goliath? Because if it is, it isn't working." He held up some fingers and began ticking them off. "One: if we can think like hivies, it's just possible he's been able to think like humans and will be all ready for us to come blazing in on him. Two: even if he *isn't* ready for us right at the start, a hive mind learns pretty damn quickly. How many passes is it going to take us to hit a vital spot and put his ship out of commission—twenty? Fifty? And three: even if by some miracle he doesn't catch on to the basics of space warfare through all of that, what makes you think we're going to be able to take advantage of it? None of *us* are soldiers, either."

"What do you think *I* am?" I asked.

"A former Services engine room officer who got everything he knows about tactics by pure osmosis," he shot back.

I forced down my irritation with an effort. The fact that he was right didn't make it any easier. "Okay," I growled. "But by osmosis or otherwise, I've still got it. And as far as *that* goes, you and Fromm have both had more than *your* share of experience using the meteor laser. Haven't you."

I had the satisfaction of seeing him flinch. He and Fromm had had a private duel of LaserWar going on down in the game room for the past six months, and I knew for a fact that they both occasionally brought the competition into duty hours, using the *Volga*'s lasers for live practice. Strictly against regulations, naturally. "A little, maybe," he muttered. "But mostly that's just a game."

"So? Hivies don't get even *that* much practice—they don't play LaserWar or any other games. Which brings me to our second advantage over them: a hive mind may learn fast, but all eighteen thousand bodies on that ship are going to start exactly even. It's not as though there's going to be anyone there who has even a smattering of practical experience with tactics, for instance, or anyone who excels at hitting small, fast-moving targets. We do, and I intend to use that advantage to the fullest."

"By making Fromm and me your chief gunners?" Waskin snorted.

"By making Fromm my chief gunner," I corrected. "You I'm making my second-in-command."

His eyes bulged. "You're—*what*? Oh, now wait a minute, sir—"

"Sorry, Waskin, the job's yours." I glanced at my watch. "All right. We'll be having a meeting to set up practice sessions in the lounge in exactly one hour. Be there."

For a moment I thought he was going to argue with me. But he just took a deep breath and nodded. "Yes, sir. Under protest, though."

"I wouldn't have expected it any other way."

He left, and I took a deep breath of my own. There was nothing like a willing team, I reflected, letting my eyes defocus with tiredness. None of the six I'd chosen had any real enthusiasm for what they saw as a stupid decision on the captain's part, but at least only Waskin was even verbally hostile about it.

That would probably change, of course, at the meeting an hour away, when I told them about the rest of my plan. It wasn't something I was especially looking forward to.

But in the meantime . . . Stretching hard, I cracked the tension out of my back and settled more comfortably into my seat. *One: hivies won't be able to think in terms of small-group efficiency. Two: a given hivey mind-segment won't have the same range of abilities and talents that a human force will have. Three: . . .*

No good. Whatever that third hivey weakness was, it was still managing to elude me. But that was okay; I still had a couple of days until breakout, and surely that would be enough time for my subconscious to dig it out of wherever it was I'd tucked it away.

They didn't like the plan. Didn't like it at all.

And I couldn't really blame them. The landing boat assault was bad enough, relying as strongly as it did on Hive Mind Weaknesses One and Two—weaknesses they had only my unsupported word for. But the full plan was even worse, and none of them were particularly reticent about voicing their displeasure.

It could have come to mass mutiny right there, I suppose, with the crew going to the captain en masse and demanding either a decent plan of action or else that he scrap this whole thing. And I suppose that there was a part of me that hoped they would do so. It had been rather pleasant, for a change, to be treated with a little respect aboard the ship—to be Tactician Travis, the man who was guiding the *Volga* into battle, instead of just plain Third Officer Travis, who always lost at poker. But none of that could quite erase the knowledge that I could very well be on the brink of getting some of us killed, me included. I'd already burned my own spaceport behind me, but if the captain decided to quit now, I for one wasn't going to argue too strenuously with him.

But he didn't. Perhaps he felt he'd also come too far to back down; perhaps he really believed that he was obligated to Colonel Halveston's dying order. But whatever the reason, he came out in solid support of both me and my plan, and in the end everyone fell grudgingly into line behind him. Perhaps, with so much uncertainty still remaining as to whether we'd even catch the Drymnu ship, no one wanted to stick his or her neck too far out.

A fair portion of that uncertainty, though, was illusory. True, we had only the Drymnu's departure vector to guide us, and it was true that he could theoretically break out and change his direction anywhere along a path a hundred light-years long. But in actuality, his choices were far more limited: by physics, which governed how long a ship could generate heat in hyperspace before it had to break out and dump it; and by common sense, which said that in case of breakout problems you wanted your ship reasonably close to raw materials and energy, which meant somewhere inside a solar system.

There was, it turned out, exactly one system along the Drymnu's vector that fit both those constraints.

So even while my team complained and muttered to one another about the chances this would all be a waste of time, I made sure they worked their butts off. Somewhere in that system, I was pretty sure, we would find the Drymnu.

Four days later, we broke out into our target system, a totally unremarkable conglomeration of nondescript planets, minor chunks of rock, a dull red sun . . . and one Drymnu ship.

He wasn't visible to the naked eye, of course, but by solar system standards we arrived practically on his landing ramp. He was barely three million klicks away, radiating so much infrared that Waskin had a lock on him two minutes after breakout. Captain Garrett gave the order, and we turned and drove hell for leather straight for him.

The *Volga* was capable of making nearly two gravs of acceleration, but even at that, the Drymnu was a good seven hours away. There was, therefore, no question of sneaking up on him, especially since half that time we would be decelerating with our main drive blasting directly toward him. There was little chance he would escape into hyperspace—not with the amount of heat he clearly had yet to get rid of—but I'd expected that he would at least make us chase him through normal, gain himself some extra time to study us.

We were less than half an hour away from him when we all were finally forced to the conclusion that he really *did* intend to simply stand there and hold his ground.

"Damn," Waskin muttered under his breath at the scanners. "He knows we're here—he *has* to have seen us by now. He's waiting for us, like a—a giant spider in his web—"

"That'll do, Waskin," the captain told him, his own voice icy calm. "There's no need to create wild pictures; I think we're all adequately nervous. Just remember that chances are at least as good that he's waiting because he figures we're a warship and that running would be a waste of time."

"Running doesn't sound like a waste of time to *me*," Kittredge said tensely.

The captain turned a brief stare on her, then looked at me. "Well, Travis, looks like this is it. Any last-minute changes you want to make in the plan?"

I shook my head. *One: hivies don't form small groups. Two: all members of a hive mind have the same experience level. Three: . . . Three, where the hell are you, damn it?* "No, sir," I told him with a quiet sigh. Half an hour to battle. No way around it; we were just going to have to make do without Hive Mind Weakness Number Three, whatever it was. "I'd better get the team into the boat."

He nodded and motioned someone else to take Waskin's place at the scanners. "We'll signal just before we drop you," he told me. "And we'll let you know if there's any change in the situation out there. Good luck."

"Thank you, sir."

Waskin beside me, I headed out the bridge door and did a fast float down the cramped corridor toward the landing boat bay. "So this is it, isn't it?" Waskin murmured. "Your big chance to be a hero."

"I'm not doing this for the heroics of it," I growled back.

"No? Come on, Travis, I'm not *that* stupid. You and the captain dreamed up this whole landing boat assault just so that he can pretend he's obeying Halveston's damned order while still keeping the *Volga* itself from getting blasted to dust."

"The captain has nothing to do with it," I snapped. "It's—it just happens to make the most sense this way."

"Aha," he nodded, an entirely too knowing look on his face. "So you're trying to con the captain along with the rest of us, are you? I should have guessed that. He wouldn't have been able to send us out to get fried on his behalf. Not with a straight face, anyway."

I gritted my teeth. Somehow, I'd thought I'd covered my intentions better than that. "You're hallucinating," I snarled. "There's not a scrap of truth to it—and you'd sure as hell better not go blabbing nonsense like that to the rest of the team."

"Don't get so mad—it's working, isn't it? The *Volga*'s going to come out okay, and you're going to get to go out in a blaze of glory. Along with six more of us lucky souls."

I gritted my teeth some more and ignored him, and we covered another half corridor in silence. "There wasn't really any Services list of hive mind weaknesses, was there?" he said as we maneuvered through a tight hatchway. "You made all that up to justify this plan."

I exhaled in defeat. "No, it was—it is—an actual list," I told him. "It's just that—look, it was a long time ago. The two I gave you are real enough. And there's one more—an important one, I'm pretty sure—but I can't for the life of me remember what it was."

"Uh-huh. Sure."

Or in other words, he didn't believe me. "Waskin—"

"Oh, it's all right," he interrupted. "If it helps any, I actually happen to agree with the basic idea. I just wouldn't have picked myself to be one of the sacrificial goats."

"I'm hoping we'll come out of it a bit better than that," I told him.

"Uh-huh. Sure."

We finished the rest of the trip to the bay in silence, to find that the captain had already had the other five members of the team assemble there.

I tried giving them a short pep talk, but I wasn't particularly good at it and they weren't much in the mood to be pepped up, anyway. So instead we spent a few minutes checking one last time on our equipment and making as sure as we could that our specially equipped suits and weapons were going to function as desired.

Afterward, we all sat in the boat, breathed recycled air, and sweated hard.

And I tried one last time to think. *One: hivies don't form small groups. Two: all members of a hive mind have the same experience level. Three: . . . .*

Still no use.

I don't know how long we sat there. The plan was for the captain to take the *Volga* as close in as he could before the Drymnu's inevitable attack became too much for the ship to handle, but as the minutes dragged on and nothing happened, a set of frightening possibilities began to flicker through my already overheated mind. The *Volga*'s bridge blown so quickly that they'd had no time even to cry out . . . the rest of us flying blind

toward a collision or to sail forever through normal
space . . .

"The Drymnu's opened fire," the captain's voice crackled abruptly in our headsets. "Antimeteor lasers; some
minor sensor damage. Get ready—"

With a stomach-jolting lurch, we were dumped out
through the bay doors . . . and got our first real look at
a Drymnu hive ship.

The thing was *huge.* Incredibly so. It was still several
klicks away, yet it still took up a massive chunk of the
sky ahead of us. Dark-hulled, oddly shaped, convoluted,
threatening—it was all of those, too, but the only word
that registered in that first heart-stopping second was
huge. I'd seen the biggest of the Services' carriers up
close, and I was stunned. God only knows how the
others in the boat felt.

And then the first laser flicked out toward us, and the
time for that kind of thought was thankfully over.

The shot was a clean miss. We'd been dropped along
one of the Drymnu's flanks, as planned, and it was
quickly clear that lasers designed for shooting oncoming
meteors weren't at their best trying to fire sideways.
But the Drymnu was a hive mind, and hive minds
learned fast. The second and third shots missed, too,
but the fourth bubbled the reflective paint on our nose.
"Let's get moving," I snapped.

Kelly, our pilot, didn't need any coaxing. The words
weren't even out of my mouth when she had us jammed
against our restraints in a tight spiraling turn that sent
us back toward the stern. Not *too* close; the drive that
could actually move this floating mountain would fry us
in nanoseconds if it occurred to the Drymnu to turn it
on. But Kelly knew her job, and when we finally pulled
into a more or less inertial path again, we were no more
than two-thirds of the way back toward the stern and
maybe three hundred meters from the textured hull.

This close to a true warship, we would be dead in
seconds. But the Drymnu wasn't a warship . . . and as
we flew on unvaporized, I finally knew for a fact that

my gamble had paid off. We were inside the alien's defenses, and he couldn't touch us.

Now if we could only turn that advantage into something concrete.

"Fromm, get the laser going," I ordered. "The rest of you, let's find some targets for him to hit. Sensors, intakes, surface radiator equipment—anything that looks weak."

My headset crackled suddenly. "*Volga* to Travis," the captain's voice said. "Neutrino emission's suddenly gone up—I think he's running up his drive."

"Acknowledged," I said. "You out of his laser range yet?"

"We will be soon. So far he seems to be ignoring us."

A small favor to be grateful for. Whatever happened to us, at least this part of my plan had worked. "Okay. We're starting our first strafing run—"

Abruptly, my headset exploded with static. I grabbed for the volume control, vaguely aware of the others scrambling with similar haste around me. "What happened?" Kelly's voice came faintly, muffled by two helmets and the thin atmosphere in the boat.

"It's occurred to him that jamming our radios is a good idea," I shouted, my voice echoing painfully inside my helmet.

"Took him long enough," Waskin put in. "What was that about the drive? He trying to get away?"

"Probably." But no matter how powerful the Drymnu's drive, with all that mass to move, he wouldn't be outrunning us for a while, anyway. "We've still got time to do plenty of damage. Get cracking."

We tried. We flew all the way around that damn ship, skimming its surface, blasting away at anything that looked remotely interesting . . . and in the process we discovered something I'd somehow managed not to anticipate.

None of us had the faintest idea what Drymnu sensors, intakes, or surface radiator equipment looked like.

Totally unexpected. Form follows function, or so I'd

always believed. But there was clearly more room for variation than I'd ever realized.

Which meant that even as we vaporized bits of metal and plastic all over that ship, we had no idea whatsoever how much genuine damage we were doing. Or even if we were doing any damage at all.

And slowly the Drymnu began to move.

I put off the decision as long as possible, and so it wound up being Waskin who eventually forced the issue. "Gonna have to go all the way, aren't we?" he called out. "The full plan. It's either that or give up and go home."

I gritted my teeth hard enough to hurt. It was my plan, and even while I'd been selling it to the others I'd been hoping like hell we wouldn't have to use it. But there was literally no other choice available to us now. If we tried to escape to the *Volga* now, it would be a choice of heading aft and being fried by the drive or going forward and giving the lasers a clean shot at us. There was no way to go now but in. "All right," I sighed, then repeated it loudly for everyone to hear. "Kelly, find us something that looks like a hatchway and bring us down. Anyone here had experience working on rotating hulls?"

Even through two helmets I could hear Waskin's sigh. "I have," he said.

"Good. You and I will head out as soon as we're down."

The hatches, fortunately, *were* recognizable as such. Kelly had anchored us to the hull beside one of them, and Waskin and I were outside working it open, when the Drymnu seemed to suddenly realize just what we were doing. Abruptly, vents we hadn't spotted began spewing gases all over the area. For a bad minute I thought there might be acid or something equally dangerous being blown out the discharge tubes, but it registered only as obvious waste gases, apparently used in hopes of confusing us or breaking our boots' pseudoglue grip. Once again, it seemed, we'd caught the

Drymnu by surprise; but Waskin and I still didn't waste any time forcing the hatch open.

"Looks cramped," he grunted, touching his helmet to mine to bypass the still-jammed radio.

It was, too, though with Drymnu bodies half the size of ours, I wouldn't have expected anything else. "I think there's enough room for one of us to be inside and still have room to work," I told him, not bothering to point out we didn't have much choice in the matter. "I'll go. You and Fromm close the outer hatch once I'm in."

It took a little squeezing, but I made it. There didn't seem to be any inside controls, which was as expected; what I hadn't expected was that even as the hatch closed behind me and I unlimbered my modified cutting torch, my suit's exterior air sensors suddenly came alive.

And with the radio jammed, I was cut off from the others. I waited, heart thumping, wondering what the Drymnu had out there waiting for me. . . . As the pressures equalized, I threw all my weight upwards against the inner hatch. For a second it resisted. Then, with a *pop!* it swung open and, getting a grip on the lip, I pulled myself out into the corridor—

To be faced by a river of meter-high figures surging directly toward me.

There was no time for thought on any rational level, and indeed I later had no recollection at all of having aimed and fired my torch. But abruptly the hallway was ablaze with light and flame . . . and where the blue-white fire met the dark river there was death.

I heard no screams. Possibly my suit insulated me from that sound; more likely the telepathic bodies of a hive mind had never had reason to develop any vocal apparatus. But whatever else was alien about the Drymnu, its multiple bodies were still based on carbon and oxygen, and such molecules were not built to survive the kind of heat I was focusing on them. Where the flame touched, the bodies flared and dropped and died.

It was all over in seconds, at least that first wave of the attack. A dozen of the bodies lay before and around me, still smoldering and smoking, while the others beat an orderly retreat. I looked down at the carnage just once, then turned my eyes quickly and firmly away. I was just glad I couldn't smell them.

I was still standing there, watching and waiting for the next attack, when a tap on my helmet made me start violently. "Easy, easy, it's me," a faint and frantic voice came as I spun around and nearly incinerated Waskin. "Powers is behind me in the airlock. Are there any buttons in here we have to push to cycle it?"

"No, it seems to be set on automatic," I told him. "You have everyone coming in?"

"All but Kelly. I thought we ought to leave someone with the boat."

"Good." Experimentally, I turned my radio up a bit. No good: the jamming was just as strong inside the ship as it had been outside. "Well, at least he probably won't have any better hand weapons than we do. And he ought to be even worse at hand-to-hand than he is at space warfare."

"Unfortunately, he's got all those eighteen thousand bodies to spend learning the techniques," Waskin pointed out sourly.

"Not that many—we only have to kill maybe fourteen or fifteen thousand to destroy the hive mind."

"That's not an awful lot of help," he said.

Actually, though, it was, especially considering that the more bodies we disposed of the less of the mind would actually be present. *Weakness Number Three: destroying segments of the mind eventually destroys the whole?* No, that wasn't quite it. But it was getting closer. . . .

The Drymnu was able to get in two more assaults before the last four of our landing party made it through the airlock. Neither attack was particularly imaginative, and both were ultimately failures, but already the mind was showing far more grasp of elementary tactics than I cared for. The second attack was actually layered, with a torch-armed backup team hiding under cover while the main suicide squad drew us out into the corridor, and it was only the fact that we had heavily fire- and heat-proofed our suits beforehand that let us escape without burns.

But for the moment we clearly still held the advantage, and by the time all six of us were ready to begin moving down the corridor the Drymnu had pulled back out of sight.

"I don't suppose he's given up already," Fromm called as we headed cautiously out.

"More likely cooking up something nasty somewhere," Waskin shouted back.

"Let's kill the idle chatter," I called. My ears buzzed from the volume I had to use to be heard, and it occurred to me that if we kept this up we would all have severe self-inflicted deafness long before the Drymnu got us. "Keep communication helmet-to-helmet as much as possible," I told them.

Fromm leaned over and touched his helmet to mine. "Are we heading anywhere specific, or just supposed to cause as much damage as we can?"

"The latter, unless we find a particular target worth going for," I told him. "If we analyze the Drymnu's defenses, say, and figure out that he's defending some place specific, we'll go for that. Pass the word, okay?"

Good targets or not, though, we were equipped to do a lot of incidental damage, and we did our damnedest to live up to our potential. The rooms were already deserted as we got to them, but they were full of flammable carpeting and furnishings, and we soon had a dozen fires spewing flames and smoke in our wake. Within ten minutes the corridor was hazy with smoke—and, more significantly, with *moving* smoke—which meant that whatever bulkheading and rupture-control system the Drymnu was employing, it was clear that the burning section wasn't being well sealed off from the remainder of the ship. That should have meant big trouble for the alien, which in turn should have meant he would be soon throwing everything he had in an effort to stop us.

But it didn't happen. We moved farther and farther into the ship, setting fires and torching everything that looked torchable, and still the Drymnu held back. For a while I wondered if he was simply waiting for us to run out of fuel; for a shorter while I wondered if he had indeed given up. But the radio jamming continued, and he didn't seem to care that we were using up our fuel destroying his home, and so for lack of a better plan we just kept going.

We got up a couple of ramps, switched corridors twice, and were at a large, interior corridor when we finally found out what he had in mind.

It was just the fortune of the draw that Powers was point man as we reached that spot . . . just the fortune of the draw that he was the one to die. He glanced around the corner into the main corridor, started to step through—and was abruptly hurled a dozen meters sideways by a violent blast of highly compressed air. Waskin, behind him, leaned into the corridor to spray torch fire in that direction, and apparently succeeded in neutralizing the weapon. But it cost us precious seconds, and by the time we were able to move in and see what was happening to Powers, it was too late. The dark tide of bodies withdrew readily from before our flames, and we saw that Powers, still inside his reinforced suit, had nevertheless been beaten to death.

"With tools, looked like," Fromm said. Even through the muffling of the helmets his voice was clearly shaking. "They clubbed him to death with ordinary tools."

"So much for him not understanding the techniques of warfare," Waskin bit out. "He's figured out all he really needs to know: that he's got the numbers on his side. And how to use them."

He was right. Inevitable, really; the only mystery was why it had taken the Drymnu this long to realize that. "We'd better keep moving," I shouted as we pressed our helmets together in a ring.

"Why bother?" Brimmer snarled, his voice dripping

with anger and fear. "Waskin's right—he knows what he's doing, all right. He's suckered us into coming too far inside the ship and now he's ready to begin the slaughter."

"Yeah, well, maybe," Fromm growled, "but he's going to have one hell of a fight before he gets us."

"So?" Brimmer shot back. "What difference does it make to *him* how many of his bodies he loses? He's got *eighteen thousand* of them to throw at us."

"So we kill as many as we can," I put in, struggling to regain control. "Every bit helps slow him down."

"Oh, *hell*!" Brimmer said suddenly. "Look—here they come!"

I swung around . . . and froze.

The entire width of the hallway was a mass of dark bodies charging down on us—dark bodies, with hands that glinted with metal tools.

This was it . . . and down deep I knew Brimmer was right. For all my purported tactical knowledge, I'd been taken in by the oldest ploy in human military history: draw the enemy deep inside your lines and then smother him. I glanced around; sure enough, the bodies filled the corridor in the other direction, too.

And for the last time in my life I had wound up in the wrong place at the wrong time. Except that this time I wouldn't be the only one who paid the price.

We had already shifted into a back-to-back formation, and three lines of torch fire were licking out toward each half of the imploding waves. Leaning my head back a few degrees, I touched the helmet behind me. "Looks like this is it," I said, trying hard to keep my voice calm. "Let's try to at least take as much of the Drymnu down with us as we can—we owe Messenia that much. Go for head shots—pass it down to the others."

The words were barely out of my mouth when I was deafened by another of the air blasts that had gotten Powers. Automatically, I braced myself; but this time they'd added something new. Along with the burst of air threatening to sweep us off our feet came a cloud of metal shrapnel.

It hit Waskin squarely in the chest.

I didn't hear any gasp of pain, but as he fell to his knees I clearly heard him utter something blasphemous. I gave the approaching wave one last sweep with my torch and then dropped down beside him. "Where does it hurt?" I shouted, pressing our helmets together.

"Mostly everywhere," he bit out. "Damn. I think they got my air system."

As well as the rest of the suit. I gritted my teeth and broke out my emergency patch kit, running a hand over his reinforced air hose to try and find the break. Suit integrity per se shouldn't be a big problem—we'd modified the standard suit design to isolate the helmet from everything else with just this sort of thing in mind. But an air system leak in an unknown atmosphere might easily prove fatal, and I had no intention of losing Waskin to suffocation or poisoning while he could still fight. I found the leak, gripped the piece of metal still sticking out of it—

"Oh, hell, Travis," he gasped. "Hell. What am I using for brains?"

"What?" I called. "What is it?"

"The Drymnu, damn it. Forget the head shots—we got to stop killing them."

Hysteria so quickly? "Waskin—"

"Damn it, Travis, don't you see? It's a hive mind—a *hive mind*. All experiences are shared commonly. *All* experiences—*including pain!*"

It was like a tactical full-spec bomb had gone off in the back of my brain. *Hive Mind Weakness Number Three: injure a part and you injure the whole.* "That's *it!*" I snapped, standing up and slamming my helmet against the one behind me. "Fire to injure, everyone, not to kill. Go for the arms and legs—try and take the bodies out of the fight without killing them. Pass the word—we're going to see if we can overload the Drymnu with pain."

For a wonder, they understood, and by the time

Waskin and I were back in the game ourselves it was already becoming clear that we indeed had a chance. It was far easier to injure the bodies than to kill them—far easier and far quicker—and as the incapacitated bodies fell to the deck, their agonized thrashing hindered the advance of those behind them. The air-blast cannon continued its attacks for a while, but while all of us got painfully pincushioned by the flying shrapnel, Waskin's remained the only seriously life-threatening injury. We kept firing, and the bodies kept charging, and I gritted my teeth waiting for the Drymnu to switch tactics on us.

But he didn't. I'd been right, all along: for all his sophistication and alien intelligence, the Drymnu had no concept of warfare beyond the brute-force numbers game he'd latched onto. Even now, when it was clearly failing, he could come up with no alternative to it, and with each passing minute I could feel the attack becoming more sluggish or more erratic in turn as the Drymnu began to lose his ability to focus on us. Eventually, it reached the point where I knew there would be no more surprises. The Drymnu, agonized probably beyond anything he had ever felt before, and with more pain coming in faster than it could be dealt with, had literally become unable to think straight.

Approximately five minutes later, the attacking waves finally began to retreat back down the corridor; and even as we began to give chase, the radio jamming abruptly ceased and the Drymnu surrendered.

The full story—or at least the official story—didn't surface from the dust for nearly two months, but it came out pretty nearly as we on the *Volga* had already expected it to. The Drymnu—either the total thing or some large fraction of it—had apparently decided that having a fragmented race out among the stars was both an abomination of nature and highly dangerous besides, and had taken it upon himself to see whether humanity could indeed be destroyed. Point man—or point whatever—in a war that was apparently already over. The

Drymnu, defeated by a lowly unarmed freighter, had clearly learned his lesson.

And I was left to meditate once more on the frustrations of my talent.

Sure, we won. Better than that, the *Volga* was actually famous, at least among official circles. To be sure, our medals were given to us at a private ceremony and we were warned gently against panicking the general public with stories about what had happened, but it was still fame of a sort. And we *did* save humanity from having to fight a war of survival. At least this time.

And yet. . . .

If I hadn't been standing there next to Waskin—hadn't decided to take the time to repair his air tube—we would very likely all have been killed . . . and I would have been spared the humiliation of having to sit around the *Volga* and listen to Waskin tell everyone over and over again how it had been *his* last-minute inspiration that had saved the day.

The wrong place at the wrong time.

MAGIC MATTER

And now for something absolutely different in propulsion technology: Magic Matter. Since its initial conception, the harnessing of anti-matter has been The Impossible Dream. Well, maybe impossible to the primitive science of the 1970s, but, after all, times do change . . .

MAGIC MATTER

Dr. Robert L. Forward

You watch the screen as the aging executive ponders the stocks you suggested: Rotavator, Ltd. and MirrorMat, Inc., the new subsidiary of General Energy. They are equally good investments. Your eyes wander to the clock at the top of the screen. It is near quitting time.

"Thank God it's Thursday," you mutter as the image on the screen finally decides to invest 35,000 international accounting units in MirrorMat, Inc. You politely inquire about the weather in Paris, then switch back to local. With relief you place the buy order, make your weekly sales report to the home office in Australia, and initiate shut-down as the clock reaches 16:00:00.

A hard day's work is done. You deserve the long holiday weekend coming up. With the Fourth of July falling on Monday, you are going to enjoy four days at the glamorous Sahara Copernicus in Las Lunas, with its fabulous casinos and non-stop entertainment. What you want to see is the new "Holiday in Flight" show, with swooping chorus lines of aerobats flying about in shimmering white wings in the low lunar gravity.

You open the door to the office, step out into the

Excerpted from *Future Magic*, to be published by Avon Books

Arizona sunshine, and walk over to your Chevy Astro-Cruiser. Checking to make sure that the propellant tanks are topped off with water and there is plenty of magic matter in the storage bottle, you take off. Under controlled power, the 'Cruiser mutters off into the deep desert, heading for the greenly glaring pillar of fire that streaks upward into the sky. As you approach, you see others riding up on that green beam, boosted into low Earth orbit by laser tugs that collect the light from a battery of lasers surrounding the launch site, then use the energy to heat water into a blazing plasma exhaust that is too hot to be called steam.

The waiting line is too long. This is your vacation, so hang the expense. You shoot your 'Cruiser into orbit using magic matter, despite the price per milligram of the stuff. Once up in orbit, you set the computer for the nearest space station and the jet spouts a flare of incandescent hydrogen and oxygen as invisible particles of magic matter are mixed with buckets of water. At the orbital space station, you refill the tank with water and replace the magic matter capsule with a new one from the MirrorMat filling station. It has a full load of 30 milligrams of magic matter. You then take off on the long trip across the black desert between the workaday Earth and the glamorous oasis above you in space, jets booming as you start a holiday away from the dreary reality of the work-screen.

Fiction or Future Magic?

What is magic matter? How can it let us escape the dreary bounds of Earth and let us shoot upward into the skies?

To travel you must move. To move you must have energy. To get energy you must convert mass. Every time you burn a tankful of gasoline to take you and your automobile farther down the highway on a long week-end trip to Las Vegas, mass has disappeared. In the process of burning gasoline, some of the mass of the gasoline has been converted into energy.

With chemical fuels such as gasoline and rocket fuels,

the amount of mass that gets converted is parts in a thousand million. With fission energy, using uranium or plutonium as fuels, the amount of mass converted becomes parts in a thousand. With fission fuels like hydrogen and deuterium, the mass conversion ratio reaches almost one percent. Yet all of these fuels are eclipsed by magic matter, for when magic matter meets normal matter *all* of the mass in both the magic matter and the normal matter gets converted into energy. (Since normal matter is easy to come by, one could say that magic matter is the only fuel that is 200 percent efficient!) Magic matter has had many names, such as contraterrene and antimatter, but perhaps the most descriptive term is "mirror matter," for it is a new form of stable matter that is the "mirror image" of normal matter.

The world is made of normal matter, in the form of atoms. The atoms have a heavy nucleus at the center made up of particles called protons and neutrons. Surrounding the nucleus of each atom is a cloud of electrons. Everything we normally experience is made up of these three stable particles: protons, neutrons, and electrons.

Each of these three particles consists of a bundle of raw energy, wrapped up by nature into a compact, stable ball that we call matter. We don't really know why the proton and neutron weigh about the same, and yet are 1,800 times heavier than the electron. We don't really know why the charge on the electron is *exactly* equal and opposite in sign to the proton. We don't really know why all the other characteristics of each particle are the way they are. These are still mysteries. It is as if each of the particles has some special kind of quantum-mechanical "glue" to hold it together. The type of glue defines the amount of energy that can be bundled up into a particular kind of particle and the properties that the resulting bundle has.

For a long time after the electron and proton were discovered in the atom, scientists were puzzled at the asymmetry of nature. Why does the carrier of the positive electric charge weigh so much more than the carrier of the negative electric charge? Then, in the mid-1900's, scientists solved the puzzle by finding that each particle has a "mirror" twin. The mirror particle for the electron is called the positron. It has the same mass as the electron, but the sign of its electric charge is reversed. Like the electron, the positron also acts as if it were spinning like a top, generating a detectable magnetic field. Since the positron has a positive charge while the electron has a negative charge, the magnetic fields are oppositely directed to the spin axis in the two particles. Thus the positron is the mirror image of the electron [see Figure 1].

The mirror particle for the proton is called the antiproton. It has the same mass as the proton, but its charge and magnetic moment are reversed. There is also a mirror twin for the neutron, called the antineutron. Since neither the neutron nor the antineutron has a charge, it is hard to tell them apart. The neutron spins about its axis, however, and even though it is electrically neutral, it does have a magnetic field (indicating it is not a simple object, but is made up of a proton and electron). The mirror neutron also has a magnetic field, but its spin is in the opposite direction.

Since normal matter is made up of atoms built from electrons, protons, and neutrons, then it should be possible to make mirror matter out of atoms built up from positrons, antiprotons, and antineutrons. Mirror matter is just like normal matter, but with the properties reversed. For example, normal hydrogen is made of a single electron orbiting a proton, while mirror hydrogen is made of a positron orbiting an antiproton.

There is an important difference between the two forms of matter. Whereas a particle made of normal matter is a bundle of energy held together with quantum-mechanical "glue," the mirror particle is a similar bundle of energy held together with "antiglue." Each "glue" turns out to be a solvent for the other! Thus, when a mirror particle meets a normal particle, the two glues dissolve each other, and the energy con-

15195-1

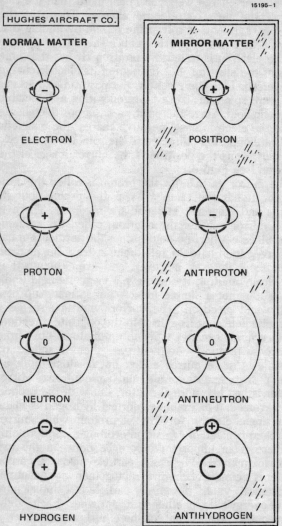

Figure 1. Normal matter and mirror matter.

tained in the two particles is released in a micro-explosion. The mass of both particles is *completely* converted into energy. The amount of energy that is released is given by the famous Einstein equation, $E = mc^2$. This complete conversion of mass to energy makes mirror matter a highly efficient, compact, light-weight, almost magical source of energy. One milligram of mirror matter combined with one milligram of normal matter produces the same energy as 20 tons of the most energetic chemical fuel in use today—liquid oxygen and liquid hydrogen.

Where can we get this magic matter? As far as scientists have been able to determine, it seems that the universe is made up of only one kind of matter—the normal kind that you, and I, and the Earth, Moon, Sun, stars, and galaxy are made of. Some theorists have speculated that this is just a local anomaly and that many of the galaxies that we see far from us in the deep skies could be mirror galaxies. We might be able to communicate with the mirror beings in them some day, but we could visit them only at our peril! Whatever the reason, the experimental fact is that only regular matter occurs in nature. If we want magic matter, we will have to make it.

It is at this point that you might think, "This is nothing but science fiction," but mirror matter has graduated to the dimly perceived realm of future magic. Recent advances in a number of seemingly unrelated sciences have combined to show that it is now physically feasible to make, capture, store, and utilize mirror matter in useful quantities. Whether it can ever be done at reasonable cost is a task for future technologists to determine.

You may have heard that mixing mirror matter with normal matter produces gamma rays. The first mirror matter that was produced was the positron, the mirror particle to the electron. When positrons are mixed with electrons they *do* produce all of their energy as gamma rays, which are very difficult to cope with. When antiprotons are mixed with normal protons, however, the resulting energy does *not* come out as gamma rays.

Instead, the proton and its mirror twin turn into a collection of particles called pions. On the average there will be three charged pions and two neutral pions. The neutral pions almost instantly produce gamma rays. These gamma rays can be stopped by a shield to produce heat to run the auxiliary systems.

The other 60 percent of the energy released is in the form of highly energetic charged pions. The charged pions have a short life, but since they are traveling at 94 percent of the speed of light, they cover a distance of 21 meters (60 feet) during their lifetime, which is more than enough to extract the kinetic energy from them [see Figure 2]. After they decay, they turn into other charged particles called muons. The muons will travel 1.85 kilometers (over a mile) before they decay, turning into positrons and electrons. Since all these particles are electrically charged and moving near the speed of light, they act like a heavy, high-speed electrical current. This current can be directed by magnetic fields and perhaps used to drive power generators. The charged pions can also be used to heat normal matter, such as water or hydrogen, to produce a hot plasma. The hot plasma can be ejected out a rocket nozzle to provide thrust or used to power electric generators.

Because the mixing of protons and antiprotons produces easily used charged particles, the key to the utilization of mirror matter for space power and propulsion is the generation, capture, storage, and use of the mirror twin of the proton, the antiproton. Most people are not aware of it, but antiprotons are being made, collected, and stored today, so the production of mirror matter is no longer a question of technical feasibility, but one of economic feasibility.

The only known major producer of antiprotons is the European Center for Nuclear Research (CERN) in Geneva, Switzerland. In 1980, it was reported that the U.S.S.R. Institute for High Energy Physics in Novosibirsk was constructing an antiproton production facility, but there have been no further publications since that date. The United States Fermi National Accelerator Labora-

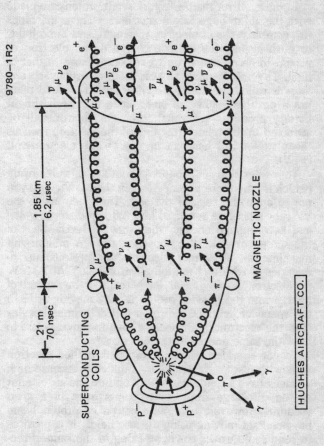

Figure 2. Thrust from proton-antiproton annihilation.

tory in Batavia, Ill., started the operation of its antiproton facility in late 1985.

In these mirror matter factories, antiprotons are made with the aid of huge "atom smashers." These machines use combinations of electric, magnetic, and radio fields to push against the electric charge on an electron or proton to accelerate it up to velocities close to that of light. The unit of energy that is used in particle accelerators is called the electron-volt or eV. If a metal plate has a positive voltage of one volt (a regular flashlight battery produces 1.5 volts), then an electron will be attracted to that plate. Just before the electron reaches the plate, it will have an energy of one electron-volt (1 eV).

Your television set produces about 20,000 volts inside (which is why there is a message on the back telling you not to open the back of the set). The electrons in the TV tube therefore reach 20 keV (20 kilo-electron-volts) and have enough energy when they strike the back of the screen to make the phosphor glow. A million-volt machine can accelerate electrons (or protons) up to energies of 1 MeV (1 million electron-volts). At 1 MeV, an electron is moving at 94 percent of the speed of light, while the heavier proton is only moving at $\frac{1}{20}$th the speed of light. (The proton is 1,800 times heavier than the electron, so it doesn't have to move as fast to have the same energy as the electron.)

To get energies greater than a few million electron volts with just an electric field is difficult, because high voltages have a tendency to leak off into the air or emit corona discharge from sharp points even in a good vacuum. However, once an electron or proton beam has been set moving using electric fields, it is possible to send radio waves traveling along in the same direction as the beam of particles. If the radio waves are properly tuned, the charged particles can gain energy from the moving radio waves just as a surfboard gains energy from a water wave. By this technique, energies of thousands of millions of volts, or giga-electron-volts (GeV) have been reached. Fermilab has completed construction of a superconducting proton accelerator that is designed to produce protons with an energy of a million-million electron-volts or a tera-electron-volt (TeV) machine. The Fermilab machine is aptly called the Tevatron.

The amount of energy bound up into the mass of a proton is 0.938 GeV. Thus, any proton with a kinetic energy greater than 1 GeV has more energy in its motion than it has in its internal mass. A proton with a total energy of 100 GeV has within itself enough energy to make 99 more protons (or antiprotons!).

When the scientists in Geneva, Batavia, or Novosibirsk want some antiprotons to play with, they take the proton beam that is circling around in their multi-kilometer circumference machine, add more radio energy, boost the energy until the protons are moving at nearly light speed, then dump the high-energy protons into a tungsten target. As the rapidly moving protons strike the heavy tungsten nuclei, their kinetic energy is converted into a spray of elementary particles, including antiprotons, antielectrons, and antineutrons, moving at speeds close to that of light.

You would think that the task of capturing the rapidly moving antiprotons from the cloud of debris emanating from the tungsten target would be as impossible as trying to catch the queen bee in a swarm of bees emanating from a kicked-over hive. But with the aid of a lens made of magnetic fields and a magnetic particle selector, the negatively charged antiprotons can be separated from the remainder of the debris, which consists of particles which have a different charge and mass from the antiproton. The antiprotons that are collected are then directed into a magnetic storage ring where they are accumulated.

The antiproton accumulator consists of a long, stainless steel vacuum tube bent into a large ring many hundreds of meters in circumference. Spaced at intervals along the ring, like beads on a wire, are dozens of various kinds of magnets. They are huge—one to three meters long—full of iron and heavy wire, and weigh over a ton each.

Some of the magnets are used for "bending" the beam of antiprotons. As the negatively charged antiproton passes through the magnetic field penetrating the vacuum tube from top to bottom, the charge on the antiproton experiences a sidewards force that is at right angles to both the direction of the magnetic field and the direction of travel of the antiproton. This sidewards force causes the path of the antiproton to be bent slightly, so the antiproton follows the curvature of the vacuum pipe. If everything is lined up properly, the antiprotons circle around endlessly inside the storage ring. The scientists at CERN in Switzerland have stored antiprotons in this manner for days.

Other magnets in the storage ring use more complex magnetic field shapes to keep the beam focused in the center of the tube, so none of the antiprotons strike the walls and are lost. There are also smaller, stronger magnets that can be pulsed to move the beam around inside the vacuum pipe, or to switch the beam into an extraction vacuum line when it is time to do experiments with the antiprotons.

When the antiprotons are generated in the tungsten target, they have a wide spread of energies. Before they can be used further, it is necessary to "cool" the antiproton beam so that all the antiprotons have the same velocity. Two techniques for reducing the spread in velocity have been demonstrated and both have been found to work well.

One technique, invented by Carlo Rubbia at CERN in Switzerland, is called "stochastic cooling." Stochastic is a scientific word meaning "random" (even though the Greek root word means "skillful in aiming"!). With the wide spread in velocities, some of the antiprotons move faster than the average and some move slower, so as they move around inside the vacuum tube, they pass each other and "clumps" of charged antiprotons temporarily form. These clumps of charge are detected by a current sensor.

The signal from the sensor is amplified, switched in sign, then quickly sent by cable from one side of the ring to the other. Since the cable cuts across the center of the ring, while the antiprotons have to circle around the circumference of the ring, the signal arrives before the clump of antiprotons are moving at nearly the speed of light. The signal then drives a "kicker" that accelerates or decelerates the "clump" of current, smoothing it out. By using hundreds of sensors and kickers, the scientists and engineers at CERN can decrease the randomness in the antiproton energies by an order of magnitude in less than two seconds. They also use other sensors to detect antiprotons which are not moving straight down the vacuum pipe, but snaking from side to side. Signals from those sensors are then sent to transverse kickers, which straighten out the antiproton paths.

Stochastic cooling works well on the high-speed antiprotons that are initially collected from the tungsten target. After this preliminary stochastic cooling, the antiprotons are then switched out of the capture and stochastic cooling ring into a particle decelerator. At CERN, the antiproton decelerator is just a proton accelerator run backwards. The antiprotons enter the decelerator with an energy of 3500 MeV and leave with an energy of 200 MeV. This seventeen-fold decrease in energy means that the antiprotons, which used to be moving at relativistic velocities, are now moving well below the speed of light.

In Switzerland, the decelerated antiprotons are then sent to another storage ring, called the Low Energy Antiproton Ring (LEAR). For various reasons, the scientists wanted some long straight sections to do experiments with. So LEAR is not actually a ring, but a square, with sides of about 20 meters and rounded corners. At each corner is a set of bending magnets that take the antiproton beam, turn it through an angle of 90 degrees, and send it shooting down the next straight section of vacuum pipe to the bending magnets at the next corner.

After stochastic cooling, but before deceleration, the antiprotons' spread in energy has been reduced from 1.5

to 0.17 percent of the average energy of 3500 MeV, or 6 MeV. After the antiprotons are decelerated to 200 MeV, however, that 6 MeV spread is now 3 percent of the average antiproton energy, so it is necessary to cool the beam of antiprotons some more after deceleration. It is possible to continue to use stochastic cooling, and the scientists at CERN in Switzerland have decided to continue to use that technique in the Low Energy Antiproton Ring, even though stochastic cooling is not as efficient at low energies as it is at high energies.

At Novosibirsk, in Russia, the Soviet scientists are using another cooling technique (which was invented by Soviet scientists) called electron cooling. To carry out electron cooling, a carefully designed electron gun is used to make a beam of electrons that all have the same energy. The average velocity of the electrons is chosen to be exactly the average velocity of the antiprotons. Since the electrons have very little variation around their average velocity, they can be called "cold" electrons.

This cold stream of electrons is then inserted into one of the straight sections of a low-energy antiproton storage ring to travel along with the beam of "hot" antiprotons. The negatively charged antiprotons interact with the much lighter negatively charged electrons through their mutually repulsive electric fields. Those antiprotons that are moving faster than the electrons will bump into the electrons and be decelerated, while those antiprotons that are moving slower than the electrons will be bumped by the electrons and be accelerated. The much smaller electrons will be "heated" during the process, so the electron beam is removed farther on down the straight section and new "cold" electrons are reinserted until all the antiprotons are moving at the same speed as the electrons.

The electron cooling technique works equally well on those antiprotons that have the right average speed, but have a direction that is at an angle to the average direction. The best way to see how electron cooling works on the antiprotons is to switch to a point of view that is moving along at the average speed of the electrons. From that viewpoint, we would see a cloud of slowly moving electrons and rapidly moving antiprotons. The antiprotons that are moving too slowly or too rapidly are coming toward us or going away, while those antiprotons that are at the wrong angle are weaving from side to side through the nearly stationary cloud of electrons. The moving antiprotons bump into the electrons and "heat" them up, but are themselves "cooled" in the process.

The scientists at CERN have stored up to a trillion (10^{12}) antiprotons in their Antiproton Accumulator. To give some scale to what has already been accomplished, a trillion antiprotons have a mass of about 2 trillionths of a gram. When this infinitesimal amount of mirror matter is mixed with an equivalent amount of normal matter, it will release 300 watt-seconds (70 calories), an engineeringly significant quantity of energy. To obtain this "firecracker" amount of energy requires the use of multimillion-dollar machines that use an enormous amount of electric energy. Yet it is important to recognize that scientists working in basic physics, using research tools not designed for the job, have produced and continue to produce significant quantities of mirror matter.

The production efficiency of the present machines is abysmally low. It ranges from parts in a thousand million in Switzerland to parts in a million in the U.S.S.R. Fortunately, the efficiency can be improved by orders of magnitude. The reason for the low efficiency is that all of the production facilities have been built as crash projects under limited budgets. Production efficiency has been sacrificed to such considerations as speed, cost, science requirements, and national pride.

The motives of the scientists building the mirror matter machines are interesting and have a significant impact on the present low efficiencies. The ordinary layman might think that the making of this magical form of matter would be enough motive. The real motive of the scientists, however, is to win Nobel prizes. Since the Nobel prize for the discovery of the positron was awarded in 1936 and for the antiproton in 1959, the study of mirror matter is no longer science to elementary particle physicists—it is engineering. To win a Nobel prize in physics today, you have to discover a new "elementary" particle. To discover these new particles, you have to be the first one to build a machine that slams normal particles together with a collision energy greater than anyone else has achieved and hope you are lucky enough to find a new particle in the resulting debris.

The scientists in Switzerland knew that the U.S. scientists at Fermilab were building a new machine that would be the first to explore the next highest energy range. They then realized that they might be able to beat the Americans if they used their old machine to collide two beams of protons head on instead of colliding a beam of protons with a stationary target.

They came up with two possible design approaches. One approach was to build a copy of the machine that they already had, in the same tunnel as the first one. (A major cost factor in the building of a new machine is digging the tunnel to put it in.) One machine would accelerate protons clockwise and the other counterclockwise, with a crossover point where the two beams would interact. The alternative approach was to use the old machine just by itself, but have it accelerate positively charged protons clockwise while it simultaneously accelerated negatively charged antiprotons counterclockwise. To carry out the second approach meant the scientists had to construct a separate antiproton production, capture, and storage facility.

Amazingly enough, their cost studies showed it was faster and *cheaper* to build an antiproton factory than to build a new accelerator ring. The Europeans hurriedly threw together a facility with limited funds, made enough antiprotons to do the job and found two new elementary particles. Two European scientists, Carlo Rubbia and Simon van der Meer, won the 1984 Nobel prize in physics—not for the study of mirror matter, but for using mirror matter as an engineering tool to do physics. Fermilab, having been beat, belatedly started its own antiproton factory, to explore the next highest range of energies and, hopefully, win the next batch of Nobel prizes.

Because of this race to be first, and because of limited budgets, many shortcuts are being taken in the designs of the mirror matter factories. For example, in Switzerland, the scientists had to use the proton accelerator machine available, even though they knew it generated protons with marginal energy for producing antiprotons. If they had had a machine of the right energy, they could have produced 20 times the number of antiprotons per proton. Then, of the antiprotons coming out of the target, they only manage to collect one out of a thousand in the collector ring. The rest are allowed to get away because the scientists could only afford one focusing lens and one capture ring. An array of magnetic lenses would allow the capture of antiprotons coming from the target area at many different angles, while the ring tunnel could hold many capture rings, each designed to capture antiprotons at a different energy.

Another factor that is limiting the research groups is that their proton accelerators are designed for precision, not production. The proton current in these machines is designed to be low so that the machines can produce protons of extremely high and quite precise energy. Thus, when the protons strike a target, the scientists know their exact energy and can make precise measurements on the new particles that are produced so they can compare the measurements with the predictions from the latest version of elementary particle theory. As a result, these research tools have proton currents that are too low for optimum antiproton production. The machines are also not very efficient; typically, only 5 percent of the electrical energy from the power lines ends up as energy in the proton beam.

There are designs for proton accelerators that are much more energy-efficient. They are called linear accelerators. As the name implies, they are built in a straight line, instead of a large circle. In the circular proton accelerator rings, the protons circle around and around the ring, each time getting a kick from the single section of radio energy kickers. In a linear accelerator, there are many more radio energy accelerating sections and the protons only pass through once. Such linear accelerators would have an energy efficiency of 50 percent from the "wall plug" to energy in the proton beam. You can't do much better! A linear accelerator needed to produce protons with the optimum energy to make antiprotons, however, would be very long—40 to 100 kilometers (25 to 60 miles). But there is plenty of room in the deserts in Texas and New Mexico, and there is even more room in space.

In a recent study I carried out for the Air Force Rocket Propulsion Laboratory, I showed that if an antiproton factory were designed properly by engineers, instead of by scientists in a hurry to win a Nobel prize, the present energy efficiency (electrical energy in compared to mirror matter recombination energy out) could be raised from a part in a billion to a part in 10,000—or 0.01 percent. At this energy efficiency, mirror matter would cost about $10 million per milligram.

This low production efficiency and the resulting high cost estimate has two significant implications. First, mirror matter cannot be used to make an "antimatter bomb." A single antimatter bomb of the size of the small Hiroshima nuclear bomb (20 kilotons) would require a *gram* of mirror matter, costing $10,000,000,000. (This amount of money is about 1 percent of the national budget of the United States.) Any country trying to make antimatter bombs would go broke in the attempt.

Second, it is unlikely that mirror matter will be a cost-effective fuel for power and propulsion except in space, where any fuel is expensive because it must be lifted into space first. Even at $10 million per milligram, however, mirror matter is already cost-effective for space propulsion and power. At the present subsidized price of a Space Shuttle launch, it costs about $5 million to put a ton of anything into low Earth orbit.

Since a milligram of mirror matter produces the same amount of energy as 20 tons of the most energetic chemical fuel available, then $10 million of mirror matter would be a more cost effective fuel in space than $100 million of chemical fuel.

How do you "hold on" to this magical mirror matter that disappears in a burst of energy the instant it touches normal matter? The scientists in Switzerland have demonstrated one solution to this problem. Their "bottle" is an evacuated tube about two inches in diameter and bent into a ring about 300 feet in circumference. As it goes around, the beam of antiprotons is directed and focused by magnetic fields to keep it from hitting the walls of the tube.

Scientists working in atomic physics and plasma physics have come up with a very compact trap for mirror matter. The side walls of the trap consist of a carefully machined solid metal ring about two inches (five centimeters) in diameter. Above and below the hole in the ring are two domed metal end caps. This trap is placed in a vacuum chamber inside the bore of a superconducting magnet in a thermos jug containing liquid helium. The magnetic field from the superconducting magnet runs along the axis of the trap from one end cap to the other.

To capture an antiproton once it has been inserted into the trap, the end caps are given a negative charge and the ring a positive charge. The negative charge on the caps repels the negatively charged antiproton, keeping it from going in the axial direction. The antiproton will attempt to move out toward the positively charged ring electrode, but the magnetic field will keep the antiproton moving in a circle and it will never get to the ring.

These compact traps have already demonstrated their ability to store mirror matter. At the University of Washington in Seattle, one of these traps has held a positron for over a month, demonstrating that the trap is stable over long periods of time and the vacuum inside a supercold container is extremely low. The atomic scientists will soon be taking their traps from Seattle to Switzerland. The American scientists have received permission from the European particle physicists to attempt to trap a few of their precious antiprotons. If they are successful, the American scientists will pick up their trap and carry it to a quieter room to carry out their scientific experiments.

The purpose of their experiments is not to demonstrate the trapping of mirror matter. In fact, if the University of Washington scientists accidentally trap more than one antiproton, they will eject all but one, since the purpose of the experiment is to measure the mass of the antiproton to a part in 100,000,000,000, and the experiment is more accurate if there is only one antiproton in the trap. Everyone knows that the antiproton mass should be exactly the same as the normal proton mass, but if it isn't, then there is a Nobel prize waiting for the person who first finds out.

The simplest mirror atom is antihydrogen. It consists of a single positron orbiting an antiproton. Since the Europeans have had antiprotons in abundance for a number of years, and it is relatively easy to make positrons, you would think that they would have made antihydrogen long ago. In fact, four European scientists made such a proposal right after the first antiprotons became available. They proposed to produce a beam of positrons and run them side by side with the beam of antiprotons going around in the low-energy antiproton storage ring. They would then use a laser to stimulate the attachment of the positively charged positron onto the negatively charged antiproton to produce a beam of neutral antihydrogen. When their proposal came up before the experiment selection committee it got a very low priority rating. The reason? Everyone knows that when you put an electron next to a proton, it will react to form hydrogen. Demonstrating this experiment with mirror matter is not only not particle physics, it is not even *physics*. It is a trivial *chemistry* experiment. Thus, unless someone in the U.S. or U.S.S.R. does it sooner, the first manufacture of antihydrogen will have to wait until all the other possible "physics" experiments that can be done with the beam of antiprotons at CERN have been done.

Once mirror hydrogen has been made, it can be slowed, cooled, trapped, and stored using a combination of electric fields, magnetic fields, and laser beams. If a laser beam is tuned to exactly the right wavelength, the laser photons will be absorbed by an atom. The energy in the photon causes the electron around the atom to jump into a higher orbit, while the momentum in the photon pushes the atom slightly in a direction away from the laser. The electron soon jumps down into its old orbit, emitting a photon. That photon goes off in some random direction, in the process kicking the atom in the opposite direction. The process is repeated thousands of times per second. The laser photons always push the atom in the same direction, so their little pushes add up, while the reemitted photons go in all directions and their kicks average out. Thus, if a laser beam is tuned to the right wavelength, it can push on atoms without touching them.

Atomic scientists at the National Bureau of Standards and elsewhere have used lasers to deflect atom beams to one side, cool atoms in a beam until they are all moving at the same velocity, and stop a beam of atoms in its tracks. Other scientists at Bell Labs have trapped a drop of oil using lasers. These atomic scientists are now in a race to build an apparatus using an array of lasers to trap and cool individual atoms, then a cloud of atoms. It won't be long before they produce a cloud of atoms cooled to less than one degree above absolute zero.

The atoms the scientists are presently attempting to trap are atoms of metals such as sodium, that absorb visible laser light. Soon other scientists will be demonstrating the same cooling and trapping techniques on hydrogen—first on atoms of hydrogen, then on molecules of hydrogen consisting of two hydrogen atoms combined together. This has required them to develop sources of tunable narrow-band ultraviolet laser light, since hydrogen atoms and molecules only respond well to laser light in the short ultraviolet wavelengths.

Molecular antihydrogen, like its mirror cousin, molecular hydrogen, is nearly magnetically neutral when it is in its lowest energy state. The two antiprotons and the two positrons each have a magnetic moment, but in the ground state of the molecule, the two antiprotons have their spins pointing in the opposite direction and the two magnetic fields cancel out, while the same thing is true for the two positrons. The only magnetic response that is left is called the "diamagnetic" response. When there is no magnetic field applied to a hydrogen molecule, it has zero net magnetic moment. When an external magnetic field is applied, however, the orbits of the positrons about the antiprotons are changed. The changed orbital motion is equivalent to an additional current. This induced current causes an induced magnetic field of opposite sign to the applied field. This induced magnetic field property is called diamagnetism.

A diamagnetic molecule has the tendency to move toward a region with low magnetic field and stay there. We can use this property to make a magnetic "bottle" for antihydrogen. The bottle will consist of a vacuum chamber kept at very low temperature, with two superconducting metal rings built into the wall. In the superconducting rings will flow a persistent supercurrent that will generate a magnetic field that is strong near the walls of the vacuum chamber and weak at the center of the chamber. Any antihydrogen put into this container will avoid the strong magnetic fields near the walls and collect in the center as a ball of antihydrogen ice. The ice ball would be so cold only a few mirror atoms per day would evaporate from the surface.

Electric fields can also be used to store and manipulate antimatter. If a ball of antihydrogen ice has a slight excess electric charge, electric fields can be used to move it around. A weak beam of ultraviolet light can be used to drive positrons off the antihydrogen ice ball to keep it charged. Experimenters at the Jet Propulsion Laboratory have been experimenting with such traps for use in zero-gee laboratories on Spacelab and the Space Station. They have already used such traps to levitate balls of water ice.

The JPL traps consist of two large, curved metal plates about four inches (10 centimeters) apart in a vacuum chamber. Between the two plates is a ball of ice that is kept charged by ultraviolet light that kicks electrons off the ice, leaving the ice ball positively charged. The top plate of the trap is charged negatively and the bottom plate is charged positively, so the ice ball is levitated in the Earth's field by the electric fields from the charged plates. The curvature of the two plates keeps the ice ball centered radially.

The vertical position of the ice ball is not stable. If the ice ball approaches the upper plate, the attraction of the charges on the plate becomes stronger. Thus, unless prevented, the ice ball will quickly slam into the upper plate. In the JPL trap, the voltage between the plates is varied by a fast-acting voltage generator that is controlled by a television camera watching the position of the charged ice ball, so that the ball stays levitated in the center of the chamber.

It will by many years before mirror matter becomes a product that is bought and sold like gasoline or diesel fuel. There are many, many, many difficult problems left to solve in the production, capture, cooling, storage, transport, and use of this extremely potent, extremely expensive, nearly magic source of raw energy. But as one skeptic after another takes a look at the problems that have been overcome and the problems still left to be solved, it begins to look as if there are no "showstoppers." There is no physical reason why mirror matter, in some form, cannot be made and stored in enough quantity to produce the kilowatts and megawatts of prime power and propulsion power needed for rapid space travel.

The scientific and engineering interest in mirror matter is broad and growing. The particle physicists at the European Center for Nuclear Research in Switzerland, the Institute for High Energy Physics in the U.S.S.R., and Fermilab in the U.S. are all upgrading their antiproton production facilities to aid in their quest for Nobel prizes, while at the same time allowing some preliminary engineering experiments critical to the understanding of the problems of storing antiprotons and the generation of mirror matter. Scientists at the University of Washington will shortly be taking their cryogenic traps across the ocean and one day may be returning carrying mirror matter through Customs. Scientists and engineers at Los Alamos National Laboratory are busy with a number of interlinked studies to generate antiprotons with an upgraded particle accelerator, collect them in magnetic traps, study their interaction with normal matter atoms, and design magnetic chambers and nozzles to extract energy from the high-temperature plasmas produced by the interaction of mirror matter with normal matter. Engineers at the RAND Corporation are looking at the space system implications of the availability of mirror matter.

The Air Force Rocket Propulsion Laboratory has been supporting studies of advanced propulsion using mirror matter at Lawrence Livermore Laboratories and Hughes Aircraft Company. They are also initiating an in-house program to study the slowing and cooling of molecular hydrogen with laser light sources. The Air Force Rocket Propulsion Lab interest in propulsion is augmented by studies of mirror matter-powered missions to the planets by engineers and mission analysts at the NASA Jet Propulsion Laboratory. Similar mission studies and preliminary design studies of mirror matter-powered rocket engines are underway at Boeing Aerospace and United Technology Research Center.

This "mirror matter underground" primarily consists of optimists. But they are intelligent optimists who have better things to do than to waste professional time on something that will not work. They are convinced that making mirror matter is feasible. The real question is cost.

Mirror matter at the present cost of $100 billion per milligram has already been proven cost-effective for scientific experiments to win Nobel prizes. Mirror matter at $100 million per milligram would definitely be cost-effective for unmanned probe missions to the rings of Saturn. When the cost of mirror matter starts to drop below $10 million per milligram, many new applications will come to the fore, for mirror matter would be cheaper in energy delivered to orbit than any chemical fuel, and possibly even cheaper than nuclear fuel.

Where will we get the energy to run these magic matter factories? Some of the prototype factories will be built on Earth, but for large-scale production, we certainly don't want to power these machines by burning fossil fuels. There is plenty of energy in space. At the distance of the Earth from the Sun, the Sun delivers over a kilowatt of energy for each square meter of collector, or a gigawatt (1,000,000,000 watts) per square kilometer. A collector array of 100 kilometers on a side would provide a power input of 10 terawatts (10,000,000,000,000 watts)—enough to run a number of antimatter factories at full power, producing a gram of antimatter a day.

Once we have learned how to make and store antimatter, we can start using it for propulsion. In science fiction stories in the past, the usual assumption has been that antimatter rockets would use equal parts of matter and antimatter. Instead, it is now recognized that for any trip speed less than one-third the speed of light, you do not want to use equal parts of matter and antimatter. Instead, you use a small amount of antimatter to heat a much larger amount of matter (either hydrogen, water, or anything else convenient). What is most remarkable is that when the engineers calculated the optimum mix of matter and antimatter for a given payload and a given mission, they found that the amount of normal matter you need is practically independent of the journey planned.

For any journey, whether it is from one orbit to another, from Earth to the Moon, to Mars, or to the nearest stars, the optimum ratio is about two tons of water for one ton of spaceship. The only thing that varies is the amount of antimatter needed, but in all cases, the amount of magic matter fuel needed is so small that its mass can be neglected in the calculations.

To give some examples: If we wish to go to the Moon in four hours, we will want to travel the 384,000 kilometer distance at a speed of better than 30 kilometers per second. For a 2033 Chevy Astro-Cruiser weighing one ton, this will require 30 milligrams of antimatter mixed with two tons of water.

If we want to take longer journeys in larger vehicles, then 10 grams of antimatter heating 20 tons of water can propel a 10-ton space vehicle to Mars in a week. Similarly, a kilogram of antimatter will send the same 10 tons to Pluto in a month, while 100 kilograms could send a 10-ton deep space probe to the nearest stars at a speed of 10 percent that of light, reaching Alpha Centauri in less than 50 years.

We know how to make antimatter. We know how to store antimatter. With a fully developed magic matter technology, the solar system and the nearby stars can be ours. There is no question about the feasibility of the technology; it is only a matter of scaling and cost. The question is not: "Can we do it?" It is: "Do we *want* to do it?"

The long trip to Las Lunas is over. The autopilot beeps and you tear your gaze from the retreating blue marble. You monitor the Chevy Astro-Cruiser's rendezvous with the outer end of the Lunar Rotavator as it cartwheels about the Moon, its ends touching down to the surface once every hour. There are a hundred cables splayed out from the upper end in a seeming rat's nest of threads, each one designed to lower a passenger ship down to the lunar surface on its next long, slow swing. There are no empty cables. You are not about to wait. This is your vacation. You go down on jets.

You touch the controls, and deep inside a zero-cold bottle, a tease of laser light extracts another microgram of magic matter from the frozen ball that rests in darkness there, suspended in an invisible cat's cradle of magnetic lines of force. The speck of magic matter is carried off by controlled pulses of electric and magnetic fields to the roaring hot hell of the rocket chamber, where the still-icy speck of ultrapure magic meets a glob of dirty water. The two explode in a blaze of purifying fire as the lunar dust rises to hide the glittering casino signs towering in the distance.

IRON

This story is set in Larry Niven's Known Universe, and chronicles the events that led up to the second Man-Kzin War. Part I was published in the final edition of Far Frontiers (#7). If you missed it, here is

WHAT HAS GONE BEFORE

On board the asteroid mining town of Tiamat, ROBERT SAXTORPH is walking to a meeting with COMMISSIONER MARKHAM when he is subjected to an unprovoked attack by a kzin whom he has never seen before. No unarmed human could prevail hand-to-hand against one of the tiger-like sophonts, but because Saxtorph was a member of an elite assault force during the late Man-Kzin War, he manages to fend his assailant off for a while as he yells bloody murder. He is aided in this by the kzin's apparent unfamiliarity with the odd effects of centrifugal gravity. (Completed just before the introduction of the gravity generator, Tiamat was one of the last of the giant spin habitats.) As a human peace enforcer arrives upon the scene, the kzin flees to anonymity in Tigertown, a section of Tiamat occupied by kzinti since before the war.

While her husband recovers, DORCAS SAXTORPH meets with elderly PROFESSOR TREGENNIS and his wealthy young graduate student, LAURINDA BROZIK. Laurinda has big news: her father has approved a grant for Laurinda's proposed expedition to a sun she's discovered that may be as old as the universe. Robert and Dorcas' vessel Rover will carry the expedition. Both Laurinda and Tregennis will be going along.

A little later Saxtorph finally meets with Markham, and finds that although the Commissioner's attempts to have the unauthorized expedition forbidden as "too dangerous" have failed, he has managed to have himself named an official observer. He claims this move was largely motivated by his still lively sense of adventure; he disapproves, but since there will be an expedition in any event he might as well have the fun of taking part in it. Also, he admits, as a member he will be in a position to try to keep the expedition within what he regards as proper scientific and bureaucratic bounds.

Saxtorph is doubtful of the aristocratic Markham's joie de vivre—though Markham was a leader in the Centaurian Resistance during Kzinti occupation, Saxtorph finds him a cold and repellent martinet. Alas, there is nothing for it; the Commissioner goes or nobody does.

Rover's crew includes Saxtorph's long-time friend KAMEHAMEHA (KAM) RYAN and Jinxian CARITA FENGER, who because of her planetary-ethnic background is rather short and immensely strong, and JUAN YOSHII. Rover's two shuttles are Fido and Shep. As the expedition shakes down, Markham proves himself a cold-blooded pain and is ostracized. But not all shipboard encounters are painful: Laurinda and Juan find themselves falling in love.

None too soon (for all save Laurinda and Yoshii), Rover is orbiting the strange sun. The immensely old, metal-impoverished dwarf has five planets, christened Prima, Secunda, Tertia, Quarta, and Quinta.

Secunda and Tertia show signs of a faint atmosphere. Of more immediately compelling interest, the supposedly desolate Secunda is emitting radio waves. Markham seems immensely disturbed by this news, and Ryan finds him later in parts of the ship open only to crew. What is the man up to?

Such is the situation when Rover receives a hostile message from a kzin warship. It is Markham who has brought this upon them. He says he has been broadcasting signals to Secunda in an attempt to provoke a response from the mysterious radio emitters. How was he to know there were kzinti about?

The only hope, a pale one, is for most of them to secretly flee aboard Rover's two shuttles, but for this trick to work,

*at least a few humans must remain aboard. A deserted ship
would give the game away instantly. Kam, Tregennis and—
rather to everyone's surprise—Markham volunteer to stay,
knowing that the kzinti are as ruthless in their interrogation practices as in all else.*

The Saxtorphs and Laurinda will go in Shep, *Yoshii and
Carita in* Fido; *even if one group is discovered the other may
evade notice. When the kzinti board* Rover, *Kam and
Tregennis learn that Markham has betrayed them. Long a
kzin agent, he believes that the only "cure" for human
decadence is to submit to the austere discipline of the kzinti.
To help usher in the New Order, he has earlier passed to them
the secret of the new space drive that ended the last war on
human terms, and he tells Kam and Tregennis that with
the aid of the new drive the kzinti are using Secunda as a
secret staging base to launch yet another war against men.*

*Meanwhile, the Saxtorphs and Laurinda have landed on
Secunda where they find evidence of a race that died billions
of years ago, doomed by the lack of metal to never advance
out of the stone age. Yoshii and Carita have found that
what seemed a safe haven on Tertia is anything but: the
surface of the planet is one immense voracious molecule that
flows over and eats everything, and has a special taste for
the metals with which its solar system is so poorly endowed. It
has been busy for some time eating their ship.*

*The kzinti captain to whom they appeal finds the very
notion of risk-laden rescue of enemies yet another example of
monkey grotesquerie. They are trapped. Soon the shuttle will
be eaten through, and the molecule will begin to digest their
suits.*

IRON

Part II of II

Poul Anderson

16

The sun in the screen showed about half the Sol-disc at Earth. Its light equaled more than 10,000 full Lunas, red rather than off-white but still ample to make Secunda shine. The planetary crescent was mostly yellowish-brown, little softened by a tenuous atmosphere of methane with traces of carbon dioxide and ammonia. A polar cap brightened its wintered northern hemisphere, a shrunken one the southern. The latter was all water ice, the former enlarged by carbon dioxide and ammonia that had frozen out. These two gases did it everywhere at night, most times, evaporating again by day in summer and the tropics, so that sunrises and sunsets were apt to be violent. Along the terminator glittered a storm of fine silicate dust mingled with ice crystals.

The surface bore scant relief, but the slow rotation, 57 hours, was bringing into view a gigantic crater and a number of lesser neighbors. Probably a moon had crashed within the past billion years; the scars remained, though any orbiting fragments had dissipated. A sister moon survived, three-fourths Lunar diameter, dark yellowish like so many bodies in this system.

Thus did Tregennis interpret what he and Ryan saw as they sat in *Rover's* saloon watching the approach. Data taken from afar, before the capture, helped him fill in details. Talking about them was an anodyne for both men.

Markham entered. Silence rushed through like a wind.

"I have an announcement," he said after a moment.

Neither prisoner stirred.

"We are debarking in half an hour," he went on. "I have arranged for your clothing and hygienic equipment to be brought along. Including your medication, Professor."

"Thank you," Tregennis said flatly.

"Why shouldn't he?" Ryan sneered. "Keep the animals alive till the master race can think of a need for them. I wonder if he'll share in the feast."

Markham's stiffness became rigidity. "Have a care," he warned. "I have been very patient with you." During the 50-odd hours of 3-g flight—during which Hraou-Captain allowed the polarizer to lighten weight—he had received no word from either, nor eye contact. To be sure, he had been cultivating the acquaintance of such kzinti among the prize crew as deigned to talk with him. "Don't provoke me."

"All right," Ryan answered. Unable to resist: "Not but what I couldn't put up with a lot of provocation myself, if I were getting paid what they must be paying you."

Markham's cheekbones reddened. "For your information, I have never had one mark of recompense, nor ever been promised any. Not one."

Tregennis regarded him in mild amazement. "Then why have you turned traitor?" he asked.

"I have not. On the contrary—" Markham stood for several seconds before he plunged. "See here, if you will listen, if you will treat me like a human being, you can learn some things you will be well advised to know."

Ryan scowled at his beer glass, shrugged, nodded, and grumbled, "Might as well."

"Can you talk freely?" Tregennis inquired.

Markham sat down. "I have not been forbidden to. Of course, what I have been told so far is quite limited. However, certain kzinti, including Hraou-Captain, have been reasonably forthcoming. They have been bored by their uneventful duty, are intrigued by me, and see no immediate threat to security."

"I can understand that," said Tregennis dryly.

Markham leaned forward. His assurance had shrunk enough to notice. He tugged his half-beard. His tone became earnest:

"Remember, for a dozen Earth-years I fought the kzinti. I was raised to it. They had driven my mother into exile. The motto of the House of Reichstein was '*Ehre*—' well, in English, 'Honor Through Service.' She changed it to 'No Surrender.' Most people had long since given up, you know. They accepted the kzin order of things. Many had been born into it, or had only dim childhood memories of anything before. Revolt would have brought massacre. Aristocrats who stayed on Wunderland—the majority—saw no alternative to cooperating with the occupation forces, at least to the extent of preserving order among humans and keeping industries in operation. They were apt to look on us who fought as dangerous extremists. It was a seductive belief. As the years wore on, with no end in sight, more and more members of the resistance despaired. Through the aristocrats at home they negotiated terms permitting them to come back and pick up the pieces of their lives. My mother was among those who had the greatness of spirit to refuse the temptation. 'No Surrender.' "

Ryan still glowered, but Tregennis said with a dawn of sympathy, "Then the hyperdrive armada arrived and she was vindicated. Were you not glad?"

"Of course," Markham said. "We jubilated, my comrades and I, after we were through weeping for the joy and glory of it. That was a short-lived happiness. We had work to do. At first it was clean. The fighting had caused destruction. The navy from Sol could spare few units; it must go on to subdue the kzinti elsewhere. On the men of the resistance fell the tasks of rescue and relief.

"Then as we returned to our homes on Wunderland—I and many others for the first time in our lives—we found that the world for whose liberation we had fought, the world of our vision and hope, was gone, long gone. Everywhere was turmoil. Mobs stormed manor after manor of the 'collaborationist' aristocrats, lynched, raped, looted, burned—as if those same proles had not groveled before the kzinti and kept war production going for them! Lunatic political factions rioted against each other or did actual armed combat. Chaos brought breakdown, want, misery, death.

"My mother took a lead in calling for a restoration of law. We did it, we soldiers from space. What we did was often harsh, but necessary. A caretaker government was established. We thought that we could finally get on with our private lives—though I, for one, busied myself in the effort to build up Centaurian defense forces, so that never again could my people be overrun.

"In the years that my back was turned, they, my people, were betrayed." Markham choked on his bitterness.

"Do you mean the new constitution, the democratic movement in general?" Tregennis prompted.

Markham recovered and nodded. "No one denied that reform, reorganization was desirable. I will concede, if only because our time to talk now is limited, most of the reformers meant well. They did not see foresee the consequences of what they enacted. I admit I did not myself. But I was busy, often away for long periods of time. My mother, on our estates, saw what was happening, and piece by piece made it clear to me."

"Your estates. You kept them, then. I gather most noble families kept a substantial part of their former holdings; and Wunderland's House of Patricians is the upper chamber of its parliament. Surely you don't think you have come under a . . . mobocracy."

"But I do! At least, that is the way it is tending. That

is the way it will go, to completion, to destruction, if it is not stopped. A political Gresham's Law prevails; the bad drives out the good. Look at me, for example. I have one vote, by hereditary right, in the Patricians, and it is limited to federal matters. To take a meaningful role in restoring a proper society—through enactment of proper laws—a role which it is my hereditary duty to take—I must begin by being elected a consul of my state, Braefell. That would give me a voice in choosing who goes to the House of Delegates— No matter details. I went into politics."

"Holding your well-bred nose," Ryan murmured.

Markham flushed again. "I am for the people. The honest, decent, hard-working, sensible common people, who know in their hearts that society is tradition and order and reverence, not a series of cheap bargains between selfish interests. One still finds them in the countryside. It is in the cities that the maggots are, the mobs, the criminals, the parasites, the . . . politicians."

For the first time, Ryan smiled a little. "Can't say I admire the political process either. But I will say the cure is not to domesticate the lower class. How about letting everybody see to his own business, with a few cops and courts to keep things from getting too hairy?"

"I heard that argument often enough. It is stupid. It assumes the obvious falsehood that an individual can function in isolation like an atom. Oh, I did my share of toadying, I shook the clammy hands and said the clammy words, but it was hypocritical ritual, a sugar coating over the cynicism and corruption—"

"In short, you lost."

"I learned better than to try."

Ryan started to respond but checked himself. Markham smiled like a death's head. "Thereupon I decided to call back the kzinti, is that what you wish to say?" he gibed. Seriously: "No, it was not that simple at all. I had had dealings with them throughout my war career, negotiations, exchanges, interrogation and care of prisoners, the sort of relationships one always has with an opponent. They came to fascinate me and I learned everything about them that I could. The more I knew, the more effective a freedom fighter I would be, not so?

"After the . . . liberation, my knowledge and my reputation caused me to have still more to do with them. There were mutual repatriations to arrange. There were kzinti who had good cause to stay behind. Some had been born in the Centaurian System; the second and later fleets carried females. Others came to join such kinfolk, or on their own, as fugitives, because their society too was in upheaval and many of them actually admired us, now that we had fought successfully. Remember, most of those newcomers arrived on human hyperdrive ships. This was official policy, in the hope of earning goodwill, of learning more about kzinti in general, and of—frankly—having possible hostages. Even so, they were often subject to cruel discrimination or outright persecution. What could I do but intervene in their behalf? They, or their brothers, had been brave and honorable enemies. It was time to become friends."

"That was certainly a worthy feeling," Tregennis admitted.

Markham made a chopping gesture. "Meanwhile I not only grew more and more aware of the rot in Wunderland, I discovered how much I had been lied to. The kzinti were never monsters, as propaganda had claimed. They were relentless at first and strict afterward, yes. They imposed their will. But it was a dynamic will serving a splendid vision. They were not wantonly cruel, nor extortionate, nor even pettily thievish. Humans who obeyed kzin law enjoyed its protection, its order, and its justice. Their lives went on peacefully, industriously, with old folkways respected—by the commoners *and* the kzinti. Most hardly ever saw a kzin. The Great Houses of Wunderland were the intermediaries, and woe betide the human lord who abused the people in his care. Oh, no matter his rank, he must defer to the lowliest kzin. But he received due honor for what he was, and could look forward to his sons rising higher, his grandsons to actual partnership."

"In the conquest of the galaxy," Ryan said.

"Well, the kzinti have their faults, but they are not like the Slavers that archeologists have found traces of, from a billion years ago or however long it was. Men who fought the kzinti and men who served them were more fully *men* than ever before or since. My mother first said this to me, years afterward, my mother whose word had been 'No Surrender.'"

Markham glanced at his watch. "We must leave soon," he reminded. "I didn't mean to go on at such length. I don't expect you to agree with me. I do urge you to think, think hard, and meanwhile cooperate."

Regardless, Tregennis asked in his disarming fashion, "Did you actually decide to work for a kzin restoration? Isn't that the sort of radicalism you oppose?"

"My decision did not come overnight either," Markham replied, "nor do I want kzin rule again over my people. It would be better than what they have now, but manliness of their own is better still. Earth is the real enemy, rich fat Earth, its bankers and hucksters and political panderers, its vulgarity and whorishness that poison our young everywhere—on your world too, Professor. A strong planet Kzin will challenge humans to strengthen themselves. Those who do not purge out the corruption will die. The rest, clean, will make a new peace, a brotherhood, and go on to take possession of the universe."

"Together with the kzinti," Ryan said.

Markham nodded. "And perhaps other worthy races. We shall see."

"I don't imagine anybody ever promised you this."

"Not in so many words. You are shrewd, Quartermaster. But shrewdness is not enough. There is such a thing as intuition, the sense of destiny."

Markham waved a hand. "Not that I had a religious experience. I began by entrusting harmless, perfectly sincere messages to kzinti going home, messages for their authorities. 'Please suggest how our two species can reach mutual understanding. What can I do to help bring a détente?' Things like that. A few kzinti do still travel in and out, you know, on human ships, by prearrangement. They generally come to consult or debate about what matters of mutual concern our species have these days, diplomatic, commercial, safety-related. Some do other things, clandestinely. We haven't cut off the traffic on that account. It is slight—and, after all, the exchange helps us plant our spies in their space.

"The responses I got were encouraging. They led to personal meetings, even occasionally to coded hyperwave communications; we have a few relays in kzin space, you know, by agreement. The first requests I got were legitimate by anyone's measure. The kzinti asked for specific information, no state secrets, merely data they could not readily obtain. I felt that by aiding them toward a better knowledge of us I was doing my race a valuable service. But of course I could not reveal it."

"No, you had your own little foreign policy," Ryan scoffed. "And one thing led to another, also inside your head, till you were sending stuff on the theory and practice of hyperdrive which gave them a ten- or twenty-year leg up on their R and D."

Markham's tone was patient. "They would inevitably have gotten it. Only by taking part in events can we hope to exercise any influence."

Again he consulted his watch. "We had better go," he said. "They will bring us to their base. You will be meeting the commandant. Perhaps what I have told will be of help to you."

"How about *Rover?*" Ryan inquired. "I hope you've explained to them she isn't meant for planetfall."

"That was not necessary," Markham said, irritated. "They know space architecture as well as we do—possibly better than you do, Quartermaster. We will go down in a boat from the warship. They will put our ship on the moon."

"What? Why not just in parking orbit?"

"I'll explain later. We must report now for debarkation. Have no fears. The kzinti won't willingly damage *Rover.* If they can—if we think of some way to prevent future human expeditions here that does not involve returning her—we'll keep her. The hyperdrive makes her precious. Otherwise *Kzarr-Siu—Vengeful Slasher*, the warship—is the only vessel currently in this system which has been so outfitted. They'll put *Rover* on the moon for safety's sake. Secunda orbits have become too crowded. The moon's gravity is low enough that it won't harm a freightship like this. Now come."

Markham rose and strode forth. Ryan and Tregennis followed. The Hawaiian nudged the Plateaunian and made little circling motions with his forefinger near his temple. Unwontedly bleak of countenance, the astronomer nodded, then whispered, "Be careful. I have read history. All too often, his kind is successful."

17

Kzinti did not use their gravity polarizers to maintain a constant, comfortable weight within spacecraft—unless accelerations got too high even for them to tolerate. The boat left with a roar of power. Humans sagged in their seats. Tregennis whitened. The thin flesh seemed to pull back over the bones of his face, the beaky nose stood out like a crag and blood trickled from it. "Hey, easy, boy," Ryan gasped. "Do you want to lose this man . . . already?"

Markham spoke to Hraou-Captain, who made a contemptuous noise but then yowled at the pilot. Weightlessness came as an abrupt benediction. For a minute silence prevailed, except for the heavy breathing of the Wunderlander and the Hawaiian, the rattling in and out of the old Plateaunian's.

Harnessed beside Tregennis, Ryan examined him as well as he could before muttering, "I guess he'll be all right in a while, if that snotbrain will take a little care." Raising his eyes, he looked past the other, out the port. "What's that?"

Close by, a kilometer or two, a small spacecraft—the size and lines indicated a ground-to-orbit shuttle—was docked at a framework which had been assembled around a curiously spheroidal dark mass, a couple of hundred meters in diameter. The framework secured and supported machinery which was carrying out operations under the direction of suited kzinti who flitted about with drive units on their backs. Stars peered through the lattice. In the distance passed a glimpse of *Rover*, moon-bound, and the warship.

The boat glided by. A new approach curve computed, the pilot applied thrust, this time about a single g's worth. Hraou-Captain registered impatience at the added waiting aboard. Markham did not venture to address him again. It must have taken courage to do so at all, when he wasn't supposed to defile the language with his mouth.

Instead the Wunderlander said to Ryan, on a note of awe, "That is doubtless one of their iron sources. Recently arrived, I would guess, and cooled down enough for work to commence on it. From what I have heard, a body that size will quickly be reduced."

Ryan stared at him, forgetting hostility in surprise. "Iron? I thought there was hardly any in this system. What it has ought to be at the center of the planets. Don't the kzinti import their metals for construction?"

Markham shook his head. "No, that would be quite impractical. They have few hyperdrive ships as yet—I told you *Vengeful Slasher* alone is so outfitted here, at present. Once the transports had brought personnel and the basic equipment, they went back for duty closer to home. Currently a warship calls about twice a year to bring fresh workers and needful items. It relieves the one on guard, which carries back kzinti being rotated. A reason for choosing this sun was precisely that humans won't suspect anything important can ever be done at it." He hesitated. "Except pure science. The kzinti did overlook that."

"Well, where do they get their metals? Oh, the lightest ones, aluminum, uh, beryllium, magnesium, . . . manganese?—I suppose those exist in ordinary ores. But I don't imagine those ores are anything but scarce and low-grade. And iron—"

"The asteroid belt. The planet that came too close to

the sun. Disruption exposed its core. The metal content is low compared to what it would be in a later-generation world, but when you have a whole planet, you get an abundance. They have had to bring in certain elements from outside, nickel, cobalt, copper, et cetera, but mostly to make alloys. Small quantities suffice."

Tregennis had evidently not fainted. His eyelids fluttered open. "Hold," he whispered. "Those asteroids . . . orbit within . . . less than half a million kilometers . . . of the sun surface." He panted feebly before adding, "It may be a . . . very late type M . . . but nevertheless, the effective temperature—" His voice trailed off.

The awe returned to Markham's. "They have built a special tug."

"What sort?" Ryan asked.

"In principle, like the kind we know. Having found a desirable body, it lays hold with a grapnel field. I think this vessel uses a gravity polarizer system rather than electromagnetics. The kzinti originated that technology, remember. The tug draws the object into the desired orbit and releases it to go to its destination. The tug is immensely powerful. It can handle not simply large rocks like what you saw, but whole asteroids of reasonable size. As they near Secunda—tangential paths, of course—it works them into planetary orbit. That's why local space is too crowded for the kzinti to leave *Rover* in it unmanned. Besides ferrous masses on hand, two or three new are usually en route, and not all the tailings of worked-out old ones get swept away."

"But the heat near the sun," Ryan objected. "The crew would roast alive. I don't see how they can trust robotics alone. If nothing else, let the circuits get too hot and—"

"The tug has a live crew," Markham said. "It's built double-hulled and mirror-bright, with plenty of radiating surfaces. But mainly it's ship size, not boat size, because it loads up with water ice before each mission. There is plenty of that around the big planets, you know, chilled well below minus a hundred degrees.

Heated, melted, evaporated, vented, it maintains an endurable interior until it has been spent."

"I thought we . . . found traces of water and OH . . . in a ring around the sun," Tregennis breathed. "Could it actually be—?"

"I don't know how much ice the project has consumed to date," Markham said, "but you must agree it is grandly conceived. That is a crew of heroes. They suffer, they dare death each time, but their will prevails."

Ryan rubbed his chin. "I suppose otherwise the only spacecraft are shuttles. And the warcraft and her boats."

"They are building more." Markham sounded proud. "And weapons and support machinery. This will be an industrial as well as a naval base."

"For the next war—" Tregennis seemed close to tears. Ryan patted his hand. Silence took over.

The boat entered atmosphere, which whined as she decelerated around the globe. A dawn storm, grit and ice, obscured the base, but the humans made out that it was in the great crater, presumably because the moonfall had brought down valuable ores and caused more to spurt up from beneath. Interconnected buildings made a web across several kilometers, with a black central spider. Doubtless much lay underground. An enterprise like this was large-scale or it was worthless. True, it had to start small, precariously—the first camp, the assembling of life support systems and food production facilities and a hospital for victims of disasters such as were inevitable when you drove hard ahead with your work on a strange world—but demonic energy had joined the exponential-increase powers of automated machines to bring forth this city of warriors.

No, Ryan thought, a city of workers in the service of future warriors. Thus far few professional fighters would be present except the crew of *Vengeful Slasher*. They weren't needed . . . yet. The warship was on hand against unlikely contingencies. Well, in this case kzin paranoia had paid off.

The pilot made an instrument landing into a cradle. Ryan spied more such units, three of them holding shuttles. The field on which they stood, though paved, must often be treacherous because of drifted dust. Secunda had no unfrozen water to cleanse its air; and the air was a chill wisp. Most of the universe is barren. Hawaii seemed infinitely far away.

A gang tube snaked from a ziggurat-like terminal building. Airlocks linked. An armed kzin entered and saluted. Hraou-Captain gestured at the humans and snarled an imperative before he went out. Markham unharnessed. "I am to follow him," he said. "You go with this guard. Quarters are prepared. Behave yourselves and . . . I will do my best for you."

Ryan rose. Two-thirds Earth weight felt good. He collected his and Tregennis' bags in his right hand and gave the astronomer his left arm for support. Kzinti throughout a cavernous main room stared as the captives appeared. They didn't goggle like humans, they watched like cats. Several naked tails switched to and fro. An effort had been made to brighten the surroundings, a huge mural of some hero in hand-to-hand combat with a monster; the blood jetted glaring bright.

The guard led his charges down corridors which pulsed with the sounds of construction. At last he opened a door, waved them through, and closed it behind them. They heard a lock click shut.

The room held a bed and a disposal unit, meant for kzinti but usable by humans; the bed was ample for two, and by dint of balancing and clinging you could take care of sanitation. "I better help you till you feel better, Prof," Ryan offered. "Meanwhile, why don't you lie down? I'll unpack." The bags and floor must furnish storage space. Kzinti seldom went in for clothes or for carrying personal possessions around.

They did hate sensory deprivation, still more than humans do. There was no screen, but a port showed the spacefield. The terminator storm was dying out as the sun rose higher, and the view cleared fast. Under a pale red sky, the naval complex came to an end some distance off. Tawny sand reached onward, strewn with boulders. In places, wind had swept clear the fused crater floor. It wasn't like lava, more like dark glass. Huge though the bowl was, Secunda—much less dense than Earth, but significantly larger—had a wide enough horizon that the nearer wall jutted above it in the west, a murky palisade.

Tregennis took Ryan's advice and stretched himself out. The quartermaster smiled and came to remove his shoes for him. "Might as well be comfortable," Ryan said, "or as nearly as we can without beer."

"And without knowledge of our fates," the Plateaunian said low. "Worse, the fates of our friends."

"At least they are out of Markham's filthy hands."

"Kamehameha, please. Watch yourself. We shall have to deal with him. And he—I think he too is feeling shocked and lonely. He didn't expect this either. His orders were merely to hamper exploration beyond the limits of human space. He wants to spare us. Give him the chance."

"Ha! I'd rather give a shark that kind of chance. It's less murderous."

"Oh, now, really."

Ryan thumped fist on wall. "Who do you suppose put that kzin up to attacking Bob Saxtorph back in Tiamat? It has to have been Markham, when his earlier efforts failed. Nothing else makes sense. And this, mind you, this was when he had no particular reason to believe our expedition mattered as far as the kzinti were concerned. They hadn't trusted him with any real information. But he went ahead anyway and tried to get a man killed to stop us. That shows you what value he puts on human life."

"Well, maybe . . . maybe he is deranged," Tregennis sighed. "Would you bring me a tablet, please? I see a water tap and bowl over there."

"Sure. Heart, huh? Take it easy. You shouldn't've come along, you know."

Tregennis smiled. "Medical science has kept me functional far longer than I deserve.

" 'But fill me with the old familiar Juice,
    'Methinks I might recover by-and-by!' "

Ryan lifted the white head and brought the bowl, from which a kzin would have lapped, carefully close to the lips. "You've got more heart than a lot of young bucks I could name," he said.

Time crept past.

The door opened. "Hey, food?" Ryan asked.

Markham confronted them, an armed kzin at his back. He was again pallid and stiff of countenance. "Come," he said harshly.

Rested, Tregennis walked steady-footed beside Ryan. They went through a maze of featureless passages with shut doors, coldly lighted, throbbing or buzzing. When they encountered other kzinti they felt the carnivore stares follow them.

After a long while they stopped at a larger door. This part of the warren looked like officer country, though Ryan couldn't be sure when practically everything he saw was altogether foreign to him. The guard let them in and followed.

The chamber beyond was windowless, its sole ornamentation a screen on which a computer projected colored patterns. Kzin-type seats, desk, and electronics suggested an office, but big and mostly empty. In one corner a plastic tub had been placed, about three meters square. Within stood some apparatus, and a warrior beside, and the drug-dazed telepath huddled at his feet.

The prisoners' attention went to Hraou-Captain and another—lean and grizzled by comparison—seated at the desk. "Show respect," Markham directed. "You meet Werlith-Commandant."

Tregennis bowed, Ryan slopped a soft salute.

The head honcho spat and rumbled. Markham turned to the men. "Listen," he said. "I have been in . . . conference, and am instructed to tell you . . . *Fido* has been found."

Tregennis made a tiny noise of pain. Ryan hunched his shoulders and said, "That's what they told you."

"It is true," Markham insisted. "The boat went to Prima. The interrogation aboard *Rover* led to a suspicion that the escapers might try that maneuver. *Ya-Nar-Ksshinn*—call it *Sun Defier*, the asteroid tug, it was prospecting. The commandant ordered it to Prima, since it could get there very fast. By then *Fido* was trapped on the surface. Fenger and Yoshii broadcast a call for help, so *Sun Defier* located them. Just lately, *Fido* has made a new broadcast which the kzinti picked up. You will listen to the recording."

Werlith-Commandant condescended to touch a control. From the desk communicator, wavery through a seething of radio interference, Juan Yoshii's voice came forth.

"Hello, Bob, Dorcas, Lau-laurinda—Kam, Arthur, . . . Ulf, if you hear—hello from Carita and me. We'll set this to repeat on different bands, hoping you'll happen to tune it in somewhere along the line. It's likely goodbye."

"No," said Carita's voice, "it's 'good luck.' To you. Godspeed."

"Right," Yoshii agreed. "Before we let you know what the situation is, we want to beg you, don't ever blame yourselves. There was absolutely no way to foresee it. And the universe is full of much worse farms we could have bought.

"However—" Unemotionally, now and then aided by his companion, he described things as they were. "We'll hang on till the end, of course," he finished. "Soon we'll see what we can rig to keep us alive. After the hull collapses altogether, we'll flit off in search of bare rock to sit on, if any exists. Do not, repeat do not risk yourselves in some crazy rescue attempt. Maybe you could figure out a safe way to do it if you had the time and no kzinti on your necks. Or maybe you could talk them into doing it. But neither one is in the cards, eh? You concentrate on getting the word home."

"We mean that," Carita said.

"Laurinda, I love you," Yoshii said fast. "Farewell, fare always well, darling. What really hurts is knowing you may not make it back. But if you do, you have your life before you. Be happy."

"We aren't glum." Carita barked a laugh. "I might wish Juan weren't quite so noble, Laurinda, dear. But it's no big thing either way, is it? Not any more. Good luck to all of you."

The recording ended. Tregennis gazed beyond the room—at this new miracle of nature? Ryan stood swallowing tears, his fists knotted.

"You see what Saxtorph's recklessness has caused," Markham said.

"No!" Ryan shouted. "The kzinti could lift them off! But they—tell his excellency yonder they're afraid to!"

"I will not. You must be out of your mind. Besides, *Sun Defier* cannot land on a planet, and carries no auxiliary."

"A shuttle—No. But a boat from the warship."

"Why? What have Yoshii and Fenger done to merit saving, at hazard to the kzinti for whom they only want to make trouble? Let them be an object lesson, gentlemen. If you have any care whatsoever for the rest of your party, help us retrieve them before it is too late."

"I don't know where they are. Not on P-prima, for sure."

"They must be found."

"Well, send that damned tug."

Markham shook his head. "It has better uses. It was about ready to return anyway. It will take Secunda orbit and wait for an asteroid that is due in shortly." He spoke like a man using irrelevancies to stave off the moment when he must utter his real meaning.

"Okay, the warship."

"It too has other duties. I've told them about Saxtorph's babbling of kamikaze tactics. Hraou-Captain must keep his vessel prepared to blow that boat out of the sky if it comes near—until Saxtorph's gang is under arrest, or dead. He will detach his auxiliaries to search."

"Let him," Ryan jeered. "Bob's got this whole system to skulk around in."

"Tertia is the first place to try."

"Go ahead. That old fox is good at finding burrows."

Werlith-Commandant growled. Markham grew paler

yet, bowed, turned on Ryan and said in a rush: "Don't waste more time. The master wants to resolve this business as soon as possible. He wants Saxtorph and company preferably alive, dead will do, but disposed of, so we can get on with the business of explaining away at Wunderland what happened to *Rover*. You will cooperate."

Sweat studded Ryan's face. "I will?"

"Yes. You shall accompany the search party. Broadcast your message in Hawaiian. Persuade them to give themselves up."

Ryan relieved himself of several obscenities.

"Be reasonable," Markham almost pleaded. "Think what has happened with *Fido*. The rest can only die in worse ways, unless you bring them to their senses."

Ryan shifted his feet wide apart, thrust his head forward, and spat, "No surrender."

Markham took a backward step. "What?"

"Your mother's motto, ratcat-lover. Have you forgotten? How proud of you she's going to be when she hears."

Markham closed his eyes. His lips moved. He looked forth again and said in a string of whipcracks: "You will obey. Werlith-Commandant orders it. Look yonder. Do you see what is in the corner? He expected stubbornness."

Ryan and Tregennis peered. They recognized frame and straps, pincers and electrodes; certain items were less identifiable. The telepath slumped at the feet of the torturer.

"Hastily improvised," Markham said, "but the database has a full account of human physiology, and I made some suggestions as well. The subject will not die under interrogation as often happened in the past."

Ryan's chest heaved. "If that thing can read my mind, he knows—"

Markham sighed. "We had better get to work." He glanced at the kzin officers. They both made a gesture. The guard sprang to seize Ryan from behind. The Hawaiian yelled and struggled, but that grip was unbreakable by a human.

The torturer advanced. He laid hands on Tregennis.

"Watch, Ryan," Markham said raggedly. "Let us know when you have had enough."

The torturer half dragged, half marched Tregennis across the room, held him against the wall, and, claws out on the free hand, ripped the clothes from his scrawniness.

"That's your idea, Markham!" Ryan bellowed. "You unspeakable—"

"Hold fast, Kamehameha," Tregennis called in his thin voice. "Don't yield."

"Art, oh, Art—"

The kzin secured the man to the frame. He picked up the electrodes and applied them. Tregennis screamed. Yet he modulated it: "Pain has a saturation point, Kamehameha. Hold fast!"

The business proceeded.

"You win, you Judas, okay, you win," Ryan wept.

Tregennis could no longer make words, merely noises.

Markham inquired of the officers before he told Ryan, "This will continue a few minutes more, to drive the lesson home. Given proper care and precautions, he should still be alive to accompany the search party." Markham breathed hard. "To make sure of your cooperation, do you hear? This is your fault!" he shrieked.

18

"No," Saxtorph had said, "I think we'd better stay put for the time being."

Dorcas had looked at him across the shoulder of Laurinda, whom she held close, Laurinda who had just heard her man say farewell. The cramped command section was full of the girl's struggles not to cry. "If they thought to check Prima immediately, they will be at Tertia before long," the captain's wife had stated.

Saxtorph had nodded. "Yah, sure. But they'll have a lot more trouble finding us where we are than if we were in space, even free-falling with a cold generator.

We could only boost a short ways, you see, else they'd acquire our drive-spoor if they've gotten anywhere near. They'd have a fairly small volume for their radars to sweep."

"But to sit passive! What use?"

"I didn't mean that. Thought you knew me better. Got an idea I suspect you can improve on."

Laurinda had lifted her head and sobbed, "Couldn't we . . . m-make terms? If we surrender to them . . . they rescue Juan and, and Carita?"

" 'Fraid not, honey," Saxtorph had rumbled. Anguish plowed furrows down his face. "Once we call 'em, they'll have a fix on us, and what's left to dicker with? Either we give in real nice or they lob a shell. They'd doubtless like to have us for purposes of faking a story, but we aren't essential—they hold three as is—and they've written *Fido*'s people off. I'm sorry."

Laurinda had freed herself from the mate's embrace, stood straight, swallowed hard. "You must be right," she had said in a voice taking on an edge. "What can we do? Thank you, Dorcas, dear, but I, I'm ready now . . . for whatever you need."

"Good lass." The older woman had squeezed her hand before asking the captain: "If we don't want to be found, shouldn't we fetch back the relay from above?"

Saxtorph had considered. The same sensitivity which had received, reconstructed, and given to the boat a radio whisper from across more than two hundred million kilometers, could betray his folk. After a moment: "No, leave it. A small object, after all, which we've camouflaged pretty well, and its emission blends into the sun's radio background. If the kzinti get close enough to detect it, they'll be onto us anyway."

"You don't imagine we can hide here forever."

"Certainly not. They can locate us in two-three weeks at most if they work hard. However, meanwhile they won't know for sure we are on Tertia. They'll spread themselves thin looking elsewhere too, or they'll worry. Never give the enemy a free ride."

"But you say you have something better in mind than simply distracting them for a while."

"Well, I have a sort of a notion. It's loony as it stands, but maybe you can help me refine it. At best, we'll probably get ourselves killed, but plain to see, Markham's effort to cut a deal has not worked out, and—we can hope for some revenge."

Laurinda's albino eyes had flared.

—"*Aloha, hoapilina.*—"

Crouched over the communicator, Saxtorph heard the Hawaiian through. English followed, the dragging tone of a broken man:

"Well, that was to show you this is honest, Bob, if you're listening. The kzinti don't have a telepath along, because they know they don't need the poor creature. They do require me to go on in a language their translator can handle. Anyway, I don't suppose you remember much Polynesian.

"We're orbiting Tertia in a boat from the Prowling Hunter warship. 'We' are her crew, plus a couple of marines, plus Arthur Tregennis and myself. Markham stayed on Secunda. He's a kzin agent. Maybe you've gotten the message from *Fido.* I'm afraid the game's played out, Bob. I tried to resist, but they tortured—not me—poor Art. I soon couldn't take it. He's alive, sort of. They give you three hours to call them. That's in case you've scrammed to the far ends of the system and may not be tuned in right now. You'll've noticed this is a powerful planar 'cast. They think they're being generous. If they haven't heard in three hours, they'll torture Art some more. Please don't let that happen!" Ryan howled through the wail that Laurinda tried to stifle. "Please call back!"

Saxtorph waited a while, but there was nothing further, only the hiss of the red sun. He took his finger from the transmission key, which he had not pressed, and twisted about to look at his companions. Light streaming wanly through the westside port found Dorcas' features frozen. Laurinda's writhed; her mouth was stretched out of shape.

"So," he said. "Three hours. Dark by then, as it happens."

"They hurt him," Laurinda gasped. "That good old man, they took him and hurt him."

Dorcas peeled lips back from teeth. "Shrewd," she said. "Markham in kzin pay? I'm not totally surprised. I don't know how it was arranged, but I'm not too surprised. He suggested this, I think. The kzinti probably don't understand us that well."

"We can't let them go on . . . with the professor," Laurinda shrilled. "We can't, no matter what."

"He's been like a second father to you, hasn't he?" Dorcas asked almost absently. Unspoken: But your young man is down on Prima, and the enemy will let him die there.

"No argument," Saxtorph said. "We won't. We've got a few choices, though. Kzinti aren't sadistic. Merciless, but not sadistic the way too many humans are. They don't torture for fun, or even spite. They won't if we surrender. Or if we die. No point in it then."

Dorcas grinned in a rather horrible fashion. "The chances are we'll die if we do surrender," she responded. "Not immediately, I suppose. Not till they need our corpses, or till they see no reason to keep us alive. Again, quite impersonal."

"I don't feel impersonal," Saxtorph grunted.

Laurinda lifted her hands. The fingers were crooked like talons. "We made other preparations against them. Let's do what we planned."

Dorcas nodded. "Aye."

"That makes it unanimous," Saxtorph said. "Go for broke. Now, look at the sun. Within three hours, nightfall. The kzinti could land in the dark, but if I were their captain I'd wait for morning. He won't be in such a hurry he'll care to take the extra risk. Meanwhile we sit cooped for 20-odd hours losing our nerve. Let's not. Let's begin right away."

Willingness blazed from the women.

Saxtorph hauled his bulk from the chair. "Okay, we

are on a war footing and I am in command," he said. "First Dorcas and I suit up."

"Are you sure I can't join you?" Laurinda well-nigh beseeched.

Saxtorph shook his head. "Sorry. You aren't trained for that kind of thing. And the gravity weights you down still worse than it does Dorcas, even if she is a Belter. Besides, we want you to free us from having to think about communications. You stay inboard and handle the hardest part." He chucked her under the chin. "If we fail, which we well may, you'll get your chance to die like a soldier." He stooped, kissed her hand, and went out.

Returning equipped, he said into the transmitter: "*Shep* here. Spaceboat *Shep* calling kzin vessel. Hello, Kam. Don't blame yourself. They've got us. We'll leave this message replaying in case you're on the far side, and so you can zero in on us. Because you will have to. Listen, Kam. Tell that gonococcus of a captain that we can't lift. We came down on talus that slid beneath us and damaged a landing jack. We'd hit the side of the canyon where we are—it's narrow—if we tried to take off before the hydraulics have been repaired; and Dorcas and I can't finish that job for another several Earthdays, the two of us with what tools we've got aboard. The ground immediately downslope of us is safe. Or, if your captain is worried about his fat ass, he can wait till we're ready to come meet him. Please inform us. Give Art our love; and take it yourself, Kam."

The kzin skipper would want a direct machine translation of those words. They were calculated not to lash him into fury—he couldn't be such a fool—but to pique his honor. Moreover, the top brass back on Secunda must be almighty impatient. Kzinti weren't much good at biding their time.

Before they closed their faceplates at the airlock, Saxtorph kissed his wife on the lips.

—Shadows welled in the coulee and its ravines as the sun sank toward rimrock. Interplay of light and dark was shifty behind the boat, where rubble now decked the floor. The humans had arranged that by radio detonation of two of the blasting sticks Dorcas smuggled along. It looked like more debris than it was, made the story of the accident plausible, and guaranteed that the kzinti would land in the short stretch between *Shep* and glacier.

Man and woman regarded each other. Their spacesuits were behung with armament. She had the rifle and snub-nosed automatic, he the machine pistol; both carried potentially lethal prospector's gear. Wind skirled. The heights glowed under a sky deepening from royal purple to black, where early stars quivered forth.

"Well," he said inanely into his throat mike, "we know our stations. Good hunting, kid."

"And to you, hotpants," she answered. "See you on the far side of the monobloc."

"Love you."

"Love you right back." She whirled and hastened off. Under the conditions expected, drive units would have been a bad mistake, and she was hampered by a weight she was never bred to. Nonetheless she moved with a hint of her wonted gracefulness. Both their suits were first-chop, never mind what the cost had added to the mortgage under which Saxtorph Ventures labored. Full air and water recycle, telescopic option, power joints even in the gloves, self-seal throughout. . . . She rated no less, he believed, and she'd tossed the same remark at him. Thus they had a broad range of capabilities.

He climbed to his chosen niche, on the side of the canyon opposite hers, and settled in. It was up a boulderful gulch, plenty of cover, with a clear view downward. The ice cliff glimmered. He hoped that what was going to happen wouldn't cause damage yonder. That would be a scientific atrocity.

But those beings had had their day. This was humankind's, unless it turned out to be kzinkind's. Or somebody else's? Who knew how many creatures of what sorts were prowling around the galaxy? Saxtorph hunkered into a different position. He missed his pipe. His heart slugged harder than it ought and he could smell himself in spite of the purifier. Better do a bit of meditation. Nervousness would worsen his chances.

His watch told him an hour had passed when the kzin boat arrived. The boat! Good. They might have kept her safe aloft and dispatched a squad on drive. But that would have been slow and tricky; as they descended, the members could have been picked off, assuming the humans had firearms—which a kzin would assume; they'd have had no backup.

The sun had trudged farther down, but *Shep*'s nose still sheened above the blue dusk in the canyon, and the oncoming craft flared metallic red. He knew her type from his war years. Kam, stout kanaka, had passed on more information than the kzinti probably realized. A boat belonging to a Prowling Hunter normally carried six—captain, pilot, engineer, computerman, two fire-control officers; they shared various other duties, and could swap the main ones in an emergency. They weren't trained for groundside combat, but of course any kzin was pretty fair at that. Kam had mentioned two marines who did have the training. Then there were the humans. No wonder the complement did not include a telepath. He'd have been considered superfluous anyway, worth much more at the base. This mission was simply to collar three fugitives.

Sonic thunders rolled, gave way to whirring, and the lean shape neared. It put down with a care that Saxtorph admired, came to rest, instantly swiveled a gun at the human boat 50 meters up the canyon. Saxtorph's pulse leaped. The enemy had landed exactly where he hoped. Not that he'd counted on that, or on anything else.

His earphones received bland translator English; he could imagine the snarl behind. "Are you prepared to yield?"

How steady Laurinda's response was. "We yield on condition that our comrades are alive, safe. Bring them to us." Quite a girl, Saxtorph thought. The kzinti wouldn't wonder about her; their females not being sapient, any active intelligence was, in their minds, male.

"Do you dare this insolence? Your landing gear does not seem damaged as you claimed. Lift, and we fire."

"We have no intention of lifting, supposing we could. Bring us our comrades, or come pry us out."

Saxtorph tautened. No telling how the kzin commander would react. Except that he'd not willingly blast *Shep* on the ground. Concussion, in this thick atmosphere, and radiation would endanger his own craft. He might decide to produce Art and Kam—

Hope died. Battle plans never quite work. The main airlock opened; a downramp extruded; two kzinti in armor and three in regular spacesuits, equipped with rifles and cutting torches, came forth. The smooth computer voice said, "You will admit this party. If you resist, you die."

Laurinda kept silence. The kzinti started toward her.

Saxtorph thumbed his detonator.

In a well-chosen set of places under a bluff above a slope on his side, the remaining sticks blew. Dust and flinders heaved aloft. An instant later he heard the grumble of explosion and breaking. Under one-point-three-five Earth gravities, rocks hurtled, slid, tumbled to the bottom and across it.

He couldn't foresee what would happen next, but had been sure it would be fancy. The kzinti were farther along than he preferred. They dodged leaping masses, escaped the landslide. But it crashed around their boat. She swayed, toppled, fell onto the pile of stone, which grew until it half buried her. The gun pointed helplessly at heaven. Dust swirled about before it settled.

Dorcas was already shooting. She was a crack marksman. A kzin threw up his arms and flopped, another, another. The rest scattered. They hadn't thought to bring drive units. If they had, she could have bagged them all as they rose. Saxtorph bounded out and downslope, over the boulders. His machine pistol had less range than her rifle. It chattered in his hands. He zigzagged, bent low, squandering ammo, while she kept the opposition prone.

Out of nowhere, a marine grabbed him by the ankle. He fell, rolled over, had the kzin on top of him. Fingers clamped on the wrist of the arm holding his weapon. The kzin fumbled after a pistol of his own. Saxtorph's free hand pulled a crowbar from its sling. He got it behind the kzin's back, under the aircycler tank, and pried. Vapor gushed forth. His foe choked, went bug-eyed, scrabbled, and slumped. Saxtorph crawled from beneath.

Dorcas covered his back, disposed of the last bandit, as he pounded toward the boat. The outer valve of the airlock gaped wide. Piece of luck, that, though he and she could have gotten through both with a certain amount of effort. He wedged a rock in place to make sure the survivors wouldn't shut it.

She made her way to him. He helped her scramble across the slide and over the curve of hull above, to the chamber. She spent her explosive rifle shells breaking down the inner valve. As it sagged, she let him by.

He stormed in. They had agreed to that, as part of what they had hammered out during hour after hour after hour of waiting. He had the more mass and muscle; and spraying bullets around in a confined space would likely kill their friends.

An emergency airseal curtain brushed him and closed again. Breathable atmosphere leaked past it, a white smoke, but slowly. The last kzinti attacked. They didn't want ricochets either. Two had claws out—one set dripped red—and the third carried a power drill, whirling to pierce his suit and the flesh behind.

Saxtorph went for him first. His geologist's hammer knocked the drill aside. From the left, his knife stabbed into the throat, and slashed. Clad as he was, what followed became butchery. He split a skull and opened a belly. Blood, brains, guts were everywhere. Two kzinti struggled and ululated in agony. Dorcas came into the tumult. Safely point-blank, her pistol administered mercy shots.

Saxtorph leaned against a bulkhead. He began to shake.

Dimly, he was aware of Kam Ryan stumbling forth. He opened his faceplate—oxygen inboard would stay adequate for maybe half an hour, though God, the stink of death!—and heard:

"I don't believe, I can't believe, but you did it, you're here, you've won, only first a ratcat, must've lost his temper, he ripped Art, Art's dead, well, he was hurting so, a release, I scuttled aft, but Art's dead, don't let Laurinda see, clean up first, please, I'll do it, we can take time to bury him, can't we, this is where his dreams were—" The man knelt, embraced Dorcas' legs regardless of the chill on them, and wept.

19

They left Tregennis at the foot of the glacier, making a cairn for him where the ancients were entombed. "That seems very right," Laurinda whispered. "I hope the scientists who come in the future will—give him a proper grave—but leave him here."

Saxtorph made no remark about the odds against any such expedition. It would scarcely happen unless his people got home to tell the tale.

The funeral was hasty. When they hadn't heard from their boat for a while, which would be a rather short while, the kzinti would send another, if not two or three. Humans had better be well out of the neighborhood before then.

Saxtorph boosted *Shep* inward from Tertia. "We can get some screening in the vicinity of the sun, especially if we've got it between us and Secunda," he explained. "Radiation out of that clinker is no particular hazard, except heat; we'll steer safely wide and not linger too long." Shedding unwanted heat was always a problem in space. The best array of thermistors gave only limited help.

"Also—" he began to add. "No, never mind. A vague notion. Something you mentioned, Kam. But let it wait till we've quizzed you dry."

That in turn waited upon simple, dazed sitting, followed by sleep, followed by gradual regaining of strength and alertness. You don't bounce straight back from tension, terror, rage, and grief.

The sun swelled in view. Its flares were small and dim compared to Sol's, but their flame-flickers became visible to the naked eye, around the roiled ember disc. After he heard what Ryan knew about the asteroid tug, Saxtorph whistled. "Christ!" he murmured. "Imagine swinging that close. Damn near half the sky a boiling red glow, and you hear the steam roar in its conduits and you fly in a haze of it, and nevertheless I'll bet the cabin is a furnace you can barely endure, and if the least thing goes wrong—Yah, kzinti have courage, you must give them that. Markham's right—what you quoted, Kam—they'd make great partners for humans. Though he doesn't understand that we'll have to civilize them first."

Excitement grew in him as he learned more and his thoughts developed. But it was with a grim countenance that he presided over the meeting he called.

"Two men, two women, an unarmed interplanetary boat, and the nearest help light-years off," he said. "After what we've done, the enemy must be scouring the system for us. I daresay the warship's staying on guard at Secunda, but if I know kzin psychology, all her auxiliaries are now out on the hunt, and won't quit till we're either captured or dead."

Dorcas nodded. "We dealt them what was worse than a hurt, a humiliation," she confirmed. "Honor calls for vengeance."

Laurinda clenched her fists. "It *does*," she hissed. Ryan glanced at her in surprise; he hadn't expected that from her.

"Well, they do have losses to mourn, like us," Dorcas said. "As fiery as they are by nature, they'll press the chase in hopes of dealing with us personally. However, they know our foodstocks are limited." Little had been taken from the naval lockers. It was unpalatable, and stowage space was almost filled already. "If we're still missing after some months, they can reckon us dead. Contrary to Bob, I suppose they'll return to base before then."

"Not necessarily," Ryan replied. "It gives them something to do. That's the question every military command has to answer, how to keep the troops busy between combat operations." For the first time since that hour on Secunda, he grinned. "The traditional human solutions have been either (a) a lot of drill or (b) a lot of paperwork; but you can't force much of either on kzinti."

"Back to business," Saxtorph snapped. "I've been trying to reason like, uh, Werlith-Commandant. What does he expect? I think he sees us choosing one of three courses. First, we might stay on the run, hoping against hope that there will be a human follow-up expedition and we can warn it in time. But he's got Markham to help him prevent that. Second, we might turn ourselves in, hoping against hope our lives will be spared. Third, we might attempt a suicide dash, hoping against hope we'll die doing him a little harm. The warship will be on the lookout for that, and in spite of certain brave words earlier, I honestly don't give us a tax collector's chance at Paradise of getting through the kind of barrage she can throw.

"Can anybody think of any more possibilities?"

"No," sighed Dorcas. "Of course, they aren't mutually exclusive. Forget surrender. But we can stay on the run till we're close to starvation and then try to strike a blow."

Laurinda's eyes closed. *Juan*, her lips formed.

"We can try a lot sooner," Saxtorph declared.

Breaths went sibilant in between teeth.

"What Kam's told us has given me an idea that I'll bet has not occurred to any kzin," the captain went on. "I'll grant you it's hairy-brained. It may very well get us killed. But it gives us the single possibility I see of getting killed while accomplishing something real. And we might, we just barely might do better than that. You see, it involves a way to sneak close to Secunda, undetected, unsuspected. After that, we'll decide what, if anything, we can do. I have a notion there as well, but first we need hard information. If things look impossible, we can probably flit off for outer space, the kzinti never the wiser." A certain vibrancy came into his voice. "But time crammed inside this hull is scarcely lifetime, is it? I'd rather go out fighting. A short life but a merry one."

His tone dropped. "Granted, the whole scheme depends on parameters being right. But if we're careful, we shouldn't lose much by investigating. At worst, we'll be disappointed."

"You do like to lay a long-winded foundation, Bob," Ryan said.

"And you like to mix metaphors, Kam," Dorcas responded.

Saxtorph laughed. Laurinda looked from face to face, bemused.

"Okay," Saxtorph said. "Our basic objective is to recapture *Rover*, agreed? Without her, we're nothing but a bunch of maroons, and the most we can do is take a few kzinti along when we die. With her—ah, no need to spell it out.

"She's on Secunda's moon, Kam heard. The kzinti know full well we'd like to get her back. I doubt they keep a live guard aboard against the remote contingency. They've trouble enough as is with personnel growing bored and quarrelsome. But they'll've planted detectors, which will sound a radio alarm if anybody comes near. Then the warship can land an armed party or, if necessary, throw a nuke. The warship also has the duty of protecting the planetside base. If I were in charge—and I'm pretty sure What's-his-screech-Captain thinks the same—I'd keep her in orbit about halfway between planet and moon. Wide field for radars, optics, every kind of gadget; quick access to either body. Kam heard as how that space is cluttered with industrial stuff and junk, but she'll follow a reasonably clear path and keep ready to dodge or deflect whatever may be on a collision course.

"Now. The kzinti mine the asteroid belt for metals, mainly iron. They do that by shifting the bodies into eccentric orbits osculating Secunda's, then wangling them into planetary orbit at the far end. Kam heard as how an asteroid is about due in, and the tug was taking station to meet it and nudge it into place. To my mind, 'asteroid' implies a fair-sized object, not just a rock.

"But the tug was prospecting, Kam heard, when she was ordered to Prima. Afterward she didn't go back to prospecting, because the time before she'd be needed at Secunda had gotten too short to make that worthwhile. However, since she was in fact called from the sun, my guess is that the asteroid's not in need of attention right away. In other words, the tug's waiting.

"Again, if I were in charge, I wouldn't keep a crew idle aboard. I'd just leave her in Secunda orbit till she's wanted. That needs to be a safe orbit, though, and inner space isn't for an empty vessel. So the tug's circling wide around the planet, or maybe the moon. Unless she sits on the moon too."

"She isn't able to land anywhere," Ryan reminded. "Those cooling fins, if nothing else. I suppose the kzinti put *Rover* down, on the planet-facing side, the easier to keep an eye on her. She's a lure for us, after all."

Saxtorph nodded. "Thanks," he said. "Given that the asteroid was diverted from close-in solar orbit, and is approaching Secunda, we can make a pretty good estimate of where it is and what the vectors are. How 'bout it, Laurinda?

"The Kzinti are expecting the asteroid. Their instruments will register it. They'll say, 'Ah, yes,' and go on about their business, which includes hunting for us— and never suppose that we've glided to it and are trailing along behind."

Dorcas let out a war-whoop.

20

The thing was still molten. That much mass would remain so for a long while in space, unless the kzinti had ways to speed its cooling. Doubtless they did. Instead of venting enormous quantities of water to maintain herself near the sun, the tug could spray them forth. "What a show!" Saxtorph had said. "Pity we'll miss it."

The asteroid glowed white, streaked with slag, like a lesser sun trundling between planets. Its diameter was ample to conceal *Shep*. Secunda gleamed ahead, a perceptible tawny disc. From time to time the humans had ventured to slip their boat past her shield for a quick instrumental peek. They knew approximately the rounds which *Vengeful Slasher* and *Sun Defier* paced. Soon the tug must come to make rendezvous and steer the iron into its destination path. Gigantic though her strength was, she could shift millions of tonnes, moving at kilometers per second, only slowly. Before this began, the raiders must raid.

Saxtorph made a final despairing effort: "Damn it to chaos, darling, I can't let you go. I can't."

"Hush," Dorcas said low, and laid her hand across his mouth. They floated weightless in semi-darkness, the bunk which they shared curtained off. Their shipmates had, unspokenly, gone forward from the cubbyhole where everyone slept by turns, to leave them alone.

"One of us has to go, one stay," she whispered redundantly, but into his ear. "Nobody else would have a prayer of conning the tug, and Kam and Laurinda could scarcely bring *Rover* home, which is the object of the game. So you and I have to divide the labor, and for this part I'm better qualified."

"Brains, not brawn, huh?" he growled half resentfully.

"Well, I did work on translation during the war. I can read kzin a little, which is what's going to count. Put down your machismo." She drew him close and fluttered eyelids against his. "As for brawn, fellow, you do have qualifications I lack, and this may be our last chance . . . for a spell."

"Oh, love—you, you—"

Thus their dispute was resolved. They had been through it more than once. Afterward there wasn't time to continue it. Dorcas had to prepare herself.

Spacesuited, loaded like a Christmas tree with equipment, she couldn't properly embrace her husband at the airlock. She settled for an awkward kiss and a wave at the others, then closed her faceplate and cycled through.

Outside, she streaked off, around the asteroid. Its warmth beat briefly at her. She left the lump behind and deployed her diriscope, got a fix on the planet ahead, compared the reading with the computed coordinates that gleamed on a databoard, worked the calculator strapped to her left wrist, made certain of what the displays on her drive unit meters said—right forearm—and set the thrust controls for maximum. Acceleration tugged. She was on her way.

It would be a long haul. You couldn't eat distance in a spacesuit at anything like the rate you could in a boat. Its motor lacked the capacity—not to speak of the protections and cushionings possible within a hull. In fact, a large part of her load was energy boxes. To accomplish her mission in time, she must needs drain them beyond rechargeability, discard and replace them. That hurt; they could have been ferried down to Prima for the saving of Carita and Juan. Now too few would be left, back aboard *Shep*. But under present conditions rescue would be meaningless anyway.

She settled down for the hours. Her insignificant size and radiation meant she would scarcely show on Kzin's detectors. Occasionally she sipped from the water tube or pushed a foodbar through the chowlock. Her suit took care of additional needs. As for comfort, she had the stars, Milky Way, nebulae, sister galaxies, glory upon glory.

Often she rechecked her bearings and adjusted her

vectors. Eventually, decelerating, she activated a miniature radar such as asteroid miners employ and got a lock on her objective. By then Secunda had swollen larger in her eyes than Luna over Earth. From her angle of view it was a scarred dun crescent against a circle of darkness faintly rimmed with light diffused through dusty air. The moon, where *Rover* lay, was not visible to her.

Saxtorph's guess had been right. Well, it was an informed guess. The warship orbited the planet at about 100,000 klicks. The supertug circled beyond the moon, twice as far out. She registered dark and cool on what instruments Dorcas carried; nobody aboard. Terminating deceleration, the woman approached.

What a sight! A vast, brilliant spheroid with flanges like convulsed meridians; drive units projecting within a shielding sheath; no ports, but receptors from which visuals were transmitted inboard; recesses for instruments; circular hatches which must cover steam vents; larger doors to receive crushed ice— How did you get in? Dorcas flitted in search. She could do it almost as smoothly as if she were flying a manwing through atmosphere.

There—an unmistakable airlock— She was prepared to cut her way in, but when she had identified the controls, the valves opened and shut for her. Who worries about burglars in space? To the kzinti, *Rover* was the bait that might draw humans.

The interior was dark. Diffusion of her flashbeam, as well as a gauge on her left knee, showed full pressure was maintained. Hers wasn't quite identical; she equalized before shoving back her faceplate. The air was cold and smelled musty. Pumps muttered.

Afloat in weightlessness, she began her exploration. She'd never been in a kzin ship before. But she had studied descriptions; and the laws of nature are the same everywhere, and man and kzin aren't terribly unlike—they can actually eat each other; and she could decipher most labels; so she could piecemeal trace things out, figure how they worked, even in a vessel as unusual as this.

She denied herself haste. If the crew arrived before she was done, she'd try ambushing them. There was no point in this job unless it was done right. As need arose she ate, rested, napped, adrift amidst machinery. Once she began to get a solid idea of the layout, she stripped it. Supplies, motors, black boxes, whatever she didn't think she would require, she unpacked, unbolted, torched loose, and carried outside. There the grapnel field, the same force that hauled on cosmic stones, low-power now, clasped them behind the hull.

Alone though she was, the ransacking didn't actually take long. She was efficient. A hundred hours sufficed for everything.

"Very well," she said at last; and she took a pill and accepted ten hours of REM sleep, dreams which had been deferred. Awake again, refreshed, she nourished herself sparingly, exercised, scribbled a cross in the air and murmured, "Into Your hands—" for unlike her husband, she believed the universe was more than an accident.

Next came the really tricky part. Of course Bob had wanted to handle it himself. Poor dear, he must be in absolute torment, knowing everything that could go wrong. She was luckier, Dorcas thought: too busy to be afraid.

Shep's flickering radar peeks had gotten fair-to-middling readings on an object that must be the kzin warship. Its orbit was only approximately known, and subject both to perturbation and deliberate change. Dorcas needed exact knowledge. She must operate indicators and computers of nonhuman workmanship so delicately that Hraou-Captain had no idea he was under surveillance. Thereafter she must guess what her best tactics might be, calculate the maneuvers, and follow through.

When the results were in: "Here goes," she said into the hollowness around. "For you, Arthur—" and thought briefly that if the astronomer could have roused in his grave on Tertia, he would have reproved her, in his gentle fashion, for being melodramatic.

Sun Defier plunged.

Unburdened by tonnes of water, she made nothing of ten g's, 20, 30, you name it. Her kzin crew must often have used the polarizer to keep from being crushed, as Dorcas did. "Hai-ai-ai!" she screamed, and rode her comet past the moon, amidst the stars, to battle.

She never knew whether the beings aboard the warship saw her coming. Things happened so fast. If the kzinti did become aware of what was bearing down on them, they had scant time to react. Their computers surely told them that *Sun Defier* was no threat, would pass close by but not collide. Some malfunction? The kzinti would not gladly annihilate their iron gatherer.

When the precalculated instant flashed onto a screen before her, Dorcas punched for a sidewise thrust as great as the hull could survive. It shuddered and groaned around her. An instant later, the program that she had written cut off the grapnel field.

Those masses she had painstakingly lugged outside—they now had interception vectors, and at a distance too small for evasion. *Sun Defier* passed within 50 kilometers while objects sleeted through *Vengeful Slasher*.

The warship burst. Armor peeled back, white-hot, from holes punched by monstrous velocity. Missiles floated out of shattered bays. Briefly, a frost-cloud betokened air rushing forth into vacuum. The wreck tumbled among fragments of itself. Starlight glinted off the ruins. Doubtless crew remained alive in this or that sealed compartment; but *Vengeful Slasher* wasn't going anywhere out of orbit, ever again.

Sun Defier swooped past Secunda. Dorcas commenced braking operations, for eventual rendezvous with her fellow humans.

21

The moon was a waste of rock, low hills, boulderfields, empty plains, here and there a crater not quite eroded away. Darkling in this light, under Sol it would have been brighter than Luna, powdered with yellow which at the bottoms of slopes had collected to form streaks or blotches. The sun threw long shadows from the west.

Against them, *Rover* shone like a beacon. Saxtorph cheered. As expected, the kzinti had left her on the hemisphere that always faced Secunda. The location was, however, not central but close to the north pole and the western edge. He wondered why. He'd spotted many locations that looked as good or better, when you had to bring down undamaged a vessel not really meant to land on anything this size.

He couldn't afford the time to worry about it. By now the warboats had surely learned of the disaster to their mother ship and were headed back at top boost. Kzinti might or might nor suspect what the cause had been of their supertug running amok, but they would know when *Rover* took off—in fact, would probably know when he reached the ship. Their shuttles, designed for strictly orbital work, were no threat. Their gunboats were. If *Rover* didn't get to hyperspacing distance before those overtook her, she and her crew would be *ganz kaput*.

Saxtorph passed low overhead, ascended, and played back the pictures his scanners had taken in passing. As large as she was, the ship had no landing jacks. She lay sidelong on her lateral docking grapples. That stressed her, but not too badly in a gravity less than Luna's. To compound the trickiness of descent, she had been placed just under a particularly high and steep hill. He could only set down on the opposite side. Beyond the narrow strip of flat ground on which she lay, a blotch extended several meters across the valley floor. Otherwise that floor was strewn with rocks and somewhat downward sloping toward the hill. Maybe the kzinti had chosen this site precisely because it was a bitch for him to settle on.

"I can do it, though," Saxtorph decided. He pointed at the screen. "See, a reasonably clear area about 500 meters off."

Laurinda nodded. With the boat falling free again, the white hair rippled around her delicate features.

Saxtorph applied retrothrust. For thrumming minutes he backed toward his goal. Sweat studded his face and darkened his tunic under the arms. Smell like a billy goat, I do, he thought fleetingly. When we come home, I'm going to spend a week in a Japanese hot bath. Dorcas can bring me sushi. She prefers showers, cold.—He gave himself entirely back to his work.

Contact shivered. The deck tilted. Saxtorph adjusted the jacks to level *Shep*. When he cut the engine, silence fell like a thunderclap.

He drew a long breath, unharnessed, and rose. "I can suit up faster if you help me," he told the Crashlander.

"Of course," she replied. "Not that I have much experience."

Never mind modesty. It had been impossible to maintain without occasional failures, by four people crammed inside this little hull. Laurinda had blushed all over, charmingly, when she happened to emerge from the shower cubicle as Saxtorph and Ryan came by. The quartermaster had only a pair of shorts on, which didn't hide the gallant reflex. Yet nobody ever did or said anything improper, and the girl overcame her shyness. Now a part of Saxtorph enjoyed the touch of her spidery fingers, but most of him stayed focused on the business at hand.

"Forgive me for repeating what you've heard a dozen times," he said. "You are new to this kind of situation, and could forget the necessity of abiding by orders. Your job is to bring this boat back to Dorcas and Kam. That's *it*. Nothing else whatsoever. When I tell you to, you throw the main switch, and the program we've put in the autopilot will take over. I'd've automated that bit also, except rigging it would've taken time we can ill afford, and anyway, we do want some flexibility, some judgment in the control loop." Sternly: "If anything goes wrong for me, or you think anything has, whether or not I've called in, you go. The three of you must have *Shep*. The tug's fast but clumsy, impossible to make planetfall with, and only barely provisioned. Your duty is to *Shep*. Understood?"

"Yes," she said mutedly, her gaze on the task she was doing. "Besides, we have to have the boat to rescue Juan and Carita."

A sigh wrenched from Saxtorph. "I told you—" After Dorcas' flight, too few energy boxes remained to lift either of them into orbit. *Shep* could hover on her drive at low altitude while they flitted up, but she wasn't built for planetary rescue work, the thrusters weren't heavily enough shielded externally, at such a boost their radiation would be lethal.

Neither meek nor defiant, Laurinda replied, "I know. But after we've taken *Rover* to the right distance, why can't she wait, ready to flee, till the boat comes back from Prima?"

"Because the boat never would."

"The kzinti can land safely."

"More or less safely. They don't like to, remember. Sure, I can tell you how they do it. Obvious. They put detachable footpads on their jacks. The stickum may or may not be able to grab hold of, say, fluorosilicone, but if it does, it'll take a while to eat its way through. When the boat's ready to leave, she sheds those footpads."

"Of course. I've been racking my brain to comprehend why we can't do the same for *Shep*."

The pain in her voice and in himself brought anger into his. "God damn it, we're spacers, not sorcerers! Groundsiders think a spacecraft is a hunk of metal you can cobble anything onto, like a car. She isn't. She's about as complex and interconnected as your body is. A few milligrams of blood clot or of the wrong chemical will bring your body to a permanent halt. A spacecraft's equally vulnerable. I am *not* going to tinker with ours, light-years from any proper workshop. I am not. That's final!"

Her face bent downward from his. He heard her breath quiver.

"I'm sorry, dear," he added, softly once more. "I'm sorrier than you believe, maybe sorrier than you can imagine. Those are my crewfolk down and doomed. Oh, if we had time to plan and experiment and carefully test, sure, I'd try it. What should the footpads be made of? What size? How closely machined? How detached—explosive bolts, maybe? We'd have to wire those and—Laurinda, we won't have the time. If I lift *Rover* off within the next hour or two, we can pick up Dorcas and Kam, boost, and fly dark. If we're lucky, the kzin warboats won't detect us. But our margin is razor thin. We don't have the days or weeks your idea needs. *Fido*'s people don't either; their own time has gotten short. I'm sorry, dear."

She looked up. He saw tears in the ruby eyes, down the snowy cheeks. But she spoke still more quietly than he, with the briefest of little smiles. "No harm in asking, was there? I understand. You've told me what I was trying to deny I knew. You are a good man, Robert."

"Aw," he mumbled, and reached to rumple her hair.

The suiting completed, he took her hands between his gloves for a moment, secured a toolpack between his shoulders where the drive unit usually was, and cycled out.

The land gloomed silent around him. Nearing the horizon, the red sun looked bigger than it was. So did the planet, low to the southeast, waxing close to half phase. He could make out a dust storm as a deeper-brown blot on the fulvous crescent. Away from either luminous body, stars were visible—and yonder brilliancy must be Quarta. How joyously they had sailed past it.

Saxtorph started for his ship, in long low-gravity bounds. He didn't want to fly. The kzinti might have planted a boobytrap, such as an automatic gun that would lock on, track, and fire if you didn't radio the password. Afoot, he was less of a target.

The ground lightened as he advanced, for the yellow dust lay thicker. No, he saw, it was not actually dust in the sense of small solid particles, but more like spatters or films of liquid. Evidently it didn't cling to things, like that horrible stuff on Prima. A ghostly rain from space, it would slip from higher to lower places; in the course of gigayears, even cosmic rays would give some slight stirring to help it along downhill. It might be fairly deep near the ship, where its surface was like a blot. He'd better approach with care. Maybe it would prove necessary to fetch a drive unit and flit across.

Saxtorph's feet went out from under him. He fell slowly, landed on his butt. With an oath he started to get up. His soles wouldn't grip. His hands skidded on slickness. He sprawled over onto his back. And he was gliding down the slope of the valley floor, gliding down toward the amber-colored blot.

He flailed, kicked up dust, but couldn't stop. The damned ground had no friction, none. He passed a boulder and managed to throw an arm around. For an instant he was checked, then it rolled and began to descend with him.

"Laurinda, I have a problem," he managed to say into his radio. "Sit tight. Watch close. If this turns out to be serious, obey your orders."

He reached the blot. It gave way. He sank into its depths.

He had hoped it was a layer of just a few centimeters, but it closed over his head and still he sank. A pit where the stuff had collected from the heights—maybe the kzinti, taking due care, had dumped some extra in, gathered across a wide area—yes, this was very likely their boobytrap, and if they had ghosts, Hraou-Captain's must be yowling laughter. Odd how that name came back to him as he tumbled.

Bottom. He lay in blindness, fighting to curb his breath and heartbeat. How far down? Three meters, four? Enough to bury him for the next several billion years, unless— "Hello, *Shep*. Laurinda, do you read me? Do you read me?"

His earphones hummed. The wavelength he was using should have expanded its front from the top of the pit, but the material around him must be screening it. Silence outside his suit was as thick as the blackness.

Let's see if he could climb out. The side wasn't vertical. The stuff resisted his movements less than water would. He felt arms and legs scrabble to no avail. He could feel irregularities in the stone but he could not get a purchase on any. Well, could he swim? He tried. No. He couldn't rise off the bottom. Too high a mean density compared to the medium; and it didn't allow him even as much traction as water, it yielded to every motion, he might as well have tried to swim in air.

If he'd brought his drive unit, maybe it could have lifted him out. He wasn't sure. It was for use in space. This fluid might clog it or ooze into circuitry that there had never been any reason to seal tight. Irrelevant anyway, when he'd left it behind.

"My boy," he said, "it looks like you've had the course."

That was a mistake. The sound seemed to flap around in the cage of his helmet. If he was trapped, he shouldn't dwell on it. That way lay screaming panic.

He forced himself to lie quiet and think. How long till Laurinda took off? By rights, she should have already. If he did escape the pit, he'd be alone on the moon. Naturally, he'd try to get at *Rover* in some different fashion, such as coming around on the hillside. But meanwhile Dorcas would return in *Shep*, doubtless with the other two. She was incapable of cutting and running, off into futility. Chances were, though, that by the time she got here a kzin auxiliary or two would have arrived. The odds against her would be long indeed.

So if Saxtorph found a way to return topside and repossess *Rover*—soon—he wouldn't likely find his wife at the asteroid. And he couldn't very well turn back and try to make contact, because of those warboats and because of his overriding obligation to carry the warning home. He'd have to conn the ship all by himself, leaving Dorcas behind for the kzinti.

The thought was strangling. Tears stung. That was a relief, in the nullity everywhere around. Something he could feel, and taste the salt of on his lips. Was the tomb blackness thickening? No, couldn't be. How long had he lain buried? He brought his timepiece to his faceplate, but the hell-stuff blocked off luminosity. The blood in his ears hammered against a wall of stillness. Had a whine begun to modulate the rasping of his breath? Was he going crazy? Sensory deprivation did bring on illusions, weirdnesses, but he wouldn't have expected it this soon.

He made himself remember—sunlight, stars, Dorcas, a sail above blue water, fellowship among men, Dorcas, the tang of a cold beer, Dorcas, their plans for children—they'd banked gametes against the day they'd be ready for domesticity but maybe a little too old and battered in the DNA for direct begetting to be advisable—

Contact ripped him out of his dreams. He reached wildly and felt his gloves close on a solid object. They slid along it, along humanlike lineaments, a spacesuit, no, couldn't be!

Laurinda slithered across him till she brought faceplate to faceplate. Through the black he recognized the voice that conduction carried: "Robert, thank God, I'd begun to be afraid I'd never find you, are you all right?"

"What the, the devil are you doing here?" he gasped.

Laughter crackled. "Fetching you. Yes, mutiny. Court-martial me later."

Soberness followed: "I have a cable around my waist, with the end free for you. Feel around till you find it. There's a lump at the end, a knot I made beforehand and covered with solder so the buckyballs can't get in and make it work loose. You can use that to make a hitch that will hold for yourself, can't you? Then I'll need your help. I have two geologist's hammers with me. Secured them by cords so they can't be lost. Wrapped tape around the handles in thick bands, to give a grip in spite of no friction. Used the pick ends to chip notches in the rock, and hauled myself along. But I'm exhausted now, and it's an uphill pull, even though gravity is weak. Take the hammers. Drag me along behind you. You have the strength."

"The strength—oh, my God, you talk about *my* strength?" he cried.

—The cable was actually heavy-gauge wire from the electrical parts locker, lengths of it spliced together till they reached. The far end was fastened around a great boulder beyond the treacherous part of the slope. Slipperiness had helped as well as hindered the ascent, but when he reached safety, Saxtorph allowed himself to collapse for a short spell.

He returned to Laurinda's earnest tones: "I can't tell you how sorry I am. I should have guessed. But it didn't occur to me—such quantities gathered together like this—I simply thought 'nebular dust,' without stopping to estimate what substance would become dominant over many billions of years—"

He sat straight to look at her. In the level red light, her face was palely rosy, her eyes afire. "Why, how could you have foreseen, lass?" he answered. "I'd hate to tell you how often something in space has taken me by surprise, and that was in familiar parts. You did realize what the problem was, and figured out a solution. We needn't worry about your breaking orders. If you'd failed, you'd have been insubordinate; but you succeeded, so by definition you showed initiative."

"Thank you." Eagerness blazed. "And listen, I've had another idea—"

He lifted a palm. "Whoa! Look, in a couple of minutes we'd better hike back to *Shep*, you take your station again, I get a drive unit and fly across to *Rover*. But first will you please, please tell me what the mess was that I got myself into?"

"Buckyballs," she said. "Or, formally, buckminsterfullerene. I didn't think the pitful of that you'd slid down into could be very deep or the bottom very large. Its walls would surely slope inward. It's really just a

. . . pothole, though surely the formation process was different, possibly it's a small astrobleme—" She giggled. "My, the academic in me is really taking over, isn't it? Well, essentially, the material is frictionless. It will puddle in any hole, no matter how tiny, and it has just enough cohesion that a number of such puddles close together will form a film over the entire surface. But that film is only a few molecules thick, and you can't walk on it or anything. In this slight gravity, though—and the metal-poor rock is friable—I could strike the sharp end of a hammerhead in with a single blow to act as a kind of . . . piton, is that the word?"

"Okay. Splendid. Dorcas had better look to her standing as the most formidable woman in known space. Now tell me what the—the hell buckyballs are."

"They're produced in the vicinity of supernovae. Carbon atoms link together and form a faceted spherical molecule around a single metal atom. Sixty carbons around one lanthanum is common, galactically speaking, but there are other forms too. And with the molecule closed in on itself the way it is, it acts in the aggregate like a fluid. In fact, it's virtually a perfect lubricant, and if we didn't have things easier to use you'd see synthetic buckyballs on sale everywhere." A vision rose in those ruby eyes. "It's thought they may have a basic role in the origin of life on planets—"

"Damn near did the opposite number today," Saxtorph said. "But you saved my ass, and the rest of me as well. I don't suppose I can ever repay you."

She got to her knees before him and seized his hands. "You can, Robert. You can fetch me back my man."

22

Ponderously, *Rover* closed velocities with the iron asteroid. She couldn't quite match, because it was under boost, but thus far the acceleration was low.

Ominously aglow, the molten mass dwarfed the spacecraft that toiled meters ahead of it; yet *Sun Defier*, harnessed by her own forcefield, was a plowhorse dragging it bit by bit from its former path; and the dwarf sun was at work, and Secunda's gravity was beginning to have a real effect. . . .

Arrived a little before the ship, the boat drifted at some distance, a needle in a haystack of stars. Laurinda was still aboard. The tug had no place to receive *Shep*, nor had the girl the skill to cross safely by herself in a spacesuit even though relative speeds were small. The autopilot kept her accompanying the others.

In *Rover's* command center, Saxtorph asked the image of Dorcas, more shakily than he had expected to, "How are you? How's everything?"

She was haggard with weariness, but triumph rang: "Kam's got our gear packed to transfer over to you, and I—I've worked the bugs out of the program. Compatibility with kzin hardware was a stumbling block, but— Well, it's been operating smoothly for the past several hours, and I've no reason to doubt it will continue doing what it's supposed to."

He whistled. "Hey, quite a feat, lady! I really didn't think it would be possible, at least in the time available, when I put you up to trying it. What're you going to do next—square the circle, invent the perpetual motion machine, reform the tax laws, or what?"

Her voice grew steely. "I was motivated." She regarded his face in her own screen. "How are you? Laurinda said something about your running into danger on the moon. Were you hurt?"

"Only in my pride. She can tell you all about it later. Right now we're in a hurry." Saxtorph became intent. "Listen, there's been a change of plan. You and Kam both flit over to *Shep*. But don't you bring her in; lay her alongside. Kam can help Laurinda aboard *Rover* before he moves your stuff. I'd like you to join me in a job around *Shep*. Simple thing and shouldn't take but a couple hours, given the two of us working together. Though I'll bet even money you'll have a useful suggestion or three. Then you can line out for deep space."

She sat a moment silent, her expression bleakened,

before she said, "You're taking the boat to Prima while the rest of us ferry *Rover* away."

"You catch on quick, sweetheart."

"To rescue Juan and Carita."

"What else? Laurinda's hatched a scheme I think could do the trick. Naturally, we'll agree in advance where you'll wait, and *Shep* will come join you there. If we don't dawdle, the odds are pretty good that the kzinti won't locate you first and force you to go hyperspatial."

"What about them locating you?"

"Why should they expect anybody to go to Prima? They'll buzz around Secunda like angry hornets. They may well be engaged for a while in evacuating survivors from the warship; I suspect the shuttles aren't terribly efficient at that sort of thing. Afterward they'll have to work out a search doctrine, when *Rover* can have skited in any old direction. And sometime along about then, they should have their minds taken off us. The kzinti will notice a nice big surprise bound their way, about which it is then too late to do anything whatsoever."

"But you— How plausible is this idea of yours?"

"Plausible enough. Look, don't sit like that. Get cracking. I'll explain when we meet."

"I can take *Shep*. I'm as good a pilot as you are."

Saxtorph shook his head. "Sorry, no. One of us has to be in charge of *Rover*, of course. I hereby pull rank and appoint you. I am the captain."

23

The asteroid concealed the ship's initial boost from any possible observers around Secunda. She applied her mightiest vector to give southward motion, out of the ecliptic plane; but the thrust had an extra component, randomly chosen, to baffle hunter analysts who would fain reduce the volume of space wherein she might reasonably be sought. That volume would grow fast, become literally astronomical, as she flew free, generator cold, batteries maintaining life support on a minimum energy level. Having thus cometed for a time, she could with fair safety apply power again to bring herself to her destination.

Saxtorph let her make ample distance before he accelerated *Shep*, also using the iron to conceal his start. However, he ran at top drive the whole way. It wasn't likely that a detector would pick his little craft up. As he told Dorcas, the kzinti wouldn't suppose a human would make for Prima. It hurt them less, losing friends, provided the friends died bravely; and few of them had mastered the art of putting oneself in the head of an enemy.

Mainly, though, Carita and Juan didn't have much time left them.

Ever circling, the planets had changed configuration since *Rover* arrived. The navigation system allowed for that, but could do nothing to shorten a run of 30-odd hours. Saxtorph tried to compose his soul in peace. He played a lot of solitaire after he found he was losing most of the computer games, and smoked a lot of pipes. Books and shows were poor distraction, but music helped him relax and enjoy his memories. Whatever happened next, he'd have had a better life than 90 percent of his species—99 percent if you counted in everybody who lived and died before humankind went spacefaring.

Prima swelled in his view, sallow and faceless. The recorded broadcast came through clear from the night side, over and over. Saxtorph got his fix. *Fido* wasn't too far from the lethal dawn. He established a three-hour orbit and put a curt message of his own on the player. It ended with "Acknowledge."

Time passed. Heaviness grew within him. Were they dead? He rounded dayside and came back across darkness.

The voice leaped at him: "Bob, is that you? Juan here. We'd abandoned hope, we were asleep. Standing by now. Bob, is that you? Juan here—"

Joy surged. "Who else but me?" Saxtorph said. "How're you doing, you two?"

"Hanging on. Living in our spacesuits this past—I

don't know how long. The boat's a rotted, crumbling shell. But we're hanging on."

"Good. Your drive units in working order?"

"Yes. But we haven't the lift to get onto a trajectory which you can match long enough for us to come aboard." Unspoken: It would be easy in atmosphere, or in free space, given a pilot like you. But what a vessel can do above an airless planet, at suborbital speed, without coming to grief, is sharply limited.

"That's all right," Saxtorph said, "as long as you can go outside, sit in a lock chamber or on top of the wreck, and keep watch, without danger of slipping off into the muck. You can? . . . Okay, prepare yourselves. I'll land in view of you and open the main personnel lock."

"Hadn't we better all find an area free of the material?"

"I'm not sure any exists big enough and flat enough for me. Anyhow, looking for one would take more time than we can afford. No, I'm coming straight down."

Carita cut in. She sounded wrung out. Saxtorph suspected her physical strength was what had preserved both. He imagined her manhandling pieces of metal and plastic, often wrenched from the weakened structure, to improvise braces, platforms, whatever would give some added hours of refuge. "Bob, is this wise?" she asked. "Do you know what you're getting into? The molecule might bind you fast immediately, even if you avoid shining light on it. The decay here is going quicker all the while. I think the molecule is . . . learning. Don't risk your life."

"Don't you give your captain orders," Saxtorph replied. "I'll be down in, m-m, about an hour. Then get to me as fast as you prudently can. Every minute we spend on the surface does add to the danger. But I've put bandits on the jacks."

"What?"

"Footpads," he laughed childishly. "Okay, no more conversation till we're back in space. I've got my reconnoitering to do."

Starlight was brilliant but didn't illuminate an unknown terrain very well. His landing field would be minute and hemmed in. For help he had optical amplifiers, radar, data-analysis programs which projected visuals as well as numbers. He had his skill. Fear shunted from his mind, he became one with the boat.

Location . . . identification . . . positioning; you don't float around in airlessness the way you can in atmosphere . . . site picked, much closer to *Fido* than he liked but he could manage . . . coordinates established . . . down, down, nurse her down to touchdown. . . .

It was as soft a landing as he had ever achieved. It needed to be.

For a pulsebeat he stared across the hollow at the other boat. She was a ghastly sight indeed, a half-hull pocked, ragged, riddled, the pale devourer well up the side of what was left. Good thing he was insured; though multi-billionaire Stefan Brozik would be grateful, and presumably human governments—

Saxtorph grinned at his own inanity and hastened to go operate the airlock. Or was it stupid to think about money at an hour like this? To hell with heroics. He and Dorcas had their living to make.

Descent with the outer valve already open would have given him an imbalance: slight, but he had plenty else to contend with. He cracked it now without stopping to evacuate the chamber. Time was more precious than a few cubic meters of air. A light flashed green. His crewfolk were in. He closed the valve at once. A measure of pressure equalization was required before he admitted them into the hull proper. He did so the instant it was possible. A wind gusted by. His ears popped. Juan and Carita stumbled through. Frost formed on their spacesuits.

He hand-signalled: Grab hold. We're boosting right away. He could be gentle about that, as well as quick.

Or need he have hastened? Afterward he inspected things at length and found Laurinda's idea had worked as well as could have been hoped, or maybe a little better.

Buckyballs scooped from that sink on the moon. (An open container at the end of a line; he could throw it far in the low gravity.) Bags fashioned out of thick plastic, heat-sealed together, filled with buckyballs, placed around the bottom of each landing jack, superglued fast at the necks. That was all.

The molecule had only eaten through one of them while *Shep* stood on Prima. Perhaps the other jacks rested on sections where most of the chemical bonds were saturated, less readily catalyzed. It didn't matter, except scientifically, because after the single bag gave way, the wonderful stuff had done its job. A layer of it was beneath the metal, a heap of it around. The devourer could not quickly incorporate atoms so strongly interlinked. As it did, more flowed in to fill the gaps. *Shep* could have stayed for hours.

But she had no call to. Lifting, the tension abruptly off him, Saxtorph exploded into tuneless song. It wasn't a hymn or anthem, though it was traditional, "The Bastard King of England." Somehow it felt right.

24

Rover drove though hyperspace, homeward bound.

Man and wife sat together in their cabin, easing off. They were flesh, they would need days to get back the strength they had spent. The ship throbbed and whispered. A screen gave views of Hawaii, heights, greennesses, incredible colors on the sea. Beethoven's Fifth lilted in the background. He had a mug of beer, she a glass of white wine.

"Honeymoon cruise," she said with a wry smile. "Laurinda and Juan. Carita and Kam."

"You and me, for that matter," he replied drowsily.

"But when will we get any proper work done? The interior is a mess."

"Oh, we've time aplenty before we reach port. And if we aren't quite holystoned-perfect, who's going to care?"

"Yes, we'll be the sensation of the day." She grew somber. "How many will remember Arthur Tregennis?"

Saxtorph roused. "Our kind of people will. He was . . . a Moses. He brought us to a scientific Promised Land, and . . . I think there'll be more explorations into the far deeps from now on."

"Yes. Markham's out of the way." Dorcas sighed. "His poor family."

The tug, rushing off too fast for recovery after it released the asteroid to hurtle toward Secunda—if all went as planned, straight at the base— Horror, a scramble to flee, desperate courage, and then the apparition in heaven, the flaming trail, Thor's hammer smites, the cloud of destruction engulfs everything and rises on high and spreads to darken the planet, nothing remains but a doubled crater plated with iron. It was unlikely that any kzinti who escaped would still be alive when their next starship came.

At the end, did Markham cry for his mother?

"And of course humans will be alerted to the situation," Saxtorph observed superfluously.

It was, in fact, unlikely that there would be more kzin ships to the red sun. Nothing was left for them, and they would get no chance to rebuild. Earth would have sent an armed fleet for a look-around. Maybe it would come soon enough to save what beings were left.

Dorcas frowned. "What will they do about it?"

"Why, uh, rebuild our navies. Defense has been grossly neglected."

"Well, we can hope for that much. We're certainly doing a service, bringing in the news that the kzinti have the hyperdrive." Dorcas shook her head. "But everybody knew they would, sooner or later. And this whole episode, it's no *casus belli*. No law forbade them to establish themselves in an unclaimed system. We should be legally safe, ourselves—self-defense—but the peace groups will say the kzinti were only being defensive, after Earth's planet grab following the war, and in fact this crew provoked them into overreacting. There may be talk of reparations due the pathetic put-upon kzinti."

"Yah, you're probably right. I share your faith in the infinite capacity of our species for wishful thinking." Saxtorph shrugged. "But we also have a capacity for muddling through. And you and I, sweetheart, have some mighty good years ahead of us. Let's talk about what to do with them."

Her mood eased. She snuggled close. The ship fared onward.

NOT FOR COUNTRY, NOT FOR KING

To fight and kill and die for mere pomp and grandeur is to fight and kill and die for illusion. Indeed, even "National Honor" may ring a little hollow as you watch your blood pouring into the sand. Is there anything *worth the terrible price of war?*

We walked into a corridor, slid along a walkway, bounced up a jumpshaft, then eased ourselves down another corridor in low-weight, toward the inspector's office. I understand why the local inspectors tend to put their offices and quarters up toward the hub of their complexes—low-weight is addictive, once you get past the queasiness—but I wish that just *once* I'd be able to confront one under higher gravity. I was raised in Metzada's twelve hundred centimeters-per-second-squared gravity, and anything less than half of a standard gee makes my stomach tie itself in knots.

We waited for a solid half hour in the inspector's outer office. I wasn't going to complain; I'd felt the vibration through the deck as the shuttle was booted away, and I knew that I'd have to wait for the next departure. It's just that I once spent an idle hour figuring out how many man-centuries busy people have been kept waiting in bureaucrats' offices. I won't show the figure; it's just too damn depressing.

Finally, his secretary beeped, and the door to his inner office slid open. "You may come in now, General Hanavi."

At that, I sighed. *Here we go again.*

Thousand Worlds Commerce Department Inspector Arthur McCawber was a chubby little man, with brown hair receding back toward the top of his skull and a rather bad case of low-gee acne speckling his face. His handshake was tentative, as though he was afraid that the big, bad Metzadan would crush it to a pulp if he exerted any pressure.

I don't like the short, nervous, weak-handshaking type; they tend to sublimate their fear. It almost always comes out in other ways.

"I'm pleased to meet you, mister inspector," I said, releasing his hand. "But it's not general—it's *inspector-*general. I'm here to witness the Eighteenth Regiment's fulfillment of its contract with the Montenier colony."

He waved me to a seat, two guards taking up positions on either side of me and one behind. "Or lack thereof," McCawber said. "When last I'd heard, the

Dutch still had them bogged down on the banks of the
. . . Nouveau Loire."

I raised an eyebrow. "Loire? I thought that the river
was generally known as the Neu Hunse. Named after
the river in Der Nederlands, Earthside, no?"

"For the time being, that is the name that's being
used. But as soon as the Metzadan Mercenary Corps
regains control of the chartered region for the French, I
expect that the original name will become more . . .
appropriate." He smiled at his little joke, then sighed.
"Quite a mess."

Alsace was a mess, of course. The chartering colony
had been French—hence the French name of the planet.
But the original Montenier colony had died off in one of
the harsh winters that sweep across Alsace's only habitable continent. The Dutch settlers had managed to
hang on, but neither they nor their countrymen back
home had the political leverage to get the Montenier
charter lifted.

If you're into morality as opposed to legality, you'd
probably agree that the Dutch had the better claim:
they had managed to survive and even flourish a trifle—
and it was a Dutch settler who had taken the time to
examine the properties of hempwood, and turned Alsace
from a dumping ground into a financial bonanza for the
Thousand Worlds.

And, of course, indirectly stimulated the second wave
of French immigration. Old Van Huysen was probably
regretting, from the safety of his grave, that he'd discovered that the hempwood tree's fibers were long,
tangled monofilament chains with an incredible tensile
strength and heat resistance, usable as linings for rocket
nozzles or as the basic building material for Skystalks on
small, low-gee worlds.

His discovery had brought the French back. And,
indirectly, brought some employment to the Metzadan
Mercenary Corps, when the Dutch started to express
their resentment at Montenier taxation of goods flowing
south on the Neu Hunse to the launcher.

McCawber went on: "I'm sure you're wondering why I had you taken off the shuttle."

He was ready for me to snap back at him, so I didn't answer for a moment. Besides, I wasn't at all curious: McCawber's Dutch sympathies had been part of my Intelligence briefing, back on Metzada.

Not that I had any complaint about that. My sympathies were similar. And, similarly, beside the point. Since when does what you have to do have anything at all to do with your personal sympathies?

I'd let him stew long enough. I dropped a few words into the silence: "You want to negotiate a settlement."

The Commerce Department people *always* want to negotiate a settlement. There's a belief on Metzada that the Commerce Department was actually founded by Neville Chamberlain, but that's a canard. Chamberlain had been dead for more than a century before even the predecessor to the Commerce Department was founded.

"Obviously." He quirked a smile. "The Commerce Department's only interest is in improving the hempwood trade."

And, as usual, trying to put some shorts in the MMC's circuits, I thought.

I shrugged. "As I'm sure General Davis told you, that's not what the MMC does. If Phillipe Montenier wanted negotiation, he could have taken it up with you."

He shrugged. "Monsieur," he pronounced it Mon-*sewe*r, "Montenier says that he isn't interested in settlement, just in collecting his taxes on Dutch shipping. I'd hoped that—"

"I'd betray an employer?" I shook my head. "The Metzadan Mercenary Corps has a contract with Montenier. For the next five-minus-a-fraction standard years, the Eighteenth will do its damnedest to keep the lower river under French control." I shrugged. "As far as we're concerned, he can take one hundred percent of the cargo of Dutch shipping, not the seventy-five he's demanding."

I didn't discuss Montenier's response when a Dutch

paddlewheel would try to evade the tax; McCawber knew it as well as I did.

But he pressed. "Perhaps you'll consider forfeiting your performance bond, and pulling the regiment off Alsace? I'm authorized to rebate most of the bond. My only interest is in seeing the planet develop, helping them sell enough fiber to bring their technology up to—"

I held up a hand. "And if word gets out that the MMC can be bought off? Even by the Thousand Worlds Commerce Department?"

"Really, I—"

"No; the matter is closed." I can be diplomatic, when the situation calls for it. It's just that it rarely does. "Now, when can I shuttle down? I'm looking forward to getting to work."

He smiled thinly. "Almost immediately. We have a shuttle leaving for—"

His secretary beeped. "Deputy Inspector Celia von du Mark is—"

It shut off as she barged in. Celia von du Mark was a medium-height, rail-thin woman, with shortish black hair that whipped around her face as she squared off with McCawber. "I thought we agreed that my people would go over this Metzadan's gear. They're tricky, Arthur. You can take my word for it."

"Hello, Celia. How are you?" I kept my voice casual.

She hadn't stopped to take a good look at me before; she did now.

"Tetsuo Hanavi. Aren't you supposed to be dead?"

"It's good to see you, too."

She glanced at my collar. "General?"

"Inspector-General, actually. I was just a line colonel when we met, wasn't I? And I seem to recall you were a full inspector; don't quite remember for sure . . ."

"*I* remember," she hissed. "I was demoted to deputy after that Indess affair. You and your uncle came close to ruining my career."

I allowed myself a smile. "You are too kind. How do you like your new post?"

Ignoring me, she turned back to McCawber. "I was saying that I thought we'd agreed that I'd take care of screening the Matzadan's gear. Your monkeys are swarming all over it."

I raised an eyebrow. "Find anything interesting?" Someday, I swear I'm going to leave a bomb in a locker—no timing device or anything like that, just a gimmick to set off a kilo of HE if someone opens my bag. Negative feedback can correct many a problem.

I stood. "I'll leave you to your argument. Inspector McCawber, please let me know when I'm cleared for the surface." I didn't bother to tell them where I'd be; no doubt McCawber's people would be keeping an eye on me.

He glared at me. "You're cleared *now*. Your shuttle leaves in . . . fifty-three minutes."

"Fine. Then I should be in Marne in—"

"Not Port Marne. Port Leewenhoek. Shuttles down to French territory are full for the next . . . seventeen hundred hours," he said, clearly picking the figure out of the air. "Perhaps you would prefer to wait? Or would you rather shuttle down to Port Leewenhoek? I'm sure that the Dutch have some things that they would like to . . . discuss with you."

I looked carefully from the guard on my right to the one on my left, then back to McCawber. Clearly, I was not going to be getting on a shuttle into French territory. Not now. And not in seventeen hundred hours, either. "I'll take the Leewenhoek shuttle."

He didn't know what to make of that. I was supposed to refuse.

Celia didn't like it, either. "I'll be going along, Hanavi," she said.

"Be a bit dangerous around me, won't it?" An inspector-general is, technically, a noncombatant; officially, the Dutch couldn't touch me.

I wasn't worried about that; it was the possibility of unofficial touching that bothered me. As I understand it, your body cools to room temperature just as quickly when you're killed unofficially as when all the forms have been met.

She shook her head. "I'll have a squad of Peacemakers. This way," she said as she turned to McCawber, "I can keep an eye on him. I don't understand people who kill for money."

No, Celia, I thought. *You don't understand*. I forced a smile. "I didn't know that you cared. Going to protect me, eh?"

"Don't count on it."

I wasn't counting on it.

Not at all.

II

I can understand why the Commerce Department initially set up its launcher down south, at the mouth of the Neu Hunse, or Nouveau Loire, or whatever you want to call it: it's always easier, at least technically, to ship downriver than up.

As it turned out, they would have been better off with the port about a thousand klicks north of where the river dumps into the sea; there was nothing in French—southern—territory that was worth enough to absorb the cost of shipping it offworld. All the hempwood grows up north; it seems that the plant needs an occasional cold winter in order to keep its sometimes-commensal, sometimes-parasitic bacterial partner under control.

But once the Commerce Department had built the launcher, it and the locals were stuck with the placement. That's one of the more reasonable regulations of the Thousand Worlds Commerce Department: while it will build landing strips for skipshuttles wherever the trade justifies it, the Thousand Worlds supplies one and *only* one laser launcher per colony world. Launching complexes are expensive to build and maintain; Alsace wouldn't have another until it developed the capital for a hefty down payment, and either the technology to support it, or still more capital to finance the import of technicians and equipment.

So while the Dutch controlled the north and the hempwood, the French controlled the south, and their chartered area around the launching port.

Hmm, make that "mostly controlled." The Dutch irregulars had made significant inroads into French territory along the river, in an attempt to give their ships free passage through Port Marne to the Commerce Department launcher.

Which was why, of course, the French had hired the MMC, and why the war in the south had brought the hempwood trade to a virtual standstill, and why a Thousand World Commerce Department inspector had me landed deep in Dutch territory.

And why there was a reception committee of sorts waiting for me at the Leewenhoek docks—that's pronounced *lay*-ven-hook, by the way. Somebody should teach the Dutch how to spell.

Celia looked at me, her mouth pursed in self-satisfaction. "I guess this is goodbye." She moved off to the side, beckoning to her five black-suited Peacemakers to follow.

I took a moment to size up the crowd. Fifty-three blocky men, mainly middle-aged, but with a leavening of younger ones, all dressed in dull gray shirts and trousers. The hempwood tree's inner bark makes excellent thread, but the locals hadn't developed a dye that would last through more than a couple of washings.

They all carried beltknives, of course; on a frontier world, you'll more often find a local without pants than without a knife. A dozen of them had rifles as well— flintlocks and wheellocks. Alsace had yet to develop the manufacturing base to produce cartridges, but saltpeter, sulfur, and charcoal were easy to obtain locally. For the first, all that's needed is a well-used outhouse; natural deposits and local wood provided the other two.

I eyed the warehouses around the dock and the paddlewheel steamer, the *Bolivar*. No good. I'd have to go through the mob to get to the cover of the buildings, and the only way to the boat would be by crossing fifty meters of open dock. Don't be fooled: those primitive rifles can be very accurate.

But if I could get to the boat, I'd be safe. Even with a war on, it was still in both sides' interests for a neutral ship to be able to carry limited amounts of heavily taxed Dutch hempwood to Port Marne. Both French and Dutch needed the offworld credits to import medical tech and supplies, among other things, so the *Bolivar* and her two sister sidewheelers had achieved a sacrosanct status, backed up, when necessary, with the two turret guns just aft of the bridge.

And even if someone decided to forget the forms, the skipshuttle we'd ridden down on had been mounted on the rear deck of the *Bolivar* for transport south; the hatch was only about two meters off the deck and standing slightly ajar—a skipshuttle's outer skin is tough.

But the boat was just too far away. I turned to face the crowd.

"We want a word with you," a large, black-bearded man said. He planted himself in front of me, and tapped me on the chest with a gnarled stick almost the diameter of my arm. "You're with the killers?" He glared at my khakis.

No, I was tempted to respond, *I just like to dress up in uniforms.*

I sighed. He wasn't necessarily as stupid as he sounded. It usually takes civilians a while to work up to killing an unarmed man. "My name is Tetsuo Hanavi. Hanavi family, Bar-El clan. Inspector-General, Metzadan Mercenary Corps. You?"

"Amos Sweelinck. What are you doing here?"

Another silly question. But it didn't quite seem politic to point that out. "And these are . . . ?" I gestured at the two men at his side.

"Friends. Of mine, and of the Roupers." He tapped me on the sternum again—not gently. "I asked you a question."

"I am preparing to get on the boat. Obviously."

Behind the crowd, three men in gray shirts and

pantaloons stepped out of the clutter of boxes in front of the nearest warehouse.

Sweelinck tapped me again, his forehead creased in puzzlement. When he hit me, I was supposed to react, not just stand there—either attack him, or cringe. Either would set the mob off. It's standard primate psychology. I don't have any grievance with that; I'm a primate, too. It's just that a professional can't let his reactions be standard.

He sneered. "We know that you want to join up with your French friends—"

"Employers."

"Eh?"

"Not friends. The French have bought the MMC's services, *not* our friendship; we don't take our passions to the marketplace. Now, can we just leave it at that? I'll just be getting aboard—"

"No. We can*not* just leave it at that."

The three men behind the crowd took up positions on top of a stack of boxes; their compound bows strung, each nocked an arrow. It was about damn time.

I held up three fingers. "Last chance."

Sweelinck took a step forward.

I stepped back, and pointed to Sweelinck and the other two at the front of the mob.

When a powerful compound bow looses an arrow, you don't see the shaft in flight unless you're looking for it; it seemed as though arrows *spang*ed out of the backs of the three men's heads. Sweelinck and the other two crumpled.

I snatched my knife from my belt while I kicked Sweelinck's body into the crowd, then turned, grabbed another local by the hair, and spun him around to serve as a shield. He didn't seem eager to hold still, so I tapped him on the temple with my knife's hilt—being damn careful to keep the tap light. When the adrenaline starts pumping, it's easy to cave in a skull without intending to.

I rested the blade against his throat as I faced the

crowd. "Three dead, so far. You want more?" I raised my voice. *"Run or you're all dead men."*

It worked: the mob broke and ran, weapons unfired. No shame there; if they had been ready for a fight, they would have fought. But they were after a simple lynching, not a battle.

One by one, the three bowmen climbed down, and then, arrows nocked, walked over, keeping a careful eye on the three bodies. Too many soldiers have been killed by supposedly dead men.

I checked the unconscious man I was holding. Good—he was still breathing. Lowering him to the ground, I frisked him quickly, relieving him of his knife and a crude flintlock pistol. It didn't seem likely he would object; he'd gotten off easily. Relatively.

The oldest of the three newcomers, a lanky man with a badly scarred forehead, stopped in front of me. He didn't salute; he wasn't in uniform. "Skirmisher-Sergeant Dov Levin, sir."

"You took your time," I said, pleased to find that I could still punch for a calm voice and get it.

"The general told us to stay out of it unless and until I was sure you couldn't handle the situation by yourself."

I guess I shouldn't complain; at least Yonni Davis had taken most of the right steps. Sometimes, though, I think he violates policy just for the fun of it. Standard procedure is to assume that the Commerce Department busies will do all that they can within regulations to sabotage an operation of the MMC, and to take proper precautions to safeguard late arrivals.

'Safeguarding late arrivals' includes sending out a detail to watch over an inspector-general's possible arrival at a bad drop spot. It does *not* include ordering the leader of the detail to roll dice with the inspector-general's life. But Yonni was an Aroni, after all, and had to show off.

"Well, at least he sent you. Plan on sleeping in shifts—I don't exactly trust those Peacemakers."

Levin smiled at the five men, giving their wireguns a quick glance.

His smile could have been mistaken for a friendly grin, if you didn't notice the way his eyes narrowed. They noticed. "Do you think, sir," he asked casually, "that you could find some use for a handful of wireguns?"

"*No*. And particularly not in front of witnesses."

The youngest of the Skirmishers, a blue-eyed blond who couldn't have been more than seventeen, eyed the bodies of the three dead men. "Standard booty rights?"

I shook my head. "No. Let's get—"

"But we earned—"

"*Save it*," Levin snapped. He shrugged an apology at me. "Sorry, sir. My fault."

I was beginning to like Skirmisher-Sergeant Dov Levin. He took responsibility for his man. Granted, he'd probably chew the boy's head off later, out of my sight, but any discipline should properly come from him, not me.

A blast from the boat's steamwhistle spun me around, the pistol coming up as if by its own volition. That was silly; I hadn't checked to see if it was loaded. I guess I was a bit more shaken than I'd thought. "We'll let it pass, sergeant. It looks like the captain's getting a bit nervous. Let's get aboard."

III

The nights on Alsace are bright; its moon is even larger than Earth's, and a trifle closer to Alsace's surface than Luna is to Earth's. You'd think that the tides would be the cause of the dramatic rising and falling along the banks of the river—but you'd be wrong. It's nothing so exotic; it's all caused by the spring thawing up in the mountains. While we were well into spring, the high-water markings stood two, three metres above low-water in some spots along the banks.

I stood at the *Bolivar*'s stern railing, watching the stars dance on the water behind us, spray from the twin paddlewheels giving me an occasional jolt when the light breeze would catch it and blow it my way.

As we passed by another of the riverfront houses belonging to the wealthier Dutch hempwood planters, the boat slowly turned to follow one of the river's immense curves. It reminded me of a passage from Twain, so I pulled out the copy of *Life on the Mississippi*, and thumbed the pageglow on.

> The water cuts the alluvial banks of the "lower" river into deep horseshoe curves; so deep, indeed, that in some places if you were to get ashore at one extremity of the horseshoe and walk across the neck, half or three quarters of a mile, you could sit down and rest a couple of hours while your steamer was coming around the long elbow, at a speed of ten miles an hour, to take you aboard again.

I hadn't truly understood that from looking at the topo maps; it had been an intellectual game.

Here on Alsace, it came alive. As the river turned endlessly, it often would have been possible to leave the *Bolivar* at one of its stops, and catch up with it by walking straight across one of the Dutch plantations while the boat followed the twists in the river.

In fact, despite the fact that the paddlewheel was almost twice as fast as the sort Twain described—the boilers were of offworld manufacture, and could easily hold twenty times the pressure—I could have walked the eight hundred klicks from Leewenhoek to Marne in little more than three times the thirteen local days it was taking us to steam the distance.

Lay a ruler on the map, and it will read out as eight hundred klicks; measure in all the twists and turns, and you'll find that the trip is more than eight times that distance.

Figuring orbits is a lot easier than dealing with a twisting river.

There was a whisk of leather soles on the deck behind me. I shut the book, trying not to seem too hurried.

"Good evening, inspector-general." Celia von du Mark stood nearby. Only one of her Peacemakers was with her, a careful five paces behind.

The pages were still glowing; I thumbed the glow off. No need to draw attention to the book. It wouldn't have hurt if she'd read most of it, but the next few sentences after the passage I'd been reading . . . well, there were things in there that she didn't need to know.

"Call me Tetsuo." I shot a glance at the upper deck, behind the wheelhouse. Soloveczik, the young Skirmisher who had wanted to exercise standard booty rights, was up there, on guard. Well, he might not have been much on discipline, but he was a good shot.

"I'd rather not," she said. "I really don't like getting friendly with murderers," she added, in a voice so flat and even as to suggest that she was commenting on the weather.

"The docks today?" I pulled a tabstick from my pocket, and puffed it to life. In the darkness, the lit end glowed with a comforting redness. "That bothering you?"

"Yes." She held out her fingers in a "v". I passed her the tabstick and lit myself another. A slow draw, then, "Filthy habit," she said.

"Smoking? Or killing?" I shrugged. "We've got both on our consciences, you and me. If you have a conscience, that is."

"Me?" She was offended; Celia von du Mark was not used to being lectured to on morality by such as I.

"You. You could have had your Peacemakers disperse the mob. It might have taken a whole ten seconds."

She snorted. "You know a lot about mobs, eh?"

"Standard part of officer training on Metzada. Now," I said, warming to the subject, "Africans are tricky. Say you take your basic Eastern mob—Earthside designations: Pharsi, Indians, Hmong, Chinese, like that. Present them with a superior force, and they martyr themselves all over you. Messy. But when you've got Westerners, almost any organized group can make them run. Usually." I spent a moment examining the glowing head of the tabstick, then flicked it overboard. "Doesn't always work. But it usually does. It would have, today."

"You're saying that I could have saved their lives."

"Exactly. They would have known that they couldn't stand up to wireguns. You," I raised my voice and called out to her guard, "how many rounds do you have in a clip? Fifty? Seventy?"

"Plenty."

I shrugged. "It really doesn't matter. The Dutch would have known that they couldn't stand up to your Peacemakers' fire. In order to get the same result out of Levin's three bows, we had to kill."

She was silent for a long moment. Then, "You're just trying to rationalize your way out of it."

"Or you are. Or both. Fact: three men died today. I don't know that the lives of three reasonably nice Dutch settlers are properly any of your concern—"

"Don't you *dare* say that to me. You hated them enough to—"

I silenced her with a snort. "No, I didn't hate them. Matter of fact, Sweelinck impressed me as a good man, trying to make the best of a bad situation. Hell, Celia, if he'd really wanted me dead, I'd be cold by now. Decent man; had to work himself up to it."

"You say you liked him but you had him killed?"

I shrugged. She didn't understand. "One has nothing to do with the other. As I was saying, I don't know if their lives were properly any of your concern, but if they were, then you let your judgment be swayed by an old grudge, by a desire to see me dead, without having the blood—"

"They weren't going to *kill* you! I sent word to Sweelinck. They were just going to rough you up a little, scare you off. That's all. And you—"

I snorted. "Don't talk nonsense. Even if that's true, even if that's what you arranged with Sweelinck and his friends, there's no way I could have known that. And if I had known, I really wouldn't have cared, Celia—"

"That's Inspector von du Mark."

"*Deputy* Inspector von du Mark. A bit of free advice:

you'd be better off looking out for yourself, instead of trying to figure out what I'm going to do and how to mess that up. You're not going to catch us violating any of your precious import regs. Besides," I said, just to add a bit of misdirection, "if we already did, it's too late."

" 'Not going to catch us'—that sounds as though it would be fairly dangerous for me if I *did* catch you, doesn't it?"

"You're not thinking it through, again. Metzada's position is always precarious; I'd hardly take the chance of killing even a Commerce Department *Deputy* Inspector."

"I saw one of your men eyeing the Peacemakers' weapons. So tell me what you'd to if you found that you really needed, say, five wireguns."

"The only thing I could think of is that—given that we really needed them—it would be kind of convenient if six Commerce Department personnel had been killed in a Dutch ambush. All surviving witnesses would swear to that. The rumors would hurt, but witnesses are dangerous."

She started to open her mouth to call for her guard; I silenced her with a quick shake of my head. "Go easy. You've got three deaths on your conscience. Isn't that enough for today?"

Celia gave me a long, slow look. "You might be bluffing. I don't think you'd really kill everyone aboard this boat, just to avoid a beating."

I just smiled. "Would you?"

"No, of course not. I—"

"Would rather take a beating. Which suggests you've never been on the receiving end of a good working-over."

"And you have."

"Once." I shrugged. "I didn't like it much." I lit another tabstick. "I'm not bluffing, Celia. I can't afford to. Never, Deputy Inspector von du Mark, *never* try me. Metzada has a reputation, the Bar-El clan and its Hanavi family have a reputation . . . and I'm busy building one for myself. Don't try and find out if it's well-founded. Just take my word for it."

"Reputation is worth killing for?"

I smiled, remembering a deserted Kabayle hut on Endu. In their flight, the occupants had left behind a demon doll, a good representation of a MMC private, that the mothers had used to frighten the children with. We'd taken the village without a shot fired, although there hadn't been a Metzadan on Endu for fifty years.

"Perhaps," I said.

Without another word, she walked off. Thinking, no doubt, black thoughts; wondering, certainly, what I'd smuggled down to use on the poor, innocent Dutch.

It can get annoying when someone clever starts wondering, and just maybe Celia had developed a bit of cleverness in the past few years. Or maybe I'd lost some.

"Damn." I stared down at the book in the palm of my hand. It was too much of a risk keeping it around. A pity, that: an affection for books runs in my family. Still . . .

So I tossed it overboard, and watched it splash into the Nouveau Loire. Or Neu Hunse, or whatever you want to call it. The *Bolivar* steamed away from the ever-expanding ripples.

What have I smuggled down? Just an idea, Celia.
Just an idea.

And a need, of course. People from rich worlds don't understand that. For Metzada, a million credits isn't merely a number on a fiche, but perhaps a shipment of iodine-heavy Endu kelp that will mean that none of my children get goiter.

I walked to my cabin, stretched out on the bunk, and pillowed the back of my head on my hands. I didn't bother to undress. No need to go through the motions of trying to make myself comfortable; I wouldn't sleep much or well.

I never do, off Metzada.

IV

I'd always thought that Colonel Yonaton Davis looked more like a shopkeeper than an officer. He was a short, wide man with only traces of hair on his shiny scalp, an easygoing smile on his broad face, and a slow way of moving, as though all he had to worry about was getting around to turning on his waldoes to unload a pallet or two.

Was. General Yonaton Davis wasn't taller or slimmer than Colonel Davis had been, and he didn't move any faster.

But the smile was gone. Not just from his face; he stood with his feet planted far apart, his back straight, as though he was carrying all two-thousand-plus men of the Eighteenth Regiment on his back. It's a cliche that a general's stars weigh heavily. The reason it's a cliche is because it's true.

He waited for me on the outskirts of the encampment, his fifteen bodyguards spread out along the riverbank, their eyes on the forest.

"Tetsuo," he said, taking my hand, "it's been a long time."

I nodded. "The years have a way of adding up."

Just his mouth smiled. "You don't show it."

I matched his light tone. "I'll have you know that my second wife is now officially the third best reconstructive surgeon on Metzada. When she had to rebuild my right side after that Rand mess, she decided to bring back the face of the twenty-year-old she married."

"And how is Suki? And Rachel, too?" he added quickly. You don't ask after one of a man's wives and neglect another.

"Both are fine. As are yours; I brought some letters," I said, reaching into my bag. "And it seems that Shmuel is doing well; he told me to tell you that he just accepted that promotion you've been nagging him about, and he's too busy getting his new company ready for combat to write—serves you right for nagging him. You should be proud of your son." I handed him three letters; he opened and glanced through the bottom-most, then tucked all three in his left-hand shirt pocket, velcroing the pocket carefully closed.

"All your children are doing well, far as I know," I said. I let that hang in the air. It would have been strictly contrary to protocol for me to ask directly.

But, thank God, it wasn't improper for him to answer my unvoiced question.

"When you have the kind of casualties we've been getting, you also get a few field promotions, Tetsuo. Matter of fact, one Daniel Hanavi of the Bar-El clan has been bumped all the way from private to sergeant. You might see him around camp, rubbing dirt into his shiny new chevrons, trying to make it look as though he's had them for a while." He nodded slowly. "A good boy. I'm thinking about recommending him for officer training." He snorted. "Even if he is a Bar-El."

A good boy. There was a time in our people's history when that phrase didn't refer to a blooded seventeen-year-old warrior.

"I've got a Commerce Department deputy inspector and five Peacemakers cooling their heels back in Marne. She's busy trying to get in to see Montenier, work out some sort of compromise," I said.

"She's just wasting breath. I know Montenier."

I shrugged. "Air's free, here—but I don't want to leave them alone too long. How about you giving me a quick tac briefing, then we head into Marne? I want to meet this Phillipe Montenier."

"I doubt that. Strongly."

"That's my problem, isn't it? The tac briefing, please. You don't expect me to fix everything while I'm blind-folded, do you?"

For just a moment, he relaxed. "You've got a way to do it?" he asked, more prayer than question.

There's long been a bit of tension between our Bar-El clan and Davis's Aronis. My answer didn't do much to relieve it. "Of course. It just took a little thought—

something we specialize in. You don't think I'm stupid as an Aroni, do you?"

"*How?*"

"With this." I tossed him the implement I'd borrowed from Skirmisher-Sergeant Levin.

"A shovel?" He raised an eyebrow.

"You're supposed to call it an entrenching tool."

He snorted. "I'm a general. One nice thing about the rank is that I can call a fucking shovel a fucking shovel. Now . . . what are you planning to do with this—hit the Dutch over the head?"

It only took me a few minutes to tell him.

Smiling broadly, he shook his head. "A typical bit of Bar-El insanity. How the hell did you think of—? But it might work. And there'll be one fine butcher's bill to pay, win or lose."

"This way, perhaps we don't have to pay the bill. And maybe we can give a lesson to the French about trying to hire the MMC for the impossible. Besides, when it comes to butcher's bills, it's better to collect than to pay, no?" I lit a tabstick. "And what do you mean, it *might* work? It damn well *better* work. Now . . . I'd better go deal with Montenier."

V

" 'Best efforts' clause be damned." Phillipe Montenier's eyes flashed. "Three million quid a year for this *merde?* You little piece of filth. If the Dutch swine don't pay my taxes—*my taxes*, I say—then you will *make them pay*. Is that understood? You will *not* allow them to raid our farms."

He paced across the stone floor of the high-ceilinged salon as though he was a caged beast waiting for dinner—whoever dinner might be.

Just sitting still and staying wary took a little effort; even all together, Montenier's three retainers/bodyguards wouldn't have been more than a moment's work, and I've always believed that a decently trained soldier

should be able to go through ten times his weight of
Frenchmen like a hot knife through butter. I know it's
just prejudice, but as my uncle Shimon says, "There's
only three things in the universe I despise: frogs, krauts,
and bigots."

I didn't like being called a little piece of filth, and I
didn't much like Montenier. In other circumstances, I
would have enjoyed feeding him his favorite eyeball—
after all, I'm only *officially* a noncombatant—but this
was neither the time nor the place, and I wasn't likely
to find one. Pity.

Raising an eyebrow, I looked over at Celia. "Would
you like to give the peace-pitch now, inspector? May as
well get it over with."

She spent a good half-second restraining herself from
ordering the nearest of her Peacemakers to gun me down,
then launched into the saccharine you-really-ought-to-
be-good-boys routine that some strong-stomached person must teach them at Commerce Department bureaucrat
school. I tuned it out. It wouldn't work. It never works.

Finally, well-oiled machine though she was, Celia
ran down. Too many sandy Montenier objections in the
gears.

"Enough." I held up a hand. "Seems to me that
we're getting nowhere. Monsieur Montenier?"

"Yes?"

"Am I to believe that you doubt that the Eighteenth
Regiment is adhering to the best efforts clause?"

For a moment, Gallic temperament threatened to
burst a blood vessel, but then, sensing that I wanted
him to blow his stack, he forced himself to calm down.

"Yes," he hissed. "Your . . . *regiment* is doing nothing. They are not engaging the Dutch—"

I punched for my command voice. "*Shut up.*" Sur-
prisingly, the flow of sound ceased. "They aren't engaging the Dutch," I went on, "because any movement
upriver would leave Marne open to an assault by the
Dutch irregulars, and because a Dutch company could
carve its way through what you idiots call a defense."
Not that a Dutch expeditionary force could destroy the

launcher—the Peacemakers protecting it wouldn't let them, and they wouldn't even if they could—or even maintain control of it for long, but a decent-sized Dutch force could leave Port Marne burning.

Which would tend to take the spirit out of the French.

"So," he said with another sniff, "you intend to try to fulfill the best efforts clause by having your regiment sit on their hands, *protecting* Port Marne? I'll have your bond forfeit."

I snickered. "Read your contract, Montenier. Forgetting the fact that you can't afford to pay interest on our bond while waiting three, maybe four standard years for a court date—paragraph twenty-seven "Forfeiture of Bond," subparagraph (j)—the moment you move to seize the bond, the Eighteenth will pull up and head for home—subparagraph (l)."

Celia smiled slyly. So, she probably thought, *that* was really what I was after: pushing Montenier into slapping a lien on the performance bond so that the Eighteenth could withdraw without losing much face.

Wrong, Celia, but not a bad guess, I thought.

Montenier apparently decided the same thing that Celia did. "So," he said. "There will be no best efforts payment made, General Hanavi—"

"Inspector-General."

"I'll have papers prepared ordering the regiment into combat against the Dutch. They are to assault the Dutch regiment stationed at—"

"No." I shook my head. "Read the contract again. Tactical decisions are General Davis's prerogative, not yours. If you want the Dutch attacked, you'll get it, but—"

"When—and where?"

"General Davis will decide. The regiment will move out in eight days, to give you time to arrange a better defense. As to when and where we'll attack, it's none of your damn business. I'll expect to see written orders or notice of a lien by nightfall."

I turned and walked away, my heels clicking on the stone.

Celia's words echoed after me: "Is this what you do for your money, Tetsuo Hanavi?" And, unspoken, *Do you kill for someone like Montenier*.

No, Celia. Never.

Yonni Davis was in his tent playing bridge with a short colonel, a major, and his message runner when I got back to the encampment.

"Well?"

I chuckled. "Orders will be on their way shortly. Can you have the Eighteenth ready to move out in a week or so?"

He nodded. "It can be arranged. Or sooner, if need be."

"Don't rush. You're going to have to break them down to companies, maybe down to platoons, then have everyone sneak upriver about five, six hundred klicks. And that's going to take a good forty days, what with slipping through Dutch lines and all."

"They can do it in thirty," he said.

"They'll do it in forty. The river will be fully swollen in forty days."

"Right." He turned to his two opponents. "I claim," he said. "If the queen of diamonds doesn't fall, I've got an automatic double squeeze. Tetsuo, I'll want you to stay with HQ comm—" He caught himself, and smiled. "Make that HQ squad."

VI

Yonni Davis was no Shimon Bar-El; my uncle's kind of genius is a rare talent. Still, he impressed me. There's a reason why generals who are authorized to run low-tech operations on worlds like Alsace, Rand, and Indess are generally considered the elite of the elite. On high-tech worlds, reasonably sophisticated comm gear can let a commanding general shortcut down to running a regiment by company, sometimes by platoon, with the rest of the chain of command listening in, ready to take over if the enemy takes out either the communications system, or the general.

With sound intelligence and good troops, running a high-tech battle is relatively easy—when you compare it to what Yonni Davis was up against on Alsace. On low-tech worlds, $C^3 + I$ is never easy. Even in a set-piece meeting engagement, a general has to give up almost all tactical control for everything beyond HQ company and, more often than not, he has to run most of HQ company as a formation, not a tactical unit; even a loud voice can only carry so far.

And here, Yonni had had to break the Eighteenth down to loosely linked sections of even more loosely linked platoons, the whole regiment spread out along hundreds of klicks of riverbank, trusting to his officers and senior enlisted to keep everything quiet, doing everything right on the numbers. Particularly the withdrawal. Granted, the Dutch irregular force would soon evaporate, but there was sure to be at least one assault through to Port Marne. The Eighteenth would have to be back, and well dug in.

All of which explains why I was impressed with the way that Yonni's round face was unworried as it gleamed, sweaty in the bright moonlight.

He straightened for a moment, rubbing at the small of his back as he leaned on his shovel.

His headquarters section was spread out along the bank of the rising river and into the woods, three bowmen posted to watch for any sign of movement from the planters in the house a klick away, out on the promontory.

The other thing that stretched out into the woods was a narrow ditch, perhaps a meter wide and not much deeper, that cut all the way across the peninsula of the Haugen plantation. Working hard, twenty men could each dig through ten meters of the soft riverside dirt per hour, and we had been at it since just after dark.

One foot in the water, one foot out, I pitched another shovelful into the waist-high earth dam that was already melting away into the swirling river.

A low whistle was picked up in the distance and relayed, quickly becoming louder.

"Fine," Yonni said. "Signal back: move out. We've got another one to do before morning." He turned to me. "You may do the honors."

It only took me a couple of minutes to clear away the improvised dam. The water quietly rushed into the ditch, the newly made stream rolling off into the night, pulling little morsels of dirt from the edge. It almost seemed to grow as we watched; by noon, the rising river would have established the cut-off as a solid new path.

He shook his head in amazement. "Are you sure they won't be able to do anything about it?"

I shrugged. "We've been through this before." My memory isn't eidetic, but sometimes it is good. I closed my eyes, seeing the shining page in front of me once again.

The water cuts the alluvial banks of the "lower" river into deep horseshoe curves; so deep, indeed, that in some places if you were to get ashore at one extremity of the horseshoe and walk across the neck, half or three quarters of a mile, you could sit down and rest a couple of hours while your steamer was coming around the long elbow, at a speed of ten miles an hour, to take you aboard again. When the river is rising fast, some scoundrel whose plantation is back in the country, and therefore of inferior value, has only to watch his chance, cut a little gutter across the narrow neck of land some dark night, and turn the water into it, and in a wonderfully short time a miracle has happened: to wit, the whole Mississippi has taken possession of that little ditch, and placed the countryman's plantation on its bank (quadrupling its value), and that other party's formerly valuable plantation finds itself out yonder on a big island; the old water-course around it will soon shoal up, boats cannot approach within ten miles of it, and down goes its value to a fourth of its former worth.

"Nothing they can do about it," I said. The Haugens, who lived out on the peninsula that would soon become an island, wouldn't necessarily think that their inland neighbors did it, although perhaps they might suspect them. It wouldn't matter. The news would fly to the Dutch forces in the south. Any of the Haugen sons in the Dutch irregulars would find it hard to fight for their inland cousins. The inland cousins would find defending their newly valuable plantation more appealing than fighting the French.

The scene would be repeated, up and down the river, as the Eighteenth shortened the New Hunse this night, putting the ownership of a good portion of Dutch territory into question.

No, it wasn't over. We'd have to get back downriver. Surely, whoever was commanding the Dutch irregulars would try for one last push before his command collapsed underneath him, and the Eighteenth and the French forces would have to hold the line.

The Eighteenth would hold—even without the French forces—and Phillipe Montenier would win, at least in the short run. It would surely take more than the remaining five years of our contract for the Dutch to straighten things out well enough to support a unified fighting force. More likely than not, they'd split up and end up feuding among themselves for most of a century. The French could play divide and conquer, and their coffers would overflow.

For now. But that was enough.

Boots pounded on the riverbank as a message runner ran up. "Report from Lieutenant Roth's group," he said, half out of breath. "Begins. Spotted by a householder. As work was completed, I ordered a withdrawal. One casualty, minor. Ends."

"Not bad." Yonni clapped a hand to my shoulder.

"Let's get out of here. We've got another ditch to dig tonight."

And then a few hundred klicks of traveling. South to the defense of Port Marne and its environs for Davis and the Eighteenth; south to the launcher for me.

And home.

"You'll carry mail?" he asked.

"Of course. You'll hold the line in the south?"

He laughed. "Of course."

VII

Just over two thousand hours later, I was back on Metzada, walking down my home tunnel, the mail sack safely in the hands of Central Distributing. I waved happily to cousins as I let my feet break into a run for the last klick. Homecoming is a joyous time in the Bar-El warrens; most Bar-El men spend far too much time offplanet.

I always see the children first. If it's daytime—not surface daytime, of course, but the twenty-four hour clock we use, always set to Jerusalem time—I pull them out of school. RHIP.

But it was night.

Rachel knows my habits even better than Suki; the moment I dropped my bag in the foyer, she led me down the hall and into the nursery. "Suki'll be home in a couple of hours," she whispered. "She's doing a . . . mandouble reconstruction—"

"Mandible," I said. "Mandible."

She squeezed my hand and shook her head for a moment, her black hair whipping around her face like Celia's had, when she and her Peacemakers had escorted me into the shuttle at Port Marne.

"Good work," Celia said, her voice dripping with sarcasm. "Very, very good. Now the Dutch will lose their unity, start fighting among themselves, and the French will walk all over them. Seventy-five percent taxes?

Nonsense. Montenier will probably carve the upper river into French holdings, and turn the Dutch into peons."

I nodded. *It was true, of course.*

The two youngest children were in their cribs. Deborah was sound asleep, curled in her blankets. I let my hand rest against the back of her head for a moment. I've always wondered why the hair on my children's heads is so much softer, so much finer than anybody else's.

Tetsuo Hanavi, how can you be proud of what you do for money? she asked, sneering. For filthy money?

Little Benyamin was sleeping restlessly, as though he knew what his own future held, starting sixteen years hence.

"Take your time," I whispered. "There's no rush."

"A bit of good news," Rachel whispered. "That new shipment of medicines came in just last week. All of the children's immunizations are up-to-date."

"The new payment from the Rand monarchists must have come through."

"That's right."

No, Celia, nobody ever fights for money. Not for money.

Still asleep, Benyamin reached out and grasped my forefinger, gripping it more tightly than his little hand had any right to.

We don't fight for money. We fight, and kill, and die for the credits that keep Metzada alive. The distinction is important.

"What did you say?" Rachel asked, wrapping her arms around my waist as she leaned up against me.

I shook my head, as little Benyamin's grip grew stronger. "Doesn't matter."

IN PRAISE OF SOCIOBIOLOGY

The fundamental tenet of Sociobiology seems at first blush so unarguable as to be trite: that genetic endowment influences behavior, including social behavior. In other words you cannot teach a horse to do quadratic equations or vote the Party Ticket no matter how supportive the horse's environment.

Alas, the Powers That Be have declared this nascent science to be Anti-Marxist, and so it has become rather more controversial on American campuses than you might otherwise expect . . .

IN PRAISE OF SOCIOBIOLOGY

John and Mary Gribbin

Sociobiology is the study of all forms of social behavior in all animals, including humans. That sounds innocuous enough, but sociobiology naturally includes the genetic bases of behavior. A hyena has a very different social life from an albatross, say, and this is fundamentally because the DNA inside the cells of the two species codes for different things. The fact that an albatross has two wings and two legs, and is covered by feathers, while a hyena has four legs and no wings, and is covered by hair, is due to their different genetic inheritance. So, clearly, a very large part of sociobiology is about genetic inheritance, which predisposes individual members of different species to do certain things well, and others badly, or not at all.

Of course, the more interesting aspects of this study concern differences more subtle than those between wings and legs. Why do lions, for example, find it advantageous, in terms of evolutionary success, to form groups (prides) in which one male dominates and mates with all the females? Why do most birds spend so much time and effort raising their young, while most frogs simply abandon their eggs to take their chance in the world? And so on. The principle is still the same. A bird behaves like a bird, and a frog behaves like a frog, because of its genetic inheritance.

It is when this straightforward line of biological and evolutionary reasoning is applied to humans that it causes such a strong reaction in some quarters that the very term "sociobiology" has become almost a dirty word to a small minority of biologists. The problem does not lie, as you might guess, with those who believe in the literal word of the creation story told in the Bible, and therefore cannot accept that people should be regarded by science in the same way as other animals. Ironically, the vehement opposition to human sociobiology has come from the other end of the religious spectrum—from self-acknowledged Marxists and atheists who mistakenly believe that sociobiologists are claiming that all human behavior is so rigidly programmed by our genes that there is little or no scope left for free will.

In recent years, there have been two extreme views put forward to explain human behavior, and much of human history. Konrad Lorenz and Robert Ardrey espoused the view that human beings are driven by innate aggression, genetically determined, which has molded the development of human society through repeated warfare and which finds an outlet today in activities such as football hooliganism. B. F. Skinner, on the other hand, has postulated that each newborn human infant is a blank slate, capable of being molded in any direction, depending on the kind of stimuli it receives from the world around it. Train the child to be a warlike aggressor, and you will get an aggressive adult; train the child to be a peaceful farmer, and you will get an adult agriculturalist.

As is the case with most extreme views of the world, the truth lies somewhere in between. People are born with certain innate abilities and inclinations, but they are also molded by their cultural surroundings. We are born with a predisposition to speak, for example, but the language we speak as adults depends on what we hear when we are young.

If culture were the *overriding* influence on being

human, then surely it would be possible to raise a pygmy chimp from birth in a human household, and end up with a passable imitation of a human being. In fact, the genetic difference of only one percent between ourselves and such a chimpanzee makes this impossible. Humankind is indeed a cultural animal, but our cultural nature and our instincts alike are themselves genetically determined, like our naked skin and our large brains.

The extreme opponents of human sociobiology are concerned that any evidence for a genetic basis for human behavior will strengthen the case of the Lorenzes and Ardreys who argue that human aggression is innate and cannot be controlled. But that misses the point—sociobiology does *not* presume that our fate is determined by biology in this way. Culture *is* a big influence on human behavior, and we have the intelligence to analyze situations and act on the basis of reasoned argument, instead of by instinct. People are rather *unusual* African apes, and our unusual attributes have to be taken into account. Indeed, what matters is that we should try, through sociobiology, to understand what our animal inheritance predisposes us for, so that we can decide whether that predisposition is good or bad, and can take suitable steps to overcome it where necessary. If, for instance, people are innately somewhat aggressive and suspicious of foreigners, it should be advantageous to understand that and to ensure that we use our intelligence to avoid conflicts. Discarding sociobiology because a few neo-Nazis claim that it implies certain races are inferior is like banning the manufacture of knives because a few people commit murder with them. Or like banning radio, because some evil dictators use the medium to spread their message.

The power of the sociobiological approach is best seen by looking at how the behavior of animals, including human animals, is so effectively tailored to maximize their chances of reproducing, and passing on copies of their genes to succeeding generations.

That, after all, is what life on Earth is all about.

Replication—copying—of strands of DNA. The complexity of life we see around us, including our own species, is a result of competition and selection which has produced a variety of different ways to ensure the copying of DNA, and has produced many kinds of DNA—many genes—along the way. This is a blind process operating in accordance with the laws of physics and chemistry, and statistics, with no guiding intelligence behind it. But with that clearly understood, it is often convenient to anthropomorphize somewhat, and use everyday expressions to discuss how the genes ensure their replication. We may say, for example, that a gene "wants" to ensure that copies of itself get spread among subsequent generations. Obviously, one effective way to do this is to "help" the body in which it lives to reproduce and leave many offspring behind.

That is basic Darwinian evolution. Genes that make a body better fitted to its environment will inevitably be selected and will spread. But this is not the full story. Because of the way genes are inherited—half from each parent—there is a fifty-fifty chance that two offspring who share the same two parents will have any one of their genes in common. On average, half the genes of full siblings will be identical in each body. Or, from the "point of view" of a particular gene residing in the cells of one body, there is a fifty-fifty chance that the cells of the body of a sibling carry copies of that same gene. So, if one sibling helps another to find food, or a mate, and, ultimately, to reproduce, then he or she is helping to ensure the spread of very many of the genes that are in his or her own body. If a gene arises which causes the body it inhabits to behave in such a way that the survival of siblings is encouraged—even if this is merely a side effect of whatever influence the gene has on the body it inhabits—then the gene will spread, because half the siblings carry the same gene.

At a stroke, this concept explains, in a qualitative way, why close relations should cooperate with one another—and, indeed, members of a pride of lions will, in general, be relatives. It is quite straightforward to put numbers into all this. And when this is done, the combination of the idea of selfish genes and games theory can very often account for otherwise puzzling biological phenomena.

We might as well think in human terms here, although what we have to say applies to any species that reproduces in the way we do. Each new human being has a unique genetic blueprint which is made up of a combination of genes inherited from each parent. In most cases, the mother and father are not close relations, so we can regard each of them as having an independent set of the possible genes available in the human gene pool. Half of their child's genes come from each parent, so geneticists say that there is a relatedness of 1/2 between a child and either of its parents. What about the children's relatedness to each other?

All children of the same mother inherit half her genes. But they do not all inherit the same genes from her. On average, though, there is a 50-50 chance that one of the genes copied and passed on to one child will also be passed on to its sibling. So, on average, half the genes that each child inherits from the mother will be the same as those in any other child that has the same mother. And, since half the total genotype is provided by the mother, that means that, on average, siblings that share the same mother have a relatedness of 1/4 (half of one half). Exactly the same reasoning applies to siblings who share the same father. So for full siblings, which share *both* parents, we simply add up the two contributions to find that their relatedness is, on average, 1/2—the same as the relatedness of parent to offspring.

It is very simple to extend this argument to other relations. The next closest kin, after siblings and parents, are full cousins. You share half your genes with your mother, who, on average shares half her genes with her sister, who, in turn, shares half her genes with her daughter. You and your cousin therefore have a relatedness of $1/2 \times 1/2 \times 1/2$, or 1/8. And this kind of calculation immediately puts a new complexion on Darwinian evolution.

If an individual helps a close relation, such as a sibling or a cousin, to reproduce, then that altruistic act is actually helping many copies of genes that are also present in the altruistic individual's body to reproduce. Sometimes, the genes that are caused to spread in this way will include copies of the genes that made the altruistic individual act in this helpful way. And that is all you need to understand altruism in Darwinian terms. A gene, or set of genes, that causes individuals to behave in what we think of as an altruistic way can spread among the population, because its presence in some bodies (phenotypes) will lead to action which allows copies of that same gene to reproduce in other bodies! This is all best summed up by a remark that J.B.S. Haldane is supposed to have made in a Cambridge pub in the 1950s. Discussing the puzzle of altruism over a pint or two with some colleagues, he was asked if he would lay down his life for his brother. Haldane thought for a while, and then replied, according to legend, "Not for one brother. But I would for two brothers, or eight cousins." The point is that, on average, behavior that ensures the reproductive success of two of your full siblings, or eight of your cousins, ensures the survival of copies of every gene that you carry, simply by adding up the relatednesses. It is as good, Haldane realized, as if you lived to reproduce yourself.

Of course, Haldane's remark should not be taken too literally. People—let alone other animals—don't sit around calculating degrees of genetic relatedness before deciding whether to jump into a river to save a drowning child. But the fact that people are more likely to risk their own lives to save a close relation is so firmly established that, for example, the award of the Carnegie Medal is specifically excluded for such acts. If you want to win this bravery award, you have to save the life of someone outside your immediate family.

Nature is not quite so red in tooth and claw as naive

Darwinism would have us believe. From the original Darwinian standpoint, it is a complete mystery why individual members of the same species should bother to work together at all. But sociobiology can explain why we are predisposed to be nice to each other. In the small family groups and tribes that were the basic human societies before the invention of civilization, the chances were that anyone you met would be a relation. So being nice to people would help some copies of your own genes, and a tendency for general niceness would spread. Although we now live in very different societies, we still carry this genetic inheritance, and we are still basically predisposed to be nice to one another.

This may seem a surprising claim in view of the publicity given to the ideas of Lorenz and Ardrey, but it certainly stands up to inspection. After all, muggings and violence make news in our society not because they are normal, routine events, but because they are aberrations. All the little old ladies who *don't* get mugged don't make the headlines, because being nice to old ladies really is a fundamental part of human nature. Sociobiology, it seems, is not such a bad thing after all. It tells us that people are quite nice, really—and it tells us a great deal more about why we do the things we do.

Take just one example of the application of sociobiology to humans—the conflict between the generations, which repeats itself inexorably every time a man and a woman get together to raise a family. Sociobiological insight may lessen some of the pain of the conflict, even if it cannot remove the grounds for the hassles. And it can also explain the spectacular careers of a certain kind of movie star.

Why *is* the helpless, dumb blond, as portrayed so memorably by Marilyn Monroe, a successful role for some individual members of human society? The reasons lie in our genes as much as in our culture, and have to do with the size of our brains and the resulting helplessness of human babies.

Human babies are physically helpless. They survive only because their helpless appearance promotes a strong response among most adults. Even male chauvinists who profess a profound dislike of infants will coo over a newborn baby, responding to some deep-seated biological imperative, while a mother is able to identify the whimper of her own baby in a busy maternity ward, and when at home will wake at the first cry in the night, even if she was previously a heavy sleeper. It is easy to see how such responses must have evolved in tandem with the helplessness of the human baby at birth—a helplessness which is itself directly related to the evolution of the large brain that makes us so successful as adults.

In primitive societies, human beings who are repelled by helpless infants do not, for obvious reasons, leave many offspring to carry their genes forward into future generations. Some men may, but scarcely any women. Things are different in the development of a civilized society in which it is possible for child-rearing to be taken over almost at birth by people who are not the biological parents of the infant. But those are not the conditions under which we evolved. Parents who respond more lovingly to the helpless appearance of their own babies will be more effective at rearing children and ensuring the spread of their own genes, including the package of interacting genes that makes them love babies. And this raises the possibility of an interesting evolutionary feedback.

This kind of feedback can best be understood by considering the peacock's tail. This is a wonderful accoutrement, which is used by the male bird solely as a lure to attract females and to obtain a mate. The female birds are, obviously, attracted by the tail. We don't have to know why this should be so in order to understand the feedback process—which is just as well, since some of the arguments put forward to "explain" the phenomenon are quite tortuous. Some people have suggested that the appearance of the tail, with the colors of the feathers making a pattern of a myriad eyes, may hypnotize the hen into submission; others argue that since such a large tail is a physical handicap to the peacock, only an otherwise very "fit" bird could survive while carrying such a handicap, and so females mate with the males with the biggest tails, who must be very good at survival in order to cope with such a handicap. Whatever the reason, though, in the world today peahens *do* prefer to mate with peacocks with large, colorful tails.

Because the peahens are, in human terms, obsessed by this characteristic, any male with a bigger tail will mate successfully and have many offspring. So genes that provide for large, colorful tails spread rapidly through the population, and the present extravagant display can evolve from a much smaller feature over many generations.

Now let's get back to parents and babies. Successful parents are those who respond to the helplessness of their babies with love and attention, so packages of genes that promote this parenting response are widespread in human populations—almost universal. In such a situation, it may actually be in the best interests of the baby to seem to be even more helpless than it really is, because that will promote a stronger parenting response. The baby, in other words, may actually be manipulating its parents, psychologically, from the moment it is born. It has to—as American sociobiologist Robert Trivers has pointed out. Because the infant is much smaller and weaker than its mother, it cannot physically fling her to the ground and suckle when it is hungry. Psychological weapons are the only ones it has to achieve its objectives.

Of course, even newborn babies are not completely helpless. They can suck, cry, see, hear, and grasp. They certainly do look even more helpless than they are. But the relationship is not all one way. Evolution has provided the baby with a powerful means of rewarding its parents for all the attention it gets—the smile. Crying communicates a baby's distress, and this essential means to stimulate adults into action is present at birth. Within a very few weeks, the baby also develops a smile, so heartwarming that many other adults (especially women) apart from its parents respond to it. The smile encourages adults to interact with the baby, play with it, goo over it, and tickle its toes. It also makes the adult feel good; it is a reward to the adult for bothering to pay attention to the infant. And, once again, it is easy to see how such a system has evolved through a feedback process like the one which has made the peacock's tail so big.

There is no conscious thought involved, any more than a peacock thinks "Hm, I'd like to grow a big tail." It is all instinctive—that is, it is coded in our genes. Once babies started to smile, back in evolutionary history, (and it may have been simply a grimace connected with wind pain to start with) then adults who responded to the smile were favored by selection, because they gave their babies more attention and helped them to grow up successfully. So infants that smiled more were favored more, and so adults who responded were further favored, generally speaking, and so on. The result is that we all carry genes which ensure that we smile a lot as babies (whatever culture may do to change that pattern of behavior as we get older), and we all carry genes that make us respond warmly to smiling people— especially helpless, smiling infants.

Which brings us back to Marilyn Monroe. Just as infants are physically weaker than their parents, so women are, by and large, physically weaker than men. Abhorrent though the image may be to many women today, the stereotype of a big, husky male and a weaker female is unfortunately close to the truth, and just as babies use psychological weapons to get their way with adults, so women can, consciously or unconsciously, use psychological weapons rather than brute force to get their way with men. And what better weapon to use than the one which has proved such a success with the babies—an appearance of helplessness, combined with a fetching smile? The success of the not-so-dumb blond in melting the heart of a husky he-man is no surprise at all to the sociobiologist, but simply reflects a distortion for adult use of the infant's prime weapons in the generation game.

But why should there be any conflict between parents and offspring at all? It might seem that what is good for the child must be good for its parents, who want to ensure that it survives to carry their genes on into the future. But this misses the point that parents are also able to "invest" in other children. To the parent, one child is as good as another as a gene carrier; but each child, sharing only half its genes with a sibling (or indeed with a parent) "cares" much more for its own good than for theirs, in evolutionary terms. And that is where things get interesting.

This is still a new and developing area of scientific research, and the detailed implications, especially for human beings, are very far from being fully worked out. But that doesn't make the broad outlines of the work in progress any less fascinating.

It all began in 1974, when Trivers published a scientific paper on parent-offspring conflict. The important point is the degree of genetic relatedness between different individuals in a family group. It doesn't have to be a human family, although that is the one we are especially interested in. People are animals. We have exactly the same kind of genetic material as other animals, and share up to 99 percent of the DNA with our closest relations. We obey the same evolutionary rules as other animals—and even the things that set us apart from our closest relations are not all unique to our species.

People are in the minority in the animal world as a species where the male takes on a degree of responsibility for the offspring. But this is a respectably large minority of species, and includes birds, where there is a similar sharing of parental responsibility. But in bird or human, or other species, the only way in which an individual can be successful, in terms of evolution is to leave copies of his or her genes, and to be sure that his or her children have reproduced in their turn. Leaving aside the possibility for doubts about paternity, each parent has a 50 percent genetic investment in each child—parent and offspring have a genetic relatedness of 0.5. On average, two offspring of the same set of parents also have a relatedness of 0.5. Without going into the mathematical details, we can see that in everyday terms each parent "needs" to raise at least two offspring in order to ensure that all of its own genes are copied, and would "like" to raise more. Each infant, on the other hand, only really cares about its own survival, although it will be happy to see siblings also doing well, provided that their success is not at its own cost.

In other words, the strategy by which a parent can maximize its own reproductive success is not necessarily compatible with the strategy by which the child maximizes its own reproductive success, and, in particular, parents will try to produce more offspring when existing children prefer, in evolutionary terms, to see more attention given to themselves than to new siblings.

At some point, of course, the growing infant becomes able to stand on its own two feet, or fly on its own two wings, and make a living without further parental help. The parent's interests are best served by getting the offspring off her hands (usually, it is the mother who is primarily concerned here) as soon as possible, and getting on with the job of raising another infant. The offspring's interests are best served by getting the mother—and father, if possible—to continue to provide help, or food, as long as possible. But the offspring do share part of the mother's investment in their siblings, so there comes a point when *even in terms of the best strategy for their own genes* it makes better evolutionary sense for them to cut loose from the proverbial apron strings and make their own way in the world, so that the parents can raise more offspring unhindered.

Because of the simple relatedness of 0.5 that is involved, each infant should be inclined to seek aid from the parent as long as the cost to the parent—in reproductive terms—is less than half the benefit to the infant. But once the cost to the parent is more than twice the benefit to the offspring, the infant should be willing to leave her to raise another sibling. To the parent, however, the time to start concentrating on the next infant is when the benefit of so doing is *equal* to the cost of continuing to help an older offspring. And therein lies the conflict.

Inexorably, the arithmetic dictates that parents want their offspring to fly the nest before the offspring are willing to do so. And the evolutionary rules also dictate that, no matter how strongly each teenager may vow to treat his or her own children differently, by the time we grow up to be parents ourselves, we will act out the same role models that our parents acted out before us. As well as what we might call the weaning conflict, the children will inevitably be more adventurous, take more risks, and be less inclined to settle down than their parents desire. To the kids, with a long life ahead, there is plenty of time for settling down later. The parents, with their best reproductive years behind them, want to see their investment in their children paying off, in the form of grandchildren, and paying off quickly.

For once, understanding why we act the way we do doesn't seem to be a great deal of help in tackling the day-to-day problems this causes. Have you ever tried to explain to a teenage son that the conflict between his wishes and yours is an inevitable result of human evolution, and that he'll see things your way when he gets older? Never mind. At least father and son can agree on one thing—we both like dumb blondes, and knowing *why* we like them doesn't seem to reduce the pleasure one bit.

The best book about human sociobiology published to date is Edward Wilson's *On Human Nature* (Harvard University Press, 1978). Robert Trivers has produced a fascinating and readable textbook called *Social Evolution* (Benjamin/Cummings, 1985). And John and Mary Gribbin are now completing a book, *Being Human*, which will be published in 1987.

LIFEGUARD

Any resemblance between Astar of the LeGrange Water Depository, Heinlein, and the young lady who starred in RAH's immortal "The Menace from Earth" is purely intentional, I suspect. But somehow I don't think Robert will mind. . . .

LIFEGUARD

Doug Beason

Heinlein, Robert A. (hĭn lĭn), n. 1. 1907 –, American writer and space enthusiast. 2. Water depository for the stable (L-4, L-5) Lagrange colonies. Two water tanks, each 1 kilometer thick and 2 kilometers in diameter, counterrotate (10 rev/hr) at opposite ends of a 2-kilometer-long cylinder. A byproduct of the revolving water tanks is a vacillating, water-free tunnel extending along the zero-gee core of each water tank; low air pressure and high water temperature in the water tank result in a boiling point near 52 degrees Centigrade for the water . . .

Second Triumvirate Dictionary

No matter what you've heard, being a sixteen-year-old female in the *Heinlein* is not exciting. And no, we don't swim with our clothes off. The water is much too hot for that—you'd boil after two minutes, no matter what the holos show you. Besides, it's all trick holography, and the touri *really* get upset when they find out we wear wetsuits. But we keep the air pressure low enough that the water boils to make up for it.

Anyway, I was 'guarding when the *Forward* docked, so I missed the first gaggle of touri this month. They're probably out gawking at the Swimmers now, so I have to make doubly sure no one gets hurt on my shift. This was my last run anyway, and things are pretty quiet.

I peered through the tunnel of water that surrounded me and made out the shimmering electrostatic curtain that protected the restcove. The water tank's wall was coming up fast—too fast for a safe landing. It was still over four hundred meters away, but I had to start thinking about slowing down; I was moving at least twice as fast as I should have. The body has these certain warning signals that kick in when you're doing something stupid: my heart started palpitating and I grew suddenly chilled—which was ridiculous, because the tank was up to at least fifty-five Cee today, lots warmer than usual.

The restcove grew larger through the tunnel; it couldn't have been more than two hundred meters away by now. Oh well, this was the end of my shift, and I hadn't spotted any Jumpers—might as well make the most of it and Jump myself.

I threw my buoy up at the water above me. The motion sent me moving slowly in the opposite direction—down, toward the bottom of the tunnel. This is the hard part—I didn't leave much room to spare . . .

The buoy skipped across the water, grabbed at the surface, then dove outcore, toward deep water. I was jerked up when the buoy hit and smacked against the water. It hurt—stopping forward momentum in zero-gee makes you a believer!—but I had other things to worry about. I was trolled in the water as the buoy picked up speed on its way down.

When I passed the twentieth glowglobe, I drew my legs up under me. I should hit bottom . . . any . . . second . . . *now!* I jumped for the tunnel, clawing my way up through the kilometer of water above me. As the gravity decreased, I pulled myself up faster, pointing slightly inward to adjust for coriolis.

The pseudosurface was a warbling ripple above me. I felt cocky, so I angled toward the restcove. If I planned it right, I'd pop out just at the viewports, break the pseudosurface, and manage to get eight flips in before I hit the water at the top of the tunnel. That oughta pop a few eyeballs out . . .

I misjudged the surface. I must have caught a bubble as it burst, because I only had time to get five flips off before I realized that I was going to hit the top of the tunnel sooner than I thought. Instead of twenty meters of open air, I flew through fifteen. That's not much when you're trying to get in those extra turns.

I hit the water on my back with a *pop*. The spray was something else. It must have taken five minutes for all the water to diffuse from the zero-gee core back down to where the pseudosurface boiled.

Feeling foolish, I half-dog paddled, half-skipped across the pseudosurface to the restcove, then trudged up the stickum and entered through the electrostatic curtain. Soloette was there with three touri, all male.

She looked like she was in heaven. I was about to sail past her to post my report when she said to the men, "Oh, and this is my best friend I've been telling you about. Astar, meet Randall, Justin, and Phillip. They're laying over for a few days until the lunar shuttle gets back; they're with the Computer Upgrade Project at Tycho Station."

One of the men grinned stupidly—from the size of his arms he had to be a weight lifter. Or walk on his hands. Another was a runt, and the last—the cute one, of course—couldn't keep his eyes off Soloette.

I said, "Hi, glad to meet you," and turned away, but a male voice stopped me. The weight lifter.

"Hey, wait." He looked me up and down; I wasn't used to being stared at. My face grew warm as he said, "I'm Justin Kenlai. Do you swim here a lot?"

I managed to make one of my typical brillant statements. "Uh?" Then, "Sure, what do you think I am—a touri?"

Soloette interrupted and motioned with her eyes to the chronometer embedded over the entrance to the water tank. "Astar, aren't you about done with your shift?"

"Uh, yeah. That was my last run before my lunch break."

Soloette looked smug. "I tell you what—why don't you join us for lunch at the Bifrost? It won't take more than an hour. How does that sound?"

I smiled sweetly. "Soloette, don't you think the men would like to try somewhere a little less formal?" Translated: *The Bifrost will blow my food allowance for the month!*

She batted her eyes. "Now, Astar, they're only going to be here a few days. We might as well show them the high spots." In other words: *Don't blow it for me!*

She's flipped over every new guy for the past two months; might as well let her have her fun. "All right," I grudgingly agreed. "If they want to."

"Well?" asked Soloette, looking to the men.

"Sounds good to me, if you're both coming with us," said Justin, smiling at me.

I shrugged. "Sure, why not."

"Great." Soloette was practically drooling. She said, "Astar, I'll take them there while you change out of your 'suit. Ten minutes?"

"If you want." I turned to go. "Uh, nice meeting all of you. See you there."

"Sure."

They managed to make it out of the restcove without hurting themselves. I quickchanged, then bounced to my apartment to get something a little more appropriate for the Bifrost Lounge. After all, if I'm going to use up Daddy's rations, might as well go in style.

The apartment was empty. Daddy's the *Heinlein*'s chief hydrologist and was still at the L-4 colonies for the week, so I was able to grab the ration cube without him protesting.

They were already seated by the time I got there. Aalicen was doing the ballet today, so Soloette had managed to wrangle an area nearby the dance space. Justin attempted to get up when I approached, but was jerked back into his seat by the webbed belting. His arms bulged as he strained against the straps; I thought he was going to break the belt. He looked sheepish. "Sorry."

"S'all right." I grinned. "Sometimes that's the only way to tell the touri in here. Don't want you floating into the middle of Aalicen's dance." I looked around. "We're missing someone." *The runt*.

"Phillip's stomach didn't feel too well," said Randall. "He wanted us to go on without him."

"Whatever." It was fine with me; the fewer people here meant the faster I could get back to 'guarding.

We punched in our orders and sat in silence until the weight lifter—sorry, until Justin—spoke up. "You said something about a dance?"

I nodded toward the dance space, demarcated by bundles of fine-mesh netting. "Aalicen is doing the floorshow today: classic punk ballet. The netting ensures she doesn't stray too far from the dance space. Sometimes she can get pretty worked up if the crowd interacts well with her."

"Umm, I've never seen zero-gee ballet."

"It's great. In fact, next to swimming, it's the most popular attraction here."

We were interrupted by Aalicen's entrance. She spun around the volume encompassing her dance space, then bounced through a train of holographs projected around the chamber. The music seemed to change with every swirl. It still strikes me every time I watch her—which isn't often, because of the prices in here.

We were finally served; Aalicen's dance set a pleasant mood for lunch. Justin turned to me and said, "I've seen holos on swimming in your water tanks. It looks exciting."

"It is," I agreed. "I really enjoy it. In fact, I could probably do it forever. If it wasn't for school, I'd probably be lifeguarding most of the time."

"Is it hard swimming here?"

"Are you kidding? Three- and four-year-old kids do it all the time. They even make Jumping look easy."

Justin was quiet for a moment. "Do you think I could try it?"

"Swimming? Why not? If you want, I'll take both of you after lunch."

Justin looked pleased. "That would be fun."

I toyed with my food. "What about you—did you ever 'guard back on Earth?"

Randall looked abruptly up, then back down at his plate. Justin poked at his food and said, "To tell you the truth, I never had the chance. You see, when I was younger, I—"

He was drowned out by applause as Aalicen completed her set. Randall leaned over the table and said, "She's great. If she wanted, I bet she could make a million on Earth." He looked to Soloette. "Do you think she'll ever try?"

The table grew quiet. Soloette managed to answer quickly, "No, I don't think so; she likes it too much here. Besides, she wouldn't be able to do half of what she does here down there." She turned her attention to me and said urgently, "Astar, isn't it time for your shift?"

The atmosphere seemed tense. "Er, yes . . . I guess it is." I unstrapped and floated up. I wasn't quite finished, but Randall had touched a nerve best left alone for now. "Randall, Justin—sorry to cut this short. I've got to get back to the tank."

"No problem. We understand."

"Fine, then I'll see you all later?"

Soloette answered, "We'll be right behind you." She held my eye. "Go on. I'll get these guys fitted out in wetsuits. We'll meet you in the restcove."

I overrode their objections to my paying for my own meal, and left. Reaching the water tank, I changed and made it into the restcove just as my shift started.

I scanned the sonarholo for traffic in the water; it was virtually deserted. Then I kicked into the water tank. The tunnel was boiling in a Dantean frenzy, water popping as bubbles fought their way up from the bottom of the tank. Sailing through the tunnel, I thought about lunch: Soloette would do *anything* to get a man to come back here. Lucky I was more particular than she is;

besides, I wasn't ready to get involved. I'm having too much fun just 'guarding.

Oh, *bother*. The restcove on the outer wall was coming up fast. I'd have to let the buoy slow me down. That's what I get for thinking about men.

I spotted them on my approach to the main restcove. Soloette had done a pretty good job of fitting them with wetsuits; they resembled neon signs in their hot-pink novice suits.

The colonists spruced their suits up a little more to style: Soloette's radiated an ever-changing hue of colors, rippling through the rainbow from blood maroon to deep indigo and back again. If there had been gravity in the restcove, the guys' eyes would be rolling on the floor.

My own suit was the straight dayglow orange Lifeguards wear on duty. My last "civilian" wetsuit was more of a mockup of a wraparound toga—but I'd outgrown that years ago, and since taking my Lifeguard duties seriously, had saved Daddy money by not investing in a mantrap like Soloette's.

Soloette hadn't worn this one lately—there hadn't been any men as eligble as these around for a while—but I had to admit that she filled the suit rather nicely. She had bulges and curves in just the right places, and the suit seemed to play on that, making her more attractive than usual. In fact, you couldn't tell the signs of near zero-gee living—which infested everyone who lived here for more than six months.

I closed in on the restcove at a safe speed. It was about twenty meters away. I flipped and hit feet first, trudged up the stickum, through the electrostatic curtain, and into the restcove. I tried to sound cheery. "How do the suits feel?"

Justin answered my call, "Confining." He grunted and leaned over to tighten a strap, and began to float up from the effort. I grabbed a handhold, reached out and hauled him back. He looked bewildered, but managed to get out, "Thanks."

"Sure. Just be careful; it takes a while to get acclimated to zero-gee."

"I guess. But what do we need this gear for?"

"You'd boil if you didn't wear the wetsuit; the water tanks are a heat sink. The *Heinlein* doesn't have heatvanes or IR transmitters like the other colonies to get rid of waste heat, so we dump it in the water."

Justin twisted his forehead. "If you say so, but what about the mask?"

It dawned on me that Soloette was being awfully quiet. I glanced over at her, but she ignored me. I said, "It's for the low air pressure. The combination of the low pressure and high temperature puts the vapor pressure at just the right point for the water to boil."

"Why do you want to do that?"

Soloette dimpled and looked at Randall. She said, "So touri like you will come here. Since we're the water depository for the consortium, it's the only drawing point we have over the other, newer colonies. It's just another way to get more touri to visit."

I said under my breath, "And it still doesn't pack them in."

Randall tried to join in. "I don't understand why you can't just dump the heat into space. Isn't space supposed to be cold—three degrees, or something like that?" He looked quizzically at Soloette, who just smiled.

I rolled my eyes and started to explain—was it because they were *men*, or because they were groundhogs, that they didn't know better? As I opened my mouth, Soloette's face went vacant and she said: "I don't know much about the mechanics of it, but I do know it's fun to swim in boiling water."

Soloette was hanging all over Randall. If there had been any obscenity laws here, she'd be in the pokey for life. I asked, "How's his suit?"

"Couldn't be better." She almost purred. If she was bad at lunch, this was worse. It could get sickening.

"All right, then," I said. "Check your masks and we're ready to go."

I showed Justin how to make sure his mask was snug—something they should have checked at the equipment rental—then turned to exit the restcove. "When you leave, you'll feel a slight tingling. Don't worry, that's just the electrostatic curtain that keeps most of the water out, and the restcove dry. If you're scared, use the handholds. If you want to walk, there's stickum all around the port; just be sure to keep one foot on the stickum until you're ready to go into the tunnel. Otherwise, you'll float out and it could take a while to get you back."

Soloette spoke up, sounding intelligent for the first time all day. "Are you going to tell them about the buoys?"

"I was getting to that." I pulled a buoy from my waist belt. "There are two restcoves. One here," I pointed behind me with the buoy, "and another at the end of the tunnel, one kilometer away. If you're moving too slowly, or find yourself moving too fast toward either restcove, just toss your buoy toward the water. The little bugger is a waterjet with a homing device that makes a geodesic for the bottom of the tank. You don't have to go all the way to the bottom, of course, when the buoy pulls you down. But if you do go to the bottom, you can kick back up to the tunnel. I recommend that as soon as you hit the water, you let go of the buoy. I guarantee you'll slow down once you hit the pseudosurface."

Randall spoke nervously. "How far is the bottom?"

"A kilometer from the axis—about nine hundred ninety meters below the water's surface. That's approximate; the tunnel is about twenty meters in radius, plus or minus several meters, taking into account the pseudosurface."

It didn't help any; Randall seemed more upset. "Uh, nine hundred and ninety meters seems awfully deep to go swimming. I know I can't go any deeper than a few meters or so back—"

"—on Earth." I finished for him. "Don't worry. The pressure at the bottom of the water tank corresponds to about three meters of water on Earth. The difference is that our gravity is variable. It increases from zero at the center of the tunnel, to a max of about two percent of a gee at the rim. It's very comfortable, and you don't even have to worry about the bends: you can't get them at these pressures. Also, there are glowglobes floating every fifty meters apart, radially and axially, so you won't have to worry about having enough light to see.

"One more thing. If you get disoriented in the water, shoot out your buoy. It'll take you to the bottom, and from there you can get back to the surface by crawling to a wall. But don't try blowing bubbles to find out which way is up, 'cause it won't work. The bubbles move too slowly, and with the coriolis force acting on them, it will only make things worse."

Randall had a blank stare. I started to explain, but noticed that Justin nodded, so I closed my mouth. Soloette still hadn't pitched in to help me. She was playing the dumb-wahoo role to attract Randall, and it looked like it was working.

I needed to get back on my patrol through the tunnel. I briskly went through the remainder of the ingress procedures, and when there were no questions, led them out through the electrostatic curtain. Justin stayed at the edge of the restcove, still hanging on to the handhold. I had to speak louder than normal to get over the roar of the boiling water and the muffling of the mask. "Any questions?" They shook their heads.

Soloette called out, "I'll take them on out, Astar. Go ahead with your patrol."

"Thanks." I ducked back in to check the sonarholo. There were one or two Drifters in the tunnel and maybe half a dozen Jumpers actually in the water. No problem. I got back into the tank, crouched, then leapt out toward the far end of the tunnel and flipped over to watch Soloette and the guys as they receded. They left the restcove holding hands as a group and moved slowly into the tunnel. They weren't traveling anywhere near as fast as I, but at least they made the incursion into the water tank.

I flipped back over to see where I was heading as I approached the halfway mark. I was traveling a little too fast, so I released a buoy. As it hit I was jerked backwards, and headed for the water. I skipped on the surface and managed to flail my arms to get back on track in the center of the tunnel. It looks hard, but all it takes is practice.

I landed on the outer restcove and checked the sonarholo again. All Swimmers—Drifters and Jumpers—were still active. There was nothing out of the ordinary, so I jumped back toward the main restcove to take a blow for a while.

Soloette, Randall, and Justin were about a third of the way through the tunnel. I timed the buoy just right so I stopped about ten meters ahead of them. Soloette caught me by the arm to join them, slowing their progress even more.

As I started to speak, a Jumper broke water ahead of us, coming up from the surface, through the tunnel, and up into the water. She had done a good job of keeping control as she broke surface; Randall and Justin's mouths sagged in their masks.

The guys looked a little wary. "How do you like it so far?" I yelled.

"S'all right." Justin was craning his neck all around. "I feel as though the water will collapse all around me."

I laughed. "Don't worry—it can't. The worst that could happen would be for the colony to stop rotating—then the water would just float up into the tunnel. With your mask and wetsuit on, you're safe."

Justin flashed me a smile through the mask. "I'd like to try the water."

"Sure. Randall, how about you?"

Randall clung to Soloette's arm. He refused to answer, but Soloette didn't seem to mind. I turned back to Justin. "Want to Jump through the tunnel?"

"Huh?"

"All we do is get to the bottom of the water tank, kick off, and head for the surface. It's not as easy as it looks, though. You'll not only have to judge the pseudosurface when you pop through the tunnel, but you'll have to fight the coriolis on the way up. It will push you sideways, and the faster you go, the more you'll have to fight it."

"How do you get around it?"

"By stroking and leaning into the force. If you try to glide, you'll get all screwed up."

"Sure, when do we go?"

I glanced over to Soloette and Randall. She shook her head slightly. Randall didn't speak; he was trembling slightly. Soloette motioned with her head for me to go on without them. She shouldn't have any trouble if he didn't lose his head.

When we were about three hundred meters from the far restcove, I shouted to Justin, "Ready?" All he could do was grin and give a thumbs up. I motioned for him to grab his buoy. "After you toss it, just hold on tight and let it take you to the bottom."

"Right."

I counted to three out loud, then in tandem we threw the buoy down. It hit water and immediately started down. We had drifted up from the momentum of tossing the device, but as soon as the line grew taut, we were jerked down with it.

Justin hit water first—with an audible "ooof" as he was pulled under. (Once in the water I kicked to catch up, then grabbed onto his hand.) He nodded; he was all right. I motioned for him to turn off the buoy, and he complied, so we sank downward at a slower pace than usual. We passed several glowglobes on the way; Justin motioned excitedly at the first one, but quickly became accustomed to them.

I caught myself grinning. I don't know why—it sure wasn't because of Justin. He was okay for a guy: cute, I guess fairly bright if he was a programmer, and he *did* have muscles.

Then it hit me what I was really grinning about: I was getting caught up in Soloette's incessant drive to *find a man*. That's the last thing I needed. I shoved the thought firmly out of my mind and let go of his hand.

As we approached bottom, I tapped Justin on the shoulder and rotated till I was feet down, ready to absorb the landing with my legs. Justin should have been following my lead, but he remained head down, flexing his arms as though he was going to land with his hands rather than his feet. I frantically pulled at him, but he waved me off. The idiot wants to kill himself!

I tried to reach over to him, but he batted me away. I got ready to grab him and make a geodesic for the restcove after he cracked his skull. We passed the final glowglobe before the bottom. Two meters . . . one meter . . .

I hit bottom and collapsed to the deck, not bouncing. As I turned to grab Justin, he sprang from the bottom using his arms, and shot up, into the water. Zen! I followed, not holding back. He flipped over and started stroking against the coriolis. As we moved faster, we were pushed even harder in a direction perpendicular to our motion. Justin did a pretty good job of compensating for it.

The surface was coming up. I was wary about trying anything fancy when we popped up, so I decided just to follow Justin and shoot through the tunnel.

There was a Drifter right in our path as we broke air. I screamed for Justin as I tossed a buoy behind me. Justin did the same, and we both were jerked backwards to where we had popped out of the water. I let go of the buoy and hit the water.

Justin let out a whoop. He's hurt! I *knew* something would happen. I stroked over to him, grabbed his elbow, and hauled him up to the surface. We bounced around in the breaking bubbles as I yelled into his mask, "Are you all right?"

He was grinning. "Yeah, that was great! It was like having the universe revolve around you whan we hit the tunnel. I've never had so much fun—"

"You mean you're okay?" I demanded.

"Sure. Let's go again. I could do this forever." He must have noticed my look through my mask. "Hey,

Astar, what's the matter? We missed the person floating in the tunnel, didn't we?"

I pulled away, angry. "Yeah, we did. Now what were you trying to pull by landing on the bottom with your hands? You could have broken your neck." He shrugged and avoided answering. I pointed toward the restcove. "Come on, we can talk in there." I started the half-dog paddle, half-skimming it took to get up to the tunnel. Justin followed—slowly, because he was only using his arms—but he was still pretty proficient for a beginner.

When we reached the restcove, Justin stopped me. "Hey, why the sudden turnaround? What's going on?"

I recited the first nine 6-j symbols under my breath and tried to cool down. "Look, Justin. That was a stupid thing to do out there."

"So?"

Oh, bother! "So, look: I shouldn't have taken you down to the bottom on your first time out. And if I had known what kind of hare-brained stunt you'd pull—" I sputtered, trying to bawl him out, but I wasn't too good at it.

Justin shrugged. "I did all right."

"Sure, but you could have cracked your skull and killed yourself—and on my shift. Even if you hadn't been killed, it could have meant I'd never pull Life-guard duty again."

"So what's the big deal? It's not that important, is it?"

"Justin Kenlai, you just don't understand. I'm sorry. Perhaps you'd better get hooked back up with that friend Randall of yours. If you'll excuse me, I've got to make another pass through the tunnel. Just go into the restcove and stay out of the water, would you?" I turned to go, and just as I kicked, Justin grabbed on to a handhold and pulled me in.

"Now wait one damn minute. Just what the hell is going on? One minute we're having a great time swimming, and the next you're bawling me out for landing on the bottom with my hands. If you really want to know why I did it, I'll tell you. But I want to know what's wrong with you, first."

Daddy told me that I could freeze a Tokamak with my stare if I wanted to. He said I inherited that—and my looks—from Mom.

So I stared at Justin, and to leave no mistake about the matter, I froze the air in the restcove with my reply: "I *said* I have a job to do, Mr. Kenlai. Now, if you please." I kicked through the electrostatic curtain and into the tunnel.

I wiped away water from my eyes that just happened to splash in, making them all red and teary. As I shot to the other side, I nearly missed colliding with a Drifter. Funny . . . that's *never* happened twice in one day before.

Daddy was still gone, but I didn't mind. I liked being alone in the apartment sometimes so I could just think. The week had been going fine until those guys had shown up.

The door beeped angrily. I ignored it until I realized it wasn't going to stop, then flung it open. Soloette slowly drifted in.

"What's the matter?" she asked. I lowered my eyes and muttered something about being asleep.

Soloette nodded, obviously unimpressed. "Justin wanted to know where you were. Said he hadn't seen you since swimming yesterday."

"What did he say?"

Soloette frowned. "Say? He just wanted to know where you were, that's all."

"He didn't say anything about the swim?"

Soloette answered slowly. "No, should he?"

It didn't make sense—but then again, men never do. I tried to sluff it off. "No, I guess not." I pushed over to the kitchen and scanned the menu for something sweet.

Soloette floated beside me. "What's wrong?"

"Nothing!" I punched up a glucose-covered tofu bar.

Soloette raise an eyebrow. "Oh? Miss Calorie-Conscious getting surly again?" She twirled me by the elbow, sending us both spinning. "Astar, something happened in that water tank. This is your best buddy talking. Now what's up?"

After I got through explaining Justin's near miss with the Drifters in the tunnel, and how he was *a lot* better swimmer than I thought he should be, Soloette tried to chase down my tears as they started floating around the kitchen. We laughed, and she held my hands. "Astar, I'm asking Randall to visit me after he's through at Tycho Station."

"For how long?"

"As long as he wants."

I stopped sniffing and managed to raise a brow. "After two days? You're starting to sound like the holos. Besides, you're only seventeen."

Soloette ignored it. "He's not as intelligent as Justin is, but he's cute and he's well off. I think I can talk him into staying; I've almost convinced him to move here after he's done."

I bit my lip. "Soloette, if he comes back, are you going to propose to him?"

"You bet!"

"Before or after you tell him about the *Heinlein*?"

Silence. Then Soloette spoke with a trace of anger. "That's between Randall and me, Astar. Don't you *dare* tell him—or Justin, for that matter."

"Just be fair to him, Soloette."

After a few more minutes of forced conversation, Soloette found an excuse to leave. I never did eat that tofu bar. Darn those tears!

I saw Justin three more times after that. He took me back to the Bifrost the night after my talk with Soloette. I don't think he cared much for our home-grown version of tequila, but we had fun anyway. He wouldn't let me take him to any of the gravity decks, so we stayed in zero-gee the whole time, which was fine with me. And I didn't take him swimming.

I even let him kiss me twice too, but each time I put off the other advances. I mean, it just wasn't *fair* to him. It would never work with us. And besides, I couldn't tie him down here. I'd seen what happened to Daddy, and I've heard Daddy talk after he'd had too much to snort. He really misses Earth, and for all it's worth, I couldn't tie Justin down like that.

I was pulling Lifeguard duty on the day Justin's shuttle was supposed to leave. I couldn't believe it had been only three days.

I sailed through the tunnel, and as I approached the restcove, I caught sight of him. No way to get around it. I passed through the electrostatic curtain and removed my mask. I said, "Sorry I couldn't see you off; we're kinda busy with the new touri who just came in."

"I understand."

Did he really? I doubted it. "Well, thanks for everything—it's been nice knowing you." I stuck out my hand.

He stared at it. "Is that all? Astar, I thought we had something more than that going between us."

Oh, *bother*! I shook my head. "It was fun, Justin, but . . ." I tried to change the subject. "We can always keep in touch through Randall."

"Randall isn't coming back through here."

My jaw dropped. "What?"

"Randall changed his ticket two hours ago. He won't talk about it, but he's going back by way of the L-4 group. He doesn't want to lay over here again."

"Oh." I repositioned myself. "Did he say why?" Justin shook his head. I scanned the sonarholo. There was a large group—probably that new gaggle of touri—drifting in the tunnel. They were safe for now; I had time to talk. I drew in a breath. "Justin, I like you *a lot*, but I can't ask you to come back. And I think that's the reason Randall decided not to either."

"Huh?"

"Look. Soloette and I were born here on the *Heinlein*. We've never been off of it." I tried to make a point by switching gears. "What's the max gravity here?"

Justin looked startled. 'Why, two one-hundredths that of Earth. At least, that's what you told me. Why?"

I sighed. "That's why. I've *never* experienced more

gravity than that, and for most of my life, I've lived in zero-gee. You wanted to know why being a Lifeguard is so important to me? It's because it's the only thing I can do to keep in shape. Some people dance, some are tour guides: I lifeguard. If I didn't, my joints would meld from calcification and I'd turn into an oversized balloon. I can never leave the *Heinlein*, can't you see? I can't even go to other colonies. They have too much gravity at their outer core, and they're not built in decks like the *Heinlein*, so they don't have a zero-gee living space. I'm stuck here forever, Justin. *I can't leave*.

"That's why I can't ask you to come back. If something did happen between us, you'd be stuck here forever. And I bet that's why Randall didn't want to get involved with Soloette; he could never take her off the *Heinlein*." I wonder how he found out. I'll bet Soloette sure didn't tell him.

My voice trembled. "I can't do that to you, Justin. I've already got one man to worry about: my father. Since Mother died, he's trapped here because of me. The only time he gets away is on business trips, but he still has to come back to me. I can't let that happen to you."

Justin opened his mouth to say something when the alarm went off. *Collisin!* The sonarholo showed a large group near the restcove, skimming the pseudosurface.

I shot out the restcove, adjusting my mask while in flight. There was a gaggle of people—at least seven touri, judging from their hot-pink wetsuits—clawing at the air in the tunnel. Bodies were separating and I could hear screams over the roar of the boiling water. I couldn't tell what happened, but it's even money some hotdog Jumper probably thought she could impress them by Jumping through their group.

As I closed in, I spotted several objects tumbling away from the gaggle. Some of their masks were ripped off! There must have been four or five masks drifting in the tunnel, whirling aimlessly away from the crowd.

I picked out those who needed help the most and flailed myself toward them. I shot off a buoy, which skipped against the water when I stopped it, and bounced, putting me right in front of one group. I gathered up three kids and an adult and started kicking for the restcove.

Two more groups were splashing around. *Unspeakable!* We should never have let that many in here at once. And if anyone drowns, they'll close the water tanks forever.

I pushed the first group toward the restcove, kicking in the water to give me support. Although they were weightless, their mass gave them a hefty amount of inertia I had to overcome.

I got them on the stickum, pushed them through the electrostatic curtain, and bounced back for the other two groups. Two people were splashing around at the surface of the water, and a third twirled wildly in the tunnel. I made a split-second decision and went for the two. The lone one would have to wait. I let off my last buoy, managed to grab the two, and started hauling them back to the restcove. One of them was going nutso on me. I tried to slug him.

The groundhog ripped my mask off! I drew in several breaths of near-nothing. I tried to concentrate: just make for the restcove, and forget about the other one still out here. The silvery stickum delineating the restcove seemed light-years away. I stroked, kicked, and pushed the squirming groundhogs ahead of me. It looked as though we were going to make it.

A dark object shot out from the restcove over me; another Lifeguard must have been nearby. At least I wouldn't have to rescue the last one myself. We reached the restcove and I pushed them onto the stickum, then inside the electrostatic curtain, where I gasped pressurized air for the first time in a minute.

I ran my hands over the touri I had hauled in. Everything seemed to be all right. At least they were still breathing. I looked up at one in the first group I rescued. "How's the Lifeguard doing that went after your buddy?"

The touri coughed. "It wasn't a Lifeguard—or at least

not one in a wetsuit—just somebody who was in the restcove."

Turning my attention back to the tunnel, my body yammered with adrenaline: *Where's Justin!* The idiot had shot into the water, *sans* wetsuit, mask, or anything. The sonarholo showed them about five meters below the surface, fifty meters out. I grabbed a mask and shot out of the restcove, into the tunnel. I couldn't see anything below me—maybe they were farther from the side than I thought.

That's when it hit me that I didn't have a buoy to slow me down.

I started rotating, gyrating, and everything else I could think of, trying to hit water, but nothing helped. I was helpless—so I fumed all the way over to the other side. Finally reaching the farside restcove, I grabbed three buoys and shot back to the main restcove, craning my neck, scanning the water for any sight of them.

I thought I saw something, so I let off a buoy, dropped, and looked around—just a couple of kids from the *Heinlein.* I dog-paddled and skipped across the surface until I was up in the tunnel again.

The inner restcove was about fifty meters away when I spotted them. They had reached the stickum, and Justin was using his hands, trying to pull the touri past the electrostatic curtain. An arm reached through from the restcove and hauled them both inside.

I hit the stickum too fast, bounced, and headed back in the opposite direction. Cursing, I let go with another buoy, which grabbed the water, and I made it on my own to the restcove.

Breaking through the electrostatic curtain, I just made it as they were fitting Justin with an oxygen bottle. I reached over and touched his face. It was Mars red—at least second-degree burns. I started crying and they pushed me away. He felt so *hot!*

After what seemed to be forever, they finally started to move him out. I collared one of the medics and demanded, "Is he all right?"

Justin coughed. I pushed my way to him. He was

barely audible as he bleared at me and grinned. "It takes a lot more than a little swimming pool to kill this ole boy."

I held his head in my hands. "You stupid . . ." I was at a loss for words; if Daddy could see me now, he'd faint. "Why did you do it?"

The medics tried to move him, but Justin stopped them. He coughed again and said, "You were in trouble, and the kid might have died."

"Still—!"

He made an effort to pat my arm. "And I didn't get a chance to finish what we were talking about."

And *I* thought I switched gears fast! Oh, no. Tears started to well in my eyes. "I already told you, Justin. I *can't*—"

"Let me finish," he interrupted. "You made a comment about my arms. Why do you think I never use my feet to push off . . . or to swim with . . . or why I never go down to your gravity decks? Because I *can't*, that's why. Look, Astar, I've been paralyzed from the waist down since I was a child. I was in a diving accident and the doctors couldn't grow the nerve endings back. Back on Earth, the only thing I can do is work with my arms.

"But here I'm a whole person . . . and if I come back, I won't be trapped. It's the only place I can be like everyone else. Now will you at least give me a chance when I come back?"

Funny. To this day, I can't ever recall saying yes to him. As they moved him to emergency, I think I was crying too hard to remember.

But I do remember everyone in the restcove clapping.

HOW TO STOP A SPACE PROGRAM

In the late 50's, the Russians made a major mistake: they made a big deal of their fledgling rocket program. Their aim was to strike fear of the Soviet Monolith into the heart of the imperialists. They achieved the same result as the Japanese at Pearl Harbor. In the words of one worried Japanese admiral: "We have awakened a sleeping giant, and filled him with a terrible resolve."

Since then a major goal of Soviet diplomacy has been to lull the giant back to sleep. Now it would seem that the emphasis has gone from lulling the giant to sleep to putting him to sleep.

One further note: Harry's views regarding the relative likelihood of actual physical sabotage are his own.

THE SPACE BEAT

HOW TO STOP A SPACE PROGRAM

G. Harry Stine

How would you stop a space program dead in its tracks?

This isn't an academic exercise. Nor is it an intellectual pursuit engaged in by science fiction authors working out the scenarios for contemporary SF novels and stories. It's speculation based on the fact that the massive, multi-billion-dollar military and civilian space programs of the United States have effectively been halted. In little more than a year, the pride and joy of a nation, the most visible exhibit of its enormous and even overwhelming lead in the highest of high technology, and the confident symbol of its faith in the future and the frontier is gone.

How? Why? What happened?

As I mentioned above, I can only speculate.

However, the space program could have been brought to its knees accidentally through a perverse combination of bizarre circumstances—bad engineering, poor management, and political shenanigans.

On the other hand, it *might* have been deliberately brought to its knees.

193

Let's look at the various factors which could accidentally or deliberately bring the American space program— or any other government project—to a standstill:

1. SMAT—sabotage, mutiny, attack, and terrorism.
2. Dis-information.
3. International legal developments.
4. The American negative-power system.
5. Simple garden-variety overconfidence—the tortoise-hare syndrome.
6. Ordinary bureaucracy.

The first three factors depend upon either outside intervention or a hugely dissatisfied domestic faction. The last three need no external forces; we are perfectly capable of activating those all by ourselves, and we've done it before. But they could be encouraged and thus used by either domestic or foreign elements whose goals were to bring the space program to a halt.

First of all, it is very difficult for me to understand why any American would want to halt the space program, Senator Proxmire notwithstanding. While there were and still are those people who believe that we "shouldn't spend all that money in outer space"—we should spend it on *their* pet projects instead—the opinion polls for the last ten years have shown that the American people support the space program. For one thing, most of us feel in our gut that it's the new frontier, the adventure of our age, and the one government program that makes us feel good about ourselves as a nation. The anti-space people who were so vocal during the Apollo moon landings have almost disappeared. Or they've gone underground. They were only one aspect of the general anti-technology and anti-intellectual movement of those times.

Any American who wanted to stop the space program would find it extremely difficult, if not impossible, *without outside help from other nations*.

Aha, here's the nub. Is there another country that would like to see the demise of the American space program, both military and civilian? Who? And why?

And, if so, what would they be most likely to do to bring this about?

As pointed out in some detail in the *Space Beat* department of the December 1986 issue, there exists in the world a nation of 272 million people under an authoritarian collectivist government whose economic and foreign policy are geared up to function on a continual wartime basis. This is the *Soyuz Sovietskii Socialistichestkay Republik*, the Union of Soviet Socialist Republics.

Most Americans engage in a great deal of wishful thinking about the Soviets. We hear a continual refrain that "they are no different than we are." While it is true that they put on their pants one leg at a time and are friendly enough when you get them away from a situation where they feel they're being watched, there is a very basic difference. *The Soviets think differently because of their language.* This is also due in part to their history and to the sort of authoritarian and totalitarian regimes that have governed them both in Czarist and Communist periods. Although they had a revolution in 1917, they simply exchanged one set of imperial bosses for another set of *aparatchik* bosses. The foreign and domestic policies of the U.S.S.R. merely built upon the foundation laid by the Czarist regime. They threw the rascals out for yet another set of rascals. These are the combined descendants of Genghis Khan, the Golden Horde, Attila, and the lords of the marches, who were never very trustful of those city and castle dwellers sitting there in western Europe in the security of Burgundy, Bohemia, Bavaria, and Britain.

The basic political and ideological doctrines of the U.S.S.R. are straightforward, have been openly published, and have never been repudiated. Very few Americans have read Karl Marx, much less the works of V.I. Lenin, which form the very foundation of Soviet ideology. It seems strange that we do not understand or even attempt to understand the basic thinking of those who have said for more than three-quarters of a century that we were their enemies and they were pledged to destroy us, no matter how long it took them to do it.

Although the Soviets say privately that they really don't believe it any longer, their actions speak otherwise of them.

Furthermore, the Soviets have the motive and the means to bring the American space program to a halt. They may have done it.

As I say: speculation. But let's speculate in any event. It could result in nothing more than a host of paranoid notions. But, on the other hand, this might be expected when dealing with a paranoid adversary.

They're not paranoid, you say? Herewith a direct quote of their current military doctrine, which is by fiat directly derived from the military policy of the Politburo: "A new world war, if the imperialists should unleash it, will be a decisive clash of the two social systems and will draw into its orbit the majority of the countries of the world. The powerful coalition of the socialist countries, united by unanimity of political and military goals, will oppose the aggressive imperialist bloc."

And what do they see when they look beyond their borders and across the oceans? A strong, vibrant, growing, expanding world of free-enterprise capitalists who are rapidly outdistancing the socialist and communist countries in nearly every area of technology, production, distribution, standard of living, and vivacity of the creative and performing arts. They look at themselves and, since they aren't stupid, they clearly see that they cannot produce and distribute in competition with the Free World, much less even feed themselves. Much of their new technology comes from the Free World either by purchase or outright theft. I challenge the readers of *New Destinies* to tell me of *one* advance in science and technology that has come from the U.S.S.R. The Tokomak is the only thing I can think of; and when Western scientists found out about the Tokomak, they rapidly built them and improved upon them, extending the Tokomak principle to its absolute limits. On the other hand, from the West have come lasers, computers, integrated circuitry, biotechnology, rocket propulsion, jet propulsion, and composite materials, to name but a few. How many Soviet rock tunes make the Top 100 here and in Europe? How many Soviet science fiction novels have you read lately? The Bolshoi puts on a striking ballet performance, but it's *classical* ballet, with none of the panache and creativity of, say, Balanchine, or for that matter, the Harlem Dance Theater. Seen any great paintings or sculpture or architecture come out of the Soviet Union recently? Or at all? True, in the Soviet Union and its satellite countries, no one starves and everyone has a job. If you get sick, you get free medical care (even if it kills you; the Soviet space pioneer Sergei Pavlovich Korolev died undergoing an hemorrhoidectomy at the hand of Dr. Boris Petrovskiy, the Soviet Minister of Health). Even if you take away the KGB and other secret police organizations, the socialist countries are no fun to live in. Imagine living in an apartment building where you share both the kitchen and the bathroom with four other families. (I've been there and I've been in those apartments.)

So here we have this backward socialist totalitarian state which, in 1957 and 1961, made the mistake of bragging about its great technological feats in space, Sputnik I and Vostok, the first unmanned and manned earth orbital flights, respectively. Japanese Admiral Isoroku Yamamoto could have told the Soviets what would happen; they "awakened a sleeping giant and filled him with a terrible resolve." Less than a decade after the Soviets achieved their historic Sputnik launch, America pulled away in terms of its ability to do things in space . . . and held that lead for the next five years. The Soviets may be paranoid, but they are not stupid. It's unlikely that they'll make the same mistake twice.

As a result, the Soviets have been quite taciturn and low-key about their space achievements since 1970 or thereabouts.

Apparently, the Soviets decided that if you can't beat

'em and don't want to join 'em, at least don't challenge them.

And the Soviets also decided to use whatever means at their disposal to either slow down or destroy the American space program and thus eliminate the possibility that they'd have to compete with free enterprise capitalism in space. They have tried to do this openly in world forums so, knowing the history of the Soviet Union and its activities on the world scene, we should not be hesitant about considering that they may also have been trying for years to do the same thing covertly. When the opportunity exists to conduct redundant operations, why not do so? The philosophy of suspenders *and* belt is a good one, especially if you are trying to do something as profound as stop another nation from gaining a foothold in space.

Question: If you had the desire to destroy the space programs of the United States, and if you also had practically unlimited resources and unlimited time to achieve this, what would you do?

Answer: I would covertly try to use all six methods outlined at the start of this article.

Let's consider them one at a time.

SMAT—sabotage, mutiny, attack, and terrorism

Mutiny, attack, and terrorism are three aspects of SMAT that are likely not to work in this program because you could use them once and only once before security got too tight to permit their application a second time. Sabotage is another matter.

Many people immediately seized on the sabotage angle when three of our space launch systems failed in succession.

The most prevalent sabotage hypothesis involved "shooting a rocket"—i.e., a clandestine sharpshooter hiding in the puckerbrush with a high-powered rifle and putting one or more high-velocity rounds into the bird as it lifted off. I find difficulties with this hypothesis although it cannot be 100 percent dismissed. In the first place, no rifleman is going to be able to stay alive within 1,000–2,000 yards of either the Space Shuttle or the Titan-34D5 at launch. Reason? The sound levels are high enough to kill a person within 2,000 yards of the launch point. And one must have nerves of absolute steel; even when merely observing a launch, the impact of all that fire, smoke, and sound shakes you up. Even the most powerful of rifle rounds loses a great deal of energy at a range of 1,000 yards, and at that range it must penetrate the walls of a solid booster rocket; the thickness of the Titan-34D5 boosters is 3/8″ while the Shuttle SRBs have wall thicknesses of ½″. Furthermore, once the round has penetrated, it must do some damage. In 1954–1955, I was a test engineer on a project in which we fired .30-caliber ball and tracer rounds into RATO bottles loaded with composite solid propellant not very much different from the solid propellant used in the Titan and Shuttle. We never did get the stuff to ignite. It's the consistency of rubber. It *is* rubber. The combined binder and fuel of modern composite solid propellants is synthetic rubber . . .

Besides, neither Mission 51-L or the Titan-34D5 failed because of a bullet impact.

Mission 51-L failed because it was launched in cold weather, which caused the O-rings of the field joints to be harder than normal and the zinc chromate insulating putty also to be stiffer than required for good sealing. Mission 51-L not only flew a high-stress trajectory carrying more weight than ever before, but it flew through a strong wind shear 40 seconds into the flight. The SRB field joint on the right booster had a bad blow-by at launch, but the secondary O-ring sealed after blowing frozen water and some putty out; the joint opened up again when the shuttle went through the wind shear and encountered maximum aerodynamic forces, one right after the other.

The Air Force is not *exactly* sure why the solid rocket of the Titan-34D5 blew, but all evidence points toward debonding of the insulation from the casing. I've seen a lot of rocket motors both go and blow, and I must say that it's not necessary to postulate deliberate human intervention to account for most of the failures.

However, sabotage cannot be discounted, although some rather complex occurrences must be postulated in order to come up with a reasonable scenario. The Soviet KGB is a very powerful and covert force in international affairs. It is not beyond the capabilities of the KGB (or any other similar organization) to plant a *very* deep agent in an organization such as NASA or the USAF for ten to twenty years, said agent waiting only for one single instruction to do something. It would take more than a single hammer blow on an SRB field joint to cause trouble, but there are many points of vulnerability on a space launch system between cutting metal and pushing the launch button. Most of these are covered in the extensive quality control checks and pre-launch tests, but it's impossible to cover them all. I don't know what they are. I don't want to know. I don't think NASA or the USAF will tell you what they are, either. After reading "Shuttle Down," NASA Administrator James Beggs told me, "I'm not going to tell you where all the other system vulnerabilities are!" (He didn't need to; I'd discovered a lot of them myself in more than ten years of studying space shuttle design and operation.)

Dis-information

Formenting dis-information is easier than carrying out sabotage, and the KGB has an entire Directorate set up to do just this sort of thing.

Dis-information isn't something that originates in the Soviet Union and is heard over Radio Moscow. The most important and effective dis-information is that which is filtered carefully through several people and eventually presented in the various media by Americans. One of the most successful dis-information campaigns carried out by the U.S.S.R. is the bit, "The Soviet people are no different than we are." (We know they are; no American would long tolerate the sorts of regimentation and tight control that are calmly accepted as a part of everyday life by a Soviet counterpart.)

Another dis-information program is one which attempts to discredit the carefully studied findings of the Soviet Union which are prepared by the people we have hired to defend us against aggression in its various forms: the Department of Defense and the various intelligence agencies—CIA, DIA, etc. The implication presented by the dis-information program is that these people—many of whom have spent their entire careers studying the Soviet Union and how its leaders and people think and act—are somehow acting in their own self-interest to protect their jobs or the military-industrial complex they represent.

A secondary prong to this dis-information offensive is a corollary to the "they-are-no-different-than-we" approach, one that finds particular favor among American left-wing intellectuals and many of those whose time tracks are stuck back in the days of anti-government protests of the late 1960s. In terms of blunting the American space program, this dis-information offensive has taken the form: "The Soviet space program is a peaceful one that is far behind the United States' and nothing to be concerned about." If the Soviet Union doesn't want to rekindle the flames of the 1960s space race (which it lost), it obviously wants to downplay, hide, disguise, or otherwise muddy the picture of what is actually going on over there.

Such an article appeared following mine in the December issue of this magazine. I want to emphasize that I do not know Mr. Allen—I had to ask the editors about the man's background—and I do not accuse Mr. Allen of being a disloyal American, a Soviet sympathizer, or a Soviet dupe. However, I know his sources. Many of his facts are wrong. I have asked two real experts—Art Bozlee and Charles Vick—to rebut Mr. Allen directly, point by point. Mr. Allen has, unwillingly I am sure, presented dis-information carefully fed to him by others who may not have been so unwilling in their participation. Perhaps the kindest thing I can say of Mr. Allen is that he approaches the Soviet space program from an American point of view; to begin to understand the Soviet space program or anything else that they do, it is necessary to learn to *think* in Soviet terms. This is not easy to do. I've been at it for about thirty years. If I appear to readers to be strongly anti-Soviet, it is because I do not like what I have learned about the basic Soviet way of thinking about human beings, which is *not* the "wave of the future" but a continuation of the past clothed in the high-sounding phrases of dis-information and distorted meanings.

(For example, the Soviet definition of "peace" is quite different from ours. "Peace," according to the Marxist-Leninist doctrine, which still rules their thinking in spite of the fact that they say it doesn't, is the situation that follows the total victory of socialism over the forces of capitalist imperialism. Check it out, folks.)

George Orwell was completely right: "War is Peace. Freedom Is Slavery. Ignorance Is Truth." The meanings the Soviets have for certain words are different from ours and in some cases have actually been changed since 1917. Virginia Heinlein learned to speak Russian before she and Robert Heinlein went to the Soviet Union in 1960. She pointed out to me that some of the Russian words she learned here in the United States either no longer exist in the Soviet Union or have had their meanings changed; one of their Intourist guides could not read some of the inscriptions over the Czarist buildings in Leningrad while Mrs. Heinlein could and did.

Dis-information is one of the most insidious and difficult to detect ways to stop the American space program. But the campaign is there and well under way.

International legal developments

Yet another way to stop the United States' space program is to outlaw it.

Outlaw it? Who could outlaw it? It's a perfectly legal activity carried on for scientific and commercial purposes as well as for the passive defense of the country.

That isn't the way the Soviet Union sees it. And it is a matter of public record that the Soviet Union has attempted to get the U.S. space program outlawed and to prevent the expansion of free enterprise into space. It has attempted to do this for the past twenty-five years in various international forums such as the United Nations.

What is unknown and unsuspected by most Americans is that the Soviet Union is winning this one at the moment.

Look at what they've accomplished:

Back in 1962, the Soviets made their first move by introducing a treaty in the U.N. that would have allowed only sovereign states to conduct activities in space. Basically, it would have made private enterprise in space illegal.

Fortunately, we didn't buy that. But our U.N. diplomats and politicians compromised with the Soviets. We met them halfway. In 1967 the U.N. passed and the U.S. ratified the "Treaty of Principles Governing the Conduct of Activities of Sovereign States in Space, Including the Moon and Other Celestial Bodies." This Treaty of Principles did not have the power of international law; it was only a document in which the signatories agreed to certain principles. But it served as a foundation upon which other actual treaties could be and were founded. The Treaty of Principles said that nongovernment entities could operate in space but that the appropriate government must authorize, supervise, and bear unlimited liability for the private activities of its citizens and businesses in space.

The treaties that followed turned out to be mere exercises in international law because, in most cases, space technology hadn't yet made possible many of the things they covered. But they served the purpose of the Soviet Union in limiting the ways in which free enterprise could function in space. These treaties all sounded very good. They included one for the safe return of astronauts and space hardware, a treaty on registration of objects launched into space, and an extremely infamous one, the Treaty on Liability for Damages Caused by Objects Launched into Outer Space. The U.S. signed all but one.

Happily, the United States *didn't* sign the 1979 U.N. "Moon Treaty," which was introduced by the Soviet Union. This one says that the moon and all other celestial bodies cannot be exploited by private interests because they are the "common heritage of mankind." To the Soviet Union and most other U.N. members, this means "common property." Unknown to most people, the Soviet Union didn't ratify its own treaty.

And the Soviet Union is still at it. In 1985, it submitted a draft treaty that would create a world space organization for the purposes of preventing an "arms race in outer space and for reaching accords efficiently guaranteeing the nonmilitarization of outer space." This sounds good to most people until they realize it would mean letting the Soviets approve of everything Americans wanted to do in space.

These international treaties have already had an impact on American private activities in space. The Commercial Space Launch Act of 1984 was passed by Congress so the United States would conform to the U.N. Treaty on Liability. This has resulted in a new mass of regulations which give the federal government the right to prevent the launch of any space vehicle or payload that bureaucrats believe may not be "in the best interests of the national security or foreign policy of the United States." This federal law, an act of Congress, was slipped through without any space advocates knowing it. And it probably has far more restrictions on private space activities than the infamous Moon Treaty.

Treaties aren't the only means being used by the Soviet Union in its attempts to stop Western free enterprise in space, as well as the U.S. space program.

Only a few years ago, a Soviet space lawyer speaking at a meeting of the International Institute for Space Law of the International Astronautical Federation put forth the opinion that the intentional destruction of any single space vehicle, even a manned spacecraft, would not be considered by the Soviet Union as an act of aggression under the U.N. resolution which defines "aggression" as a "series of hostile actions."

At the same conference, another Soviet space lawyer pointed out that the Soviet Union believed it possessed a "zone of exclusive control" around its satellites, a zone in which other spacecraft could not enter. This is in violation of the 1967 Treaty of Principles which the Soviet Union itself sponsored! But the Soviets continue to make law as they go and interpret international law to their own immediate benefit. For example, the Soviet Union has stated that it considers all U.S. space activity "piratical" in nature, especially the Space Shuttle, which they say could ease up to peaceful Soviet satellites and snatch them out of space into its cavernous payload bay.

When the Soviet Union launched Sputnik 1 on October 4, 1957, the flight of that satellite technically violated the right of passage of an object through a nation's airspace. The rules in effect at that time gave each nation sovereign control over all airspace above its territory from the ground out to infinity. But no one challenged the Soviet breaking of this piece of international law. In the first place, no other nation could do anything about it. As a result, by tacit acceptance of the overflight of Sputnik 1, nations allowed other nations' satellites to fly freely in space over their territory. Now it seems the Soviets have shifted their position. General Alexei Leonov, the chief Soviet cosmonaut, recently said that the right of overflight was allowed by the Soviet Union only for peaceful purposes. The Soviet Union could, he said, revoke overflight rights at will. Leonov's statement was aimed at the NASA Space Shuttle, which has regularly been overflying the U.S.S.R. Astronauts with hand-held cameras have taken some revealing photographs of places such as the Soviet space launch center at Tyuratam. The Soviet Union has consistently called the Space Shuttle a military vehicle. In fact, the Soviet Union says the Shuttle is an antisatellite weapon (ASAT) because of its ability to recover satellites in orbit, and the shuttle is so-defined as a bargaining chip in the current Geneva arms control talks.

Furthermore, along these same lines, the Soviet Union claims that all U.S. astronauts are military personnel, regardless of their actual duties on the flight and the purposes of the mission. Some Soviet space lawyers have said that military astronauts are not "envoys of mankind" under the 1967 Treaty of Principles and the 1969 Rescue and Return Treaty and that the treaty provisions do not apply to military astronauts on military missions. Thus, if a Space Shuttle had to make an emergency landing in the Soviet Union, NASA astronauts might suffer the same treatment as U-2 pilot Gary Powers.

The Soviet Union is strongly supporting a principle of international law called "universal jurisdiction." This is a very broad concept that says if a nation's interests are threatened, said nation may unilaterally enforce existing legal norms even by the use of force. It sounds absolutely insane that a nation could unilaterally impose its interpretation of international law on other nations by force. But the Soviets go even further than that; they now claim that nations must conform to general principles of international law even if such law hasn't been recognized or ratified in the form of treaties by those nations! In their support of "universal jurisdiction" principle, the Soviets believe they have the right to enforce "international law" even if other countries haven't recognized such law.

Looking at the overall international law picture, only one reasonable, rational, logical conclusion can be drawn: The Soviets are laying down an international legal basis for literally outlawing the American space program. Furthermore, they are slowly establishing a basis whereby they would be fully justified under international law in using military force to halt a space program or deny the right of access to space to another country, especially if the recent space cooperation treaty is adopted by the U.N. If the Soviets can build a space-denial capability, they will be in a position to utilize the structure of international law they are also building. Thus, anything they want to do in space will be, in their terms, "legal."

The disturbing thing about this is that, like the disinformation program, few Americans know about it or seem to care much about it. Or they simply don't believe it.

And, even if they did believe it, trying to get the United States government to do something about it brings up another problem—the "negative power system" of nearly every government, and especially that of the United States.

The American negative power system

In any large, bureaucratic organization, there are many people who have the power to say "No!" but very few with the power, much less the inducement, motivation, or desire to say "Yes!"

It is imbecilic to try to get something accomplished in such a negative power system by frontal assault. There are far too many layers of no-sayers before one can get to a yes-sayer. NASA people themselves, members of one of the biggest bureaucracies in Washington, learned this back in the early 1960s and have since mutated to become negative-power brokers themselves. It is far easier to say "No!" and thus protect your anatomy than it is to give an affirmative answer and thereby expose yourself to the possibility of being wrong and authorizing it, to boot. Be cautious; that's the watchword. And we saw it blatantly exhibited by both the Rogers Commission and NASA administrators following the Mission 51-L disaster.

The negative power system of the bureaucracy of the United States government is perfectly capable of stopping the U.S. space program all by itself without any external help, which it is getting in any event, without asking for it.

Overconfidence

One might ask: How can overconfidence stop the

space program, in the current situation with all our launch systems down? With the Shuttle off-line until mid-1988? We're *overconfident*? Yes, because few people understand the full nature of the crisis—nay, *emergency*—that the U.S. space program, military and civilian, now finds itself in. The old fable of the tortoise and the hare is quite apropos in this regard. Our natural self-confidence has become overconfidence, blinding us to the realities of the Soviet build-up in space power. It removes all sense of urgency. We ran scared in 1957. We ran scared in 1961. We are not running scared now. In the first place, the Soviets are doing nothing to frighten us; in fact, they are providing a plethora of disinformation designed NOT to frighten us.

Ordinary bureaucracy

Finally, bureaucracy, with or without the negative power system, is stopping the U.S. space program in its tracks. We've read the horror stories about the $300 pair of pliers, the $600 coffee makers, and the $1,600 toilet seats. The media reporters and, thus, the American people don't understand what's behind these atrocious prices. It is NOT the government contractors making a profit killing. It is the fact that the government bureaucracy is covering its anatomy at every step in the procurement process. The bureaucracy has been told by Congress to make certain that the American taxpayer is getting his money's worth for everything that's purchased and that no one is making a killing selling shoddy or inferior goods to the government. As a result, the procurement regulations are a morass of checks, double-checks, inspections, quality control tests, and the like. The outfit that makes a better mousetrap cannot sell it to the government because the government cannot buy "sole source;" the supplier must release his specifications and other trade secrets to other companies so that suppliers may "compete" for the purchase or contract. Even when the contract is in hand, each nut and bolt must thereafter have a trail of paper that literally extends back to the miner who dug that shovelful of iron ore out of the ground in the Mesabi Range. At each step in the process of manufacture, there are tests and inspections to make sure that only the proper materials and the proper designs are used. Hordes of government and prime-contractor people are present to ensure that even an obsolete part is made exactly as before. The procedures are infuriating to many private firms who normally don't do the majority of their business with the government, but provide products and supplies and services to other private firms. In spite of the fact that many of these private subcontractors can provide better and cheaper products using their own standards, the government and its prime contractors will accept no compromises in their bureaucratic standards and procedures, even though they may be outdated and outmoded, even obsolete.

Yes, it would be different if performance were the criterion rather than a trail of justifying paperwork—if form, fit and function were the guides to a suitable government component or system. Then even a prime contractor could use off-the-shelf parts to replace obsolete or one-of parts, and so could the subs. The government and even the primes could then enjoy the benefits of competition among contractors and suppliers. Space Shuttle Orbiters might then cost only a billion dollars instead of three or four billion each.

In some detail, I've covered many ways in which the U.S. space program could be stopped. Observation: It is stopped. Therefore, what stopped it? You are free to draw your own conclusions, but it seems obvious that in America we have done it bigger and better than anyone else; we've let it *all* stop our space program!

We are coming up on the end of the century and the end of a millennium. If we don't do something, it may well be the end of more than that.

THE GRAPHIC OF DORIAN GRAY

The computer revolution has only begun; it will not be long before graphic systems similar to the one described in this story are quite feasible. As that happens, the question of what is real and what is not will become first a matter of philosophy and then of taste.

Alas that some have such poor taste. . . .

THE GRAPHIC
OF
DORIAN GRAY

Fred Saberhagen

Mutant palms, bearing rust-red flowers that smelled like roses, grew on the steep slopes leading up to the house, as did genegineered eucalyptus trees with real oranges growing on them. When the two men had climbed the stairs that led up from the private parking area to the terrace level, some of the treetops were at eye level, some even lower. Adjoining the terrace was the house itself. Like every other dwelling within sight of it, it was a big one, Spanish-looking, with white stucco walls and a lot of red tile, most of the doors and windows guarded with wrought iron bars that added decoration as well as offering some protection.

From the top of the stairs the two men walked a few steps forward on the flagstone terrace and stopped. Lenses were swiveling to observe them, from several emplacements along the stucco walls.

"Announce us, please," the older man called to the house. He allowed his voice to sound tired when he was only talking to machines. "Basil Hallward and Henry Lord. Mr. Hallward is Dorian Gray's graphics designer, and I am Henry Lord, his agent." Or going to be his agent, maybe, he amended silently. If we both like what we see at our first meeting. He hoped the hometronics system of the house could handle all that he had just told it, if the owner himself wasn't listening at the moment. Most of the new systems could.

Some of the lenses turned away. One set, adjoining the open entry to the house from the terrace, continued looking at the visitors. But neither system nor human being said anything in reply.

The two men continued to stand there, shifting their feet uneasily. This place was worth a bundle, Lord thought. It was a while since he'd had a client who wasn't hungry from the start. Not that you could be sure, of course, even with a place like this. For all Lord knew it might be burdened with a two-million-dollar mortgage that would be difficult to meet. According to what he'd heard, Dorian Gray had just bought the place with part of a recent large inheritance.

"Make yourselves at home, gentlemen," said the home systems voice at last, after what had felt like an unreasonable delay. It was a mechanical, subtly inhuman voice that sounded like one of the standard newer models. "Mr. Gray is expecting you and will be with you shortly."

"Thank you," said Lord. He would just as soon talk to the machine as to most receptionists. He strolled over to the balustrade that rimmed the outer edge of the terrace, gazing out over the view. Actually he was wondering whether it would be a good move now to light up a cigar. Some people were impressed to encounter a man who still smoked and others were put off.

Meanwhile, Hallward, as usual, was thinking about his art, his business. Just at the broad open doorway where terrace ended and house began, one of Gray's hometronic system terminals was sitting accessibly on a table. Already Hallward had set down his sizable toolkit beside the table, pulled up a chair, and was looking for the best way to get into the terminal.

Lord, continuing to size things up in his own way, told himself that it looked as if Mr. Dorian Gray might be still in the process of moving in. At the far end of the terrace was piled a collection of crates and boxes of various sizes, as if the stuff might just have been delivered. But at least part of the shipment must have been sitting here for a little while. One of the larger crates had already been opened, the plastic broken and peeled away from the contents it had protected. The contents consisted of a large painting, the full-length portrait of a man. It was an original oil, if Lord was not mistaken.

Hallward by now was completely lost in his technology. He had already opened the terminal, and set up his own portable computer on the redwood table beside it. He had even brought out an alpha helmet, though he wasn't wearing it yet. Somehow he was getting hooked into the house system. He was staring at the flat unfolded computer screen before him, and probing into the house terminal with a little plastic wand.

Again Lord turned away to eye the view. In the small private parking area just below the terrace, Hallward's utilitarian van waited. "Graphics to the Stars" was painted on both side doors. Across from the van was a regal blue Maserati, and close beside that an infinitely more modest Volks. The owners of any vehicles parked here at this hour of the morning, Lord surmised, had more than likely slept here.

To the west a great blur of high fog was still visible above the miles-distant Pacific, but the rest of the morning sky was as clear as a tourist's idea of what sky ought to be like in Southern California. Disjointed segments of a freeway, acrawl with traffic, were visible between other hilltop houses in the middle distance.

"Now, really announce us, you bastard," Hallward grunted with soft rage, at the same moment presumably compelling obedience with a deft prod from the plastic stick in his fingers. Good programmers, Lord had observed, seldom got angry at their systems; Hallward was definitely an exception.

This time an answer was forthcoming within seconds. "Be with you very shortly, gentlemen," boomed a male voice, sounding genuinely human, over the terminal's speaker. "Just settling up with the pedicurist." That last word was followed by a sound that might have been the start of a laugh—it cut off too abruptly for Lord to be sure. The impression he got from the voice was that it belonged to a man who wanted everyone to be impressed by his confidence.

Not unusual, but not encouraging either. The agent decided he might as well have the cigar, and stop worrying about what impression he himself was going to make. He took out a stogy and lit up. No use offering a smoke to Hallward, who was addicted to nothing but his programming.

Leaning on the marble balustrade, puffing smoke out into the sunshine over the parking area, Lord presently saw a shapely female form, dressed in a pink smock, emerge from some lower level of the house and go striding on high heels toward the Volks. He couldn't see her face, only the brown curls of the back of her head. Quite likely the pedicurist, he supposed. In a matter of seconds the Volks had vanished down the curving drive toward the public highway.

Still the client did not appear, or invite them into his house. Lord, chewing his Havana, strolled back across the terrace toward the muddle of packing crates. In the morning sunlight their tough plastic was as white as the stucco of the wall behind them.

Against that wall leaned the uncrated painting. The face of its youthful subject contemplated the California morning as if he were glad to have escaped the box. The subject was a very young and very handsome man, golden-haired and dressed in very old-time clothing. Maybe, Lord guessed, that style was from a hundred years ago. Maybe two hundred. Who knew? He could only hope that his client—if Dorian Gray did become his client—would be as good-looking as the painting. No doubt Hallward was a genius, and could create a beautiful personal graphic based on anyone who was ahead of Quasimodo in the looks department; but still, the higher the point you started from the more you could do.

The wooden frame of the painting was dark with age, and it looked as heavy as some old-time piece of furniture. It must have taken a couple of moving men to get the thing up here from the parking area; Lord wasn't at all sure it would have fit into the little elevator adjoining.

There was movement behind him. Hallward was looking up from his work. Lord turned fully around, smiling, to get his first look at his potential client.

Dorian Gray, wearing a thick gray robe, had just
come bouncing out of his house onto his terrace. It was
as if he were calculating his movements to be jaunty
and energetic, but despite his best efforts they came
out awkward, overacted. The good looks were there,
though; what looked like a promising basis for a program. Blond hair curled crisply around Gray's shapely
skull, as if it were still damp from an after-pedicurist
shower. Just as Hallward had described him, Gray was
tall, lean, and muscular, with a square jaw and a face
definitely in the casting category of tough-guy hero. The
subject of the portrait might have been his faggot brother.

Hallward was practically mute, as usual, indifferent
to all social happenings, and Gray, all the while nursing
a superior smile as if he admired his own suavity,
stumbled around trying to introduce himself to Lord.

Well, maybe together they could be made to amount
to something. Right now Lord could only hope. The
agent took charge of the faltering conversation, and
with his prompting to take up the slack everyone seemed
to hit it off pretty well. He began to explain to Gray
how, if they were going to be in this together, he intended
to organize their approach to the people at the studio.

Hallward interrupted them to announce that the light
was just great right now, and he wanted to get more
sunlight input into the graphics banks on which the
personal program would be based. Lord shut up immediately, getting out of the programmer's way; after all,
it was the graphics that were going to make or break
the deal with the studio when the time came.

Basil had his little videocam out, getting input of
Dorian in sunlight. The little camera was a real professional model, with more adjustments and controls on it
than the hometronics terminal had. With it the programmer swept the terrace from side to side, capturing
Dorian from every angle. More material for the per-

sonal program to draw on when it was finally finished and went to work; you could never, Lord gathered, have too much data in the banks. Personal programs were something new, only starting to have a real impact on the business, and he wanted to know as much about them as anyone could who was not actually a programmer.

When the personal program that Hallward would design for Gray eventually went into operation, it would work the mass of graphic material on Gray into shape, the best shape for any given scene, selecting some details and suppressing others, adding bits of behavior, putting grace into the gestures of the image and good tones into its voice, even making vocabulary choices that could improve its wit when the necessity to ad lib came up.

Not that Hallward ever showed any particular grace or wit in his own behavior. The programmer, the agent thought, was like a writer. He was a writer, in his own way, and something of a director too, developing characters for his clients, writing their parts and doing half their performances for them in the great play they had to put on for the studio people, the money people, before any of the actors ever got the chance to perform for a mass audience. And all that most of the mass audience would ever see of the performer was the performing graphic. The quality of the best graphics was so high that you would swear you were watching real people act, sing, dance, make love, or die on stage or screen. You would swear that . . . except that real people just were never really quite that good, that beautiful to watch.

Hallward grunted orders. "Now turn around, Dorian. No, just halfway. I want some more of the back of your head in this light."

Dorian, when he faced away from the videocam, was now looking directly at the old portrait that stood propped against the wall. Flicking a glance sideways at Lord, he remarked: "Wonder if the old bastard had a good life? Looks like it was a rich one, anyway."

"Old?" That was probably the last word that would have come to Lord's mind when he considered the portrait. His thoughts had immediately turned on how great it would be to be that young again. Of course you couldn't expect this kid to look at it that way. He was about the same age as the subject of the portrait had been when it was made, maybe twenty-one.

Gray waved a hand in a clumsy gesture. "Well, he'd be about two hundred if he was still around, right? Or at least a hundred fifty. He's some kind of relative of mine, way back in the family somewhere. That's how come I got all this stuff. From the last heir's estate when she died."

Lord moved a step toward the painting and took a closer look. The artist had signed it, in the lower left corner, but he couldn't read the squirrelly red letters. For all Lord could tell, the name might even have been "Hallward."

Now Dorian was being ordered to turn around again, then walk back and forth across the terrace. This was a long, uninterrupted scan, in which the camera caught plenty of input from Dorian. And from the background too; the sunlit terrace, the dimmer house interior of tile and oak beyond the open doorway, the packing crates. And the portrait, leaning almost straight upright in the California sun.

"I might suggest, Dorian," said Lord, "that you'd want to move it inside. This much sun can't be good for it."

"It'll be in the shade in a minute anyway. As the sun comes around."

And with that everyone forgot about the painting.

"We can take a look now at what we've got," Hallward told them, wrapping up his videocam. "Is that stage in there turned on?"

The three men all pitched in to move the heavy videostage from its site deep in the house out to a place near the doorway to the terrace. There Hallward's special cable, stretching from the hometronics terminal and his portable computer, could reach it. He assured the other two men that his computer had enough on-board memory to provide a fairly good presentation; and anything that looked good here ought to look really great when it was run on studio equipment.

The stage was set up just inside the house, in shadow; the polychrome lasers that generated its three-dimensional graphics were bright enough to stand up to anything but direct sun.

And then Dorian, wearing only a purple bikini brief, his robe cast aside, his muscles even bigger than Lord had expected, was standing on the stage, had somehow jumped up onto the low dais before Lord had seen him approach it.

And still, at the same time, Dorian Gray was standing just where he had been, still wearing his gray robe and slumping, a little behind Lord and to his right . . .

The robed man who stood near Lord in the sunlight was squinting slightly, and you could see the start of a small pink blemish on one of his rugged cheeks. At the moment the look on his face was expressive of stupidity more than anything else.

Lord turned his head. The image on the stage was without blemish, and taut with energy. It stood proudly erect, with one fist planted on a hip, the free arm hanging gracefully at ease. With a gaze of keen intelligence its eyes met those of Henry Lord, then moved on to each of the other men. It looked last upon its model, and its gaze rested upon him longest.

The voice of the graphic image said: "Good morning, gentlemen. Or, I suppose I should say, fellow workers." Lord supposed that the program, using input from the house cameras, could do fairly well in determining what humans were present, and where they were standing. Then a good program ought to be able to come up with a reasonably appropriate response. The tones of its speech were resonant and finely modulated; the voice of it sounded very much like Dorian's own, and yet it differed. There too things had been improved.

"Good morning," Dorian answered himself, automatically. The words came out sounding rough and awkward, almost angry, as if he were swearing in surprise.

Hallward was surprised too, muttering real swearwords, but joyfully. Lord realized that the programmer was actually delighted, and really astonished, by how good his own creation looked.

"That last input must have helped a lot," Hallward was murmuring to himself. "I don't know why. Son of a bitch, just look at this thing, would you?"

"I hope," said the holographic reproduction on the stage, "that we are all going to enjoy a long and mutually profitable relationship." Once again it looked each of the three men in the eye, one after another. And it didn't just say the words. It acted them, projected their syllables, made them the utterance of some great man on the brink of some tremendous enterprise. This thing was going to knock their eyes out at the studio, if Henry Lord knew anything at all about his business. This was going to catch them right by the balls and lift them out of their goddamn chairs. He had long since dropped his cigar and ground it out with his shoe.

Again Basil Hallward's hands were moving, easily and decisively, over his computer keyboard. Dorian-on-stage was suddenly fully clothed, garbed in the latest style of black formalwear, trousers turning into tights a little above the knee, white lace blooming at his wrists and throat. His onstage figure turned easily, one hand gracefully in his pocket, the other making a small, effective gesture. The image asked: "Is it time for us to join the ladies, gentlemen? Can't lick 'em"—here the stage face stuck out its tongue and contorted in a lewd grimace, returning next instant to smooth innocence—"if you don't join 'em."

"Tremendous," said Henry Lord, meaning it heartily for once, wishing he had a better word to use.

And now, suddenly, the image had an imaged bottle of champagne in hand. With a powerful, dexterous movement of its wrists it made the imaged cork pop out; with a dance step it slid its black dress shoes out of the way of the gushing foam.

Henry Lord had by now recovered from his happy surprise and started talking. It wasn't hard to be upbeat and encouraging about this. The only trouble was, he felt he ought to be talking to the graphic on the stage rather than to the man it represented.

Every once in a while he tried to get Hallward more involved in the conversation. But Hallward kept on staring at his little computer screen, and when Lord pressed him he insisted he wasn't sure that things were quite ready to be taken to the studio.

"Not quite ready? What is that supposed to mean? Baby, I've never seen a graphic that was readier than this one!" Not that Lord—or anyone—had seen a vast number of personal graphics in any stage of readiness. It was a new concept, just beginning to be well established.

Hallward still grumbled. He said there were things he hadn't figured out yet, about the way this particular program was working now.

"Anything that's likely to screw up a presentation?"

Hallward grumbled something.

"Well?"

"How the hell do I know? I guess not."

Five days later, in the sunlit afternoon, the three men were again together on the terrace. The presentation at the studio had gone off as well as Lord had dared to hope—but, of course, it hadn't gone in precisely any of the ways he had imagined beforehand. One thing he had long ago learned to be sure of was that such meetings never did.

Today a fourth person, a young woman, was with them on the terrace. Her name was Sibyl Vane, and she was under the patronage—perhaps for the obvious reason, perhaps not—of Alan James. James was the major power at the studio, or at least the most major power that programmers and young actors and their agents were ever going to see.

The way things looked now, Alan James was going to give Dorian Gray a contract. It looked as if he was going to give Basil Hallward a contract too, and Henry Lord was going to be collecting ten percent from both of them. But the contracts would be signed only—only—if Sibyl Vane—rather, the personal program that Hallward was now going to design for Sibyl Vane—appeared in the first commercial production with the graphic program of Dorian Gray. It was going to be feature length, for theater release, and the working title was *Prince Charming*.

As far as Henry Lord could tell so far, the requirement to use Sibyl Vane oughtn't to slow them down particularly. Dorian would have to share billing with someone. Whether Sibyl Vane was any good or not, Alan James had seen something in her, and a genius like Hallward ought to be able to connect with that something and get it to come out in a polychrome three-D graphic. Whether *Prince Charming* would be a hit or a flop when it hit the public screens and stages, was impossible to determine this early, anyway. Lord wouldn't have wanted to say that out loud to anyone in so many words, but it was so.

Already Hallward's preliminaries with Sibyl were over, and her first session in front of his videocam was well under way. Dorian, thirty seconds after he got his first look at her, had volunteered his house and terrace as a location. And there were certain advantages to working here rather than at the studio.

Lord thought that Sibyl, whose dark hair and fair skin made her look almost Taylor-like, ought to provide a fine visual foil for Dorian. And so far she had been willing to give the session all she had. It was beginning to look as if that might not be very much, beyond the naturally great starting points of her face and body.

She was growing increasingly nervous as the session went on. Henry Lord, having become her agent too, found himself having to calm her down.

"Take it easy, kid. This is only a test."

"*Only* a test!" Sibyl almost screamed the words, even though her breathless, ill-modulated voice failed to give them much real volume. She, unlike Dorian, was from a poor family. She understood as well as did Henry Lord that she could easily be throwing potatoes into hot grease for McDonald's next month if this thing didn't pan out, and if Alan James turned sour on her as a result.

"Take it easy. Yeah, only a test. I mean, if your first try doesn't look right, Basil can fix it up until it does." Basil, hearing that, gave him a look. Lord ignored it. This was a time for encouragement, not stark truth. "He's great at this, a goddamn genius. You've seen what he's done for Dorian. Take another look at that."

Something changed in Sibyl's face, as if a healing, restorative thought had come to her. "I want to do it right," she whispered to Henry Lord, "for Dorian too."

Holy shit, he thought. Both of them, really gone on each other, just like that. A complication we didn't need.

Hallward was frowning, and he kept on frowning, through the rest of that session and the next. Sibyl's graphic took shape. There was nothing grossly wrong with it, but Lord thought from the start that it would never attain anything like the magical quality of Dorian's. He was right.

Dorian said nothing about the difference. The truth was that he hadn't really looked at Sibyl's graphics yet, being busy admiring his own whenever he had the opportunity. But he took Lord aside, with the air of a man who had something he was just bursting to talk about, and told him how much he loved Sibyl, and how great and talented she was.

The agent tried to calm him down. "Great. Fine. But right now we've got this job to do."

Dorian struck his fist on a table, awkwardly. "If the job gets in the way, to hell with the job. I want to marry her."

"Marry her?" Lord didn't get it at all. Neither of these kids had struck him as the marrying kind. "And what're you talking about, the job getting in the way? Why should it?"

"I just said if."

For the time being the job went on. But Sibyl and Dorian could hardly wait until the sessions were over before they disappeared into the house together, kissing as they walked.

A number of additional recording sessions took place at Dorian's house over the next several days, mainly on the terrace. Sometime between the second and third session, Sibyl moved in with him.

Lord, arriving for a fourth session a few days after number three, made himself at home on the terrace and started to replay what he thought was the tape of the most recent Sibyl-modeling session. He didn't ordinarily look over his clients' shoulders as they worked, but this had more and more earmarks of a special situation.

What he got on the holostage, instead of a working session with either of his clients, was two Dorians and two Sibyls. A nude encounter quartet, like something from a hardcore porn show. You could tell the two personal graphics from the two recorded human bodies chiefly because the graphics were better-looking and more graceful. No matter what position they got into, they didn't sag or show little ugly bulges. And you could tell by which bodies really interacted physically. Personal graphics were still purely visual, not tactile.

If this was really porn-for-hire, then two of Lord's clients were earning some money on the side, and neither was paying him his ten percent. Even worse than that—perhaps—they were in violation of their new studio contracts, jeopardizing a lot of real money.

Lord watched for a while and relaxed a little, becoming gradually convinced that this was only something the kids had done for their own amusement. They must have got up there on the stage in the flesh, while their two images cavorted, and joined in, meanwhile recording the whole thing. Oh well, it was great to be young. But somebody really ought to scrub this tape.

Lord turned it off and thought for a while. He didn't really know what this portended.

Dorian came out of the house, wearing the robe he'd had on the first day Lord met him. His face was stony sober, white around the lips. Something had happened.

"What?" Henry Lord demanded, monosyllabic in excitement, jumping to his feet.

"She's gone."

"All right. Where? When? How? You had a fight?"

"I saw her graphic. I took a good look at it, at last, and then we had a fight."

"Her graphic. You mean this stag show that the two of you cooked up?"

"No. No. The one Hallward's trying to get ready for the studio."

"All right. You saw it. So?"

"So. You know something? She's got nothing, and I told her so. To think I was ready to marry her. I felt something for her, I really did. I felt a lot, but she killed it. What a pig. Even my own graphic was telling her what a pig she was." And moisture was welling up in the eyes of Dorian Gray.

"Even your own . . . what? That doesn't make any sense at all."

Dorian began to babble incoherencies. Lord murmured soothing words. He managed to determine that Sibyl was really gone, out of the house with all her things, Dorian didn't know where. The graphics of her—the official ones not the porn show—were still here. Lord found the disk and took a look at them. Pretty nearly worthless. They were really piss-poor.

Hallward, on arriving and being confronted with this fact, grew angry. "You keep telling everyone I'm a goddamn genius, but there are limits. Computer's like a movie camera, some people it likes and some it doesn't. I can only do so much to augment, and then the output starts looking like a cartoon character. That's not what the studios are buying this year."

After that encounter, Lord was busy with other clients and other affairs for several days. Hallward, much in demand, also had other jobs to catch up on. Lord did not see or hear from Sibyl Vane. She had dropped out of sight. When she was found, in a cheap motel room, she had been dead for two days. She had died of a pill overdose and it was pretty obvious that she had killed herself.

Henry Lord phoned Dorian as soon as he heard the news. The hometronics system answered, and the agent left a message, then hurried over in case Dorian was at home and just not answering his phone.

When Lord got to the house he found his client on the terrace, watching one short sequence of Sibyl's graphic over and over again. Her slender figure on the stage was chastely garbed, picking imaged flowers and arranging a bouquet.

"Dorian, I'm sorry."

"Yeah."

"It wasn't your fault."

"I was tough on her, that's for sure. But you know, I think I learned something about myself through all this. I think things are going to be all right now."

"That's good." Lord sighed. "That's the way to take it. I'm glad you're taking it like that."

"Yeah. I learned what it feels like to do something really rotten, you know? And I don't like it. So, no more. Today I start straightening out."

"Great. What's the first step?" Lord could hope that it might involve a new dedication to the job. It was time for another session with Hallward. And this new look on Dorian's face had graphic possibilities.

"First step is Sibyl. I'm gonna marry her after all."

Lord stared at him for some seconds in silence. Dorian didn't look as if he realized there was anything at all wrong with what he had just said.

"Dorian," the agent said finally.

"What?"

"I left a message on your system today. Didn't you read it?"

"No. I saw it there, but I . . . I was afraid it'd be something I didn't want to know." Dorian looked suddenly like a big, overgrown kid.

Lord was used to that in actors. "Dorian. Sibyl Vane is dead. As near as I could tell from the information that was given on the news, you're not mixed up in it in any way. She left a note, but I don't believe it said anything about you."

"Left a note. Then she—"

"Yeah. She did. You hadn't seen her since she walked out of here, had you? Talked to her, maybe?"

"No. No. Oh, my God. No, I didn't talk to her after she left here. I killed her, though, didn't I?" He stared at Lord. "I killed her, and I can't feel anything."

"Enough of that crap about you killed her. No one kills themselves these days because their lover tells them to get lost. She was a real flake anyway. And anyway, you don't want to step into the kind of public-

ity you'd get on this one. Especially not at this stage of
your career. When you're fifty years old and people are
starting to forget about you, then maybe. Right now no
one knows who you are yet. What we ought to do—"
He stared at Dorian.

"Yeah?"

"Call up Hallward. There's something new in your face.
I think he ought to try to get it on tape for the program."

They tried to get Hallward on the phone. His
hometronics system told them, after they had identified
themselves, that he had just left on a trip to Japan.

"It can wait, then, kid. It'll have to wait. For now
just sit tight. And don't say anything to anyone about
your fight with Sibyl. Okay?"

"Okay, Hank."

A day passed. Then Dorian, coming back to his house
from a long, aimless drive, was surprised to encounter
Hallward's van, coming down his long curving driveway
just as he was starting up.

Dorian stuck his head out of the Maserati's window and
called a greeting. The programmer grunted something in
return, and added: "I want to take a look at your master."

"What?"

"The master copy of your personal program. It's still
here in your house system. I want to take a look at
it—I've got a couple hours before my plane leaves."

"We thought you were gone already."

"I put that announcement on my home system ahead
of time. There were things I didn't want to be bothered
with. Let me see the program."

Feeling an intense reluctance, Dorian pulled in his
head and gripped the steering wheel. Hallward backed
his van up the curving drive and stood waiting for
Dorian at the foot of the stairs.

When both of them were standing on the terrace, Dorian paused and said: "I don't know if you ought to see
the master copy."

Hallward stared at him in astonishment. "Why in hell

not? I'm going to be taking it to Comdex in a couple months anyway."

"You're what?"

"You heard me, pal. Comdex. The big computer show."

"You could take another copy."

"There're shades of difference in all of 'em. It says in the contract I can designate one original and keep it. This is the one I want."

But when Hallward had the graphic up and running, he paused, staring at Dorian-on-stage in astonishment. "What've you been doing to this? Who's been working on it?"

"No one."

"Goddam it, it's changed."

"How could it have changed?"

"Look at the face. Someone's been screwing around."

"You should know, Hallward," said the graphic image on the stage. "You're an expert on screwing around. And screwing up." It laughed.

"Who's been doing this?" A vein was standing out in Hallward's forehead.

"Not me," said Dorian. "I'm no programmer."

"Neither is Hallward," said the image, and laughed again.

Hallward became abusive and threatening. This copy was his property, that was in the contract. Someone had damaged it. If the damage was something he couldn't fix, he was going to sue Dorian Gray for his whole farm. He opened up his terminal and put on his alpha helmet—a tool that allowed a degree of direct interaction between the programmer's brain and his machine—and got to work. A lawsuit seemed certain now. He had the evidence right here.

It was easy for Dorian to move close behind the programmer as he sat in furious concentration before the terminal, oblivious to everything else around him. Easy to bend over and extract a heavy mallet from the open toolbox beside Hallward's chair. The alpha helmet on Hallward's head was too flimsy to offer any real protection, so striking the blow was, in a way, the easiest thing of all. Then Dorian struck twice more, to make sure.

There wasn't much blood to be taken care of; later he would hose the terrace perfectly clean. Getting the helmet off Hallward's head was really the worst part. One of the little scalp probes had been driven right into skin and scalp and perhaps bone.

Dorian looked over the balustrade. All was quiet, and it was getting dark, but there was still light enough to see. It was as if the necessary actions had already been planned out for him.

He hoisted the body over his shoulders and carried it down to the parking area and loaded it into Hallward's van. There was another gate to the parking area, seldom used, that led to a road—a rutted track rather—used only on rare occasions by utility companies. Being careful not to leave fingerprints in the van, Dorian got the keys from Hallward's pocket and drove the paneled vehicle down the unused road until he reached the old mudslide area near the throughway.

Here the genegineered kudzu vine recently planted by the highway department was taking charge of things. The ground-hugging vine devoured petroleum products and other pollutants from the air and soil, and released the oxygen from whatever it came across. The highway was so close now that Dorian could hear the rush of traffic in the dusk, but the traffic was above the mudslide area and the headlights never came near. The last time he had been back this way he had seen another abandoned vehicle already half-covered by the relentless kudzu. Maybe in a hundred years, he had thought, someone would take the trouble to dig it out. By that time only a few plastic parts would be left. Meanwhile everyone thought Hallward had gone to Japan. Some time would certainly pass before that was straightened out.

Back in his house, Dorian discovered that Hallward had left a message on the home system this afternoon. The programmer said he couldn't wait any longer, and was heading for the airport.

All to the good. Dorian left the message unerased.

Then he went back to the stage and confronted the graphic image of himself that still stood looking at him.

Again the face of it had changed, more drastically this time. Yet it was still him, Dorian Gray, and this was something he could not allow the world to see.

"I saw what you guys did," the image announced, as its human model approached the stage. Dorian had a hard time forcing himself to look at it. The once-perfect nose of the graphic image was turning into something like the snout of a pig. The red inside of its lower eyelids showed, as if the whole face were being stretched down, and the eyes themselves were increasingly bloodshot.

"What do you think you saw us do?" Dorian asked it at last.

It raised a hand, moved it up and down slowly, and the fist as it moved turned into the blunt head of a mallet.

"Bonk," the image grated, in its once-fine voice.

"I see I have to do a little reprogramming on my own," said the man, and picked up the alpha helmet from the stones of the terrace. Then he stood there staring at the damaged helmet in his hands. No reason to panic because he had temporarily forgotten one detail. There were plenty of places where he could hide the helmet—the programmer might just have forgotten it here. No, because it showed damage, better to get rid of it entirely. Anyway, it would be a long time before anyone came here seriously looking for Hallward.

"You're not a programmer," the graphic said. "Before you put on that helmet and start screwing around, you ought to remember that. Your job in this partnership is to look beautiful. You do that well. You should leave the other jobs to other people."

"Maybe. Maybe you're right. We'll let the programming go for now. There's plenty of time."

"When is Sibyl coming back?" the graphic asked him.

"Sometime. I wish . . . oh God. Oh well. Right now, you get put to sleep for a while."

And Dorian Gray slept well that night.

During the next few weeks, the copies of the program of Dorian Gray that were working at the studio went on having a fine career. *Prince Charming*, with a new co-star, was in the can and ready for release. At Dorian's house, the original home copy, and the damaged alpha helmet, had both been hidden away.

The next time Henry Lord came visiting, he saw the orange Volks of the pedicurist in the parking area. Somehow he took it as a hopeful sign.

"That bastard Hallward," he said to Dorian. "He's always been flaky. They wanted him for publicity the night of the premiere and he wasn't around. Now no one can find him; there's even some doubt he ever went to Japan at all."

"I have a feeling," said Dorian, "he's not coming back."

"Why do you say that?"

"I killed him."

Lord gave his client a long look. "Still trying to get Sibyl out of your system? It's not gonna do you any good to talk like that. Listen, we're gonna need Hallward soon, or be looking for another programmer. With the grosses for the first week in the theaters as good as they are, we want to sign up soon for something new."

"You saw Hetty leaving just now."

"That her name?"

"She and I have kind of got back together."

"Listen, this time they'll want to team you with some established star."

"No. No, I don't mean I want to use her for a graphic." Dorian, for some reason, shuddered faintly. "I was on the verge of asking Hetty to marry me today."

"Jesus Christ, kid. What is it with you and marrying? Why complicate your life just now? If—"

"No, listen to me, Hank. I changed my mind. Because my life is so screwed up already, I couldn't drag her into it. And, you know? Deciding not to mess up her life too was about the best thing I've ever done. I think I turned some kind of a corner, doing that."

"Great," said Lord after a thoughtful pause. "I agree it was probably a wise decision. You've got the career to think of now. I haven't met Hetty but somehow I doubt she'd fit."

"Yeah," said Dorian, "there's the career to think about. The graphic career. I'm thinking about that more than ever now."

When Henry Lord was gone, Dorian opened a drawer and stared at the innocent-looking laser disc on which the master copy of his graphic image was now stored. It seemed a long time since he had looked at the graphic, though actually only a few days had passed.

He put the disc into the machine and called up the graphic image on the stage. He pulled the damaged helmet from its hiding place, and plugged it in, and fitted it on his head.

When Henry Lord came back to the house that evening, he found Dorian, with the alpha wave helmet still on his head, lying dead on the terrace. Circuit breakers in the system terminal had popped off, and Lord was alert enough to notice that the helmet appeared to have been damaged. Some of its wiring looked shorted, as if it had been beaten by a hammer or something similar. Dorian's head of blond curls looked undamaged; he wasn't going to touch him to find out.

"Henry Lord, Henry Lord," said the hideous graphic cavorting on the nearby stage. It was dressed in a Nazi uniform now, like something right from central casting. "You've got ten percent of me. I recognize you, Henry Lord."

"In that you have the advantage of me, as they said in the old days." Lord was letting his voice sound tired. "But I figure you're right about the ten percent." He stared at the shape, the face, the body, of the image. Might that thing once have looked like Dorian Gray?

He reached out a hand to a nearby phone, to call the cops, then drew it back. He didn't want to touch this house's system, or any system that had *that* in it. Something was wrong with it. He'd go down to his car and use his mobile unit.

First call to the cops, of course; and then, while he was at it, a call to someone he knew at another studio. Whoever had reworked that graphic up there, it had new possibilities. He'd heard there were plans for a remake of *The Hunchback of Notre Dame*.

RANK INJUSTICE

If war is too important to be left to soldiers, then surely peace is too precious to be left to diplomats—unless that diplomat's name is Jaime Retief! No? Read on . . .

RANK INJUSTICE

Keith Laumer

1

The ten-thousand-tonner *Expedient*, on lease to the Interplanetary Tribunal for Curtailment of Hostilities, was holed by a six-ton slab of nickle-iron just as the four hundred assorted diplomatic staff members aboard, from as many worlds, were taking cocktails in the main lounge, in expectation of planetfall within the hour. The shock, far aft, rattled ice-cubes and sent trays of glasses sliding along the hundred-foot heowood bar, dumping a beaker of Lovenbroy pale ale into the lap of First Secretary and Consul Ben Magnan, who leaped up with a shrill cry.

"Retief! That confounded chief engineer is inebriated again! I distinctly felt the jar as he mistimed his power change-over to atmospheric!"

"Maybe," Retief conceded. "But I'm afraid it's something more serious this time."

"What could be more serious than a drunken power-man in charge of re-entry?"

"A collision," Retief told him. "A mere bobble in thrust timing wouldn't open a seam in the bulkhead."

Magnan followed his glance toward a rent in the brocade wallpaper.

"A collision!" Magnan yelled before Retief could stop him. At once the cry was taken up by those near-by, who finished their drinks at a gulp and rushed off in all directions to spread the word.

"Where's the captain?" demanded a gaunt mantis-like female counsellor from Glory Eleven in a voice that cut across the rising tumult like a meat-saw.

"I *demand* to know what he's doing about this catastrophe!" she added, in case anyone was in doubt. She stood with two pairs of arms folded, staring around defiantly, until her gaze fell on Retief and Magnan. "You!" she yelped. "You people are Terrans like the captain! What are you doing to save innocent lives?"

"While, Madam," Magnan began, "I cheerfully acknowledge the accuracy of your charge that my assistant and I indeed share with Captain Suggs the honor of being Terrans, we are in no way involved in the operation of this vessel. Anyway," he added less graciously, "I don't see any innocent lives being threatened."

"You dismiss all these selfless diplomats as guilty?" the lady demanded, even more shrilly. "And of *what*, may I inquire?"

"You mistake my meaning, Madam," Magnan gobbled. "I have leveled no accusation against those present! Like yourself, I cry our captain culpable! Wherever *is* the scamp?"

"This here Terry done called Captain Suggs a scamp," someone commented loudly.

Retief touched Magnan's arm. "Let's go, Mr. Magnan," he suggested. "You're in a classic no-win situation."

"Go where?" Magnan demanded, bewildered. "We're trapped here aboard this frail perfidious bark just like everyone else! Unless, of course, you were thinking of taking to the lifeboats . . . ?"

"Back to take a look at the damage," Retief explained. "That was an impact aft, I think."

"In that case one would be mad to go aft!" Magnan objected. "If we're holed, there'll be no atmosphere!"

"We'll freeze before we asphyxiate," Retief pointed out. "Unless we aren't really holed—or if we suit up."

The irate Glorytian lady had stamped off in a huff and was eagerly collaring other bewildered passengers to demand action.

"There he is, the incompetent!" she interrupted herself to yell, as Captain Suggs hove into view from the crowd, a slight, rather bedraggled figure in soiled whites with four tarnished gold stripes, his face unshaven.

"Whassamare?" he demanded cheerfully, skillfully scooping a full glass from an adjacent table, at the same time depositing an empty. A moment later, he discarded another empty. "I gotta order all you good folks to disperse," he called to no one in particular. "Now, you, over there . . ." he waved in Magnan's general direction as the latter approached him. "Mister Magnan, ain't it? Used to be good on names, Mr. Mumble. You're a Terry like me. I hereby appoint you to head up a panel to investigate whatever clobbered my command here. Aft. We been struck aft," he elaborated. "Pretty good smack, too, registered prolly a few tons doing twenty thou or better." He turned abruptly and bolted, shooing confused bureaucrats from his path, ignoring the chorus of complaints.

"Why, the man is drunk, like his Powerman," Magnan commented in an awed tone, as he returned to Retief's side. "I shouldn't wonder if he isn't personally responsible for the malfunction, whatever it is."

"He's had a few," Retief agreed, "but he's spent forty years in space; when he says a few tons of something have hit us, I'm inclined to believe him."

"Oh, dear," Magnan moaned, then, more decisively, "But that's highly unlikely. I read somewhere that the density of matter in interplanetary space in this system is about like six jelly-flies in Marsport's Grand Concourse! Still, it's Captain Suggs's responsibility, and he's doing nothing!"

"I guess that's something, ain't it, Mr. Magnan?" Suggs's blurry voice spoke up from just behind Magnan. "When doing nothing is the best thing to do, I do it!"

"You call doing nothing doing something?" Magnan demanded, whirling to confront the Skipper.

"Sure," Suggs acknowledged cheerfully. "Can't take her into atmosphere if she ain't spaceworthy, and our best bet is just to stay in parking orbit until they send a damage-control party up to fix everything. Already got off a distress bleep," he added. "Asked for approach number, too; they tole me to stay put."

"Stay put?" Magnan echoed. "Do you realize, sir, that in mere minutes an ITCH conference of stupendous importance is about to begin without me?"

"Guess keeping alive until he'p gets here is more important than your eczema," Suggs commented indifferently. "So long, Mr. Magnan, see you around—and go see my pharmacist's mate; he'll fix that rash."

" 'Rash,' indeed!" Magnan burst out. He turned to Retief. "Retief!" he hissed. "I'm surprised that in this moment of crisis you're as passive as the rest! I expected that at the least you'd nip aft and look into the captain's allegation that we've been involved in a collision!"

"Aren't you coming along, sir?" Retief asked as he put his glass on a passing tray. Magnan recoiled as if from a blast of wintry air.

"Hardly!" he huffed. "My place as Transit Director is here, maintaining order until you return to report that all is well. Listen to them," he switched subjects with breathtaking agility. "They're already at daggers drawn over who's to take charge! Pushy of them, when it's clear you have them all outranked, if not in your diplomatic status as a lowly Foreign Service Officer of Class Two, then in your position as Chief of the Armed Forces of your native world!"

Several sets of eyes, some stalked, others recessed light-sensitive pores, turned toward the two Terrans.

A large man with crooked teeth stepped forward; Magnan turned away after a single disapproving glance.

"Kouth is the handle," the newcomer said in a gravelly bass voice which seemed to reverberate among the chandeliers. "You can call me 'Boss.'" Magnan drew back hastily.

"'Kouth' may be, as he says, the name," he commented to no one in particular, "but *not* the manner."

"Skip that, Bub," Kouth rumbled. "What we go to do, we got to set this here tub down on the inner moon. That's why I'm taking over." His gaze shifted to Retief. "You look like a pretty strong boy," he commented. "So you'll be my First Mate. Now, we better amble on back up to the bridge and set course fer Old Moon."

"Here, fellow!" piped a small, cootie-like chap in elaborate diplomatic formal dress, as he popped up between the two much larger beings,

"I'm Ambassador Phoop," he clarified. "And as senior Career Ambassador aboard, I outrank all of these military chaps; why, even a mere Career Minister ranks with and after a buck general." In a less heated tone, he continued: "First, I must organize you, and dispatch a damage-control party. You—" he pointed at Kouth's knee, "—and you as well," he added as he stepped back to stare up at Retief's six-foot-three towering over him. "You two lads are hereby designated as top sergeants to shape up this mob into squads of ten individuals, regardless of species, pigmentation, or mystical alignment with regard to the Big Goober in the Sky."

"To fail to grasp the enormity of your cheek, Mr. Ambassador," a breathy Groaci voice spoke in the local stunned near-silence which had followed Phoop's pronouncement. "To admire the breath-taking audacity of such a claim to primacy," the Groaci went on, "but of course I as an Assistant UnderSecretary to Foreign Affairs, am senior diplomat aboard this vessel and as such naturally take command during the indisposition of Captain Suggs!"

"Unspeakable!" Ambassador Phoop squeaked. "It was none other than yourself, Mr. Secretary, who plied our captain with strong drink, which I myself abjure, of course, thus rendering him incapacitated in this hour of crisis!"

"What do your curious drinking habits have to do with Captain Suggs's lack of competence, small sir?" A grossly rotund Vorplisher demanded, then turned his attention to sampling the foam on a tankard of ale. "I'm Major Genreal Blow," he added, "and I'm in command here."

"You distort my meaning, sir!" Phoop squeaked, ignoring the general. "*I* had nothing to do with this Suggs's dereliction of duty!"

"This here is all academic like they say," Kouth put in bluntly. "This here is *my* turf; I'm a Stugger borned and bred, whatever that is, which that's the planet Stug figuratively like looming up on the hypothetical forward screens at the moment. I and my boys are the only native-borned Stuggies aboard, so I'm in charge here. Any objections, any of youse pansies?"

"Plenty!" Major General Blow boomed as he charged, impacting Kouth like a runaway fork-lift colliding with a semi loaded with gravel. Kouth responded by backing into a table covered with trays of empties, then hoisted the belligerent Vorplisher above his head and threw him into the faces of the fascinated onlookers.

"Some guys has wrong ideas about when to get tough," he commented. "Now the rest o' you recruits line up agin the wall over there!"

" 'Wall,' indeed!" an ornately-uniformed spider-lean fellow from Wolf Nine, a minor world listed as Booch in the New Catalog, spoke up indignantly. "It's clear, sir, you are unqualified to serve as a deck-swabber last class, to say nothing of assuming command of a deep-space vessel in dire distress! In navel parlance that's called a 'bulkhead'," he finished quite calmly.

After a moment of silence, punctuated by a single " 'ear, 'ear!" from somewhere back in the crowd, the skinny chap went on:

"I myself am Grand Captain of Avenging Flotillas Blance, representing the Boochian Combined Armed Forces. It is clear that no one here can challenge my credentials as ranking Being aboard!" He stepped out of line, leaned tête-à-tête with another of like physique, then made shooing motions.

"What I hear," a squat, burly, green-furred code clerk attached to the Hondu Military Attaché put in, "Booch ain't *got* no navy. Nor no other armed forces, neither."

"What is at issue here, my man—" Phoop started, only to be cut off by the Hondu with a peremptory gesture.

"I ain't no man, Cap, and I shore ain't yourn!" he corrected the diplomat.

"—is not a comparative assessment of military appropriations," Phoop continued, undaunted, "but a simple matter of personal rank."

"A Grand Captain of an imaginary fleet don't outrank a Deck-swabber Last Class in a first-class fighting outfit," the Hondu declared, "Like me. So you can go into a early retirement, Admiral, DS-LC Gloon is here!"

Before Grand Captain Blance could reply, he was thrust aside unceremoniously by Kouth, who in turn was jostled by General Blow as both contenders for leadership stepped forward to advance their claims.

"We set her down nice and easy on Old Moon," Kouth declared loudly.

"I have determined—" General Blow began, only to be cut off by Admiral Blance.

"A land-lubber, though of two-star rank, has no place in command in space!" he stated, but his further remarks were cut short when Gloon elbowed the wafer-thin Boochian, then to his astonishment was at once knocked flat by a snake-swift blow from the Grand Captain.

"You will not venture again to lay hands on the person of a Boochian Grand Captain," the indignant officer said harshly.

"I never laid no hand on nobody," Gloon objected as he regained his feet with an assist from a slightly smaller Hondu in NCO whites. "All I laid on you was a elbow!"

"The principle is the same, DS-LC!" Blance dismissed

the matter. "Now, I think you may as well take charge of that half of this mob of civilians, and form up in a column of ducks!"

"I don't guess no DS-LC is gonna fall me in," General Blow objected. "I done my basic thirty years ago, and I demand—"

What the general would have demanded was not to be known, as at that moment the hitherto relatively orderly crowd dissolved into a melee, as officious drill sergeants spot-promoted by half a dozen competing captains *pro tem* attempted to form the rank-concious civilian diplomats into manageable units, Kouth's polyglot supporter being the most vocal.

Magnan clutched at Retief's sleeve. "Now, for sure, it's time to slip away," he summarized. "And I've decided, yes, I shall accompany you. I don't care for that Kouth person at all. So, shall we?"

2

"It's as good a time as any," Retief agreed, fending off a belligerent Yillian with ornate rank badges, sending him reeling into a fist-fight, in which the grey-skinned flag officer cheerfully joined.

"This is all most unseemly!" Magnan exclaimed, stepping aside barely in time to avoid being swept up in a three-being wrestling match. "As designated Director of this party, I myself—"

"Forget it, Ben," a lowly Terran corporal of the Jawbone Planetary Defense Force advised just before he was struck down by a Haterakan supreme Overlord of Irresistible Armadas, a rank equivalent to a Bloovian maker of ritual Grimaces, Third Class, Magnan noted.

"Cheeky to a degree," Magnan sniffed, slapping the hypothetical dust of the near-encounter from the lapels of his Late Early Mid-morning cutaway. "It's no wonder," he added in an aside to Retief, "that Sector has reported piracy and wreckers operating in this region, if that Boss Kouth is any example of the local ruling class."

"I heard that crack, Ben," a nosy Groaci Consular Officer informed the Terran. "If you Terries are so worried about dacoits and corsairs operating in Stuggish space, hows come you decided to stage this ITCH convention right here in the middle of No Being's Land, hah?"

"Simplicity itself, Thiss," Magnan replied loftily. "It is precisely because this region is a hotbed of deep-space crime that we selected it as the appropriate site for talks designed to diminish that very problem."

"Hold! Enough!" a deep voice boomed out. All eyes turned toward a two-ton Fustian elder who had risen from his usual torpor to loom over the lesser beings all around him.

"I," he stated, "am Field Marshall Whelk, and if it's rank you're looking for, I've got rank I haven't even used yet. Get thee hence, all but you—" he pointed a stubby but massive clawed hand at Kouth—"and you— and you," designated the Hondu spac'n as well as Admiral Phoop. "You fellows are my lieutenants," he explained in a tone which invited no discussion. "Now restore order here, and do it quietly."

"I tell ya we gotta make fer Old Moon," Kouth stated boldly. He turned to address his appeal to the raggedly formed-up crowd, Welk having already resumed his slumber. "It's our only chance!" Kouth declared.

"And I say we hold orbit like the cap'n said!" someone rebutted from the rear rank. "Rescue party's on the way!" A barrel-shaped, deep-blue Krakan swaggered forth to confront Kouth.

Kouth motioned, and half a dozen of his adherents emerged from the crowd to surround the Krakan. While everyone was engrossed in the power struggle, Magnan ducked out a side door and Retief accompanied him.

3

The passage leading aft past Stores to Power Section was silent and deserted. Then a big spac'n in soiled whites with the nine blue stripes of a Chief Master

Spaceman First, Stuggish Merchant Marine, stepped from a side passage and came toward the two civilians.

"No crust-huggers allowed here," he announced in a tone of weary authority, then halted, blocking the passage. "I'm McCluskey," he added. "*Chief* McCluskey, to you."

"Where did it hit?" Magnan inquired in a tone which was almost a squeak. "Do step aside, my man," he went on, "we're on our way to inspect the damage."

"I guess maybe you don't hear so good, chum," the Chief announced. "I tole youse onct, no civilians in my Power Section, OK? So you better just turn around and tip-toe back to yer easy chairs. Now, before I start to get annoyed and all."

"Do step aside, I say, fellow," Magnan repeated. "We've no time for gossip just now."

"Oh, yeah?" the powerman came back truculently. "Well, I'm telling you, Junior, you got no business here aft. Youse could get hurt. Hot stuff could be sloshing around all over the place. Shoo! Leave us pros deal with this here."

" 'Might be,' you say," Magnan echoed. "I think we need a trifle more specific assessment of the status than that." Magnan paused, then clutched Retief's arm. "Goodness," he gushed. "What if this gorilla is right? We could receive a fatal blast of radiation as soon as we open the hard-seal doors."

McCluskey advanced a step toward Magnan, seeming, as he did so, to expand to fill the narrow passage. "I guess you never called me a gorilla," he commented mildly.

" 'Guerrilla,' " Magnan corrected breathlessly. "An heroic freedom fighter, that is. One mustn't go putting words in the mouths of others," he added.

McCluskey showed Magnan a fist as big as a cabbage. "It ain't words I'm thinking of putting in yer mush, Cull, and I never fought no freedom. You got two seconds; one t'ousan and one, a t'ousan and two—"

Magnan turned to flee, but rebounded from Retief and staggered back directly into the big powerman, who fended him off, looking puzzled.

"Never figgered the little shrimp to charge me," he mused aloud. "Backwards, too. Must be some new kinda martial arts for weaklings or like that." He picked Magnan up and paused as if uncertain what to do next.

"You'd better put Mr. Magnan down, Chief," Retief suggested gently. "Otherwise he might decide to unleash his ire on you."

"Where?" McCluskey looked over, through, and past Retief. "I don't see no leashed ire, nor no other kind neither. Had a pal once, had this here catamount on a leash, spose to be trained and all. Onney one day it got hungry and ate my pal's leg off before he could remember to say 'heel.' "

"That's a very melancholy anecdote, Chief," Retief said. "Now, about the damage aft. What hit us? And precisely where? Did it penetrate the impact hull? Is there any radioactive leakage?"

"Well, now, just a minute, Bud. What hit us, we got clobbered by a iron-nickle, looks like, and it come through the hull, all three layers and the containment bulkhead and busted the coolant system wide open, after which I didn't see no more, cause I still plan to get hitched some day and father some little deckhands, which I don't want 'em to have two heads and all."

"Reasonable enough, Chief," Retief acknowledged. "But suppose we just suit up and go take a closer look."

"Well, old Cap Suggs will split a gusset when he hears about it," the Chief grumped. "But I guess somebody got to do somethin. So, OK. Equipment lockers is right over there."

Minutes later all three men were fully clad in what McCluskey referred to as 'lead underwear.' Magnan complained bitterly at the poor fit and excessive weight of the R-garment, a Mark XV.

"One can't even breathe in this contraption," he carped. "To say nothing of walking, not to mention doing anything useful."

"Why don't you just lie down here," Retief suggested, indicating a long, padded table intended for use during fitting of the custom-tailored suits. "The Chief and I will handle it."

"Hey, I just come to think," McCluskey interjected. "I ain't said you'se are goin' *in* there with me. The both of youse better wait right here. I'll take a quick look-see and let you know what the status is."

Retief went past the Chief's bulky, R-suited figure, and cycled the entry hatch into Power Section. McCluskey, still objecting, followed. Magnan lay back with a groan.

"Hurry, Retief," he called after his departing colleague. "I'm sure I'm going to suffocate if I'm not released from this strait-jacket within the minute."

Retief paused to call over his shoulder. "Just take deep breaths, Mr. Magnan. I'll be back before you know it."

"Unless these gammas get to you, first," McCluskey added cheerfully as he clanged the hatch behind him.

Retief went across to the gaping frost-rimmed rent caused by the entry of the object the ship had struck; it was approximately sealed by a slab of tough, versatile plastron, which had been slapped in place by the automatics immediately after the penetration.

"That there rubber'll hold OK for a hour or two, maybe, before it cryodegrades," McCluskey estimated. "Before then what I got to do, I got to get a class three temporary in there."

"Meanwhile," Retief told him, "you'd better start up the contain-and-exhaust gear."

"Sure," the chief acknowledged. "I was goin' to."

"That why you were out in the passage, headed forward?" Retief inquired pointedly.

"That sounds to me like some kind of crack," McCluskey announced, and moved toward Retief with one large, gauntleted fist cocked. Retief pushed his clumsy swing aside and said, "Tsk, naughty. The C and E, remember?" The big spacer moved on, muttering. Retief studied the trajectory of the missile, clearly marked by a swath of cut pipes, conduits and cables, all leading to the missile itself, half-buried in the massive casting which housed the converter gear. He went over and looked at the slab of partly-melted iron, deep-pocked and porous, perforated by melt-holes and somewhat flattened on one side by the impact. It was warm to the touch. He turned to a wall-mounted cabinet, snapped the cover open and looked over the array of tools and equipment inside, then selected a sharp-tipped sampler and gouged a tiny fragment from the metal slab, leaving a bright scar. He put the sample in the mass spectrograph from the cabinet and waited for a read-out, jotted it down and called to McCluskey:

"Has anybody touched this thing?"

"Naw," the chief replied. "See, I was too busy to mess with it."

"Busy not cycling the spill out, eh?" Retief suggested.

"Get offa my back, for cripesakes," McCluskey came back. "Now I ain't kidding no more. You gotta get outta here, I don't mean later."

"As it happens, Chief," Retief replied casually, "I was just going forward."

"You can tell that so-called captain that Chief McCluskey has got matters well in hand aft," the belligerent powerman stated.

Abruptly, the squawk-box crackled and spoke: "Now hear this! This here is Field-Marshall—"

"Skip that," another voice cut in. "I'm UnderSecretary Frunch, and I'm ordering all hands to take to the lifeboats! Abandon ship!"

"As you were, passengers and crew," a glutinous voice countermanded the Secretary's order. "What we got to do, we got to put her down on Old Moon, like Mr. Kouth said, so—"

"Nonsense!" a faint Groaci voice dismissed the suggestion. "To man battle stations, all crew; and all passengers to their staterooms, in an orderly fashion, mind you!"

"Why don't them bums get with the program?" McCluskey demanded of the circumambient air. "It's Old Moon, just like Boss Kouth said!" He broke off to stare as if astonished as Retief paused by the power control panel and began throwing switches. "Hey!" he yelled. "What you think you're doing?" He charged, but somehow collided helmet-first with the panel as Retief palmed him off gently and stepped aside. McCluskey slid to the deck, half-stunned; as he groped to get all fours under him, Retief grabbed his helmet by the cluster of cables emerging from its top and slammed the fellow's head against the panel again. McCluskey went limp. Retief went on with his resetting of the panel. After a few seconds, the fallen space'n raised his head:

"Yer setting up for re-entry," he objected. "No atmosphere on Old Moon, and besides that you got no call to mess around here in my power section!"

"One more time, Chief?" Retief inquired interestedly as he once again took a grip on McCluskey's helmet.

"Naw, I got no beef," the latter protested. "I already got a broke moobie-bone prolly. But tryna set this bucket down on a plus-G world with her hull broached is suicide. Have a heart, Bub, and leave it lay!"

Retief dropped the Chief's head with a dull *clang!* and left the compartment. Magnan was waiting impatiently, having removed his G-suit.

"I suppose it was nothing after all," he caroled. "Where's Chief McCluskey?"

"He's lying down," Retief told him.

"Oh, no doubt quite tuckered after his ordeal, poor fellow," Magnan guessed. "But he seems to have done his duty before resting. We must remember to mention his coolness in the emergency in our despatches."

"Just one thing, Mr. Magnan," Retief cut in on his supervisor's dythrambics. "It was no accident. That supposed meteoric iron has a 1.738 percent carbon content, precisely that of standard industrial steel."

"No!" Magnan gasped. "Whyever would anyone want to fake a disaster in space?"

"The disaster's genuine," Retief told him. "It's just the meteoroid that's a fake. And judging by the angle of entry and the size of the hole, its relative velocity was zero point zero."

"You mean it was stationary?" Magnan yelped. "But

that's impossible! It would have been falling toward Stug, at escape velocity at the very least!"

"Unless someone had just dropped it off squarely in our projected path," Retief corrected.

"We must notify Captain Suggs at once!" Magnan declared.

In the equipment bay, having returned his G-suit to its locker, Retief looked over the items stored in the adjacent cabinet, selected a late-model crater-gun, strapped it on, and dumped the rest of the arms in the recycler.

"Retief!" Magan cried, "whatever *do* you intend? Bearing arms is hardly consonant with normal diplomatic procedure!"

"Neither is Kouth," Retief pointed out, "nor the rest of these king-makers, either. But I'll put it up my sleeve if that will make you feel better."

"Must you jape, even in the cannon's mouth?" Magnan demanded in an outraged tone, as he hurried off along the passage.

As they reached the axial lift, it *bang*!ed open and a disheveled Zooner pre-adult floated out, drifting with the air currents a few inches clear of the floor.

"I suppose," it began in an irritable tone, "that you people are adherents of that uncouth Vreeb person. Well, you may as well know—I'm a partisan of Captain Hoshoon."

"Never heard of him, sir or madam," Magnan hastened to declare. "Have you seen the captain, by any chance?"

"Depends on who you mean by 'captain,' " the partly-shedding creature replied, pausing to scratch its blue-furred back against the lift frame and dislodging another patch of the hairy juvenile pelt. "Itch is driving me crazy," it vouchsafed. "Looks to me like Hoshoon has the power, since Admiral Phoop threw his weight behind him."

"We really must rush off," Magnan gabbled, "if you'd be so kind as to excuse us, madam or sir."

"Ain't neither the one nor the other, till after the moult," the unhappy Zooner grumped.

"One wonders," Magnan confided to Retief as the lift door closed off his view of the shedding alien, "just what animus the creature holds against the Tribunal."

"I think it was itch, not ITCH, it was carping about," Retief suggested. The speaker in the car's ceiling cleared its throat and intoned, sounded bored:

"Tole all personnel to assemble on the boat deck in half a squat," it said, in Boss Kouth's voice.

"It's Kouth!" Magnan exclaimed.

"Damn right!" the voice confirmed. "After I finished off that Krakan wiseguy, I done talked some sense into these slobs and now we can get busy and get this here wreck down on Old Moon before she breaks up. Bad business, a piece o' arn size of a sofa cushion in yer Power Section. Over and out and all that stuff."

"Heavens!" Magnan remarked. "Candidly, I doubt that Mr. Kouth is competent to command *Expedient*. And whyever do you suppose they've elected him captain?"

"Who said anything about electing?" Kouth demanded. "And I heard that crack about me being a incompetent and all. Well, I guess I'm competent enough to shape up this here bunch of dithering diplomats! And if ya wanna utter like sedition in secret, ya better switch off the talker."

"That is hardly the point, Captain Kouth," Magnan rebuked the volunteer skipper. "I trust you've at least retained Captain Suggs in an advisory capacity. After all, he knows the vessel."

"He's sleeping it off in the dispensary," Kouth dismissed the matter abruptly. "Now you better get yer butt back up here on the double; and tell McCluskey he's busted back to Log Room Yeoman fer letting youse in Power Section. Out and over!"

The lift having reached the end of the line, they debarked and started up the narrow companionway to Command Section. Halfway up, the Hondu Deckswabber Last Class, Gloon, came tumbling down, slack, his green fur matted with ochre blood.

Magnan ducked back as the bulky Hondu fell toward

him. "Horrid!" he gasped. "And what an appalling color combination!

"Good lord, Retief," he moaned, shrinking back to give the shaggy body the widest possible berth as it fell past him, "I feared it would come to this. Fortunate indeed that I directed you to arm yourself—for self and supervisor—defense only, of course. Very well," he added, more calmly, "You may proceed now—but cautiously, mind you. There's a murderer up there."

Thumping sounds from above seemed to confirm Magnan's deduction. Retief drew his gun and waved Magnan back. He went up to the final dogged-shut hatch to the sacrosanct Control Deck. Beyond it, faint scuffling noises were audible, interspersed with muttered obscenities and an occasional louder thump such as Magnan had heard from below. Then the hatch clicked and cycled open a few inches. Captain Suggs's bleary visage peered down at Retief.

"Good thing you come along, feller," the skipper mumbled. "Had one o' them green spacers up here to help me; good hand, too, but he tried to get insubordinate on me, and I hadda coldcock him." He displayed a heavy spanner with a smear of ochre on its one-and-three-eighths end.

Retief climbed up inside the spartan, high-tech compartment, where red EMERGENCY! DO SOMETHING! lights blinked on every panel.

"Got a little trouble here, feller," Suggs explained. "That dang Hondu deck-swabber tried to take command, didn't want me to take the necessary action, like all them idiot lights is saying I got to." Suggs returned his attention to the console before him, resumed setting up a complicated sequence of relays. Retief studied the pattern, then stepped in and quietly threw in the Master Override switch. Suggs grabbed, but Retief pushed his arm aside.

"Just what do you have in mind, Captain?" he asked.

"Jest like you see, feller," Suggs snapped. "And don't get messing with my command, here. Got serious work to do."

"What you're laying out there will overload the converters," Retief told him. "And one of them already has a fake meteoroid stuck in it."

"Sure," Suggs agreed readily, then: "Whattaya mean, 'fake?' How'd you—?"

"It's burned as if it had made a fast passage through a dense oxygen-rich atmosphere," Retief elaborated. "But we're in space, well above the argon exosphere of Stug. Somebody who had only seen meteorites in a museum on Terra, and didn't know how they got full of pits and holes, faked up a slab of industrial nickle-iron to fit his idea of a piece of space-debris."

"Dumb," Suggs commented unemotionally. "But they got to get up pretty early in the afternoon to sting Calvin Suggs, Captain, SMM (Reserve)."

"Why blow the converters?" Retief persisted.

"Can't you see, feller?" Suggs demanded. "It's the only way to like thwart whatever scheme somebody got in mind."

"When you cross-link the converters," Retief stated, "you'll blow off the aft half of the ship."

"Durn right," Suggs confirmed, contentedly. "Better to scuttle my command than to have her took over by pirates or hijackers, or trash like that. And as long as I'm all the way forrad, it's no fuze off my rockets."

"What about the four hundred diplomats and their staffs you have aboard?" Retief queried.

"Some of 'em might survive," Suggs suggested indifferently. "Them's strange diplomats," he went on. "Always thought diplomats was nice, perlite fellers in striped pants, but I got about two hundred o' the four hundred pulling rank and tryna take over my command, even that green deck-ape."

"The various delegations naturally include the Ambassadorial staffs," Magnan explained, poking his head in, "including their military advisors and technical people, some of whom, as you observed, are less than gracious in their manner."

"Won't be hardly no loss to blow 'em to Kingdom Come," Suggs summed up. "Step aside, there, feller!"

He reached for the big, white EXECUTE lever. Just then Retief heard a distressed bleat from Magnan. He stepped outside the CD to help his badly shaken colleague inside.

"It—it moved!" Magnan whimpered. "I distinctly saw that nasty corpse move its arm."

"I ain't no corpse, bub," the Hondu's bass voice rumbled from below. Magnan leaped back as the wounded deckswabber clambered up into view. The big spacer paused to wipe yellow-brown blood from his viridian eye and onto the bulkhead. "Lousy little runt snuck up behind me," he grumped. "Give me a sprongache that's got 'Jazreel' wrote all over it, or like that." He thrust Magnan aside.

"What *you* doin up here in capn's country, Terry?" he demanded.

"I came up to ensure that no unauthorized personnel attempted to intrude here," Magnan told him stiffly.

"That's a hot one," Gloon grunted. "You're unauthorized personnel your ownself."

"Hardly," Magnan contradicted sharply. "I assure you that under the circumstances, my presence here is not only appropriate but mandatory; check FSR 1-923-b, if you like."

"Happens I *don't* like, Buster," Gloon said discouragingly. "So if you're authorized like you claim, who authorized you, hah?" He thrust his blood-smeared face close to Magnan's and bared his square, chartreuse teeth.

Retief took him by the shoulder and spun him around to face him. "I did," he told the astonished fellow.

"Yeah? And who are you supposed to be?" the eight-foot Hondu sneered. He reached as if to push Retief aside, then *whoof!*ed and bowed from the waist.

"Sneaky," he wheezed. "I never seen no cargo-ram."

"Life is full of trifling disappointments," Magnan put in from behind the big fellow. "Now you'd best betake yourself below before I become annoyed."

"Geeze, we can't have that, can we, mister?" The Hondu replied in an attempt at an insouciant manner, spoiled by his sudden yell and grab for support before plunging headfirst down the narrow companionway.

"Retief!" Magnan gasped. "You didn't trip him!"

"Nope," Retief replied cheerfully. "You did—he fell over your foot. I only pushed him."

"If he should strike his already wounded head on those steel treads . . ." Magnan started. "I shudder to contemplate—"

"Right," Retief confirmed. "Don't think about it. As you pointed out, ochre and vert are a tasteless combination." He broke off to step back inside in time to seize Suggs as he was about to unlock the board. As Magnan shrank back, Retief tossed the captain down on top of Gloon, eliciting sharp yells from both. He pulled Magnan inside and dogged the hatch shut.

"All right, Swabber Gloon!" the squawk-box rasped. "I see by the repeater panel here you got the CD secured."

"It's Kouth!" Magnan gasped.

"Now, I'm depending on you, Chief Gloon," Kouth went on," to set this here bucket down nice and easy on Old Moon, right dead on the target like I shown you onna chart."

"Hard lines, Mr. Kouth," Magnan said to the squawker. "I have determined that it is upon Mr. Retief and myself that the responsibility devolves to take control of this vessel. And we intend to take the necessary action to safeguard the lives and property of the passengers, as well as the vessel itself, for the safe return of which ITCH is responsible."

"You must of slipped yer moorings, Cull," Kouth came back. "If I gotta come up there—" he paused. "By the way, whereat's that Swabber Gloon I dispatched to he'p the Cap'n?"

"He fell down," Magnan supplied crisply. "And I venture to predict that if you should attempt to intrude here, you yourself might encounter the same unfortunate slippery spot."

"Frankly, Retief," he added *sotto voce* behind his hand, "I trust that Mr. Kouth less at every encounter."

"Very perceptive of you, sir," Retief congratulated his supervisor. "But this class of vessel requires at least two people to maneuver it; one up here and one aft in the Power Section, and I don't think we can count on Chief McCluskey for cooperation."

"Probably not, the cheeky fellow," Magnan agreed thoughtfully. "In fact, I think it is incumbent upon me to report him to Captain Suggs--or it would be if you hadn't thrown that officer away."

"I'm sorry to say it was necessary," Retief told Magnan. "He was intent on blowing us all up."

"Shocking," Magnan remarked, and paused. "But do you realize what this means? One of us has to return aft and do whatever is necessary."

"Quite correct, Mr. Magnan," Retief confirmed. "Unless we can recruit someone from among the naval attaches aboard."

"Dream on, Terry," Kouth's gravelly voice broke in. "Youse Terries—yeah, I reckernize youse—are gonna like roo the day youse tryda muscle in on Jerry Kouth's operation."

"Let's go aft, Mr. Magnan," Retief proposed. "Our orbit is decaying, and we're going to be in thick atmosphere and start breaking up in another ten minutes."

"Then let us by all means make haste!" Magnan ordained. Retief undogged the hatch and they went down, stepping over first Gloon, then at the foot of the steep steps, Suggs, who groaned and muttered: "I can hear atmospheric molecules whanging off the hull already. We got to hurry up here. You need a reliable boy aft, gents, and I volunteer, if I can get up. You sprained my moobie-bone, feller," he told Retief aggrievedly, as the latter helped him to his feet.

"Better get back there and give Chief McCluskey a hand," Suggs rattled on. "Seems like he done gone sour on me," he added as he staggered away, pounding his ear with the heel of his hand.

"Can we depend on him?" Magnan asked dubiously.

"Not a chance," Retief dismissed the idea. "But we can send someone back to keep an eye on him."

"Grand Captain Blance," Magnan suggested gloomily. "No doubt he's ranking naval officer aboard."

4

From one deck above, the continuing disturbance in the Grand Salon was audible. Non-Terran voices boomed, squeaked, shrilled and rasped, all, it seemed, claiming primacy.

"No one's doing anything constructive," Magnan moaned. "While they should be putting their heads together to save the ship, they're wrangling over who's to be in command of the derelict when it disintegrates. Absurd!" He pushed ahead into the salon, where the din was like a storm at sea. A few voices rose above the tumult.

". . . got my commission right here!" a tall, purple Rikk was yelling.

"My date o' rank goes back to when you were getting your first GI gill-trim!" countered a pancake-like Jaq warlord in copper bangles.

"—protocol!" an insignificant-appearing Zub from Quopp shouted.

"To natter of protocol in the face of my overwhelming credentials as Great Hivemaster of Yan!" a Groaci diplomat protested in a penetrating whisper.

"That's Shoss, a mere Assistant Military Attache," Magnan observed.

"Correction, Mr. Magnan," Retief countered. "That's Colonel Hivemaster Shoss, brevet Lieutenant-General, one of Groaci's most-decorated troublemakers."

"To have heard that, Retief!" the Groaci hissed, turning on the Terrans, his distended throat-sac a deep purple, indicating Extreme Wrath, Righteous, (B-52). "In your profound ignorance of noble Groacian tradition, you grossly mis-translate the proud honorific 'Thusfoth,' which in fact might better be rendered 'Trusty Rectifier of Egregious Wrongs' rather than 'Troublemaker,' as you so crudely suggested. I outrank a Troublemaker First Degree by nine grades!"

A preternaturally tall, long-beaked Quornt in stained fatigues without rank badges thrust Shoss aside. "I'll put it to you gents," he told Magnan. "Who ranks, a Maker of Ritual Grimaces First Class from some third-rate power, or a Quornt All-Conquering Annihilator of Hostile Armadas?"

"It's a toss-up," Retief advised him.

"So, OK, I'll toss him up," the Quornt acceded contentedly, and turned to grab an ornately-dressed Frib and throw him carelessly aside.

Magnan made an abortive lunge to intercede, but met a horny knee to the jaw, and stumbled aside, muttering, almost inaudibly:

"You fail to understand the intent of my subordinate's proposal."

"Better tone it lower, feller," the Quornt advised. "Keep it inaudible and I can't hardly take offense at what I can't hear, right?"

"Possibly," Retief said, as he stepped hard on the tall creature's unpolished boot and kicked him hard on the knee, causing him to jerk futilely at his trapped foot and then topple backward, arms windmilling, to impact the floor with an impressive *whoomp!*, knocking the cocked hat from the pointy head of a Zanubian admiral in the process. The admiral uttered a hoarse yell and drew his ceremonial sword, which Retief confiscated for safe-keeping.

"Mutiny!" the disarmed flag officer bellowed.

"Whatever you say, Admiral," a Zanubian Lieutenant Last Class replied, and knocked him down. The melee spread rapidly, heated conversation turning to inept fisticuffs in a trice.

"Good lord," Magnan mourned. "Heated conversation has given way to inept fisticuffs in a trice!" He broke off abruptly as two heavy-set aliens, identical even to their thick mops of head-tendrils except that one was bright orange, the other blue, locked in a complicated wrestler's grip and counter-grip nearly ran him down.

"Gloian and Blort, pursuing their fratricidal competition even here, in the halls of diplomatic sweet reasonableness!" The shaken First Secretary and Consul exclaimed. "Why, I do believe that's General Barf—you remember the general, Retief. Really a most reasonable chap, once he gets past that lamentable tendency to strafe first and negotiate afterward."

"What's to negotiate?" the general demanded, at the same time attempting to dislodge his adversary's gouging digit from his sensitive zatz-patch. "You think I'm gonna yield pride of place to this here Blort? Not broody likely!"

"But—he's a fellow native of Plushnik!" Magnan protested. "I should think—"

"Right!" Barf confirmed, "preferably before you talk! And I ain't no native! I got shoes on same as you, fancypants!"

"Retief!" Magnan mourned. "What's a Deputy Chief of Mission to do? They're incorrigible! Look at that great ugly Nether Furthuronian molesting that poor, pacifist Grotian. I think that's poor dear D'ong, isn't it? Why doesn't she whaffle, I wonder?"

"That would be cowardly in the extreme, Ben," D'ong reproved, even as she eluded the Furthuronian Primary War Chief by deftly extruding a flexible member ending in a large, knobby fist, with which she stunned her aggressive tormentor with a sharp rap to the barf-node. She stepped aside as he fell heavily.

"Pity to resort to violence," she commented, "but these Yahoos leave one scant choice."

" 'Yahoos'?" Magnan gasped. "My dear Madame Secretary—these are the cream of the Arm's career diplomats, chosen by their respective peoples as delegates to a tribunal which will establish peace in the Galaxy for a millenium at the least!"

"If the fate of the Galaxy depends on this bunch agreeing with each other," D'ong commented, "maybe I'd best whaffle after all. Do pass along my regards to dear Freddie." With a sharp *whap*! of imploding air, she disappeared.

"I give up," a bristly pink Spism declared loudly, and bustled to the fore, its wiry arms overhead. "I saw you vaporize old D'ong, which she wasn't a bad old dame, for a Grotian! Leave me live, and I won't say a word."

"You may relax, Mr. Ambassador," Magnan soothed the excited fellow. "I assure you I did not 'vaporize,' as you put it, her Excellency the Ambassador of Grote!"

"We're not, after all, blind, Ben," the Quornt Annihilator cut in harshly, brushing himself off after his fall. "I myself was assaulted but now by your assistant," he added, then turned to address the crowd whose scuffling members had paused in mid-attack at what they had taken to be the sound of a hardshot.

"Clearly," the tall warrior called, "we are victims of an insidious Terry plot. Was it not haughty Terra which proposed the Convention of this Tribunal? It seems we are to be done away with, one by one, whilst our attention is distracted by the petty disputes so cleverly fomented by none other than Ben Magnan and his notorious tool, Retief!"

"Yeah, I was just saying—" someone shouted. And "I seen him, too!" another contributed.

"Where's Mr. Kouth?" a hoarse voice yelled from the far side of the salon, at once seconded by a chorus of demands for Boss Kouth.

"It just might be expedient at this point," Magnan whispered to Retief, "to take a leaf from D'ong's book and whaffle. You do recall the technique, I hope?" So saying, he squeezed his eyes shut and a second *whap!* sent the close-pressing onlookers back a step, setting off a brisk renewal of the free-for-all. Retief made his way through the press, fending off random blows and charging combatants as he went. Suddenly Kouth appeared directly in his path, planted solidly and blocking the way. He looked at Retief without visible joy.

"OK, where's that tricky side-kick o' yourn?" he demanded. "I wanna talk to him."

"Oh, he must be off somewhere minding his own business," Retief told the ill-tempered Boss.

"Is that some kinda crack? Kouth inquired.

"Not unless you feel *you're* not minding your own business," Retief told him.

"Yer too smart-mouth fer yer own good," Kouth stated. "Who are ya, anyway? Some kind big general, that pal o' yours said, but I ast around, and seems like you're only one of these here Embassy Johnnies. So how about it?"

By this time Kouth's variegated retainers, many in crew uniform, had formed a loose circle around the two.

"As it happens, Mr. Kouth," Retief said calmly, "I'm not on active duty in a military capacity at this time."

"Oh," Kouth mimed surprise, grinning around at his strong-arm squad. "He ain't on active duty," Kouth sneered. He returned a threatening, gimlet-eyed gaze to Retief.

"Yer a little too active to suit me," he announced in a tone he seemed to feel was intimidating, at the same time rolling his well-developed shoulders and opening and closing the large fists that hung at his side. He brought one up in what was intended to be a deceptively lazy motion, and scratched above one badly twisted ear with a loud rutching sound, then whipped his hand, flat now, over and down in a whistling arc which ended in a sharp *smack*! as Retief casually caught the wrist and held it. Kouth tugged; Retief held firm. Kouth tried to twist his arm free, and Retief added to the torque, forcing the aggressive Boss to his knees. There was a mutter from his retainers. Retief jerked Kouth to his feet.

"Say 'I was a bad boy' three times," Retief ordered, bending Kouth's hand back until his wrist made popping sounds.

"I was a bad boy three times," Kouth gobbled. "Now lemme go, before—"

"Yes, Retief inquired interestedly, and gave him another two degrees of over-extension.

"Before you break my arm," Kouth amended, then, catching the eye of someone to Retief's right, added: "And I hafta get tough!"

Retief reached over and caught the man on his right by the hair, as the latter ducked his head for a charge. Retief jerked him close and shifted his grip to lay his forearm across the fellow's cheek-bone, and levered upward slightly, eliciting a terrified squawk from the would-be attacker.

"Yer running outa arms," Kouth muttered, and tried a snap-kick, which met a boot-sole to the shin. Kouth groaned and lunged backward, as two more of his boys closed in. Retief jerked Kouth to the left, swinging him in an arc which lifted the Boss's feet from the floor; the flailing members knocked the foremost man back among his fellows. Then Retief lifted the other man by the head, as Kouth was led off, bleeding from the mouth, by his solicitous allies, one of whom produced a snub-nosed hard-shooter and aimed it at Retief, who kicked it from his hand.

"Nicely did, pal!" a Furthuronian Marine Guard Sergeant commented, neatly catching the slug-gun on the fly. "I been meaning to speak to this Boss Kouth my ownself about his manners, which he ain't got any. So, you taking over now, or what?"

"I defer to his Eminence," Retief said graciously, inclining his head toward the Hoogan Cardinal in full canonicals who had come over to see what was going on.

"You mean you're backing down to some kinda sissy preacher?" the Furthuronian demanded in a tone of Astonishment at an Unprecedented Shift in Strategy.

"It's more of a tactical play, Clarence," Retief told the multi-tentacled, slug-like non-com. "This is Cardinal Oh-Moomy-Gooby, a redoubtable warrior in the cause of Church reform and tax-free booze."

"Sounds like a all-right guy, all right," Clarence conceded and faded back.

"In the absence of any further pretenders to the mantle of Captaincy," the Cardinal intoned, "I shall accept the responsibility." That settled, His Eminence withdrew to a shadowy alcove and his brandy bottle.

"I wun't take that too serious, pal," Kouth offered,

mumbling through his bruised mouth. "The old boy will be busy with his sauce fer awhile, and then he'll be so juiced he won't have no more big ideas about commanding no ten-thousand-tonner. So I'll jest step into the breach like they say, and ease her down nice on Old Moon."

"Not quite," Retief corrected the Boss. "I'm putting her down on Stug, as scheduled."

"You still on that kick, feller?" Kouth inquired as if amazed. "I already tole yer I and my boys are giving the orders now, and that's it." He broke off to yell, "Hey, Charlie!" to which responded a small, unshaven Terran in incredibly soiled whites, to the sleeves of which three shiny gold stripes had been stitched so hastily that Charlie was kept busy tucking the loose-flapping ends back in place.

"Yessir, Mr. Boss, sir," Charlie panted, offering a salute which resembled a wave of farewell to a departing traveler.

"This here," Kouth said importantly, "is Cap Stunkard, got more years in space than most has hours. He's my First Mate."

"Do you mind if I look at your captain's papers, Captain?" Retief inquired.

"Look ahead, if you can find 'em," Stunkard agreed carelessly.

"Mr. Kouth," Retief addressed the Boss again, "You and all your adherents are under arrest. Go lock yourselves in your quarters."

"Me?" Kouth echoed, trying for Astounded at Unparalled Impertinence, Level Four. "And whattaya mean 'my derents'? I ain't got none, nor no butterfly collection neither. Charlie, you got yer orders. Do it!"

Charlie took a brisk step to comply, but rebounded from the arm Retief had thrust out across his path. Charlie cast a dubious look at Kouth, then set about applying various Yug-Sub-Woo holds to the obstacle until Retief flipped him aside. "Now," he told Kouth, "don't wait for a police escort." He gripped Kouth's shoulder and spun him to face the aft grand passage.

"Will you walk, or shall I throw you?" Retief inquired in an interested tone.

"Naw, naw, nothin like that, pal," Kouth hastened to blurt. "I was jest going down thataways." He set off, reassembling his dignity as he went, pausing momentarily to confer hastily with various of those who had been vigorously seconding his self-nomination, each of whom faded back and began working his way toward Retief.

"Mind your flanks, Retief," the Fustian elder, Whelk, suggested from his place on the sidelines. "May I have the tall ugly one with the bread-knife?"

"Certainly," Retief agreed. "Don't spoil him for the trial, though."

Whelk moved off, as ponderous as a walking crane, and Retief watched as Kouth hastened off along the passage toward passenger country. Suddenly he halted, spun and raced back toward the salon.

"Look out!" he yelled. "They're coming!" Most of the contentuous crowd fell back in alarm, while the others rushed forward to comfort their leader.

"It's the blue Cobblies!" Kouth shouted hoarsely. "We ain't got a chancet!"

"Calmly now, everyone," Cardinal Gooby's resonant voice boomed out. "You, there, Admiral! And you too, General Blow! I'm surprised at such intemperate behavior in officers of your respective ranks. Keep calm! Blue Cobblies, indeed! All enlightened beings are aware that the term is a reference without a referent, applying as it does to mere figments of superstition!"

"Yeah, maybe," a shaken ambassador from Icebox Nine offered. "But them figments are swarming all over the place! See for yourself!"

The Cardinal, ignoring the jibe, wrapped himself in his robes and sank back into meditation. The salon was cleared now of passengers, except for those flattened against the walls, and one other, the gorgeously caparisoned Grotian Ambassadress D'ong.

"Oh, Retief," she called. "I do hope you don't mind my meddling, but it *did* seem an appropriate moment to boggle; dear Ben seemed *so* upset!"

Just then Magnan appeared from a door marked PRI-VATE AUTH PERS ONLY. He paused to glance about the vast, abruptly silent salon, frowned, and hurried across to Retief.

"Oh, there you are!" he caroled. "I do hope you weren't alarmed when I whaffled so abruptly. Actually, I wasn't sure I still remembered the technique; that's why I just nipped over to D'ong's cabin to confer with her; it was her idea to boggle; and it seems to have worked wonders. Astonishing how very sophisticated people believe in blue Cobblies when they see them advancing in full cry!"

"I'm glad you came to me, Ben," D'ong told Magnan when the latter had concluded his briefing. "Surprised, too," she added. "But I'd have assumed you'd whaffled to the planetary surface, to inform our hosts of the reason for the delay."

"Hardly," Magnan huffed. "One doesn't leave one's colleagues in the lurch, while one retreats to a safe haven, however logical, one's rationalization might appear."

"Pray accept my apologies, Ben," D'ong pled earnestly. "I meant to impute no baseness to you."

"Of course," Magnan reassured the sensitive Ambassadress. "As for your blue Cobblies, I think it's time to just boggle them back where they came from, before they drive all these fine diplomats to distraction."

"It's not quite so simple as that, Ben," D'ong told him. "You must recall that a considerable adjustment to the vorb plane is necessary to effect such a wide-scope illusion. I fear my vital energies are too depleted now to reverse the effect."

"You mean?" Magnan yelped.

D'ong nodded a head she had deployed for the purpose. "But perhaps if you'd join with me, Ben . . ."

"Of course," Ben agreed at once. "But I'm not at all sure I know how."

"It's quite simple," D'ong reassured him. "I'll show you."

"Hey, Cap," Kouth blurted, staggering up to the

threesome, "whattaya doin about these here like blue Cobblies and all?"

"Shocking!" Magnan retorted. "Now that an *unexpected* disaster rears its head, suddenly you're demanding that the very person whose credentials you rejected produce a remedy. Why don't you and your minions deal with the trifling annoyance yourselves?"

"Ain't none of my boys ever seen anything like 'em before," Kouth complained, "cept Woozy, o' course; he's so far gone on the pink stuff he seen everything, but all he can do is climb the drapes and yell *I see 'em!* No help there."

"What do these Cobblies of yours look like?" Retief asked the badly shaken Boss. Kouth's jaw dropped.

"You got bad eyesight or somethin, Cap?" he demanded. "How you gonna clear 'em outa here if you can't even see 'em?"

"The entities you see, sir," D'ong put in, "have no substantive existence: they represent your own neuroses objectivized. To no two persons do they appear the same. Since Mr. Retief is remarkably non-neurotic, the phenomenon fails to affect his optic nerves."

"Oh yeah?" Kouth came back. "I ast Little Harry, and he seen the same as me: like little flat worms, with shredding hooks all over, coming on in a solid wave. They're right there, see?" He pointed to a bare spot on the floor six inches from his ankle. "You telling me they ain't?" he demanded and raised a boot to stamp hard on the floor. "Got the sucker!" he cried happily. "Ok, everybody," he called, as he turned and strode out into the middle of the deserted floor. "Let's get 'em!" he ordered. "You, Stan, just stamp on 'em!" He began clapping his hands rhythmically. "Everybody dance!" he yelled, and proceeded to bawl out the words to a hillbilly lament. People were stirring, jittering, stamping, and in a moment the room was a sea of wildly bouncing beings. The band, caught up in the frenzy, deployed from their refuge behind the bandstand and struck up in approximate accord.

"Good lord," Magnan moaned. "It's like a convention

of St. Vitus' Dance victims." As he spoke, he began to bob erratically, then took a tentative step, and followed it with an entire series of quick hops, until D'ong extruded a tentacular member and caught his arm, stilling him. "Ben," the shy Ambassadress said, tugging Magnan back to her side. "Doubtless it's excellent therapy, but we must exert ourselves to dissipate the hallucination, not reinforce it."

"To be sure," Magnan agreed happily. "But they *do* squish so delightfully! Besides, I haven't cut a rug in years!"

"The situation is deteriorating, Retief," D'ong muttered. "We can't let it get out of hand; could you bring Ben back to his senses, do you suppose?"

Retief said, "I'll try," and stepped to Magnan's side. "If Ambassador Spoilsport saw you cutting the rug," he told the restless First Secretary, "while *he*'s struggling to keep our hosts engaged in light chit-chat to divert their attention from the fact that the members of ITCH have failed to appear for the conference *he* persuaded them to tolerate, I think your interest in terpsichore would vanish in a hurry."

Magnan went rigid for a moment, then relaxed and hastily ducked behind D'ong.

"I don't know what came over me," he started. "Do you really think the gimlet-eyed old devil was looking? Heavens, I knew he had his spies planted everywhere, but *here*, aboard ship?"

"There, there, Ben," D'ong soothed, turning to embrace him with a hastily improvised comradely arm. "No one saw you except Retief and myself, and a remarkably graceful figure you cut, too, indeed! But now we have work to do. Just cinch up the old sphincters nice and tight, and . . ." her voice dropped to a whisper. Magnan was nodding hesitantly, then eagerly.

"Yes, yes, of course I can do it!" he cried. "Nothing simpler!"

"We have to link arms, remember," D'ong continued as Magnan closed his eyes in concentration. He nodded vigorously and took D'ong's temporary arm. A moment later, the music stopped with a crash, only Kouth's off-key voice carrying on for a moment:

". . . but I didden cheer nobody prayy. . . ."

"In that connection," the booming voice of Cardinal Gooby cut through the hubbub, "as the direct representative of the vicar of God, I of course outrank any mere temporal authority. Accordingly, I have decided to put an end to this foolish disputation once and for all. It is to *me* that you may come for your instructions. Ah, Retief," the Prince of the Church added in a lower tone. "Since I have little practical experience of the operation of deep-space passenger vessels, I appoint you to the post of Advisor in that sphere. What, for example, should I do now?"

"Actually, Your Eminence," Retief told the imposing church-being, "We no longer have much choice. Do you hear that whistling sound?"

"Ah, now that the cacophonous ensemble has discontinued its efforts," the Cardinal commented, nodding, "I do indeed hear a most unpleasant screeching. It seems to be coming from all directions. What is it?"

"We've lost velocity and dipped into the atmosphere," Retief told the massive being. "So we're committed to putting down on Stug."

"Here, we cain't do that!" the runty Stuggan named Little Harry blurted. "Let's jest see what Boss has got to say about this!" He darted away.

"It appears," Magnan told the excited Kouth when he appeared moments later, loudly objecting, "that you are presented with the *fait accompli*. We're committed to landing. So you may as well lend a hand to help us get down intact."

"OK, onney first I wanna be sure nobody don't hole *me* responsible. Jest write out a free pardon or like that, letting me and my boys, too, off the hook, for any crimes we might of did."

"I fear that will not be possible, Mr. Kouth," Magnan told him distantly. "Still, if you wish to survive you'd best pitch in. Now be about it."

An undernourished fellow with a worried frown came

up and Kouth caught him by the arm and conferred briefly with him. Magnan caught the name "McCluskey." The fellow hurried away.

"OK, gents, sure, I'll save yer bacon for youse," Kouth grated in a sudden attempt at a gracious manner. "Jest wait a minute till Stan gets back . . ."

"Wherever has that ruffian, Gloon, betaken himself?" Magnan queried, peering around anxiously. "He's an experienced spacer, so perhaps we'd better send him aft to man—or rather, to hondu the Power Section."

"Good idea," Kouth commented.

"I was not addressing my remark to you, sir!" Magnan snapped. "But to Mr. Retief. Retief! Don't you agree—"

"Certainly, sir," Retief replied. "I sent him back while you were tending Captain Suggs's bruises."

"But—without my permission—" Magnan blurted.

"Hardly, Mr. Magnan," Retief corrected him. "You suggested it yourself; it was simply a matter of timing— and so I expect to explain in my report."

"To be sure," Magnan agreed, nodding sagely. "It's what I had in mind all along."

"Well, gents, I got bears to shoot," Kouth put in absently. "I gotta run along. See youse in the slammer." Just then Stan returned at a lope, his close-set eyes looking more anxious than ever. He muttered in Kouth's ear.

"Whattaya mean, 'They ain't there'?" Kouth yelled. "I put 'em in there my ownself!"

"Pity about your arms cache, Kouth," Retief told the Boss quietly. "They fell into the converter."

"Oh, yeah?" Kouth snarled, at the same time hauling out from his under-jacket holster a snub-nosed needler.

"All except this one," Retief continued, and showed Kouth the heavy-duty crater gun; then he took the Browning from the Boss's hand and gave it to Magnan.

"Try not to shoot him unless perhaps you don't like the look on his face, sir," Retief suggested. Magnan took the weapon dubiously and tucked it away.

The whine of atmospheric molecules whanging off the hull had risen to a penetrating screech. People were covering their auditory organs and converging on Retief.

"You're the captain!" the Glorytian counsellor cried in a voice which rivaled the screech of reentry. "I *demand* you *do* something at once!" Her eye fell on Magnan.

"And *you*, you horrid little Terry! What are *you* doing to save innocent lives?"

Magnan drew his needler and pointed it at the Glorytian's sensitive zotz-patch.

"Shut up," he ordered quietly. "You, Madame," he went on, "are designated as chairman of the Tidying-Up Committee. Do something about this mess." He indicated the smashed glasses and spilled booze on every side.

"What committee?" the new appointee yelled. "I don't see no committee. And whattaya you mean, telling me to shut up?"

"To be selected by yourself," Magnan clarified. "Now do be off about your business. This is a real gun," he added. "And while I should dislike to add to the mess, I will not tolerate any further vocalization from you. Scat!" he finished and jabbed the small weapon toward the gaunt female. She fled.

"Nice going, sir," Retief congratulated his colleague. "That voice of hers was precisely in resonance with one of the minor frequencies of the hull. Intolerable." He turned to Kouth, who was standing by with his mouth open.

"He'da *done* it," he muttered. "By golly, he'da done it, if she wouldn'ta shut up."

"Damn right," the blurry voice of the man called Woozy confirmed his chief's assessment.

Retief took Kouth aside and gave him his instructions. "And report to me on the bridge when you have everything ship-shape," he concluded.

5

Back in the Command compartment, Magnan wiped at his narrow face with an oversized floral-patterned tissue with the armorial bearings of the triarch of Gree, then noticed what he was using and quickly stuffed it into the waste slot as if to disassociate himself from the *lese majeste*.

"Heavens, Retief," he said, "however will you manage an already perilous approach, in a damaged vessel, without assistance from the crew?"

"Boss Kouth and his troops decided to help out," Retief told him.

"Oh," Magnan exclaimed, "I *don't* think I'd trust *him!* Though I did notice a number of his most vocal supporters scurrying about as if intent on something."

"There are a number of systems that have to be set up manually," Retief explained. "Safety interlocks to be set, for example, that are open for normal functioning."

"To be sure," Magnan murmured. "Now what? This panel looks so complex. Are you sure . . . . ?"

"I'm only sure," Retief said, "that if somebody doesn't do something, we'll break up in the atmosphere."

"Then by all means," Magnan blurted. "Can I help?"

"OK," Kouth's hoarse voice crackled from the talker. "I and my boys done like you said. Lucky fer you we're all experienced spacehands. Now what you got in mind?"

"Get up here at once," Magnan spoke up, "just as I distinctly heard Captain Retief tell you!"

"Keep yer lace britches on, Cull," Kouth admonished carelessly. "I'm onna way, ain't I?"

Retief quickly set up the panel for re-entry, first using a blast of reaction-mass to push the wounded vessel up and clear of the outer fringes of the Stuggan exosphere. The nerve-shredding whistling faded into inaudibility. Magnan heaved a sigh of relief. Carefully, Retief reduced the velocity of the hurtling mass that was the good ship *Expedient*, then gently eased her back down into the thin gas at the fringe of the soupy atmosphere below. The screeching resumed briefly, then became a deep-toned thrumming. Retief watched closely as the hull-temperature indicators crept up toward the fusing level of the outer ablative hull; then sheets of flame and an eruption of glowing particles were rushing past the look-out sensors. At last, dense air was reached and Retief deployed the airfoils, and the ship steadied into its long glide down. Magnan stayed glued to the DV screens, watching the misty surface below as it slowly resolved into the mountains and plains, seas and rivers of the world known as Stug.

"I see Big Continent coming over the horizon!" he cried happily. "There's a town, too, just as it looks on the map back at Sector. Oh, boy! The port is north of the city, of course," he added, his voice fading as he recalled that Retief was a licensed space pilot and thus familiar with all major ports in the Arm.

"Won't his Excellency be delighted to see me right on time, too," Magnan blurbed.

"I assume the question is rhetorical," Retief replied. "The last time Percy Spoilsport was delighted was when his rival for the post of Coordinator of the Academy for the Correction of Historical Errors fell into the sulphur pits at Yan and dropped out of the running."

"Yes, that was a stroke of luck for His Excellency," Magnan agreed. "Cecil Proudfoot was a fierce competitor. And as chief of ACHE, Spoilsport not only revised African history to eliminate all that horrid cannibalism and genocide, he was able so favorably to impress the Board of Examiners as to secure the additional plum as head of ITCH! A superb career plan, when he enticed poor Ambassador Proudfoot to go along on his PR tour of the Pits."

"It must warm the cockles of your heart, Mr. Magnan," Retief suggested, "to reflect that it is to this same gentle kindly man that you are about to report failure."

"Failure? I?" Magnan yelped. "How, pray, have I failed? Why, simply to survive in these circumstances is itself an achievement!"

"We haven't actually survived yet, Mr. Magnan," Retief pointed out.

"Well," Magnan pulled at his chin. "I suppose not, not *quite* yet. Still, when I make my report to His Excellency we *shall* have survived. Wherein lies the failure there?"

"Don't you think he's likely to inquire into just who it was who poked a hole in ITCH's leased vessel, and why?" Retief asked casually, having first switched off the talker.

"Well, gracious, as to that," Magnan temporized. "I suppose the nosy old thing *is* likely to introduce some crude carping note into what should be an occasion of congratulation. But unfortunately we don't have any cogent answers to this unconscionable third-degree."

"We could ask," Retief suggested.

"Ask whom, pray?" Magnan came back sharply.

"We could start with Mr. Kouth," Retief suggested.

"I doubt he'll prove helpful," Magnan predicted. "The fact is," he went on in a confidential tone, "I shouldn't wonder if he isn't in some way implicated himself. Doubtless you noticed that most of the crew quickly leaped to support his tenuous claims to the abdicated laurels of Captain Suggs. Almost as if they had worked it all out beforehand."

"Good thinking, sir," Retief congratulated his chief. "So it seems he should be well qualified to shed some light on just what's going on here."

"Going on?" Magnan yelped. "Why, we're crashing in flames, that's what's going *on!*"

"I don't think that's any part of Kouth's plan," Retief corrected. "He didn't strike me as the kamikazi type, especially for no purpose."

"Still," Magnan sighed, "what Mr. Kouth is thinking is his secret."

"I still think we could ask him," Retief pointed out.

"Yes, I feared you'd think of that," Magnan said with a modest shudder. "I *do* so dislike mayhem . . ."

6

They found the Boss in the VIP lounge, sprawled at ease in a tump-leather throne intended for use by Heads of State only, surrounded by subordinates, most of them in the uniform of the Nine Planet Line, all talking at once:

". . . this here bucket into a viable mode, Boss," A cargo officer was saying urgently.

"—break up, and I mean soon!" a burly wiper insisted.

"Let 'em know fast, maybe we can do a eevee transfer or something," a plump fellow in chef's whites suggested half-heartedly.

"Easy, boys," Kouth cut short the babble. "Boss has got it all under control, right? Now, you, Stan, get back to yer Comm Section and raise Dooley on the tightbeam. I'll be along as soon as I finish my drink here." As he sipped from the tall glass in his hand, as if in response to his own command, his eyes fell on Retief, who had gently parted the circle of admirers, wounding four, to take a position in the front row. Kouth choked on his razzle-and-zizz-water and came to his feet in a lunge.

"Looky who's here, boys," he invited in a gleeful tone, then, to Retief: "I been looking for you, feller, which you don't quite get the program. Well, they don't call me Boss for nuthin, and I don't care a good rap what that shellback preacher says, I'm in charge here, and I say we still put her down on Old Moon. Any objections?"

"Only a few," Retief told him quietly. "For a start, there's the matter that unless someone takes the necessary action right now, this vessel won't be putting down anywhere. Then there's the trifling matter of four hundred diplomatic personnel aboard who expect to participate in a conference on Stug, not Old Moon, and that brings us to you. You're a loud-mouthed trouble-maker without enough brains to do a clean job of wrecking a space vessel for the salvage."

"Hey, Boss," Little Harry spoke up in the resounding silence that followed Retief's rebuttal, "you going to let this here civilian bad-mouth you like he done?"

"Not hardly, Harry," Kouth reassured the small man. "I'll fix his wagon right, but first I got to get back to Comm and talk to Dooley, down Old Moon." He pushed through his admirers a few steps, then halted and whirled.

"Whattaya mean, I din't do a clean job, wise guy?" he yelled.

"Not yet," Retief rebuked him. "We've still got the personnel to transfer, remember?"

"Why you think I'm talkin'a Dooley?" Kouth growled defensively.

"Why, the treacherous scoundrel!" Magnan contributed, ignoring Kouth's presence. "He intended all along to transfer himself and his vile cronies to safety, while the rest of us perished!"

7

When Kouth slammed into the communications section, startling a man who sat drowsing before the big panel, Retief and Magnan were close behind him.

"All right, Spike!" Kouth yelled. "I seen you sleeping on duty! Got a good mind to leave you ride her down!" He broke off as a great shudder racked the vessel.

"She's going!" he yelled, even louder. "Hurry yer dead butt up, Spike! Get Dooley on Number One, and I mean right now!"

"Already got him standing by, Boss," Spike told his excited leader. "Tole him ya wanned'a talk, soon's you give me the squawk!"

Kouth grabbed the shore talker. "All right, Dooley," he rapped out. "I guess you got the cattle-barge standing by like yer orders tole ya. So close fast and cover both hatches; we got to get out now. We're already on airfoils!" Even as he concluded his speech the ship bucked again, and an oblique pressure on boot-soles indicated that the hulk had taken up an off-axis spin.

"Won't be long now!" Kouth yelled. He jumped to the all-stations talker and ordered:

"All crew to abandon ship stations pronto! Secure the salon with all the marks inside! Do it!" he turned and for the first time realized that he and Spike were not alone.

"You heard me!" he shouted. "Go get locked in the salon with the rest o' the losers!" He lunged toward Retief and met an oncoming fist to the jaw which loosened his knees and put a glaze on his eyeballs.

"Throw these here bums out," Spikey," he mumbled, "Watch the shrimp; he's mean as a fire-snake."

Spike rose dutifully and approached Retief. "I ain't leading with my chin like Boss, here," he told the bigger man, and set himself, then yelped as Retief spun him, grabbed him by the neck and crotch and upended him. Spike protested vigorously, but Retief stuffed him upside down into a narrow wall-locker, and turned to Kouth, who was draped, sagging, against the panel.

"Tell Dooley to make that two personnel barges," Retief ordered crisply. Kouth staggered a step and collapsed, snoring. Retief picked up the shore-talker and advised the dispatcher of the change in plan, ignoring the latter's yelp of protest.

"You expect me to pull another barge out'a my sock, or what?"

"Don't kid me, Dooley," Retief countered. "Just tell the flightline to rig Number Two for heavy cargo. Gold, in fact. The whole ITCH appropriation, in cash."

"Boy o boy," Dooley gobbled. "I guess you get a gold star on yer forehead after all, Boss! Hang loose. By the way, which part ya want us to match up with? That screen is showing three main pieces!" Kouth grabbed the talker and mumbled.

"Tell him the major fragment," Retief counseled. "No doubt she failed along the breakaway lines; she's still flying."

"The biggest one, dummy," Kouth told him. "Now get moving!" He dropped the talker and turned to

Retief. "Hope yer satisfied, bub," he grunted. "I onney hope I tole him the right piece."

Magnan plucked at Retief's sleeve. "How do you know we're aboard the major piece?" he quavered.

"This is a Code Standard hull, Mr. Magnan," Retief reminded him. "It's stressed to give along the predetermined seams, and they're designed to keep the entire personnel core intact. I'm sure you'll recall the Code provision on that point?"

"To be sure," Magnan agreed, more confidently. "But it appears we'll all be firmly in the hands of these horrid pirates, once they board. We may as well forget the conference, I suppose."

"Too right, sport," Kouth spoke up. "Dooley ain't as good natured as me. Prolly be pretty pissed when he finds out we ain't got no load of gold guck aboard."

"Oh, but we have," Magnan corrected. "Just in case some of the members of the tribunal should prove recalcitrant, I, that is, Ambassador Spoilsport, wanted to be sure to have cogent arguments available to bring the laggards into line."

"Bribes, eh?" Kouth queried respectfully.

"Hardly," Magnan sniffed. "It's called 'economic assistance.' "

"Good job it's here, anyways," Kouth commented contentedly. "But which piece is it on?"

"Right here, two decks down in the library, where miscreants of your stripe would never venture," Magnan told him smugly.

"What's that big word mean?" Kouth demanded. "Sounds to me like some kinda crack. Anyways, I read a book once. In reform school. All about the collapse o' civilization or something like that. Taken me all year, but I done it. Got a D on the test, too. Highest in the class. I ain't no dummy. So what say we sashay down and take a look. I ain't never seen no billion guck in cash before. Oh boy."

"Forget it, Mr. Kouth," Magnan advised the cocky fellow. "I've decided to lock you up right here in communications, first removing the master unscrambler disc, of course."

"And leave poor Spike and me to die, whilst youse skip out?" Kouth protested. "That there is krool, Mr. Magnan, is what it is. I guess Enlightened Galactic Opinion will have a word to say about that!"

"As it happens, Mr. Kouth," Magnan told the cheeky fellow, "I have no intention of informing EGO; nor, as it happens, of abandoning you to your richly-deserved fates."

"Oh, yeah?" Kouth countered truculently. "Uh, you mean you didn't plan to murder I and Spikey after all? See Spike," he addressed the locker, "I tole you he was a grand guy."

" 'Mean as a fire-snake' is, I believe, the term you employed," Magnan corrected tartly.

"I was onny kidding around-like, wasn't I Spikey?" Kouth appealed to his minion, whose reply was muffled by the steel door of the locker.

"Tell him to quiet down in there," Magnan ordered Kouth, who went over and muttered through the ventilation louvres in the panel. The pounding and yells subsided.

"Say, I almost forgot," Kouth spoke up brightly in the near-silence. "On account o' this here spin is making me space sick. I gotta go back to Power Section for my medicine."

"You needn't bother," Magnan told him. "I've already removed your arms cache, as I believe that fellow McCluskey has already advised you. Beside which, you must be airsick. We're in atmosphere now, you know."

"Figgered he was lying," Kouth confided. "Trynna pull a fast one."

"A great pity when one can't trust his own subordinates," Magnan commiserated. "But of course that's to be expected when one embarks on a career of crime; all one's associates are criminals."

"Same with diplomacy, I guess," Kouth offered sympathetically.

"A conscienceless criminal and a dedicated diplomat are hardly to be compared, sir!" Magnan rebuked sharply.

"Naw, I guess not," Kouth conceded. "We ain't got the scope o' your boys; you're the Big Leagues. But I guess we can get along OK anyways, right?"

There was a deep-toned *thump*! which added a new dimension to the off-center tumble of the derelict.

"That's Dooley!" Kouth blurted, and started for the door, shying as Magnan made a move.

"Just thought I'd check," Kouth explained contritely.

"We'll wait here," Retief told him. They did so, while Spike complained from the locker and the deck slowly precessed. All loose objects had gravitated to the aft outboard corner of the crowded compartment. Retief went to the big ground-talker unit, replaced the circuit-breaker and raised Stug Approach Control.

"Hey, what's going on out there?" an irritable voice demanded, almost blanketed in the static produced by the swarm of agitated particles in the midst of which the remains of the ship were slowly gyrating planetward. The buffeting and sounds of atmospheric friction were steadily increasing, amplified by the sounds of pieces tearing away from the disintegrating structure. "Looks like a meteor swarm," the controller resumed. "—that you, *Expedient*?"

"Say, there's two bandits on a closing course with you," the man on the ground said excitedly. "Might be some o' them wreckers plan to get a tractor beam on you and claim salvage rights!"

Just then, the closed-circuit talker linked to Old Moon came on line:

"Hard lines, Boss," Dooley's heavy voice came in loudly. "No can do. Seems like somebody forgot to do the annuals on the barges, the last few years, and they're grounded—prolly permanent. So you gotta get down the best way you can. Try for a nice solid impact here on Moon; we can smelt the gold out'a the remains later. Ta."

"The mug's tryna muscle me outa the picture," Boss Kouth growled. " 'Grounded', he says, and AC's got 'em on the screens ready to make contact!"

"Who'll be in command of the second unit?" Retief asked Kouth, who frowned and guessed:

"Prolly old Cuffs Dubois; useta be a line captain in the Bogan Naval Service."

"Raise him," Retief orderd; Kouth got busy with the intership gear and was rewarded with a thin, nasal voice saying:

"Right here, Boss," Dubois reported. "What's up? Dooley was all excited; said load all personnel—at first I thought he was abandoning the boys, here."

"Poor Dooley's not playing with a full deck," Retief told him. "We've got enough gold guck aboard to make every man rich, only we're in failure mode here. So get a beam on your lead barge, and then grapple onto the biggest piece of cargo-bay you can find. Over and out."

Kouth grabbed the talker and added: "We got a mutiny on our hands here, Cuffs; Dooley got a idear he can grab the whole take fer hisself. We'll fool him: hold him hard, like my, uh, aide here, Retief said, and set up a grapple to the port aft emergency hatch. Do it!" Then he used the PA to summon all crew to Emergency Stations—Plan B.

"—and we're gonna be boarded any second, by Colonel Dubois and his loyal crew," he concluded.

"Wrong, sucker!" Dooley's metallic voice cut across the squeals, whistles and rattles of the distintegrating vessel as he slammed into the compartment, a power gun in each fist. "I figgered you'd try something cute, Boss, so I got in here ahead of Cuffs and his traitors. Who's he think he is, tryna take his direct supervisor in tow?"

"Jest tryna give ya a hand, Dooley," Kouth alibied weakly. "See, we got a like little problem area here. We got to transfer all ships' complement to yer barge while we still got hull integrity here, so we got to move fast. My boys are all in place, ready to load."

The guns in Dooley's hands held steady on the Boss. There was a sudden outburst of thumping and yelling from the locker just beside Dooley; his eyes went to the source of the disturbance, and at the same moment, Magnan drew and fired the weapon he had tucked into his cummerbund; Dooley staggered back with a curse, dropping both guns so that his right hand could caress the left, ripped by the stream of small-caliber needles.

"I meant to tell you, if you wouldn't of been in such a big of a hurry," Kouth put in. "Watch this 'ere Mr. Magnan. He's a killer."

Retief thrust Kouth aside as he made a move for the fallen weapons and himself scooped them up.

"All right, Mr. Kouth," he told the frustrated Boss, "that's enough nonsense." Then he gave Kouth further precise instructions.

8

Half an hour later, after the diplomatic personnel had been herded, complaining bitterly, into the spartan accommodations of Barge Number One, and Kouth and Dooley and their respective cadres similarly crowded into the second scrow, the last habitable section of the ill-fated *Expedient* fell apart and traced a spectacular arc of fire toward the uninhabited desert area fifty miles below. Magnan heaved a sigh.

"A sad conclusion to my mission," he moaned. "Whatever am I to say to His Excellency? Why, paying off the Statement of Charges for the ship alone will require the remainder of my active life."

"They'll have to promote you, sir," Retief suggested encouragingly. "You'll need the extra salary to keep up the payments."

"That's scant solace, I fear," Magnan retorted.

"When Ambassador Spoilsport and the committee learn that you have an entire barge-load of trouble-makers out of circulation and in tow, I'm sure that will outweigh the trifling loss of a time-expired contract hauler."

"Of course—with Boss Kouth and his gang of ruffians subtracted from the equation, agreement will be reached far more readily," Magnan cooed.

"I was thinking of the other barge," Retief told him.

9

With both barges safely if informally at rest on the ground of Interplanetary House, Retief and Magnan stepped out on the pale blue lawn and were intercepted at once by Nat Sitzfleisch, Recording Secretary to ITCH, who came up breathless. "There you are at last, Ben," he greeted the senior diplomat, ignoring Retief. "His Ex is furious. You've kept all these Stuggish big shots—ah-senior officials, that is, waiting, which they were far from enthusiastic about this gab-fest in the first place! Another five minutes and you'd have been late!"

Magnan gave Nat instructions as to the disposition of the bulky scows marring the formal gardens and, with Retief, proceeded up the broad walk to the imposing structure housing the deliberations of the select tribunal. After making their way through the crowded hallways where groups of attaches were gossiping excitedly, they were confronted by His Excellency Ambassador Extraordinary and Minister Plenipotentiary Elmer Spoilsport, whose expression reflected none of the more tranquil emotions.

". . . Captain Suggs is resting comfortably in hospital, Magnan, as I'm sure you'll be glad to know," he announced excitedly. "He's not quite himself yet—keeps repeating the most extraordinary allegations regarding the proximate cause of his contusions—allegations in which your own name recurs with monotonous regularity—and by the way, there's a, ah, female counsellor from the Glory System, who has quite clearly suffered a breakdown—I hope! Says you actually menaced her with a Browning 2 mm! Under the circumstances I have no choice, of course, but to order you under close arrest, on your own recognizance, naturally, out of deference to your rank." He interrupted himself to gesture toward two large Terran Marines standing by. Magnan squeezed his eyes shut and appeared to be about to burst into tears. Instead, he smiled broadly, as Spoilsport bent his knees slightly, put his right foot forward in a jerky way, followed by his left, and exclaimed:

"Step on them—look at the vile things, Ben—! Wherever are they coming from? Rather a handsome shade of blue, though, one must admit." Then, as he leapt to left and right, stamping on the carpet, he began to sway from side to side and mutter.

". . . hunch yer honey out/hunch her in again . . . !"

"Mr. Magnan!" Retief commented admiringly. "You didn't tell me you'd learned to boggle."

Donald Kingsbury, **THE MOON GODDESS AND THE SON.** New York: Baen Books, 1986. $15.95.

Pamela Sargent, **VENUS OF DREAMS.** New York: Bantam Spectra, 1986. $3.50 paperback.

Walter Jon Williams, **HARDWIRED.** New York: Tor Books, 1985. $15.95.

Tom Clancy, **RED STORM RISING.** New York: G. P. Putnam's Sons, 1986. $19.95.

G.C. Edmondson and C.M. Kotlan, **THE CUNNING-HAM EQUATIONS.** New York: Del Rey/Ballantine Books, 1986. $2.95 paperback.

Charles Sheffield, **THE NIMROD HUNT.** New York: Baen Books, 1986. $3.50 paperback.

R.A. MacAvoy, **TWISTING THE ROPE.** New York: Bantam Spectra, 1986. $3.50 paperback.

Alan Dean Foster, **INTO THE OUT OF.** New York: Warner Books, $15.95.

A.J. Budrys (Editor), **WRITERS OF THE FUTURE, Volumes I & II.** Los Angeles: Bridge Publications, 1985 & 1986. $3.95 paperback.

Eric Frank Russell, **WASP.** New York: Del Rey/Ballantine Books, 1986 (expanded text). $2.95 paperback.

A few years ago, a fellow reviewer suggested that certain concepts about the human future in space (such as L-5 colonies) might become a repressive orthodoxy for SF. Even then, I thought it was overestimating the ability of SF to generate orthodoxies of *any* kind. If SF is a religion, it is one composed almost entirely of heretics.

With the passage of some years and many space-advocacy novels, this fear seems even less plausible. I offer as evidence three recent novels.

The Moon Goddess and the Son is the oak that Donald Kingsbury grew from the acorn of a Hugo-nominated novella of the same title. It covers two generations, from the '80s into the early 21st century, and interweaves three major plots.

First is the story of Diana Osborne and how she escaped first a brutal father and then Earth itself, using street-smarts, sex, and sheer *chutzpah* in roughly equal amounts. Second is the lives and loves of astroanut Byron MacDougall and his deceptively laid-back son Charles, the "son" of the title. Third is the operations of a thinktank using the techniques of the Society for Creative Anachronism and fantasy role-playing to generate major strategic concepts—among other things.

Kingsbury is one of those writers who reaches into his brimming stock of ideas with both hands and throws these double handfuls into his novels. This doesn't always produce a story that's easy to follow, but if the hands are skilled it produces most of the other rewards a reader can ask for.

Interwoven with the fun is some extremely cogent thinking on serious matters. Who else has suggested that the real secret to a strategic-defense system is to make it so *profitable* that neither side can afford to undercut it? Who else has suggested subverting the Soviet elite by spreading among them a computer game that shows how much they could have gained by getting rid of Stalin?

Now, if somebody would just give Donald Kingsbury his own thinktank. . . .

Pamela Sargent's *Venus of Dreams* has been proclaimed the first novel in an epic trilogy, a family saga of the terraforming of Venus. Trilogies have their uses, for sufficiently grand tales (one would not try to fit *Moby Dick* into a short story). Family sagas also have their uses (R.F. Delderfield is one of the authors on whom I would gladly have conferred immortality). Efforts to cross-breed them with SF, however, have usually produced the kind of offspring you don't write sagas about. More likely, hide them away on secluded estates.

Sargent, however, has chosen a sufficiently large story and so far is telling it very well. Clearly she has done her homework on the special requirements of the family saga, and found ways of translating them where necessary into SF terms.

Iris Angharad grows up a natural rebel against the matriarchal society that rules the 21st-century Great Plains. Her dream is to get off Earth and participate in the Venus Project, to make the planet habitable. In pursuit of that dream she acquires a husband and a son, loses the son permanently and the husband temporarily, and finally dies fighting terrorists.

This is a story dominated by its characters, and particularly by Iris. Such a *driven* protagonist may not be every reader's idea of agreeable company for 530 pages. She grows, though, as she learns compassion for those who have been sacrificed to her dreams. Most readers will end by feeling with and for her. Sargent has also done a good deal of thinking about her future societies and drawn them well, in spite of leaving the technology largely in the background.

Walter Jon Williams's *Hardwired* could technically be classified as "cyberpunk." It certainly uses much of the familiar territory of that burgeoning sub-genre—a 21st-century Earth in which high-tech gives power to corrupt corporate elites; and protagonists living on the fringes of society, if not actually at war with it.

Looking beyond categories, however, one quickly finds a well-told tale. Williams has done a painstaking job with the technology, and produced a number of real winners—such as speed-of-light stock-market manipulation through the global computer net.

He's also avoided the essentially nihilistic characters that disfigure much of the competition. Cowboy smuggles pharmaceuticals in an armored hovercraft, and Sarah lives by her wits in order to support her undeserving brother; both start off with enough loyalties so that we're not surprised to see them developing more. Nor are we happy when they finally win. It's a modest victory, and staying alive is half of it, but they know they're in a war that will take more than one battle.

Williams has dropped the ball a couple of times. I doubt if some of his high-performance machinery would run on grain alcohol. I also doubt the wisdom of telling the whole story in the present tense, a stylistic device that calls attention to itself.

Otherwise, a good, intelligent book, by an author who clearly believes in keeping his bargains with the reader.

When I finished Tom Clancy's *The Hunt for Red October* (U.S. Naval Institute press/Berkley paperback), I suspected there was more to the author than we were being told. I mean, this superb table of submarine warfare written by an *insurance agent*?

I also didn't care. A book that good could have been written by seven gnomes using a ouija board programmed by the National Security Agency and I still wouldn't have cared. (I would have had to reconsider everything I've ever said about the impossibility of writing books by committee, but that's a minor point.)

Tom Clancy, as it turns out, really is an Annapolis insurance agent. He is also an inveterate wargamer and a faithful follower of unclassified military literature. The rest, one must assume, is a natural gift for storytelling.

Red Storm Rising opens with Moslem rebels blowing up the Soviet Union's largest oil refinery. Faced with a critical fuel shortage, the Politburo decides to seize the Middle Eastern oilfields. To distract the West, they will also arrange a pretext for invading West Germany. . . .

Things start off well enough for the Russians; their seizure of Iceland gives them a fighting chance of cutting off American reinforcements to the battlefield in Europe. However, as casualties mount, things begin unraveling, first on the battlefield and finally in the Kremlin itself.

The subplot that will draw most readers is the story of an Air Force weatherman, marooned on Iceland by the Russian invasion. In company with a few Marines and an Icelandic girl he rescued from KGB rapists, this reluctant hero treks across Iceland, providing vital intelligence every mile of the way. A dozen other subplots provide something for everyone; all are advanced with technical expertise, good spare prose, and a knowledgeable respect for the fighting men and women of both sides.

Strictly speaking, *Red Storm* may not be SF. However, nobody who enjoys military action on the grand scale should overlook it. As for those trying to write military SF—Clancy is the current world standard for most of what goes into such a book.

Enough said.

Well-told tales, on a smaller scale . . .

G.C. Edmondson and C.M. Kotlan have combined hard-science SF and thriller in *The Cunningham Equations*. Blaise Cunningham, a neurotic, alcholic mathematician, has done the crucial equations in an experiment with DNA tailoring for increasing human intelligence. Unfortunately, the experiment involves implanting fly larvae in the subject's brains—larvae which turn out to be viable mutants, capable of growing in their hosts' skulls. . . .

The discovery of his lethal miscalculation sets off an equally lethal race to suppress it. Cunningham is one of the primary targets, and he, a dog, several complaisant women, and a beautifully drawn Mafia hit man are really put through the jumps. At the end Cunningham has a breathing spell, but no more than that—and the reader has an appetite whetted for the remaining two volumes of his adventures.

Charles Sheffield is one of the established emerging masters of hard-science SF. So it's no surprise that his *The Nimrod Hunt* is a fine example of the breed.

Some centuries in the future, the human race is one of four sapient species in contact with one another through the instantaneous transportation of the Matten Link. To explore the interstellar frontier, human researchers have created formidable cyborgs, the Morgan Constructs. They turned out to be so formidable, in fact, that they escaped from the space station where they were built and fled to the stars, where they are a potential menace to all four species.

All four join to hunt down the Constructs. The humans take the lead, partly because they're responsible for the mess, and partly because they are the only race capable of actually killing the cyborgs. As it turns out, there are more subtle ways of dealing with them. . . .

This is another "ideas by the double handful" book (I particularly liked the asteroid-sized Yang Diamond). One would like to see more of some of them, not to mention a lot more of some of the characters, as the story whirls along. Absorbing, intelligent entertainment nonetheless.

Roberta A. MacAvoy has produced another graceful fantasy tale in *Twisting the Rope*. It is a sequel to her *Tea with the Black Dragon*, in which a two-thousand-year-old Chinese dragon turns himself into a human being named Myland Long and takes up with a grandmotherly Irish fiddler named Martha Macnamara.

Five years later, Martha really is a grandmother and on tour with her band. Long is with them, suffering from a howling cold but in spite of that a formidable opponent. Just as well too, because they find themselves facing a sea of troubles, ending in the murder of one of the band and the kidnapping of Martha's granddaughter.

The only element of fantasy is the telepathic powers of the illegitimate brain-damaged son of one of the band. Otherwise the book's strengths are characterization, command of language, and the details of the small-group politics of the folk-music scene. This would not be enough to save the novel in the hands of a lesser author, and one hopes that MacAvoy herself will eventually return to the larger scale of her *Damiano* trilogy (Bantam paperbacks). Meanwhile, any book from such a gifted writer is better than none.

* * *

For many years Alan Dean Foster has been a prolific producer of lightweight fiction. Much of it has been so lightweight that it's been impossible to take seriously. I've even wondered if Foster took the books or his bargain with his readers seriously—a black mark in this reviewer's reckoning.

All sweeping indictments of Foster are hereby withdrawn. *Into the Out Of* is a first-class fantasy/horror novel, by no stretch of the imagination a lightweight piece.

The plot is a trifle shopworn—Earth about to face a mass assault by Evil Beings (the *shetani*) from Another Dimension (the Out Of). What Foster does with this story, however, is an object lesson in the limitations of originality. He pits against the *shetani* invasion a Masai *laibon* (wise man), an FBI agent, and a mail-order phone answerer, bringing them together in Washington, D.C., then sending them on to a final battle in Africa.

The book lacks nothing in pacing, characterization (*without* great dollops of gratuitous sex), or a genuinely repulsive alien menace. Foster has also done his homework on African mythology and traveled extensively in Kenya; my wife, who grew up in Washington, says he has done an equally good job with that city.

Whatever else Foster has done these past few years, he has clearly learned the art of storytelling. A few more books like *Into the Out Of*, and he will be honored as well as popular.

The late L. Ron Hubbard left a large and complex literary legacy. As much as I enjoyed *Battlefield Earth*, I would give pride of place in that legacy to the Writers of the Future Contest. This well-financed contest offers lavish prizes and publication to unpublished writers of short SF and fantasy. It is judged by a blue-ribbon panel of judges, and headed by A.J. Budrys, undoubtedly the best selection for the job that could have been made.

Budrys has also edited two volumes of *Writers of the Future* winners. Reading through them turns up the usual percentage of literate mood pieces and character studies without action that any contest for beginning writers inevitably draws. I've also found a fine crop of thoroughly professional pieces, both fantasy and SF.

With the markets for short fiction rising and falling (mostly falling, in spite of valiant efforts such as this magazine), any effort to encourage new short-fiction writers deserves praise. When it produces as much good reading as this, it deserves fireworks and champagne.

It also deserves to be continued, and fortunately it has just been announced that the Writers of the Future contest will continue for at least one more year.

Every so often, I feel inclined to turn my attention toward a classic. This time: *Wasp* by Eric Frank Russell.

Several centuries in the future, Terra is fighting the purple-skinned humanoid Sirians (who have a good deal in common with the World War II Japanese). James Mowry, another reluctant hero, is dropped on the Sirian planet of Jaimec to make a high-grade nuisance of himself. He succeeds admirably, to the point where the whole Sirian military establishment on the planet is chasing him and his largely mythical Sirian Freedom Party—right at the moment when Terra is about to invade. . . .

The story is intelligent, non-stop action from beginning to end. It also benefits from having been republished in a complete version, with more than ten thousand words cut from a previous edition carefully restored. (More posthumous praise for Judy-Lynn del Rey.) It's not a night-into-day transformation, as has been the case with SF novels finally republished complete as the author wrote them. But the characters are more fleshed out, and the planet Jaimec has a somewhat more lived-in quality, that most readers will find agreeable.

Much less agreeable will be a thought that comes inevitably to any reader of *Wasp* who's also been following international news the past few months. Russell has skillfully depicted the appalling vulnerability of modern society to terrorism. Chalk up another prophecy to SF's score—and hope modern democracies have better luck or more skill (I'll take either) than the Sirians. . . .